PHANTOM GAME

PHANTOM GAME

PHANTOM GAME

CHRISTINE FEEHAN

THORNDIKE PRESS
A part of Gale, a Cengage Company

GALE
A Cengage Company

LIBRARY OF CONGRESS CIP DATA ON FILE.
CATALOGUING IN PUBLICATION FOR THIS BOOK
IS AVAILABLE FROM THE LIBRARY OF CONGRESS.

ISBN-13: 978-1-4328-9609-6 (hardcover alk. paper)

Published in 2022 by arrangement with Berkley, an imprint of Penguin
Publishing Group, a division of Penguin Random House, LLC

Printed in Mexico
Print Number: 01   Print Year: 2022

For Cheryl Wilson and Domini Walker.
Thank you.

Thank you.

FOR MY READERS

Be sure to go to ChristineFeehan.com/ members/ to sign up for my private book announcement list and download the free ebook of *Dark Desserts*. Join my community and get firsthand news, enter the book discussions, ask your questions and chat with me. Please feel free to email me at christine@christinefeehan.com. I would love to hear from you.

ACKNOWLEDGMENTS

To Denise, for the invaluable research.
To Brian, for keeping me going even when I
was faltering.
To Domini and Cheryl, for editing. This one
was difficult, but we did it!

THE GHOSTWALKER
SYMBOL DETAILS

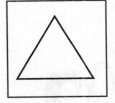

SIGNIFIES
shadow

SIGNIFIES
protection against evil forces

SIGNIFIES
the Greek letter psi, which is used by parapsychology researchers to signify ESP or other psychic abilities

SIGNIFIES
qualities of a knight—loyalty, generosity, courage and honor

SIGNIFIES
shadow knights who protect against evil forces using psychic powers, courage and honor

nox noctis est nostri

THE GHOSTWALKER CREED

We are the GhostWalkers, we live in the shadows

The sea, the earth, and the air are our domain

No fallen comrade will be left behind

We are loyalty and honor bound

We are invisible to our enemies

and we destroy them where we find them

We believe in justice and we protect our country

and those unable to protect themselves

What goes unseen, unheard and unknown are GhostWalkers

There is honor in the shadows and it is us

We move in complete silence whether in jungle or desert

We walk among our enemy unseen and unheard

Striking without sound and scatter to the winds

before they have knowledge of our existence

We gather information and wait with endless patience

for that perfect moment to deliver swift justice

We are both merciful and merciless

We are relentless and implacable in our
resolve
We are the GhostWalkers and the night
is ours

1

The mountains rose up, climbing higher and higher, towering all around, the peaks reaching for the clouds. All along the mountainsides and in the valleys between, red cedar, whitebark pine and spruce trees vied for space. This was true forest, two million acres of actual wilderness, most of it, left to the animals that were native to the area. Grizzlies, black bears, mountain lions, moose, timber wolves, mountain goats, elk, bighorn sheep and mule deer all made the vast forest home, along with a range of smaller animals.

Jonas "Smoke" Harper, Dr. Kyle Forbes and Jeff Hollister, three of the genetically and psychically enhanced members of GhostWalker Team One, continued along the nearly nonexistent game trail they'd been traveling for the past three hours.

"You still getting that bad feeling in your gut, Jonas?" Jeff asked.

Jonas scanned the dense forest with narrowed eyes, maintaining his purposefully relaxed gait while keeping his hand close to his weapon. "Yep."

Kyle sighed. "You sure it isn't just a stitch in your side?"

"Yep."

"You did notice that the higher we climb, the more bear scat we're coming across," Jeff said.

"Yep."

"Just thought I'd point that out." A small grin lit Jeff's face.

"I'm not sure he actually knows how to talk, Jeff," Kyle said. "Ryland did warn us. Said if we volunteered to come with him, we'd hear nothing but grunts for days."

"Wait." Smile fading, Jeff halted abruptly and glared at his companions. "You volunteered? Ryland *ordered* me to come with you two. Said I had to protect your asses."

Jonas and Kyle stopped as well, and Jonas took the opportunity to study Jeff without appearing to do so. It had been a couple of years since Jeff had recovered from a stroke that would have put any normal soldier out of commission for good. Jeff had fought his way back.

Jeff, like most men in the government's GhostWalker program, wasn't anyone's definition of a normal soldier anymore. These men were, instead, the products of a military experiment that hadn't quite gone as expected. They had gone into the program volunteering for psychic enhancements with the expectation of being of more use to their country, but along with removing filters in their brains, Dr. Peter Whitney had also performed experimental gene coding on them. That part they had *not* signed up for.

Worse, the first of Whitney's gene-coding experiments had been illegally performed on young orphan girls, with disastrous results. Those initial failures hadn't stopped Whitney though. Instead, he'd forged ahead with similar gene modifications on the soldiers, believing that grown men could better handle the pressures of the enhancements than the female children had. Team One had lost several of the men in their unit, and Jeff had suffered a brain bleed and stroke. He was fully recovered, but the entire team tended to watch over him, Jonas especially.

The survivors of Whitney's experiments were all admittedly stronger, and they now possessed some very incredible abilities, but those benefits had come at a steep price. They were all continuing to learn just how

17

steep that price could be. Lily Whitney-Miller, Peter Whitney's adopted daughter, who was now married to their team leader, Captain Ryland Miller, had given them all exercises to do to strengthen the barricades in their minds. That allowed the ones who had been wide open to be able to be in public without an "anchor" — one who drew emotion and psychic overload from them — at least for short periods of time.

Jeff looked good to Jonas, but still, he glanced at Kyle just to make certain. Kyle would be better at making an assessment. If the doc thought Jeff needed a break, he'd find an excuse to take one. Jeff never shirked the physical therapy designed to strengthen the weaker side of his body or the mental exercises to strengthen the barriers in his brain. He stayed in therapy the brain surgeon recommended to ensure the psychic talents he used didn't bring on another bleed. He was one of the hardest-working GhostWalkers Jonas knew — and that was saying a lot.

Their unit, GhostWalker Team One, was tight. They looked out for one another. They trusted few others, and those they brought in, they did so slowly and carefully. Years ago, their team had been set up for murder, separated and held in cages, essentially waiting to die. Ryland had planned their escape, and Lily had hidden them at her estate until they could get to the bottom of the conspiracy against them. In the end, they had managed to come out on top, thanks in no small part to their dedication to training hard and working together. They still ran missions, but they trusted and depended only on one another.

Now, there were three other GhostWalker teams. Whitney had used each team to perfect his technique so that each subsequent unit was able to handle their enhancements much better than the team before them. But he'd also added more and more genetic coding, turning the soldiers into much more than they ever expected — or wanted — to be.

There was a special place in hell reserved for sociopathic monsters like Peter Whitney — or if there wasn't, there ought to be. Jonas wouldn't mind bringing a little — or maybe a *lot* — of that hell to Whitney in the here and now, especially as more and more of his most diabolical experiments, all on orphaned girls, came to light. Unfortunately, as evil as he was, Whitney had a solid network of connections among America's most powerful, including high-ranking government officials, billionaire defense contractors, bankers, and his own private army of expendable supersoldiers, all of them would-be GhostWalkers who hadn't made the official cut. Between his connections and his army, Whitney was virtually untouchable.

Jonas sighed as his gaze swept the surrounding forest. He used every enhanced sense he had, both animal and human. They were being watched. He had been aware of it for the last few miles but hadn't been able to identify exactly where the threat was coming from — or from whom. Or rather, from what. He was certain their observers were not human.

"You feel it?" Kyle asked him quietly, turning toward him.

"Yep."

Jeff heaved an exaggerated sigh. "You ever think a word now and again might be helpful?"

"Not certain what it is yet."

Jeff shoved a hand through his perpetually sun-bleached hair. "It? Not a who. An it?" When Jonas didn't answer, Jeff rolled his eyes. "Why did I agree to keep the two of you alive? You're both a pain in the ass." He began walking again, doggedly putting one foot in front of the other. "Do we even know where we're going?"

"Nope." Jonas hid his grin. Annoying Jeff was one of his favorite pastimes, and when the tension was beginning to stretch out, like now, a little humor went a long way. In spite of his amusement, he stayed on full alert, looking for the sentries watching them.

He was fully aware Ryland hadn't sent Jeff. Jeff had come with him, like Kyle, because they were his friends, and they hadn't wanted him to check out his strange feeling alone. It had been that simple. Friendship. The feeling, at first, had been a vague calling to him. For the last mile, along with that compulsion he felt, he now felt uneasy, as if there were a threat, but he couldn't place where it was coming from.

Night was falling. In the forest, especially this deep in the interior, it was always a good thing to establish a camp before sunset. Too many wild animals hunted after dark. He could connect with them and, if he was lucky, keep them away, but it was silly to take chances. The trees were thick, the brush heavy. The trail they were on was very narrow. Tree frogs were abundant, staring at them with round eyes as they passed. In the vegetation at their feet was the constant rustle of leaves as rodents rushed to get undercover.

"We should find a place to camp for the

night. Build a fire."

"I tried to send word back to the others," Kyle said. "But I'm not getting through. Could be the density of the canopy, but I should be able to . . ." He trailed off.

"I'm not surprised." Jonas wasn't. There was something at work here. He'd gotten that feeling in his gut and wanted to check things out.

Jonas had told Ryland he had felt a strange pull toward this side of the mountain for some time and wanted to take time off to explore. They'd just recently come off a dicey hostage rescue. They'd managed to pull off the rescue without a single casualty even though things had gone sideways twice, and they all had some downtime coming. Jonas wanted — no — *needed* to explore the miles of wilderness around the fortress they had carved out for themselves close to Team Two.

"Have you noticed that we're losing visibility, Jonas?" Kyle asked. "The mist is getting thick."

Jonas could see the fog moving through the trees at times. At first it stayed low to the ground, gently rolling like ocean waves on a cloudless day. Then a few fingers of mist crept through the trees toward them in an eerie display, looking like giant hands pulling an equally giant blanket through the forest until it was impossible to see through the gray vapor. Jonas glanced down at the trail they were following, but the swirling mist had thickened so much that he couldn't see even his own boots — a strange phenomenon.

There was another component to the fog he found fascinating. A warning, or dread, that acted on their bodies. He could hear both Kyle's and Jeff's hearts accelerating. His own pulse rate had tried to increase, and he had instantly forced his heart under control. All three GhostWalkers slowed considerably, eventually halting altogether.

Jonas waited in silence for his eyes to adjust to the fog rolling off the ground and rising in dark tides nearly to his waist. Given time, he could see through just about anything. He was often called "Smoke" because he moved through and could disappear into places no one else could. He saw through things no one else could see through. It was only a matter of time before his vision would adjust to the strange mist hiding the trail.

"Looks as if the fog is dissipating in that direction," Kyle said, indicating to the right with his chin.

Jeff nodded. "And our little game trail

leads in that direction too, Jonas. If we're going to find a place to camp before nightfall, we should double-time it out of this mist."

Jonas didn't move, studying the forest and rocks in front of him. The path had wound through the trees and rocks earlier. He had a good memory. More than a good memory. His mind mapped things out for him in grid patterns. The game trail hadn't veered to the right. It had continued upward, straight ahead, winding around tree trunks and large rocks, but it hadn't really swung left or right.

"Give me a minute."

Keeping completely still, Jonas swept his gaze up and down the fog-shrouded forest floor in a grid pattern, paying special attention to the area where the game trail should have been. At first there was a strange shimmer, very reminiscent of a mirage in the desert. But Jonas persevered until the shimmer dissipated and what lay beneath became clear.

"The actual trail is straight ahead. It's being hidden from us."

"That's not good," Kyle observed. "And we're being watched to make certain we go where we're directed?"

"Yep." Jonas took the first step onto the very narrow game trail to see if it would

24

trigger an attack of some kind.

"This is some kind of crazy-ass magnetic earth thing happening, like in the Bermuda Triangle," Jeff muttered. "We're going to get misdirected all over the place, aren't we?"

"Yep."

Jonas wished the phenomenon came from a "magnetic earth thing," but he seriously doubted it. Something was going on in the mountains above the two fortresses that GhostWalker Teams One and Two had established to keep their families safe. Weirdly, the compulsion to continue forward was still on him, but the threat was still quite hazy, as if it were very, very far away.

He had to consider going back down the mountain and telling Ryland what they'd run into. The fog was manufactured, and someone had planted a very potent danger signal in it. Not only that, but they had diverted them from the real trail. Very few could manage. He wasn't going back. He *couldn't* go back. The compulsion to continue was stronger than ever. That didn't mean he wanted to risk Kyle and Jeff.

"You two could make it out of the danger zone if you hiked down fast for two hours and then camped." The offer had to be made, and he did his best to sound casual. He knew there was no way either of his friends would take him up on it, but still, he had to try.

"Can't leave you here without direction, Jonas," Jeff said. "Especially since we all know you're afraid of the dark; otherwise, I'd advise we just leave your stubborn, knife-wielding ass right here in Creepy Hollow."

"Technically," Kyle said, "a hollow is a low-lying area, not a mountainside."

"Work with me, Kyle. 'Creepy Mountain' doesn't have the same ring to it," Jeff quipped, bringing humor to the tense situation.

The tension continued to build in spite of Jonas seeing through the fog to the trail beneath it. The dark purplish beads had a strange reddish cast to them as they swirled almost hypnotically around the men.

"Seriously, it isn't a bad idea to let Rye know there's something going on up here that wasn't here before." Jonas tried a second time.

"It's that bad?" Jeff asked. He began walking, showing Jonas he wasn't about to be left behind. "Now I feel like I've got a target painted right between my shoulder blades."

"You've got a pack on. They wouldn't be able to see the target, so they would have to aim for your thick skull, Jeff," Kyle said helpfully.

"Great. Now the back of my head is all tingly. I think my psychic abilities are expanding. I can feel someone targeting me right now."

"You're so full of shit," Kyle said. "I think you need serious help. You're turning into a psychic hypochondriac."

"There isn't any such sort of thing. You're making that up."

"I'm a doctor. I would know," Kyle assured solemnly.

"Jonas, is there such a thing as a psychic hypochondriac?"

"Yep."

Jeff burst out laughing. He kept the sound low and directional so only his two companions could hear, but it was real. All the while they were walking along the game trail, Jonas continued to scout for a good place to camp for the night. He wanted somewhere they could defend if needed. With every step they took, the feeling of danger increased.

"I feel it too now," Kyle said. "Increasing, I mean. Before, the feeling of something watching us was very faint, now it's strong."

"My best guess," Jonas said, as they continued very slowly uphill. "Tree frogs.

We've now graduated to timber wolves. I noticed a disproportionate number of frogs on the trees as we passed by. The wolves are staying well back, but I've caught glimpses of them."

The trail narrowed significantly as it wound up the forested mountainside. There were fewer trees and more rocks. As they walked, the shimmer became worse. It was very disorienting, at times making it feel as if the ground had dropped out from under them.

There was a brief silence while both Jeff and Kyle looked warily around them.

"You aren't going to spot them," Jonas pointed out. "They aren't hunting to eat us, at least not at the moment. They're watching us."

"What does that mean?" Kyle asked.

"Like they've never seen humans before and they're just curious?" Jeff asked.

"I'm not getting that." Jonas reached out to the wolves with great care. There was plenty of game in the area that could sustain a small pack, and this one seemed small. "They're watching us for a reason. I have to be very careful."

Jonas kept his touch delicate as he reached out. The alpha was especially wary. Normally, Jonas had little trouble connecting with wildlife and establishing communication, even if it was just to "push" the animal in a direction away from him. This time, however, there seemed to be something blocking him from using another pathway he found that the wolf was familiar with. That pathway circumvented him from taking command of the animal.

"The ground moving continually is beginning to make me sick," Kyle said.

"You realize the ground isn't actually moving," Jonas pointed out.

"Yeah, I get that," Kyle agreed, "but it feels and looks like it. I'm trying to make my brain understand it's all an illusion."

"Are you feeling ill, Jeff?" Jonas asked.

Jeff was walking very steadily, whereas Kyle seemed a little off balance every few steps.

"No. I'm cheating a little, just like I did when I first suffered a traumatic brain injury. I take a picture of the trail out ahead of me and use it when I'm walking until I get to the end of where I was able to take the picture, and then I do it again as far out as I'm able. I don't actually look at the trail we're walking on."

"Is that how you got around all my tests so fast?" Kyle asked.

It sounded to Jonas as if he were clenching his teeth. Kyle wasn't actually Jeff's doctor and he didn't administer tests to him, but the banter helped the two keep moving.

"Absolutely."

"There's a small clearing, nothing big, but that ring of rocks just off to the right would provide cover and is large enough for a fire," Jonas said. "It looks like it might be a halfway decent defensible position."

"Head in that direction," Kyle advised, relief in his voice. "Otherwise, our orders to leave no footprints isn't going to matter. I'll be leaving my lunch behind."

Jonas stretched his senses. Kyle wasn't a man to be nauseated over a rolling trail. The shimmering mirage was difficult for him to look at, but Kyle wasn't looking at it. He was looking straight ahead at Jeff's back. There was another subtle component Jonas was missing, because he couldn't feel it.

The GhostWalkers had various talents. When Whitney had enhanced them, even the smaller gifts had grown stronger. Practicing to use those talents had developed them even more. Jonas was beginning to believe a GhostWalker or a team of Ghost-Walkers was using this particular part of the mountain for something they didn't want known, and they'd set up a perimeter of psychic defenses to keep unwanted visitors away.

"Only a GhostWalker could have produced something as complex as this," he murmured. "There's a subtle flow of acoustic energy, a low note to make you feel sick, Kyle. The sound is just below our normal hearing range. And if they decide to up the volume, we'll be in a world of hurt."

"You saying whoever's up here can weaponize sound, like what Gator and Flame can do?" Jeff asked, naming two GhostWalkers from their team. "They can kill with sound."

"That's exactly what I'm saying. I can use my voice, but I can't do what they do. And I can't do this. We're going to have to be very careful."

Knowing they were going to be facing enhanced soldiers changed everything. It was one thing to face wildlife, but this was something altogether different and very dangerous. It wasn't as if it came as a huge surprise. The moment they recognized the trail had been diverted by the illusion in the fog, they suspected they were dealing with enhanced soldiers. Or someone who was very good at building traps with illusion.

They had reached the potential campsite Jonas had spotted earlier. The circle of rocks provided a shelter from the wind and watch-

31

ing eyes. The opening at the center was large enough to allow a fire, something they wanted just in case the wolves took too big of an interest in them. And if something other than wolves came at them, well, the rocks could stop bullets too. It wasn't perfect, not a bolt-hole they could count on to last against a determined assault, but it was better than nothing. As an added benefit, when they hunkered down inside the ring, with the boulders looming over them, they escaped the strange warping of their senses.

"I'm going to take a look around while you set up camp," Jonas said. "I can negate the effects of the illusion, and if I have to, I can control the wolves. I want to see how big of an area is being affected, who or what it's protecting. Not to mention, I'd like to know how many people are behind this, who they are and what they're up to."

"Do you think they're jamming us, or we just lost signal in all this pea soup? If you run into trouble, we can't call on the others for help," Kyle reminded.

"I'm aware. But we can still talk to one another if we have to. Conserve energy, but reach out if there's trouble. Jeff, if you have to leave on the run, get Kyle out if the illusion is still making him sick."

32

Jeff nodded. "I can get around the mirage. And I can lead others back to get you out."

"Don't stick around if anything goes bad. Better you two get out and go for help." Jonas wanted to reiterate that point, because otherwise Kyle and Jeff would try coming to his aid. All GhostWalkers were intensely loyal to one another. They didn't leave their fallen behind, let alone abandon a live teammate when the shit hit the fan.

Kyle glanced up, his gaze sharp. "You think it's that bad."

"I don't know what we stumbled onto, but no one constructs a psychic defense this strong and this good without using it to hide something important. Most people would have been turned away. They never would have known this part of the forest was even here. Now, whoever put this barrier up knows it didn't work on us. They'll wonder why, and they'll either sic the wolves on us, or they'll come themselves. I want to take a look at what we're up against. How many. What we need to do to protect ourselves. I especially don't like the fact that someone in their unit can use sound to debilitate us."

"Hell, Jonas," Jeff said, once again using humor to lighten the situation. "I had no idea you knew so many words."

"I wasn't sure he knew the entire English

language," Kyle agreed. "Mostly just grunts."

"Or 'yep,' " Jeff added. "That's his go-to word when he can't think of anything else."

"Or I can just throw a knife at you," Jonas pointed out. He was very good with knives. Better than good. He'd grown up in a circus family, and he'd learned from an early age how to throw knives and stars with pinpoint accuracy, and how to balance on a high wire so he could be part of his family's act. His circus days were long behind him, but the skills he'd acquired had transferred over to combat, and he practiced every day to keep those skills sharp.

"Circus freak goes up the sides of mountains only goats go up," Kyle teased.

Jonas wasn't so certain that particular ability was completely from his circus days. Perhaps more from Whitney's gene coding. "I'll be back by sunup."

GhostWalkers were adept at disappearing into the night. They could hide in plain sight during the day, staying still for hours, but at night, they were virtually undetectable. Jonas could disappear. He was Smoke. His team had given him that name long ago for a reason. Unlike the others, Jonas didn't need the special clothing that mirrored his surroundings or the skin that changed colors to mimic his background.

He had never talked to Lily Whitney-Miller, Ryland's wife, about the science of what he could do, because he didn't want anyone looking too closely at what he'd become. He didn't want a spotlight turned on him — or any record made of his abilities. He especially didn't want anyone to know about the extremely predatory and aggressive tendencies that he'd fought so hard to keep under control. Primal animal instincts, the need to hunt, even — if he was being honest — to kill. And in the early days, keeping those impulses in check had been a real struggle.

At first he'd wanted to believe Whitney had managed to plant those urges in him, but the more he read and understood about what Whitney had done to them all, the more he realized the enhancements could only bring out what was inside of him. It was beyond disturbing to realize such ugly, violent traits were part of his own nature. It hadn't mattered that they were buried deep; they were still a part of him.

Jonas slipped over the boulder facing away from the trail, the one closest to the trees, deliberately blurring his body so that when he moved into the strange mirage, he was already becoming a part of it, so as not to disturb it. So he couldn't be seen or felt.

An owl hooted, the notes a clear warning. That told him the sentry had eyes on the men inside the ring of boulders. The bird had noticed there was one less man seated at the fire and reported immediately. He waited, staying very still, absorbing the abnormal mist and its properties, breaking it down even as he listened for the instructions to the sentries. He knew whoever was guarding the region would have to tell the lookouts what to do next.

A few short notes replied, that of a Great Gray owl calling out to its mate — at least to an untrained ear, that was what it sounded like. Jonas stayed very still, forcing his energy to remain extremely low so he couldn't be detected inside the web of mist, all the while fighting to control his surprise. That Great Gray owl cry — the orders being given to the watching animals in the woods — had come from a female. She had the sound of an owl down perfectly, but his ear was tuned so acutely, he could distinguish real from fake, no matter how good the mimicry was. And she was the best he'd ever heard.

Whitney had taken numerous girls from orphanages from countries all over the world. He'd also used in vitro to create designer babies to experiment on. His first idea had been to create pairs, a male and female. He used enhanced pheromones to make the pair attracted physically to one another so they would bond when he was certain he had the correct enhancements that would work together in the field. It was possible whatever was taking place above the homes of Teams One and Two was being run by a bonded pair.

The moment the woman had uttered her bird call, Jonas had pinpointed the direction from which the sound had come, but instead of rushing toward it, he stayed put and remained as still as stone, giving off so little energy it would be impossible to detect him, lowering his external body temperature so he gave off no heat signature. Whoever the woman was, she knew he was out here and she was, at the very least, directing the wolves and birds to keep watch on him. Rushing toward her now, while she and her sentinels were all on alert, was too risky. Best to hunker down for a while and wait for them to relax their guard.

Jonas had learned patience in a hard school when he was young. High-wire acts were dangerous, so was throwing knives. One misstep, and someone he loved could be hurt or killed. He had learned to always

37

stay calm and not make mistakes. Now, with all his predatory instincts enhanced, he had become even more patient. He could wait hours in complete stillness.

For this hunt, he knew he had to be cautious. The mist contained traps that could detect him if he made a mistake. The animals in the forest were actively looking for him. Beneath his calm surface, he could feel the familiar rush of adrenaline, the predatory instincts taking hold. That trait in him was so powerful and aggressive, so dominant, that when the alpha of the sentinel wolf pack had resisted his very subtle influence, the urge to attack that wolf and rip out his throat had welled up like a volcano.

He suppressed the urge with ruthless control. Jonas was at his most dangerous when he was in hunting mode, and while some part of him hated the savagery Whitney's experiments had unleashed in him, another part of him thrilled at the visceral intensity of those urges. He couldn't deny the joy he felt each time he allowed himself the freedom to use his abilities, in spite of the ugliness of what he knew would ultimately be his fate.

Over the years, he had come to terms with the predatory side of his nature. Now, it was a matter of always keeping it under control. He honed his hunting skills every chance he got, knowing they would be an asset to his team, so long as his killer instincts were never allowed to take over. He had seen what happened if the monster got out of control. The entire team had. That could never happen again. That meant continually strengthening his discipline. Working on restraint. He didn't let a day go by without performing the mental and physical exercises that allowed him to maintain complete control of himself.

He waited there without moving until darkness had finally fallen, bringing with it a sliver of a moon. His blood moved through his veins like thick lava, slow and hot, though from the skin out, he'd gone as cold as ice. That was the way he kept his energy level so low, it was impossible to detect.

At last he began to make his way up toward the grove of trees from which the woman had issued her earlier call. The mist grew thicker the higher up he went. He was in full predatory mode, switching between using the vision of an owl and that of a leopard to traverse the misty forest with ease. He could also use wolf vision when he needed to, but the owl and leopard both had superior night vision.

It had taken some time to sort out the fact that he had the skills of each of the three predators in him, along with their individual drives. Those weren't the only predators Whitney had put in him either. Not by a long shot. He was a mixture of far too many predatory species, all of which brought out the worst in him — this tremendous joy in the hunt. This endless, gnawing *hunger* for it.

He had tried to hide what he was from Ryland and his fellow teammates, too ashamed to let them see what he'd become, but there were times on a mission . . . And then the nightmare finally happened, when there was no going back, and he'd been forced to stare at the truth of what kind of monster Whitney had truly created. They'd all been there. His friends. His teammates. In the end, he just had to come to terms with what he was and learn control.

As he continued his prowling trek up the mountain, he was more than a little surprised to see several types of plants and trees that grew only in the rain forests with high humidity. Jonas slowed down to get a better look. This section of forest could easily be part of some bioexperiment that had been going on for years. It was as if he'd stepped into a beautiful, mythical garden.

Exotic flowering plants circled the bark of the trees, climbing high toward the canopy, draping branches in variegated or dark leaves and bright, velvety blossoms. The trees were also varieties that thrived only in warm, humid climates, yet they appeared extremely healthy, trunks wide, branches strong and leaves abundant.

His first thought was that he'd stumbled into one of Whitney's experiments. He knew Whitney was into plants, heard he kept greenhouses all over the world in his hide-aways, where he grew all sorts of plants and flowers, including some of the rarest and most exotic breeds in the world. Hell, he'd even named the girls he'd bought from orphanages after flowers. Some people might have thought that proof of a nurturing soul, but only if they didn't know the sort of cruel, torturous experiments Whitney inflicted on those same girls. All in the name of science and patriotism.

Peter Whitney. A modern-day Mengele wrapped up in an American flag.

Suppressing the sneer that curled his lips, Jonas clamped down on the rage thoughts that Whitney stirred up. This was neither the time nor the place for him to get distracted by old injustices. Because if Whitney was behind whatever was going on up here, he, Jeff and Kyle were in more danger than they suspected.

He took a careful look around, his senses flaring out, utilizing every enhancement he had in order to find any hidden traps and to identify any poisonous plants. He knew one or the other was there. More likely both. He could feel the danger surrounding him.

He pulled up the mental file of poisonous plants he kept in his head and scanned through it as he looked around. He and his team traveled all over the world and trekked through a lot of wild and dangerous places. Often they encountered a variety of environmental dangers while on a mission, including plants so toxic that one unwary scratch could cost someone an arm. Sometimes it seemed like everywhere they went, even the plants were out to kill them. Because of that, Jonas had made a point of studying books on botany, committing to memory every hazardous or helpful plant, tree, shrub or flower they might encounter.

He studied the various flowering bushes and the vines winding their way up the trees. Many of the specimens growing up high were epiphytes, plants that lived by extracting moisture out of the air rather than requiring soil for their roots. The kinds of flowers and vines he was observing just didn't grow in the Lolo National Forest. Certainly, they didn't grow in this particular high-altitude climate. Intense snow was common several months out of the year, and these exotics needed consistent care, warmth and humidity.

Jonas could feel the rising heat in the mist. At this altitude, temperatures should be dropping, but instead, the air was warm and getting downright hot the deeper into the interior he went. Whoever was able to control the temperature inside the groves of trees over such a wide range had a powerful gift. They weren't just manipulating temperatures in a controlled environment. They were manipulating the climate of several square miles of open forest and sustaining that manipulation over time. He didn't know too many of his fellow GhostWalkers capable of such a feat — if any.

He moved slowly, feeling his way with all of his senses. Plants had alarm systems, just the way animals and people did. They could shrink back from heat or cold, from loud noises, or extend their leaves or vines toward appealing music. He had always been able to hide himself from people and animals, even birds and reptiles, but he'd never considered having to include plants.

He tuned his mind to the mist and humidity. Someone had bound nature itself to them. The respect and admiration he felt rose the more he examined the full extent of the shimmering illusion hiding the grove. He was looking at an outdoor greenhouse in an impossible location where few hikers would stumble across it. Two full teams of GhostWalkers made their homes miles below, surrounded by the same national forest, yet they had no idea the phenomenon was above them. The garden had been built *after* the teams' compounds had been established, because he knew both had sent men up the mountain to ensure they had escape routes prior to building.

Jonas was capable of binding nature to him. He hadn't known any other Ghost-Walker could, not even the newer ones Whitney had perfected. He could only enhance what psychic gifts each individual already possessed. As for the gene doping, in the beginning, he'd thrown everything but the kitchen sink into the mix. He was much more cautious with his last two teams. Jonas, being a member of the first team, had no idea what was inside of him. He had discovered hidden talents accidentally and practiced hard at developing them or controlling them, whichever was needed.

The mist contained not only the illusion and the warning, driving anyone away from the area, but also the humidity, pushing the temperature up so that moisture collected in the air throughout the trees. Was there a trap for the unwary? Had vines moved overhead?

Jonas tuned his body to mimic the same molecular structure of the mist so he could disappear into it. He moved deeper into the interior of the forest and the garden. The deeper he got into it, the more he realized the garden had to have been there for some time. Someone had worked on it lovingly with a great attention to detail. Numerous footpaths wound through the forest floor, created by someone tending the various bushes and flowers.

He followed one of the paths winding in and out of the trees. He remained alert for traps and was careful not to trip alarms, but he increased his speed. He needed to find who had bound nature to them and set the mist, and where the GhostWalker team was hiding and what they were up to. Unexpectedly, he came upon several very exotic plants, flowers that were considered so rare they were only known to grow in one or two places in the world, yet here they all were.

Jonas spotted a ghost orchid growing high

in a tree, an epiphyte that required not only high heat and humidity but a certain type of fungus in order to prosper, none of which occurred naturally in the Lolo National Forest. Not far away, a beautiful jade vine was wrapped tight around another tree, its pendulous clusters of claw-shaped flowers hanging a good three meters long. The jade vine was found naturally only in the rain forests of the Philippines, yet here it was in Montana not just surviving but thriving, its magnificent hanging blooms an incredible shade of deep blue.

Jonas recognized the black bat flower. So rare as to be considered endangered in the wild, it was also quite difficult to cultivate. Thirty centimeters in diameter, the flower resembled its namesake bat, with droopy whisker-like stamen that could measure as much as seventy centimeters in length. He also spotted the Rothschild slipper orchid and a flowering Franklin tree. He found it incredible that the variety of flowers from various countries could be successfully cultivated side by side, let alone in this forest. Clearly, someone, for some reason, had brought these rare flowers to this altitude and manufactured the conditions required to grow them.

Of all the incredible blooms growing in

this unprecedented garden, he was most surprised to find the Middlemist Red Camellia. Considered by most to be the rarest flower in the world, there were only two known surviving specimens of Middlemist Red in existence, and neither was growing in the wild. But here they were, several shrubs of them, planted close together and looking very healthy, with glossy leaves and spectacular showy blooms. Although the flowers looked like beautiful roses, the plant was really a camellia. And despite being named Middlemist Red, the blooms were actually a deep, bright pink.

Jonas inched closer to the rare camellias. As he approached, the shrub's branches parted slightly, revealing a shadowy entrance hidden behind them. He went very still. The circle of shrubs were cleverly concealing the presence of a little house built into the side of the mountain. The small dwelling appeared to be constructed entirely from plants native to the forest. Evergreen tree boughs had been woven tightly together to form the walls and roof, vines threading through to tie them securely. Plants grew across the top of the roof, effectively hiding the lodging from aerial or satellite photography. The back of the house was tucked away beneath a rocky overhang, while the dense hedge of Middlemist Red shrubs completely concealed the dwelling from all other sides.

Jonas studied the little house, not moving a muscle. He doubted if the structure contained more than one or two rooms, unless it went back farther into the mountain. That was his biggest worry. Considering the mist, flowers and the woman commanding wild animals, the idea that Whitney was involved was logical. That meant the house could be an entrance to a far greater complex belowground. This could be the threat he was feeling, although it was still vague and distant. So far, he'd only sensed the presence of one woman.

He knew that women Whitney had experimented on had escaped his compound. He also knew that, rather than trusting the GhostWalker teams who aided their getaway, the women had followed their original plan and scattered to make it as difficult as possible for Whitney to reacquire them. The women were distrustful of any Ghost-Walker, any of the soldiers Whitney had experimented on. Who could blame them?

Jonas knew the women had all been taken from orphanages as children, raised under horrific conditions, used in Whitney's scientific experiments so he could perfect his enhancement methods before he tried them on his soldiers. He raised the girls in a stark environment, training them to be soldiers, only to decide later to use them in his breeding program.

At first Whitney had paired specific couples, using pheromones so they would be attracted physically. He had hoped to create surgical strike teams composed of bonded couples, a man and a woman, so it would be easier for them to slip into any country without being identified as soldiers. The paired couple's skills and enhancements would complement one another and enable the pair to handle any mission more effectively than an entire team of special ops soldiers. For all his evil, Whitney was an unswerving patriot. By creating bonded-pair teams of more efficient, more powerful supersoldiers, he was certain he would be saving American lives.

Later, he decided the next step in perfecting his enhancement program was to experiment on the children of the soldiers he created. He no longer bothered ensuring the women were attracted to the men he paired them with in his breeding program. It was no wonder the women didn't trust anyone who had been enhanced by Whitney.

Jonas inhaled slowly. The camellias gave off no real fragrance. None. Still, he was certain there was a wholly feminine feel to the mist and weaves of illusion, to the binding of nature. It was too light, too subtle, to be a man's hand. He had to be cautious. Whitney had trained female soldiers, and there could still be one or two active in his ranks. His heart wanted to accelerate, and he had to actively fight to keep the adrenaline from moving fast through his veins. He felt as if he were on the verge of a great discovery.

He couldn't take chances. Kyle and Jeff were with him. Not only were their lives in his hands, but his team counted on him. He forced air through his lungs, careful to modify each exhalation to match the temperature and vapor content of the surrounding mist. He had no choice but to settle in and wait. That was what predators did. They had patience. They waited for prey. He was a phantom, unseen. He'd disappeared into thin air, and he could outwait anyone or anything.

2

Camellia Mist paced back and forth in the confines of her small house, feeling a bit like a caged animal. She felt a threat approaching across the periphery of her senses, but not a single one of her warning systems had raised an alarm. There were three men camping just inside the lines of her property. It had never happened before, but that didn't mean it couldn't. Besides, the threat didn't feel as if it were coming from them.

The men were sick and disoriented, at least from what she could discern from the reports of the owls and wolves she had keeping a close eye on them. One of the men in particular looked to be in bad shape. He was apparently the most affected by the sonic disruptions she'd woven into the mist. She didn't like making innocent hikers ill, but she had to keep them away from her gardens — and from her. She hoped they would camp for the night and get back on the main trail. In the morning, she planned on doubling the mist around them, leaving just a slight opening to lure them away from her refuge.

Still, she had this terrible, nearly overwhelming feeling of doom. That was never good. She didn't have premonitions often, but when she did, they weren't without cause. She felt . . . hunted. Had Whitney found her? She couldn't imagine that he would. She had been very careful not to leave any trace behind. So very careful.

She'd avoided people, lived off the land, become a complete recluse. She was almost entirely self-sufficient up here in her secluded little garden, and the few times she needed supplies she couldn't harvest, hunt or make herself, she snuck into town at night and broke into stores, avoiding the cameras, careful to take only what she absolutely needed to survive. She always took enough supplies to see her through several months so she wouldn't have to make trips during the winter months, when the snow was deep and shut down the trails and roads.

How would Whitney have found her? He always planted tracking devices in the women, but she found the one in her hip and cut it out. It hadn't been that deep. Had there been a second one? If so, why would he have waited so long before he sent someone after her?

Chewing at her lower lip, a nervous habit Whitney had detested in her and in all the girls, Camellia went to the bed and lay down so she could run her fingers over her skin to feel for any foreign object, no matter how small. She had very sensitive fingertips. More, the blood in her veins was connected to nature, to the plants that grew within the perimeter of her land. She tapped into that environment now, seeking an outside source to aid her in examining her body for anything that Whitney may have surgically placed in her without her knowledge. She found nothing.

No trackers, then, that she could find, yet that feeling of dread refused to go away. If anything, the awareness of a predator closing in on her increased to such an extent that she leapt to her feet and rushed to change into clothes made of soft, organic material that would blend with her garden and allow her to disappear at will. Since no warning had been triggered, she couldn't explain why she was so certain someone was stalking her, but she was absolutely sure. She needed to be outside where she could

53

see what was happening around her and let her plants talk to her.

If the threat was beyond her garden — could it be coming from the GhostWalkers who, as she'd recently discovered, had well-established fortresses several miles below her on the steeper side of the mountain? She would reach for the reptiles, the frogs and lizards. GhostWalkers rarely suspected them, where they often did birds and mammals. Just the idea that a GhostWalker might be stalking her was terrifying.

She had made up her mind she would never return to Whitney's compound and his disgusting breeding program or his horrible experiments. She would rather spend the rest of her life alone with her plants. She'd built a life for herself here. Solitary, yes, but she had everything she needed. As long as she didn't have some kind of serious accident, like break her leg, she was almost entirely self-sufficient. She had a good first aid kit, and she knew how to take care of most injuries, even severe ones. She'd set up perimeter scouts and defenses. And just to be on the safe side, she'd thoroughly explored the surrounding forest and mapped out multiple escape routes in case Whitney's soldiers found her.

All of that had taken time, but she'd managed. She'd done everything she could think of to keep off the radar and build a comfortable, secure, solitary life in her mountaintop garden. She'd been drawn to this mountain, almost a compulsion, and it had taken months to find the perfect place out of the way, set everything up initially and be able to hike into town for supplies. It took a couple of days to backpack using the easiest trail.

Recently, she'd discovered two large compounds where quite a few families made their homes together. It looked like two fortresses developing in two separate areas fairly close together. The compounds had been on the steepest side of the mountain below her, and she had been cautious to go in that direction, not willing to risk an injury until the weather was the best and she was extremely fit.

Camellia had been drawn to that fortress, and yet, at the same time, when she approached, a kind of terror had gripped her and she'd fled without a closer recon. She intended to go back, but she hadn't yet. Every day she kept putting it off. She'd reinforced her own warning systems just in case the GhostWalkers in those buildings got too close for comfort, but even hikers and hunters rarely came around.

The Lolo National Forest was spread out over two million acres and included four wilderness areas. She had deliberately chosen one of the most isolated and inaccessible areas in which to make her home. During the winter months, the roads below were impassable for cars. She guessed those living in the fortress below her had snowmobiles. She had snowshoes — ones she'd constructed herself.

Camellia stood at her door and allowed her senses to flare cautiously out along the vast connective network of all her plants. Belowground, she tapped into the mycelium connecting all the trees together through their root systems, allowing them to communicate with one another. The mycelium ensured the health of the forest and the trees in it with its underground network. She had tapped into it the moment she'd arrived, becoming a part of the system, so it recognized her as being an unthreatening part of the wilderness.

She related to plants and animals. She felt at home with them. She "read" them. "Heard" them. Related to them. Fortunately, Whitney never realized all the things she could do with plants — nor recognized the advantages having the plant DNA from the Middlemist Red Camellia in her gave her. More than anything else, Whitney had wanted to know if his theories regarding the Middlemist were correct. She had escaped before he could ever prove them one way or the other.

Camellia took a deep breath and eased the door of her cabin open just enough to slide her body through. She waited motionless on the first step outside the door. The mist immediately surrounded her, welcoming her as part of itself, her skin absorbing the cool vaporized droplets. She closed her eyes and tuned herself to the mist's exact structure.

There was a reason she had the Middlemist Red Camellia surrounding her cabin. Like other plants, the veins in the leaves carried water and minerals, and also moved food energy around to whatever part of the plant needed it. But the Middlemist Red hid something else within its veins, something discovered in the early days in China, where it had grown in abundance. Strangely, mysteriously, the beautiful Red had vanished from its native country, where it had thrived for so many years. There were many theories, of course, but only Red knew the real reason. Whitney had come closest with his hypothesis. He had been determined to find the explanation.

Camellia looked at the blossoms, so abundant, healthy and vibrant, a deep pink that bordered on red, the petals tight and looking so much like a rose. The shrubs always reacted to her in kinship, feeling her presence, her connection to them. The plant knew what it was like to be hunted — to have someone want to destroy you because you were different. Or imprison you and take you apart because they were determined to find out your secrets.

In 1804, before the plants had vanished in China, John Middlemist, a nurseryman from West London, had brought back one of the camellias with him to donate to Kew Gardens. The plant was then housed in the Duke of Devonshire's three-hundred-foot conservatory with his camellia collection to be propagated.

During World War II, when the bombardment was at its height, a bomb exploded near the conservatory, blowing out all the glass, but the building avoided complete destruction. There was a short time when the mentally ill were housed on the property. A bomb was planted in the conservatory but failed to detonate. After the war, the conservatory fell into complete disrepair. At that time, there was no sign any of the rare camellias were left alive.

It wasn't until 1999 that the Middlemist Red Camellia was spotted and identified once again in the conservatory. Where had the flower been all that time? Why hadn't anyone seen it or been able to identify it? Granted, it took years for volunteers to restore the conservatory to its former glory and ten years for botanists to identify flower species. It took three years just to identify the Middlemist Red Camellia using historical bibliography and paintings.

Dr. Whitney had his hypothesis as to why the plant had disappeared in China so completely. Why hadn't the plant been destroyed when the bombing blew out the windows and exposed the conservatory to the elements? Why hadn't the bomb detonated inside the conservatory? Why hadn't anyone detected the Middlemist Red Camellia or any of the other rare camellias in the ten years the botanists had worked to identify the various plants? If Whitney had Camellia longer, he might have been able to prove himself right, because she knew that Middlemist Red had concealed itself in plain sight, just as Camellia was doing now.

There was far more to Middlemist Red than anyone — even Dr. Peter Whitney — could have imagined. The remarkable shrub possessed great healing properties; the oil from the plant helped to prevent cell damage and reduce inflammation due to its potent antioxidant properties. There were so many other uses, from skin care to hair strengtheners to antiaging. But that didn't even begin to cover Middlemist Red's secrets.

Red had the ability to form a network and use it to spread out in every direction, just as the mycelium connected underground to the trees in the forest. Camellia hadn't fully developed that gift before she'd escaped the compound with the other women. She wished she had, and yet the fact that she hadn't probably saved her from being shipped to one of Whitney's other facilities. Had he known what she was capable of, she might never have managed to escape.

It was possible that being completely alone had forced her to develop her talents faster. She'd concentrated on them, practicing when she had no one to talk to but her plants.

When she fled, she'd broken into Whitney's greenhouse and stolen some of his exotics. It had been a stupid thing to do, risking her life and freedom, but the compulsion had been too strong to resist. Camellia had waited in the greenhouse to make certain all the girls got away. The last one to make it out was Marigold. Mari's man and his friends, all of whom were GhostWalkers, had aided the girls' escape. While she waited, Camellia gathered up the plants that she wanted to bring with her, including Middlemist Red. She had known Middlemist Red wanted to leave with her. All along, the plant had been in on the escape plans the women had made together. Red had made it known to Camellia that it was essential the plant go with her. That was one thing that had made Camellia feel as if she wasn't entirely alone.

Due to her ability to merge with any organic and biological network, Camellia was completely tuned to the entire area she claimed. When she couldn't find a hidden threat, she expanded her search, using the mycelium beneath the ground to see outside her garden. She found the men camping. There were two of them. Hadn't the owls and wolves reported three men?

Camellia puzzled over that discrepancy. She couldn't reach out to any of her sentries because if she was right, and one of Whitney's supersoldiers was close, he might feel the surge in energy that accompanied her "talking" to the owls or wolves. It wasn't really speaking, more like pushing images into their heads, but she had established herself as the nucleus in a vast network of communication in the forest, and the creatures were used to interacting with her.

She needed to get close to those two men and ascertain if they were enhanced — if they were Whitney's supersoldiers come to take her back — or if they were innocent hikers or hunters. It was impossible to tell from this distance. Moving meant possible detection. She considered the risks. Perhaps it would be better to move the mycelium closer to the surface right beneath them. The underground network could give her a better feel of their energy. Making up her mind, she tapped into the natural grid and sent the command.

She was very aware of the two men sitting close to the fire. She knew one was feeling ill and drinking water continually. The other man was looking after him and acting as a sentry, occasionally getting up to peer over the rocks surrounding them to ensure they were safe from any wild animals. Although they were close to the fire, they weren't facing it directly. Just that small detail made her uneasy. A trained soldier would know not to look directly into flames at night if they wanted to keep their vision.

Her uneasiness increased without warning. Why? Both men rose and moved to the rocks, sitting on them, rather than on the ground. The taller of the two wrapped a blanket of some kind around the sick one and then faced out toward the forest alertly. Was that what made her so uneasy? She took a deep breath, inhaling the scents around her. The air was free of fragrance, giving her the ability to smell an intruder if he was close.

There was nothing but the fresh scent of the forest, the soil and exotic flowers she was familiar with and could catalog. Juniper? Cedar? She inhaled again to see if she could actually isolate those two scents and track them outside or inside her garden. The red cedar was common in the forest, but she'd never really isolated that scent. And juniper? Spruce? There were spruce trees. Why were the tree scents so much more prominent to her all of a sudden? Was it because she'd brought the mycelium so much closer to the surface and it was connected to the trees, trees she was unable to see?

She frowned, trying to puzzle out what she was missing. It was strange that her mind didn't want to leave the puzzle of the tree scents. She found the faint aroma exhilarating, almost intoxicating. It was as if the scent seemed to sizzle along her nerve endings. That was weird, because it wasn't moving along the network so much as actually affecting her body's nerve endings. Still, she had discipline, and she forced her mind back to the puzzle of the two men camping in the circle of boulders.

They had been sitting quietly near their fire, both on the ground until she had given the command to the mycelium network to come up closer to the surface where she could read the two men. They had moved right after she gave the order. Directly after. Within moments. Almost as if they heard it. Was that even possible?

Camellia replayed the moment in her head. She had a good memory, and she stored data like a computer might. The taller one was restless, but he didn't appear to be tuned to the network. He seemed as if he was looking into the forest for anything that might be threatening them. The other man, the sick one, had his head down. Both had reacted at the same time just after she had issued her command to the mycelium, the sick one coming to his feet and the taller man turning immediately to help him get on the boulder. Their movements were co-ordinated. Smooth. Too smooth. That sent up another red flag. Icy fingers of dread raked down her spine.

Neither looked as if they had tapped into her networks, but something had tipped them off to get off the ground. She was absolutely certain of it. That meant . . . Her breath caught in her throat. She did her best not to react. That had to mean she wasn't alone on her own network. Someone else, the man hunting her, the man smelling so faintly of juniper and spruce, had tapped into *both* her networks. It was the only way he could have known to warn them. If he was inside her garden, it meant he was capable of being part of the Middlemist Red Camellia network. So much a part of it that he wouldn't raise alarms.

She didn't think Whitney had access to the plant. She'd taken the one from his laboratory, and there just weren't dozens of others lying around. There was a specimen in London, in the Duke's conservatory, and the other in New Zealand, but would Whitney risk an international incident to steal a plant from either location?

Oh, dear God. Fear clawed at her throat. At her lungs. Would Whitney truly risk an international incident? He was an evil bastard who bought orphan girls to torture and use like lab rats. He'd planned to *breed* them like livestock. What *wouldn't* he risk to get his experiments back?

65

For a moment she couldn't breathe. If he had enhanced one of his supersoldiers with the Middlemist Red, that meant the soldier could be right there in her garden with her and she wouldn't be able to detect his presence.

Camellia tried desperately to calm down so she could think. She had always known it was possible — even probable — that she would be found. She just thought it would be much later. Much, much later. She had an escape plan. More than one. But none of those plans had included escaping from someone with the same talents she possessed. That didn't mean she couldn't use what was already in place. She might have to modify a few steps, but she'd always been flexible. And she'd always been lethal. Unlike some of the others, she had no problem defending herself or any innocent.

It was possible she could use the two men sitting on the boulders to distract the hunter. He had warned them. She hadn't seen a lot of real camaraderie among Whitney's supersoldiers, but that didn't mean that one or two of them couldn't actually feel real loyalty for one another. It seemed as if the tall man cared for the sicker one. She had cultivated weapons from the fungi to aid her should she need them. She would hate to use them so soon and tip her hand, but this might be her only chance to get away.

She knew the hunter had no more idea where she was than she knew where he was. He was a phantom, concealing himself in the mist. She was the same. She didn't dare move now. She remained very still, but she inhaled and exhaled, keeping her breath steady, her heartbeat matching that of the earth. Very softly she initiated a slight tremor in the ground just under the rocks where the two men were seated, throwing them sideways.

You hurt my friends, Jeff will burn down your garden and everything in it.

His voice was low, a sound that moved in her mind so intimately, stroking like a caress on her skin when it should have been an abrasive intrusion. While the words were a clear threat, the delivery and tone made her shiver, igniting every nerve ending in her body. That voice poured into her the way water and energy filled the Middlemist Red's vein and carried energy and nutrients throughout the plant wherever it was needed. She needed. She'd been empty until that voice filled her.

Camellia tried to trace him using his voice, but he was definitely on the wide network, and he was as tuned to it as she was. It was as if he were a ghost. She puzzled out his threat. He wouldn't burn down her garden; his friend Jeff would. She guessed Jeff was the taller of the two men sitting on the rocks. The man in her network couldn't burn down the garden and destroy the plants any more than she could.

Who are you? Three words. A simple enough question. She was positive her position was just as hidden as his was.

She felt a jolt along a thread of the Middlemist Red Camellia network. In the brief moment, all subtleties were gone. The vibration was decidedly masculine and wholly sexual as it traveled back to her. This was far worse than she'd ever imagined.

Her heart went wild. There was no way he hadn't felt her reaction, just as she felt the shock of his at the sound of her voice. He hadn't been any more prepared for her than she had been for him. There was some relief in knowing he hadn't expected their pairing — and there was absolutely no question that Whitney had paired the two of them. She was reacting to his scent, to the sound of his voice, just as he had reacted to hers.

My name is Jonas Harper. Tell me who you are.

Her stomach reacted, tied into a thousand

knots. His voice was powerful, a whisper of command, yet it held a thousand promises. She steeled herself against that lure. She would *never* go back. She'd made up her mind she'd rather be dead. She wasn't going to be trapped by his voice or anything he said to her. He knew who she was, or maybe he needed confirmation on which of the women she was. It was possible he didn't know who he'd been paired with. That would be like Whitney.

Could Whitney have paired this man with all of the escapees? She fought back a dark, unsettling surge of fury, a knot of negative emotion that was so unlike her.

I will never go back to that place. She counted off seconds before she spoke again and then threw her voice off on different strands to ensure he couldn't trace the sound back to where she was. *There is no way to lie on this network. I am willing to kill you, your friends, burn my garden and die myself.* Even as she told him the absolute truth, she knew she had spoken too many words in a row, communicated too long. Better to have given short bursts.

This soldier was too good. Not once had he given himself away, other than that faint scent she found intoxicating. He had infiltrated her garden and *both* networks, the mycelium and Middlemist Red networks, without giving his presence away, and now was stalking her using her own system to do so. She couldn't make amateur mistakes. She'd been out of the game too long.

You can hear that I'm not lying. I didn't come here seeking you. I had no idea you were here. I felt a threat and started following it to its source. I still feel it. And it isn't coming from you. Can you feel it too?

There was absolute honesty in his voice. Middlemist Red would know a lie, and so would she. Even so, she wasn't prepared to trust him. She was still feeling as if she was being hunted, and he was here. He had bypassed all her security measures, all her sentries, traps and alarms. Who knew what else he could do?

Did Whitney send you?

Absolutely not. I don't work for Whitney. He did enhance me. I work for the United States government. I'm a member of GhostWalker Team One, the first unit he experimented on. You have to be one of the women who escaped when the Nortons and Team Two went after Marigold. They hoped to get Whitney at that time, but he managed to evade them.

Camellia was silent while she processed what he'd said. Marigold had been the last woman to leave the compound, and she'd left with Ken Norton. Camellia had lost track of her. The plan had been for all of them to go in different directions. They were to rendezvous at one point where they had been stashing money collectively after every mission they went on. The money was to be divided evenly, and they would all go their separate ways to make it more difficult for Whitney's soldiers to track them.

If you truly are not here for me, then go away. Leave me alone.

This time he was the silent one. Her heart thudded. Did she really want him to leave? He was the first human being she'd talked to in so long. She wanted to see him. Put a face to that smoky voice. She tried to imagine what he looked like and couldn't. She kept herself very still, holding her breath, waiting. Needing. It was just that she didn't know how to trust.

Do you feel the threat?

She let air out slowly. It was there. The feeling of being hunted. *Yes. It is vague. I thought it was you, but you're close. If you're the one making me feel as if I'm threatened, I would think . . .* She trailed off. The feeling would be much more intense. Jonas wasn't the impending threat, but he was definitely trouble.

There are women and children living in the

GhostWalker compounds farther down the mountain. I believe you know some of them. Would you leave them to Whitney when you clearly could help them?

She pressed the heel of her hand to her forehead. Of course she wouldn't do that. *If the threat is to children, I would aid them, but I would do it my way. I am not going to allow you to draw me into the open when you could . . .* Again, she trailed off. What did she expect him to do? She believed Whitney hadn't sent him. He couldn't lie to her, not when he was using the Middlemist Red Camellia network.

Do you have a tattoo of the flower on your ankle?

She didn't like that simple question. Why would he think that she would have a flower tattooed on her ankle? She resisted the urge to touch the beautiful replica of the Middlemist Red Camellia. The tattoo artist had been a genius, his work amazing. The camellia bloom on her ankle was so beautiful, she often spent time tracing the petals of the flower with the pads of her fingers, half expecting them to feel velvet soft. The flower appeared three dimensional, the petals standing out in vivid detail. She loved the tattoo. It was the only thing Whitney had ever done for the girls that was decent. He'd named each one of them after a flower and had the artist tattoo each girl's namesake on her ankle.

Hard little knots of dread formed in her stomach. A question burned on the tip of her tongue, but she didn't want to ask. Didn't want to know. Whitney had deceived them so many times, pretending to do something nice for them, when in fact he hadn't. Her tattoo meant something to her. She didn't want that taken away too.

Abruptly, she turned to walk into the center of her garden. She didn't know if she was planning to make an escape, but she couldn't stay still. He was too close, and he was going to tell her something terrible. Take one last thing away from her.

"Don't go."

He spoke aloud. His breath was warm in her ear. He didn't block her path intentionally, but she walked right into him.

"Stay with me. Talk to me."

There was an ache in his voice. It was barely there. More felt than heard, but it was there. She was so susceptible to him. It didn't help that she hadn't spoken to another human being in so long she was desperate for company, even as the thought terrified her.

Camellia lifted her chin. She was a soldier.

She wasn't the ashamed, worthless being Whitney had reduced her to, forcing her into his breeding program after all the years of discipline and training. All of the girls' hard work to become military operatives had been for nothing. That didn't mean Camellia didn't continue to train every single day. She had always known Whitney's men would catch up with her and she would have to fight her way free.

She took a breath, braced herself and turned slightly to look at Jonas. Florentine gold looked back at her. The air left her lungs in a rush of heat. Those eyes held intelligence. A predatory, very focused stare. They devoured her hungrily. Almost possessively.

"He paired us. Whitney. He paired us." His voice was a blend of smoke and the wild of the forest. "Even if he hadn't, I would still think you're the most beautiful woman I've ever seen."

She couldn't help the answering flutter of pleasure that accompanied his declaration. There was utter sincerity in his tone. No one had ever given her a compliment before. She wasn't certain how to handle it, so she didn't acknowledge it.

His hair was thick, a mixture of every shade of blond there was. With her enhanced night vision, the colors seemed almost silvery. It was all she could do not to reach out and bury her fingers in the mass. His face was all hard angles and planes, too dangerous to be called traditionally handsome, but she was immediately drawn to him.

"I haven't spoken to anyone in a very long time," Camellia admitted. "I'm a little rusty."

"I'm going to let my brothers off the rocks. Kyle was feeling the effects of the mist. It made him pretty sick. He needs to sleep. I'd like to stay and talk with you for a little while. Maybe we can figure out where the threat is coming from."

The moment he said he wanted to stay and talk, she'd nearly panicked, but then he said the right thing — that they could figure out where the threat was coming from. He treated her like an equal. Like she had a brain. Of course, she still wasn't letting down her guard, not for a minute. She had the advantage of being on her home turf. She knew every escape route, and she was prepared to leave everything and escape. He also didn't know her resolve. Camellia was deadly when she had to be, and she wouldn't hesitate to kill if left with no other recourse.

She nodded to let him know she was amenable to allowing the two men off the boulders. She hadn't pulled back the mycelium network from close to the surface, nor would she. Had he asked her to, she would have been very suspicious, but Jonas had asked her permission before he sent word to his friends.

"Are you going to tell me your name? I'm not with Whitney, and nobody sent me to find you. So I honestly don't know your name, but I'd like to."

Camellia hesitated for a moment, weighing whether or not it would be prudent to give up her name to him. He waited patiently.

"Camellia Mist." She felt silly stating her surname. She hadn't considered a surname when she was trying to build a profile for the outside world. She didn't need a name because she had no intention of ever being around other people. "Whitney gave us the names of flowers. I chose a last name and I wasn't very inventive."

He was too close to her and he hadn't moved away. Every time she inhaled, she seemed to draw him into her lungs, and he was . . . intoxicating. Those eyes of his were difficult to look away from. All that gold. All that intelligence. More, the cunning, predatory, *animalistic* quality that aroused something in her. She didn't know if she wanted to run free with him or run from him.

She moistened suddenly dry lips, very aware of his friends stepping off the rocks into the center of the ring of boulders. She knew if she sent a command to the sentries, through either of the networks, he would know. She didn't use either of them. She reached for the alpha wolf in the pack closest to home.

Stay alert for me. Keep an eye on the visitors and report any movement. Do not engage with them.

She had to communicate using visuals, but the alpha was used to her talking to him and knew much more than he let on. When he responded in the affirmative, she reached for the pair of Great Gray owls that had stuck with her since she'd first escaped Whitney. The pair had been bonded in their first year together when she'd come across them in the mountains. Someone had shot the male. The female was beside herself, desperate to help him. Her cries had brought Camellia to the pair. She'd run off predators and taken the time to nurse the male back to health. The pair had traveled with her in spite of her repeated admonishment that she was hunted and didn't need to put them in danger. Now, she had no idea what she'd do without them.

Blue. She reached for the female. *I need eyes on the two men camping. Gray,* she added, bringing in the male, who she knew was hunting vole, their favorite meal. *Just watch them for me. Make certain they stay where they are. If they move outside that circle, let me know.* She kept her energy as low as possible, pushing the images into the minds of her sentries, hoping Jonas wouldn't feel the slight shift in power.

She felt the familiar whisper of movement the female owl used to answer her. It was always gentle, as if the owl were nudging a baby owlet. There was no sound, just that little slight touch, as if her feathers had slipped over the walls of her mind. The male was a different story if he chose to answer. He communicated with sound unless he was too far away, and then he stroked what felt like a gentle tip of his wing along her mind, a distinctive difference.

Camellia turned her focus back to Jonas. "Why did you ask me if I had a tattoo?" Her heart began to thud. She moved back deliberately, taking two steps away from him.

He had seemed very large, towering over her when she stood close, but when she

78

stepped back, she could see he probably wasn't quite six feet. He was lithe, sinewy, his muscles defined. He reminded her of a jungle cat, flexible, capable of flowing silently over the ground and concealing himself in very small spaces.

"Whitney did put trackers in all the women, but he guessed you would find them, so he had an artist design tattoos with the ability for a satellite to track hidden powder chips he embedded in either the leaves or petals. They're like dust particles. Fortunately, his ability to track is intermittent, and most of the women have had the particles removed from their tattoos. In the meantime, from what I understand, they've blocked him from tracking the tattoos, unless he's found a new way to do it."

Why was it such a surprise that Whitney hadn't done one single nice thing for the women? Not one.

"So he knew where I was all along? Why wouldn't he come after me?"

"As I understand it, he did send his men after a pregnant woman."

"Rose." She whispered her name.

"She's safe," he assured. "She's married to a GhostWalker on another team and very well protected. It was a hard-won battle though. Her husband and another Ghost-

Walker on the team nearly died, but she's good and so is the baby. She had a boy."

Camellia turned away from him, not willing for him to see how much that news affected her emotionally. Rose had made it out, was safe and had a little boy. She was married. "Who did she marry?" she asked Jonas deliberately. Another test.

Rose had told Camellia that she had begged Whitney to pair her with Kane after Kane had been transferred away from the laboratory. She didn't want Kane to be the only one living in the hell of needing to be with just that one person physically when she felt she had been the one to ask Whitney to bring Kane into the program after she'd refused every other partner. Rose had watched him, a guard on the grounds, from her window for weeks before she decided on him and had asked Whitney to partner her with him.

"He's on the third GhostWalker team, and he is the biological father of her child. He was a guard assigned to the base where Whitney was conducting his experiments. At the time, it hadn't been discovered. Kane, along with another member of that same team, brought out evidence against Whitney. Unfortunately, Whitney had too many friends in high places, and he was tipped off and was able to go underground. In any case, Rose is married to Kane Cannon."

Relief swept over her. Not once had Jonas lied to her. She honestly didn't know how to trust him, but she wanted to. She wanted to just be a normal person and have a conversation about what was going on in the outside world.

"I believe the reason Whitney didn't send anyone to get you is because once it was discovered the tattoos had the tracking devices in them, the trackers were jammed," Jonas continued.

That made sense. "Do you live in one of those homes down below me? I just discovered them about a month ago. That's the steepest side of the mountain, and I had never explored in that direction before. I caught sight of those compounds and ran like a rabbit." She forced a laugh, trying to cover up the fact that while she was telling the truth, a part of her didn't want to talk about the GhostWalkers. "I had no idea anyone was so close to me."

"You've been up here a long time. You must have gone down into town for supplies," Jonas said.

Right away, she noticed he hadn't answered her question. She took another couple of steps away from him. Distance was good. She didn't want to keep breathing him into her lungs. It was too intimate. Standing close to him in the night was too intimate. And the sound of his voice was too addictive. The more he spoke, the more she wanted to get close to him, to beg him not to leave. The chemistry between them was pretty explosive.

"There's a much easier route for me. I go straight down on the other side. I can't take a chance of breaking a leg, so until I had everything in place, I didn't explore too far from home."

He visibly winced at the idea of her breaking a bone. "It must have been difficult the first few winters you spent up here without supplies."

She shrugged. "I was free, Jonas. Freedom makes up for a lot of things."

He nodded. "We were put in cages for a brief period of time, nothing in comparison to what any of you or the other women have gone through, but it was enough to let me know I would never do well in prison. Not to say I haven't gone into a cage a time or two to get a fellow GhostWalker out since then."

They stood for several minutes looking at each other, and finally Jonas nodded toward her porch hidden behind the Middlemist Red Camellias. "Can we sit there and talk for a while?"

Her porch was small, and it would be extremely intimate surrounded by the draping branches of flowers. She nodded because there was no resisting those eyes. She turned and led the way through the camellias to her home.

3

Camellia Mist was beautiful. Just looking at her robbed Jonas of his ability to breathe. Who knew that when he'd set out to find the source of the threat to their team he'd find his other half? Jonas knew that, even without Whitney's interference, she would have been his first choice. Probably his only choice for someone permanent in his life.

Her looks, as gorgeous as they were, weren't the source of his attraction, though he found her utterly beautiful, from her lush curved body to the dark hair that blended in with the night to those eyes, blue like cornflowers or darkening into a turbulent sea, hinting at the cat in her before she turned her head to lead the way to her cabin. No, the real attraction was everything else. She had survived on her own for a very long time. Not only had she survived, but she had built this incredible, beautiful garden, a little piece of paradise that provided sustenance and protection as well as beauty. A revealing reflection of herself.

Clearly, she was highly intelligent, resourceful and no doubt lethal. She was everything a man like Jonas could possibly desire in a partner. He found her sexy. What she might not know, he was absolutely certain he could teach her. He was more than willing to learn from her.

She walked without a sound. Completely silent. Her hips had a feminine sway that drew his attention, as did the fact that the Middlemist Red parted her branches as they approached.

"So many growing free and beautiful," he commented, touching one of the limbs gently in a kind of reverence. He felt a curious sensation in his veins, a rush of power close to the towering shrubs as they formed an arc over their heads. "Look how unbelievably healthy they are, when they usually only exist in a greenhouse. You're amazing, woman."

Camellia looked over her shoulder, a small smile lighting her eyes, throwing more silvery blue into the dark blue. "*She's* truly beautiful, isn't she?"

Jonas looked at the wealth of flowers on the shrubs. The branches were covered in them. Each blossom was large and looked more like a rose with fresh, tight petals, as if they'd just blossomed, a brilliant pink.

"What's your secret with these plants? Do you talk to them? I've got a small place of my own now, but I haven't exactly got your way with plants, although I'd like to."

She sent him another look over her shoulder. When she half turned, her hair swung, a gleaming, thick mass of dark strands, flying in the air and cascading down her back. Her eyes glittered a strange silvery blue again, reminding him of a jungle cat, and her mouth — that generous mouth of hers that gave him one too many fantasies — smiled at him.

"Of course you can. How do you think you managed to tap into *both* networks?"

He raised an eyebrow, uncertain what she meant. She had waved her hand toward the single chair on the porch. He shook his head and indicated she take it.

"I'll get another one. Give me a minute." She disappeared into her house.

The moment she was gone, his gut reacted, hard knots developing. He found himself pacing, adrenaline flooding his system. He wasn't a man to get attached to a woman. He didn't think about them after spending time with them or want them in his bed all night. He never took one to his home. He knew Whitney had manipulated them with his "pairing," using pheromones and some kind of virus he put in their bodies so they were physically attracted, but already Jonas knew he was connected to Camellia on a much more emotional level. That made no sense.

Do you understand why I'm feeling this way? Do you feel it as well? Not just physical? He made up his mind he would be totally honest — or as honest as he could when it came to what was between them. He wasn't going to hide his strange, unexpected emotions from her. He couldn't hide his physical reaction to her, and she would expect that. He was laying himself pretty bare.

The door opened and a chair came through first. He took it from her, even though he could see she was extremely strong. She was enhanced. She might look delicate, but she wasn't. He could never forget that.

Deliberately, he met her gaze over the back of the chair, standing there, trapping her in the doorway, the rattan rocker between them. She didn't flinch away. She had courage. Her eyes were back to liquid sea blue. Her long dark lashes fringed the blue, making the color even deeper. He was utterly obsessed. Hell, he even noticed her skin, a beautiful silky expanse that looked as fresh and soft as the Middlemist petals that surrounded them.

"Stop, Jonas. You're broadcasting very loud. I've never had anyone think those things about me."

"I think a lot of things about you. Look at this place. The courage and the amount of work it took to build it." There was admiration and respect in his voice and mind. He didn't hide it. She deserved both. "But I would like an answer to my question. I can feel a mutual physical attraction between us. I believe it would be there, Whitney or no Whitney. But I definitely feel a much deeper connection to you in a short space of time — an emotional one. I need to know if you're feeling the same way at all. It's okay if you crush me."

He did his best to go for humor. He wasn't speaking telepathically. He wasn't using what she referred to as the "network." He spoke aloud deliberately so she wouldn't feel how much it would hurt when she said no. He expected her to say no.

Weirdly, the branches of several of the plants of the Middlemist Red shifted position as though reaching out to him. They brushed against him gently, as if consoling him. He could have sworn he heard mur-

murs, a peculiar humming melody, a song of sorts. Strangely, he did feel better. More grounded. The adrenaline rush slowed. His breathing went back to his normal rate, and his heartbeat steadied. It felt as if the plants had wrapped their arms around him and spoke to him.

The night wasn't silent by any means. He heard the wind whispering through the leaves in the trees. Night insects droned on incessantly. Lizards skittered in the vegetation on the forest floor. He could hear the rustling of mice, voles, and other creatures racing around, looking for food and doing their best to avoid the sharp eyes of the owls hunting for a meal. The night was always alive just as the day was.

Jonas kept his gaze fixed on Camellia's face. She touched her teeth to the side of her full bottom lip and bit down for a moment. Sighed. Thought about not answering him. He knew the exact moment she capitulated, and his gut clenched hard. Waiting.

"Yes." Her admission was low.

Camellia glanced at the blossoms, the way they were surrounding Jonas protectively. There was no other word for it, and he had no explanation for the plant behavior, but he had the feeling that she did. He set the chair facing out toward the garden but also angling it toward the other chair so they could easily see one another as they talked. He wanted to watch the expressions on her face, not just to see what she was thinking but also because he enjoyed looking at her. He didn't think he'd ever tire of that.

"What's it like living with so many people around you, Jonas?" Camellia sank into the rocker, curling up like a cat. Her palm curled around her ankle where the tattoo was.

Jonas could tell it was an automatic gesture. She did that often. Her thumb slid over the petals of the flower, a little sweep. Heat rushed through his veins and settled in the pads of his fingers, his mind mapping out the delicate bone structure of her face, wishing he could commit her to memory by braille. He knew she would already be forever etched into his mind, but he ached for the right for skin-to-skin contact.

One of the branches of the Middlemist Red dipped lower, a blossom sliding along Camellia's high cheekbone right where he imagined tracing the pads of his fingers. As the petals of the flower slipped over her face, he physically felt her soft skin and the small, fine bones under the pads of his own fingers as if he were the one touching her. The sensation was strong and very real.

His breath caught in his throat. His heart jerked, on the verge of a discovery that made no sense at all. Deliberately, his gaze dropped to her lips. That perfect bow of a generous mouth, with her lips the exact color of the Middlemist Red Camellia. The *exact* color. He wanted to rub the pads of his fingers over her lips to feel how soft they were.

Immediately, the branch dipped again, a blossom moving against Camellia's mouth, the petals stroking her lips. Instantly, the sensation of velvet soft was transferred to the pads of his fingers. His gaze collided with hers.

"What the hell is going on, Camellia?"

She tilted her chin. "I don't know you. That's what we're doing, right? Talking. Getting to know one another. I'm not going to just trust you because you say Whitney didn't send you."

"You know he didn't."

She shrugged. "Okay, maybe I do know that much. But I don't know why you're here. I've been here for a long time. It's obvious that you've been down below for a long while, yet all of a sudden, you decide something is wrong and you come here to my little tiny piece of the woods that no one else has ever discovered. It isn't like they haven't come this way. Other GhostWalkers have come close."

Jonas believed her. Jack and Ken Norton, the two men who had originally made their home on the mountain and leased part of their acreage to fellow team members, had roamed all over the mountain. They would have ventured to the altitude Camellia had settled in.

"No one else has ever penetrated your security?"

She shook her head. "Not once. They come close but veer away, taking the trail, believing the illusion. You're the only one who hasn't. That bothers me, Jonas."

He listened to the cadence of her voice. More, his body seemed very tuned to hers. Not just sexually, but the blood running through his veins. Up until that last sentence, everything she said seemed fine. Then his blood reacted. There was a strange rippling effect, a light churning sensation that caused his skin to prickle and his mind to reject her low, almost whispered ending.

"I don't think it does bother you, Camellia. I think you want it to bother you. You think the fact that I saw through the illusion should bother you, but it doesn't. *That's* what bothers you." He called her on it.

He kept his voice soft, a velvet caress brushing over her skin and sinking into her mind as gently as he could. He wanted to be branded there. Branded on her bones, just the way he was certain she was on his. The branches of the Middlemist Red Camellia swayed so that the blossoms seemed to hold the two of them in an embrace for a moment, and then with a slight breeze, released them again. Had Jonas not been so intently watching Camellia's face, he would have missed the small tell in her expression. She knew those branches were touching them both of their own volition. Reading the two of them.

"At least let's be honest with one another," he prompted. "I'm not trying to upset you, Camellia. I really want to get to know you and maybe get a few answers to questions I've had about myself."

Camellia regarded him in silence while that slight breeze ruffled her hair and the pink blossoms touched her face as if to soothe her. "How much do you know about Whitney's experiments?"

Jonas sighed and shoved his fingers through his hair. "We all agreed to strengthen our psychic abilities. Everyone in the GhostWalker program volunteered. We thought it was a good thing. We had a chance to prevent other soldiers from getting killed in combat. I tested fairly high in quite a number of areas. On Team One, there were several of us who did. I think Whitney was very excited about that. He convinced us he knew what he was doing. Unfortunately, he didn't."

"You look like you're a capable soldier to me," she answered.

"In the beginning, we were mostly a mess." Jonas was strictly honest. "Whitney did more than enhance our psychic abilities. He messed with our genetic coding without saying a word to any of us. He removed the filters to our brains. Some of us needed anchors to draw the energy away from us, or we got brain bleeds. Because we were unaware of the new genetics that made us more aggressive, faster and able to do things we couldn't do before, we made mistakes that hurt others." He looked down at his hands. "Not just hurt others. People were killed. Our team was separated and locked up. There were a couple of factions that took an unhealthy interest in us. One was trying to murder us and the other trying to study us."

"Whitney would want to continue his experiments," Camellia said.

He nodded. "Ryland, along with Whitney's daughter, Lily, helped us escape. Ryland runs our team and is married to Lily now. Lily taught us exercises to develop shields in our brains in order to be able to be around other people for short periods of time without an anchor. It felt like a long road learning what we were and what we could do. We're still learning. Mostly, we learned we could only count on each other to survive."

Jonas kept his eyes on her face the entire time he gave her the truth. He didn't tell her the hell they'd all been in — separated, knowing they were under a death sentence, afraid to go to sleep, knowing others were being murdered and unable to help one another. She'd been in a similar situation most of her life, imprisoned by Whitney, having to stand by while he tortured the other girls, unable to aid them.

Camellia shook her head and then looked down at her hands. "It's so terrible to feel helpless. I didn't know, for a very long time, if I had anything to contribute to my sisters. I've always been a strong telepath, but my healing abilities didn't show up until my late teens, and then they weren't strong. I had to really work at drawing that talent out. Or at least, I thought I was working at it. I didn't want Whitney to know I had that

95

gift, so I would try little experiments when I was alone in my room."

Jonas frowned. "Such as?" He knew he wasn't going to like what she did.

She sent him a little grin. The smile put a gleam in the blue of her eyes. "I'd cut myself, not deep, just a little slice, then try to close it. At first I had to make it look like I fell and hurt myself because I was lousy at healing. Eventually, I got good enough to heal the skin so there wasn't a single mark."

He not only saw it; he *felt* that she was pleased with herself. This time the ripple in his veins was a heat that flowed like slow molasses, making him so aware of her, he could barely breathe. There was no pointing out to her that it wasn't the best way to test her skills, not when she looked back on a terrible time in her life and yet somehow had a good memory.

"You're happy because you outwitted Whitney."

"He always believes he's superior to every-one, the smartest man in the room. I will give him his due: he is brilliant, and when it comes to science and scientific discovery, he's ages ahead of his time. But that bril-liance also leads him to underestimate oth-ers, and that will ultimately be his downfall. I don't know what happened to make him believe women are so inferior and incapable of genuine intelligence, but even as children, the twelve of us were often able to conceal things from him. As we got older, we became very good at it."

Jonas nodded his understanding. "We realized almost immediately that we couldn't let him or anyone else know what we could do. Like your talents, ours keep developing and growing stronger. We don't want them documented. There's a faction in the government that fears us. They send us on what basically amounts to suicide missions. Whitney does his best to throw challenges at us. Now that some of the men and women on the teams have children, Whitney does everything he can to get his hands on the kids."

Camellia looked appalled. "You can't let him."

"That's why we're building a stronghold here. Team Three has one in San Francisco and Team Four in Louisiana."

She lifted her chin, her eyes clear as they met his, but her fingers twisted together in her lap. He could tell she was emotional, not only because the branches of the Middlemist Red dipped close to her but because he felt it in the way his body reacted.

"Lily married one of your teammates, Ryland? Is she happy? Lily was always wonderful. I know some of the others thought of her as a traitor, but she couldn't help the way Whitney treated her. He filled her full of lies."

"It was very difficult for her to learn the truth about him," Jonas said, trying to be careful. "She was really thrown when she discovered what he'd done to all of you and so many other girls. You weren't the only ones he experimented on. But yes, she's very happy now. She's very loved by not only Ryland but all the teams. They have a son, Daniel. He's quite the handful."

Her eyes lit up. "I can imagine. I'm so glad she found a place where she's protected from Whitney. What about Iris? We called her Flame. He kept giving her cancer. Over and over, he'd make her so sick we all thought she would die. She wanted to die. He hated her because he couldn't break her spirit."

"She's cancer-free at the moment and married to a member of our team. Lily somehow found a way to put her cancer in remission. She and Gator are very happy together. I can tell you, he absolutely adores her."

Camellia pressed the heel of her hand to her forehead for a moment and nodded.

"You have no idea how happy that makes me. She suffered so much, Jonas. Whitney was a monster all the time, but when he detested one of us, he was worse than a monster; he was pure evil. There was another girl. She was tiny, like a little fairy. So much younger than the rest of us. He named her Jonquille. We all doted on her. Her body was like a magnet for electricity, and he wanted her to use it to attract lightning. He would put us in a meadow, and she was to direct a lightning strike to a target or he would instruct his soldiers to shoot one of us. Can you imagine a little child having that kind of pressure put on her? She couldn't direct lightning that way. He made her feel so useless. He told her she was nothing all the time. Such a failure to him and to all of us. I detested him for that. He would lock her in her room because everyone was afraid of her. She might be able to kill them if she touched them with all that electricity in her body."

There were tears in her voice. Jonas felt them running in his veins. Heard her weeping in his mind. He needed to pull her into his arms and comfort her, but he knew he couldn't do that — yet. "I've never met her, but she married a member of Team Four, a really good man. One of the best: Rubin

Campos. He's a doctor and just about the nicest man you'll ever want to meet. She's surrounded by a team that's very lethal. Rubin has a brother, Diego, and three other adopted brothers: Ezekiel, Malichai and Mordichai. Snipers, great trackers, all enhanced, all genetically engineered and elite GhostWalkers. She's safe and happy, from what I've gathered."

Camellia reached up to wrap her fingers around the Middlemist Red branch. Jonas could see she was seeking comfort.

"It's difficult to take all this in," she admitted, her voice shaky. "I thought she was dead. All this time, I thought she was dead. She had no anchor, and the energy was brutal on her."

"She lives in Louisiana near New Orleans. When you're ready, I can take you to visit her so you can see for yourself she's alive and well. I know they'd want to see you."

She moistened her lips, immediately drawing his attention to her mouth. "What of Dahlia? Do you have any news of her?"

"She's married to a teammate of mine as well. Nico and Dahlia have two homes. One up here in the mountains and another at an undisclosed area. They spend more and more time up here, but it can be difficult for her sometimes. Energy rushes to her and she has to get rid of it. Lily has been helping her to build shields, but it's a slow process. Nicolas is able to take most of the energy away from her. They'll get there. She works hard at it, and she loves Nico and wants a family with him. He would do anything for her. She's in good hands."

"I was so afraid of talking to you, Jonas, and you've brought me such great news of many of the women I regarded as sisters. We went through so much together. You told me about Rose having her baby with Kane. I know she wanted to be with him, and I'm so grateful she was able to."

"Ken Norton, one of the members of Team Two, is married to a woman you know. Marigold. She escaped the same time you did. Marigold had twin boys a few months ago, but she's been very ill since, and they can't move her. Part of the reason, when I felt this vague uneasiness, was because I knew she was having problems, and I thought it best just to be on the safe side."

Camellia took a deep breath and let it out slowly. There was a movement through his veins again, and this time as his blood circulated, he paid attention to the way it traveled through his brain. She was sending out inquiries, using two vast networks, both that he had stumbled onto but wasn't certain what they were or how he'd gotten onto them.

Next, she sent out a call to the alpha wolf. He got that one immediately. The last was to the pair of Great Gray owls. She was very familiar with them and he felt her affection for them. She called them by name, Blue and Gray.

"Do you still feel a threat, Camellia?"

She nodded. "It's still very vague, as if far off. I thought it was you."

He gave her a small smile. "And I thought it was you." He looked around him. "This place was unexpected. Your security system is amazing. I'm still not certain what you hooked into to make it work."

She tilted her head to one side, and her dark hair fell like gleaming silk, catching his eye. "You really don't know, do you?"

Jonas shook his head, watching the way that sliver of a moon played through her hair, turning sections of it into a waterfall of black silk.

"And yet you were able to tap into the networks and use them to your advantage. You hid yourself in plain sight."

He shrugged. "I've always been able to do that. My friends sometimes call me Smoke because I disappear. Completely. They don't know how."

"Do you know how you do it?" There was curiosity in her voice.

Jonas had the feeling she knew exactly how he was able to disappear, but he didn't want to get too far off the subject if the two weren't tied together. He needed to know about the security network she was using. He had women and children to protect from Whitney and the well-funded faction in the government that relentlessly kept coming after them, and what she'd set up here to hide herself in plain sight and defend her territory would go a long way toward protecting his people.

"I don't, but I'd like to learn."

She sat back in her chair, the blue in her eyes cooling to a color somewhere between silver and blue steel. "The Middlemist Red Camellia, of course. That's how you disappear as well. You're a phantom, just as Red is. A ghost, Jonas, at will. That was why the plant was slated to be stamped out. Red will defend itself vigorously, which is exactly what it did in the early days. Red's history is every bit as brutal as ours."

Jonas frowned, rubbing his left temple with the pads of his fingers. How could a plant have anything to do with her security network? Or the fact that he could disappear at will? She wasn't making sense. "I don't understand."

"You know that Dr. Whitney was obsessed with growing exotic flowers, right? He keeps greenhouses at the various laboratories he frequents. When he isn't present to tend to his plants himself, he hires specialists to look after them. If any plant dies, he kills the person that let it happen. He's ruthless when it comes to his flowers. If there is one thing he loves above all else on this planet, it's his exotics."

He nodded his head for her to continue.

Camellia tapped her fingers on her thigh. A strange habit for someone who didn't strike him as a nervous person. She had to be weighing how much she was going to tell him. He couldn't blame her. He was a stranger to her and yet he wasn't. They didn't feel like strangers. They felt as if they belonged. That was probably the biggest hurdle he had to overcome with her. Nothing real happened this fast.

It occurred to him that if she was leery, he should be doubly so. He had his team, women and children to protect after all.

"You must feel threats before they manifest, right? You know things when you're out with your team on a mission, no matter where you are."

How could she know that? He narrowed his eyes, focusing completely on her, watching every small movement, missing nothing. The entire situation with her was strange, even to a man used to constantly encountering weird shit.

She was right that he felt threats to the team when no one else could. They all had built-in radar when it came to feeling danger. The animal genetics embedded in their code gave them all kinds of abilities to know when an enemy was near, yet Jonas had the ability in spades. He always detected potential threats far in advance of the others. The team had come to rely on his early warning system.

Ryland had asked Jonas once how he did it, and when he said he didn't know, he knew Ryland thought he was lying. That he'd dodged the question because no one wanted their talent documented for fear it would somehow fall into Whitney's hands. But the truth was, Jonas *didn't* know how he did most of the shit he could do.

So how did this woman, whom he'd just met, know about the capabilities he'd never discussed with anyone?

Camellia laughed softly, shocking him. "Now you don't trust me. Just a minute ago, you were trying to convince me that because we're so connected, I had no reason not to trust you, but I can feel the waves of your suspicion rippling through my veins. No, you're not giving anything away on your face, you don't need to for me to read you. Just the way you can feel my emotions, I can feel yours."

"This is bullshit, Camellia." He didn't like what he didn't understand. "Just come out with it and tell me what's happening to me."

Camellia leaned toward him, her eyes pure blue, all cat, those dark lashes longer than he'd first thought. "It's the mycelium running beneath the ground. You're connected to that wherever you are. Whitney made certain of it, just like he did with me. That's one of the many reasons we're so connected. It's how you were able to get into the garden. You were welcomed in. The garden thought you belonged. You do know what mycelium is. I know you do. You've studied plants. Mushrooms. How it's all connected."

He couldn't stop his instinctive revulsion, an aggressive refusal that exploded through his entire being. He would *not* have fungus inside him on top of everything else. He was like some modern-day Frankenstein, a freakish monster, created by Whitney and programmed to kill. The perfect killing machine. Jonas rubbed his temples. He *had* killed. Many, many times. And now this. Fungus. Disgust permeated his mind. Abhorrence. What the fuck was this shit going to make him do?

Jonas became aware of the stillness first. There, in the garden, it was as if even the breeze had ceased. Seconds ago, he'd felt connected to Camellia on a molecular level, but suddenly she was gone, no longer in his mind. That song running through his veins had fallen silent. He searched for the connection, studying her averted face as he did so. She was looking out into the garden, her attention seemingly riveted on one of the exotics growing a few feet from the narrow path leading to her home.

The Middlemist Red blossoms framed the porch, but now they appeared to be simply normal plants, very large roselike bushes rather than something much more. He was suddenly completely alone when before, since entering the garden, he'd been saturated with awareness and vitality. His blood had buzzed with life, sparking with energy and an ever-flowing feed of sensory information. His body, his mind, forming countless connections to his surroundings, bright hot splashes of light, now completely burned out.

He took a deep breath. Whatever Whitney had done to him, he had done to Camellia first. She had been experimented on long before Jonas was. And by his instinctive revulsion over discovering yet another piece of his monstrous makeup, Jonas had broadcast a violent rejection not only of what Whitney had done to him but of Camellia herself. Everything about her. Who she was. What she was. At a basic level, he'd made her aware he was repulsed by what she was.

Jonas groaned inwardly. He'd just made a major blunder. He hadn't been thinking in terms of Camellia. How could he explain to a woman who had endured years of Whitney's experiments what it had been like for him those first years after he and his teammates had received Whitney's "enhancements"? The discoveries and the accidental deaths? The self-loathing when innocent people you'd sworn to protect paid the price because you had no idea of the power you wielded or how to control it? He hadn't marshaled his thoughts. He hadn't considered he would have to, but he should have. His response had been a knee-jerk reaction.

"Camellia, forgive me. I don't do well any time Peter Whitney's name comes up in conjunction with what he did to me. I still haven't come to terms with some of the things I did before I knew what I was capable of. Now, at the first sign of anything new or different in me, a part of me panics."

It was difficult for a man like him to confess this sort of vulnerability — this sort of weakness — to a woman he wanted to claim for his own. Yeah, maybe he had a bit too much pride, but damn it, no man wanted his woman to think he was weak.

He hoped she could hear the sincerity in his voice, because she had already distanced herself so far from him, he knew she couldn't feel the truth. In a way, that was a good thing, because he still loathed the idea of having a fungus be a part of him. What did that even mean? Why had Whitney ever thought to put that in him?

Of course, if the fungus was the source of his early warning system, he could certainly see the value. Was that possible? If so, it was an invaluable resource, and one he shouldn't have been so ready to reject simply because he didn't like the word "fungus." Or because it came from Whitney. Some of the enhancements he had given them had turned out to be assets once they learned how to control them, and Lily had taught them how to put up the barriers needed to protect their unfiltered brains.

Camellia sent him a vague smile, one that didn't quite make it to her eyes. No longer entirely blue or silver but somewhere in between, her eyes had gone to those of a cat. He found himself looking at a focused leopard, not a laughing woman. He'd hurt her. Really hurt her. She'd spent a lifetime being regarded as a science project. No doubt the guards in the laboratory had called her a freak more than once. Probably often.

"There's always a danger when listening to someone else's private thoughts of hearing no good about oneself."

Her voice was light. Just the right hint of amusement, as if she were sharing an inside joke with him, but he knew she wasn't. She wasn't sharing anything of herself at all anymore. Not only had she withdrawn completely from him, but she'd also somehow cut him off from that extraordinary network he'd tapped into.

"Don't do this, Camellia. My reaction had nothing to do with you. I'm just so damned tired of finding out all the different crap Whitney put inside me. Every time I know what I am and feel like I'm starting to get a handle on it, something new pops up." He watched her closely, hating that an unguarded reaction had damaged the growing

110

trust between them. "I never understood how I could sense danger so much faster than the rest of my team. I thought I had some kind of built-in radar no one else had. I mean all of us have the acute senses of animals. Leopards. Wolves. Owls."

Deliberately, he named the ones he knew she would be drawn to because she had those in her as well. "But I always had that little extra something they didn't. I was able to warn the team of danger long before anyone else felt it, and I couldn't tell Ryland or any of the others how I did it. Now that I know, I feel especially foolish for having such a negative reaction to the very thing that saved my team so often."

She kept that same practiced smile. "No worries, Jonas. I understand. Peter Whitney likes his little experiments with people."

"Whitney." Jonas growled. "That bastard faked his own death and left my team and me locked in cages in his laboratory, like we were fucking lab rats. At the time, most of our team couldn't operate on their own without an anchor to pull the psychic energy from them. They had no way to stop the assault on their brains, and none of us knew what was happening. We didn't know he'd messed with our DNA — that was something we never agreed to — so when some of us started getting hyperaggressive and others started manifesting strange new abilities, it made no sense to us. We didn't have any answers and had no one to tell us what was happening. Not to mention, there were people trying to murder us."

"He was probably sitting back and recording everything," Camellia said.

"Probably." That was exactly the sort of sick sociopath Whitney was.

Jonas let himself really look at her. She was quite beautiful to him. Different. Her unusual eyes were framed with thick dark lashes, and her dark hair contrasted with her pale skin. When he looked at her closely, he could see she had a dusting of freckles across her nose, like little specks of gold. Everything about her looked delicate, from her hands — the fingers of which were curled around the branch of a Middlemist Red Camellia bush — to her narrow rib cage.

She wasn't emaciated by any means — she had hips and breasts — but she was well proportioned for her height, and she looked as if she needed protection. His protection.

Jonas didn't look at women that way. He wasn't a knight in shining armor. He didn't want needy. Or clingy. He had never envisioned having a woman of his own, a permanent partner, in his bed and his life. Especially not once he was enhanced. He'd thought about it after watching Ryland with Lily and Nico with Dahlia. They worked, even when things got rough.

Jonas just didn't think that sort of relationship would work for him — until he met Camellia. The instant he'd seen her, he knew she was meant to be his. He was born for her. It was that simple. Whitney had nothing to do with it. He may have brought them together faster than it would have taken normally, but Jonas knew the moment he laid eyes on Camellia he would have gone after her, no matter what.

He detested that he had hurt her.

"Why didn't you come to our fortress, Camellia? You had to know who was living there. You get too much information not to have known that at least one of the women you grew up with was in that compound. I've been trying to understand why you wouldn't, but nothing tracks. If you thought we were holding any of your friends against their will, I doubt anything would have stopped you from coming to their aid. So why did you stay away? Why not come down and introduce yourself?"

Jonas didn't take his eyes off her. He no longer had that deep connection with her, but he was good at reading people. Maybe it was part of his predatory enhancements, but he could read every little movement, every subtle hint or change of expression.

Her lips compressed just the tiniest bit as she bit down on the inside of her mouth. Most people wouldn't have noticed that slight tell, but she had beautiful lips, and he was already very fond of them. Any small change in the shape or the way they glistened, anything at all, he was bound to notice. He also had extremely acute hearing, and he didn't miss the way her heartbeat accelerated for just a second or two. Almost as soon as her heart sped up, she took a slow breath, and her pulse dropped back to normal.

Jonas had to hand it to her: Camellia was good. Extremely good. She wasn't going to be easy to win over, and she wasn't going to be easy to read. Most of the time, when he needed answers from someone, he could either charm them into lowering their guard, or he could slip his questions into the conversation and read their resulting physical response for answers. Neither of which were going to work with Camellia. He'd destroyed his chance at charming her, and her poker face was the best he'd ever seen.

But there was a reason she'd been avoiding the GhostWalkers, and he needed to
know why.

But there was a reason she'd been avoiding the GhostWalkers, and he needed to
know why.

4

Camellia took her time, breathing in and
out slowly, not allowing herself to panic.
Jonas Harper was in her garden, surrounded
by her allies. She could escape if she needed
to. She held on to that. For a short time,
she'd had hope that she wouldn't spend her
life alone, but his unmistakable reaction to
what she was, what she would always be,
told her how she would be received no matter where she was in the world — even with
the GhostWalkers. Even with the man Whitney had paired her with.

And that man — her paired mate, who
couldn't hide his revulsion of her — seriously wanted to know why she hadn't approached the GhostWalkers once she discovered their compounds nearby? She had
more than one reason, but why would she
disclose them to someone she couldn't
trust? She wasn't going to lie to him. She
doubted if he would believe a lie from her.

So she gave him a portion of the truth. "I've been alone so long that I didn't know how to handle the thought of seeing anyone."

Jonas continued to stare at her with his golden eyes. Completely focused. The eyes of a predator. She was looking at the hunter now, and she knew it. He wasn't going to take a partial answer from her. He remained silent, waiting.

Camellia's fingers inadvertently tightened around the branch, and she knew he noticed. His gaze didn't shift toward that minute movement, but something about him conveyed his instant knowledge. She was a predator as well, but she suspected his hunter's instincts were natural-born, a part of him long before he was ever enhanced. She recognized he was very, very dangerous. She had several advantages, one being she was always underestimated. Always. She had nearly given away one of her most important advantages.

He was still waiting for her to explain why she hadn't approached the GhostWalkers or the women with them who'd once been her friends. She gave a light shrug of her shoulders. "I knew Marigold was going to stay with Ken Norton. She told me she was. I don't trust as easily."

She had nearly trusted easily, simply

because her connection to Jonas had been so strong, partly because of the mycelium network but mostly through the Middlemist Red. He wasn't even aware of that one, and she hoped he never became aware of it. She'd almost given it away with her talk of Whitney and his love of exotic flowers and greenhouses. She couldn't imagine what kind of Frankenstein he'd think her — and him — if he realized the truth of what Whitney had done to them.

Camellia regarded what she was as a miracle. Something extraordinary. Maybe because she had realized all the amazing things she could do thanks to her enhancements. Middlemist Red and the mycelium protected her and kept her company. Middlemist Red gave Camellia the opportunity to create her garden and surround herself with beautiful plants and trees. She could grow food easily all year round, even during the coldest part of the season. She was able to set up illusions and use both the mycelium and Middlemist Red networks to establish grids of alarms to alert her if anyone came near her home.

"Camellia."

Jonas continued to level that golden gaze at her. Now it appeared glittery. More cat than not. A warning. A little shiver crept down her spine.

She let out an exaggerated sigh. He had sacrificed his pride; so could she. "I know how people react to me when they find out what I am. I've learned to live without that kind of prejudice, and I'm not willing to think badly about myself again. I have no interest in having people know what I can do. I especially don't want anyone to think they can use me for experiments or even to tell me what to do ever again. I've been my own person for a long time. I don't need or want a chain of command."

She could see that resonated with him. It was the truth, or most of it, the way she saw it. She might want to see her sisters, the women she'd grown up with, but they were different. They'd moved on. They had lives completely different from hers. She didn't want to blame them and she didn't want to envy them. She wanted to be happy for them. She no longer trusted anyone. She had to fight to keep from being bitter. It wasn't in her makeup, and she refused to allow it by starting up relationships better left alone. Jonas didn't need to know any of that. She wasn't about to explain it to him.

Camellia was also aware she couldn't stay here if she didn't go down and at least let the GhostWalkers know she was on the same mountain with them. Before Jonas's arrival, she'd been wrestling with the choice between starting over somewhere else or forcing herself to actually be around a GhostWalker team. Sadly, when it came to the GhostWalkers, she just couldn't see putting herself in that position. Jonas's reaction had simply reinforced the conclusion she'd already come to. She knew her decision was based on more than that, but she didn't allow her mind to dwell on anything else. That was enough.

The moment Jonas was gone, she was going to get out.

"It doesn't make sense to go it alone, Camellia," Jonas said.

She could tell he was choosing his words carefully, trying not to dictate or use his naturally commanding voice.

"Whitney put that tattoo on you so he would always know where to find you. He'll keep sending his supersoldiers after you. If you're with a couple teams of GhostWalkers, they'll still come at us, but we'll have a much better chance of keeping them from taking you. And if they do, we'll find you."

"Now that I know he's embedded some kind of satellite tracking in the tattoo, I'll find a way to get rid of it, just the way I did the one he put in my hip," she responded.

She didn't believe for one single minute the GhostWalkers would risk their lives coming after her if she was taken. They might use her to try to find Whitney, but if they didn't think she was with him, they wouldn't come for her. She'd already seen Jonas's reaction to her, and he was paired with her.

"Do you honestly think you can outrun him forever?"

"Nothing is forever, Jonas," Camellia said. "I never thought I'd be free, but I have been. I'm not trading what I have for another kind of prison."

"Do you think I'm in prison?"

"Only you can answer that question," she countered. She was giving too much away. He knew she wasn't going to stick around. She didn't feel a threat from him, and so far, Middlemist Red hadn't reacted as if she should be on alert, but then the plant might not. Camellia was in uncharted territory. Red would consider Jonas an ally. On their side. There was no way for Red to know that he was an enemy.

"I'm not in prison, Camellia," he answered decisively. "You wouldn't be either."

"So, there isn't a chain of command? You aren't sent out on missions whenever someone deems it necessary for you to go? You just said to me, not even five minutes ago, that on more than one occasion, the mycelium beneath the ground warned you of danger, aiding you in saving your team."

"I'm a GhostWalker, Camellia, a soldier. I have certain skills, and I use them in service for my country. You don't have to do that if you don't want to. That doesn't mean you can't live in the compound with us. Not all the women work with the teams. That's where freedom of choice comes in. I told you, we don't report our talents to everyone. We don't always document them."

She analyzed his voice. It seemed to ring with truth. Red didn't protest, so she took him at his word. "Not even to Lily Whitney? You don't tell her? Or her husband?"

"Ryland is the head of our team. Sometimes a talent might be useful to the team, if we can learn to control it, and we share. But that's our choice, not a requirement. At this point, we have so many attributes suddenly emerging that we don't always know what to do with them. We have to work on the talent for months to get it under control enough to be in any way useful. Sometimes whatever comes out is more of a hindrance, like rage or the need to hunt at inopportune times. It's a balancing act all the time."

Camellia didn't want to feel for him, but

she did. She knew Whitney wanted to make his soldiers as aggressive as possible, and he'd used many of the most violent and predatory species to enhance them. Everything from leopards and wolves to reptiles and raptors, whatever he thought might make them more efficient killers.

Later, Whitney had acknowledged his mistake in blending so many strains into some of the men. Fortunately, he hadn't done it to all of them, but in the ones he had, the mixture had been lethal, and not just to their enemies. Jonas was one of the few still alive. That meant he was a well-kept secret, because otherwise, he would have been sent out on a suicide mission. Or simply terminated. That meant his team was intensely loyal to him. She was grateful for that and a bit surprised. The guards Whitney employed in the various bases and laboratories she had been taken to were not in the least bit loyal to one another.

Now that she had time to think without being so hurt by his reaction, she realized how difficult it must be for Jonas to live with the need for violence all the time. He had to be at war with himself. She hadn't been enhanced the way he had been. Whitney had gone shockingly insane with his enhancements and admittedly went too far with his first team.

Camellia acknowledged to herself that she should have cut Jonas a little slack at his first reaction to the revelation that he had mycelium in his physical makeup. No one would ever conceive of such a possibility — that Whitney could even make it a reality. By doing so, he had connected Jonas to the underground network that ran beneath the forest, or anywhere mycelium guarded the trees and shrubbery above ground. Jonas was clearly sensitive enough to tap into that network without realizing it.

Jonas had most likely believed his "danger sense" was one of many other mammalian or reptilian attributes Whitney had enhanced him with. When he realized none of the other GhostWalkers were aware of danger as early as he was, he had to have figured out that Whitney had given him something the others didn't have. Something more, when he was already contending with enough.

She suppressed a sigh. She didn't want to feel compassion for him. She wanted to sever all connection to him and make a run for it without feeling the least bit guilty. Instead, she was already remembering every word Whitney had said about these first soldiers and how they were going to be able to go undetected behind enemy lines and wipe out entire camps without anyone ever knowing they had been there. He had designed them for perfection. They weren't going to be the failures the women had been, because men were steadier and had better nervous systems and were so much stronger than women.

Whitney lectured the women, telling them he had bumped up the soldiers' levels of aggression and enhanced their abilities to see and hear in any situation. They were perfect killing machines. He had bragged to them until he realized the soldiers were having the same problems as the women, some of them unable to go out on their own without severe repercussions.

It was the first time Camellia had ever seen Whitney thrown, if only for a short time. He was furious with the soldiers but soon turned the blame on the women. Somehow, it was their fault Whitney hadn't prepared for the problems the soldiers faced. She knew some of the other women had taken his accusations to heart; by that time, thankfully, most of them knew better.

Camellia needed to change the subject, to steer it away from the things Jonas wanted to know and anything she might learn about him that would put more compassion in her heart. Already she melted each time she looked at him or heard his voice. She didn't need to know things about him that would make him more amenable to overlooking his reaction to her.

"There was another girl I grew up with, Laurel. She was very quiet. Dark red hair and the greenest eyes you ever saw. Whitney named her after the English laurel, which is often called the cherry laurel. She had that dark red hair and did when she was a baby, so I guess all that hair reminded him of a cherry laurel."

She waited, trying not to hold her breath or give any indication that finding out about the women meant everything to her. She didn't want him to have anything to hold over her. Whitney was good at finding weaknesses and exploiting them. Growing up together, the girls had inevitably formed attachments to one another, and Whitney used those feelings against them as a means of manipulation, punishment and control. She was determined that no one would ever do that to her again.

Jonas shook his head with obvious regret. "I'm sorry, Camellia. I wish I could say I knew where she was, but I haven't heard anything at all. I would think if Whitney had managed to get her back, we would have heard something. We do have a way of spying on him. We have to be very cautious, but if he had one of the women from that first group, we would know."

If she could believe him, and he seemed certain, at least Laurel was still safe, even if no one knew where she was. Like Camellia, she'd found a place to hide.

"You said that your people were able to keep Whitney from tracking the dust particle trackers in our tattoos? Laurel has one on her ankle as well. It's beautiful, with glossy leaves and clusters of cherries. She would have found the tracker in her hip and removed it, like I did. We all suspected Whitney had implanted us with microchips." She pushed her hand through her hair. "Maybe she thought of her tattoo. I didn't, but she may have." Camellia doubted it. She was the least trusting of the women, and it hadn't occurred to her that the one thing Whitney gave her that she loved was just as poisonous as all his other "gifts." She should have known.

"From what I understand, he isn't able to use that tracking system to find any of you women anymore, at least not most of the time. I'll find out more information for you," Jonas promised.

She wasn't going to stick around to find

out more information. The moment he headed back down the mountain with his friends, she was leaving. She'd planned for an escape. She had already decided on a destination if she had to leave. Middlemist Red would travel with her. The rest of the exotics would stay behind with the mycelium grid to buy them as much time as possible if anyone tried to follow them.

"There are children in the compound down below," Jonas said. "Lily has a son. Whitney would do anything to get his hands on that child. He's tried before. Ken and Marigold have twin boys. Whitney would like them as well. It has occurred to me that the threat I'm feeling is Whitney gearing up to make another try for the kids."

Camellia couldn't help but send out inquiries along both networks again, particularly the mycelium running beneath the forest, stretching far beyond her garden and even past the boundaries of the national forest into the wilderness areas. She had been using that connection for a long time and was very sensitive to every result. She could read the least little sign the mycelium returned to her, no matter if the source of the alert was many miles away. She needed the connections to spread out as far and wide as possible and tell her if there was anyone approaching the homes below her. Were there spies sent in the forest? One lone man? Two? An army? Animals that hadn't been there?

Jonas looked up at her suddenly. "Camellia. What are you doing right now? I'm feeling something very subtle, as if there is a surge in the energy around me. Barely there. I know I blew it with you by my gut reaction, but I hope you can forgive me. I swear, none of what you felt from me was aimed at you. I just despise Whitney and what he did to me." He thrust his fingers through his hair and made a sound halfway between a snarl and a growl. "Hell, maybe I was already fucked up, and all he really did was make me aware of it."

Camellia had an inexplicable desire to put her arms around him and hold him. She felt a sudden surge of rage in him, red hot. He suppressed it automatically, as if he'd been doing it forever. She also caught a small edge of despair. He knew that level of aggression in him had been multiplied by Whitney and would never go away. Living with it had to be hell.

"Whitney didn't much care how aggressive he made his soldiers, as long as he got the results he wanted," she told him. "I'm glad all of you realized you shouldn't document your talents. That must make him crazy." She allowed satisfaction to show in her voice.

"I have to admit, we do talk about that a little too much," Jonas confessed. "We hope Whitney is frustrated. We're his first team, and we know he views us as his failures. He'd want to know everything about us that he could, if only to avoid making the same mistakes in future enhancements."

Camellia had to agree with his assessment. She nodded and loosened her hold on the branch of Middlemist Red. She was able to breathe on her own and relax completely again, now that she realized just how difficult Jonas's life had to be. Looking closely at him, she could see the lines etched into his face, when Middlemist Red was renowned for her antiaging benefits. Many thought that was a myth, but Camellia had barely aged, her skin glowing and flawless in spite of Whitney's many experiments. Jonas looked young as well, but she could see those lines carved deep when he continually had to strive to control the raging instincts in him.

She sent him a genuine smile. "I know the word 'fungus' can sound off-putting. I don't remember how I reacted, because I was used to all the strange experiments he performed on us. I didn't seem to have any repercussions at the time. I was told to report anything new to him, and I honestly didn't have anything to report. The mycelium connection is extremely subtle, and Whitney didn't tell me what to look for. He never did."

Jonas leaned toward her, his eyes going completely gold, utterly focused on her. She had leopard in her, and she recognized the cat instantly, but he had gone still, become the hunter as he absorbed the information. He was the predator. He couldn't help it. That side of him was dominant. She tried not to react, not to feel uneasy. He wasn't deliberately intimidating her, but she imagined any recipient of that stare would feel threatened.

"I was out on a mission when I first became aware, most likely the way you did, that danger was closing in on me," she told him. "It was still a great distance away, so I knew the signal hadn't come from any of the animal enhancements Whitney had given me. When I returned from the mission, I filtered through everything I knew for certain he had put inside me. When he told me 'fungi,' I looked up everything I could about mycelium and how it worked. Then I studied our brains and our nervous

131

systems and how they worked together just in case. I had always been interested in plants, so I had already been studying and researching everything I could on the communication between them. I was extremely careful not to veer off course of what I was already working on, although I kept notes for myself off the computers and eventually was able to look up what I wanted."

Jonas nodded his head. "That was smart, Camellia. Was Whitney aware at all of what you were doing?"

"We couldn't use a computer without his knowledge. His techs always informed him of what we did on the Internet. I'm certain he knew, but I had researched since before I was in my teens on plants and mushrooms. My interest wasn't anything new. I didn't feel any hint of a connection with the mycelium network until my late teens. Whitney had already given up asking me. When it first happened, I wasn't positive it was the mycelium network, but I have to admit, I had the opposite reaction as you when I discovered it. I was very excited. I thought if I could find a way to tap into it and communicate with it, I could not only send and receive messages from it and through it, but I could maybe develop a few of my own weapons."

The moment the words were out of her mouth, she wanted to recall them. She even put her fingers over her mouth. She knew better than to be so loose-lipped. It was just that she hadn't had anyone to talk to since she'd been with her sisters, and even then, they'd had to be so careful. In spite of the fact that she'd broken her connection with Jonas and she no longer even knew how to trust anyone, she wanted to trust him. She wanted to talk to him, openly, honestly. To share what she'd learned with someone like her.

For years she'd had only Middlemist Red as company. Now here Jonas was. Not just another living, breathing human being, but the one person she'd been genetically altered to find irresistible. She stifled a groan and tried to marshal both her way-ward tongue and wayward thoughts, as well as build her defenses. Being close to Jonas was so difficult.

"How does the connection work?" Jonas asked. "Would you explain that to me?"

She was grateful he hadn't asked about what weapons she might be developing. She knew that slip hadn't escaped him, but he'd given her a pass, most likely knowing she would clam up if he pursued the subject.

"Fungi share more than half their DNA

133

with humans. Did you know that? Mushrooms actually inhale oxygen and exhale carbon dioxide. Quite a few of our most successful antibiotics were made possible due to shared pathogens. Fungi don't rot from bacteria."

Jonas flashed a brief smile that didn't quite make more of a glint in his golden eyes. "Good to know. So we're resistant to disease. That's what you're telling me, right?"

Her smile was wider than his. "I'm hoping that's what it means. All those neurons in our bodies are quite like the mycelium, a network delivering messages to our bodies to do what we want them to do, right? They use both chemical and electrical means to do so. Remember I told you that the average human shares more than half their DNA with fungi? You and I share more, so we're able to connect with an enormous underground system that already exists."

"That system is used to keep a forest healthy." He made it a statement but didn't sound as certain, as if he were pulling up knowledge from some time ago.

"Yes. The mycelium spreads out underground and acts as an extremely efficient communication system. The fungi send chemical, electrical and hormonal signals.

Not only do they communicate beneath the ground, but they send pheromones and scent signals."

For no reason, she found herself blushing. Those eyes on her seemed even more intense. He clearly understood the consequences of what she was telling him. It wasn't only the genetic pairing that caused their instant and very powerful physical attraction; the mycelium network they were both a part of had contributed as well. Camellia knew there was also a third influence at work, and it was a big one.

"Camellia, I would have looked at you with or without Whitney's manipulations or any mycelium-produced pheromones. I came into the garden and got so close I was practically on top of you. I couldn't see you and I couldn't smell you. For pheromones to work on someone, it requires them to be able to scent you. I didn't. And I assure you, I have an acute sense of smell. Maybe it's true that the connections gave us an extra boost, but the attraction was there between us naturally, no matter what."

Middlemist Red saw to it that Camellia hadn't put out a fragrance to give her away when she went into phantom mode. Camellia didn't know why Red hadn't protected Jonas from her in the same way. He

135

had also been in phantom mode. She had been unable to see him, but she'd caught the faint scent of those trees, one for certain not in her garden.

"The moment I actually saw you, my first thought was, 'She's the one you've been waiting for. The one you didn't think existed.' I don't know why that thought slipped into my mind, but it did. There were no pheromones involved, and it wasn't just the genetic pairing. I'd been in your garden and saw and felt the security network you set up, and I was in awe of your capabilities." He pushed his fingers through his hair. "You didn't have a team around you. You'd done it yourself. I knew you had. You were a force to be reckoned with."

There was open admiration in his voice. He couldn't fake that. A knot the size of her fist formed in her stomach, low and aching, responding to the blatant honesty in him. The way he made himself vulnerable. He might be a dominant male with aggressive, violent tendencies when it came to battle, but there was also something intrinsically honest, even noble about him. He possessed a core of decency and honor that all of Whitney's scheming and experiments hadn't tarnished. She couldn't help but react to that in him.

"Thank you, Jonas." She didn't know what else to say. The response seemed inadequate since he was laying himself out there, and she had retreated so far and wasn't willing to inch back.

"You were explaining how the mycelium network works. I think I understand now. All along, I've had that advantage and I didn't even know it. How are you able to tap into it whenever you want to?"

Again, he deliberately took the spotlight off the personal. He had done that for her more than once, and Camellia was grateful.

She pushed her hair behind her shoulder, trying not to look too closely at Jonas's golden, very focused eyes. "I'd read everything I could about mycelium prior to discovering I was connected to it. Fortunately, I'm good at retaining what I read. So once I realized what was happening, I would visualize this huge system, like the Internet but connected to my own body, and I'd send messages along my pathways to it, trying to find how and where we were actually connected. I knew there had to be a way to strengthen the link between us. I'd already made a point of practicing every skill I had, so I just began to practice strengthening that one as well."

Jonas nodded, his gaze never leaving her

face. "That's the kind of thing I do. Sometimes, though, strengthening particular skills turns out to be a mistake. More than once, I've honed a particular talent only to realize it amplifies a need for violence, which is the last thing I want."

Camellia understood. He wasn't certain what having the connection to the mycelium would do to him. She knew why he would be wary of any new talent that cropped up. She had studied Whitney and his cruelties up close.

"Are you going to tell me the real reason you didn't go down to either of the compounds and let the women know you were up here, Camellia?" Jonas asked softly. "Especially Marigold. You had to know she was there once you stumbled on the homes. She was your friend. You don't have to tell me, but it doesn't make a lot of sense that you didn't want anything to do with the teams. You could have visited with the women and then walked away. No one could have held you if you didn't want to be held. You're too good at what you do not to have studied both places for their security. You didn't just have a look and then make a run for it. That's not your personality at all." He looked around the garden. "You plan out every move. Your backup plan has backup plans."

Jonas had slipped that question in there when she was feeling relaxed with him. Now the tension coiled in her like a tight spring. She moistened her lips. He was too much like her, even though she'd cut herself off from him. He thought the way she did. What difference did it make if he said something to the others? She didn't think he would. Marigold wasn't married to a member of his team. Even if she had been, Jonas struck her as a man who kept things to himself unless he thought he needed to provide details for security.

Camellia sighed, stood up and half turned away from him, pacing across the porch toward the very edge so her face was nearly completely hidden from him. "It was a long time ago, or it seems like it now. We planned our escape as best we could, but we knew the chances of getting free of Whitney's compound were slim. He'd put us in his breeding program, and we were fighting off his chosen supersoldiers, the ones he thought had great genetics. We all wanted out of there. Whitney had gone to another base, and one of our teams of soldiers was assigned to protect Senator Freeman and his wife, Violet, from a possible assassination attempt."

She was well aware Jonas had to know about the incident. The GhostWalkers had been involved. "Marigold was friends with all the soldiers. She'd been part of their command at one time. She talked them into letting her go with them. Her goal was to talk with Violet and Senator Freeman about what was going on at the laboratory. We hoped the senator would come and put a stop to it. We didn't realize Violet was willing to sell us down the river for her own ambitions. She was raised with us, so we thought she was one of us."

"So," Jonas said, "a huge break in trust."

Camellia nodded her head slowly. "We were in dire straits. Rose was already pregnant. We had to get free. Some of the younger ones were talking about suicide. I have to admit, I was going to fight until one of them killed me. I was never going to allow Whitney to force a man on me and then take my child from me. Marigold felt the same way, so we started looking for ways to get all the women out at the same time. If Marigold could get Freeman to come to the laboratory and help us, that was one way; otherwise, we would have to overpower the guards and make a break for it. That would be risky. Our best bet was Mari."

Camellia turned to face Jonas again, pushing back against the support column, her fingers biting into the wood. Jonas listened intently, those golden eyes never leaving her face, making her feel as if everything she said was important to him — making her feel as if *she* was important to him.

"It was a huge risk for Marigold to go with the soldiers on their mission to protect Senator Freeman and Violet, but she went. There was what they thought was an assassination attempt. Mari was shot and taken prisoner. Apparently, another GhostWalker team had also been assigned to protect the senator. But it was a setup. Freeman was supposed to die. In any case, Mari was taken prisoner by Team Two, Norton's team. She fell in love with Ken Norton. Whitney's team, of course, was frantic to get her back. She wasn't supposed to have been out of the laboratory. The team found her, but apparently that was because the GhostWalker team allowed them to find her. She was determined to get back to us. Whitney always threatened that if one of us escaped, he would kill one of those left behind."

Just cracking that door open elevated Camellia's heart rate. The blood began to pound through her veins. She suddenly felt as if she couldn't breathe. She wasn't a grown woman, totally confident in her ability to defend herself. She was back to being that young girl, just finding herself, just becoming a woman, just learning about her skills and talents. She was filled with fire and defiance against a dictator who continually tore the girls down and used them cruelly.

Middlemist Red dipped its branches, and the blossoms smoothed over her face and along her arms to soothe her. Red had been her only friend, and the touch on her skin reminded her that it had been far too long since she'd felt the touch of another human. That want — or maybe need — was growing in her, and she had to push it down ruthlessly. Dredging up her past relationships would help, would be a reminder that friendships were illusions. The only person she could count on was herself.

She didn't want those eyes of Jonas's to look so closely into her. She felt exposed now, but she'd gone this far. Cracked the door open and let her secrets start spilling out.

"You know Whitney through his experiments, but we lived through them and his sadistic cruelties every day of our lives. He gave us pets to love and care for and then had them ripped to shreds in front of us as a lesson. They were all killed because we failed to teach them survival skills in a fighting ring. We didn't even know something like that existed."

Camellia pressed her fingers to her lips and found she was trembling. She couldn't look at Jonas anymore. "There were a couple of nurses who stayed with us throughout all the experiments and accompanied us to Whitney's various bases and laboratories. One of them, Beverly, was with us as long as I can remember. I loved her. We all did. It wasn't as if she was overly affectionate, but she was always there for us, no matter how much Whitney frowned at her when she picked us up off the floor when we were toddlers or instructed us when we needed to know things about growing up as females. He intimidated every caretaker he ever had for us until they quit, or he fired them because they were too nice to us. In addition to Beverly, the only other long-term nurses were Shirley and Rosa. Rosa mostly cared exclusively for Lily, although she looked after all of us when she could."

"Why would one nurse be assigned exclusively to one child?" Jonas asked.

"Lily received special treatment. Eventually, Whitney took her away from us, and

Rosa went with her. The rest of us had always been put into groups. Each group was assigned a nurse. Beverly was the nurse assigned to my group, and she ended up staying throughout our childhood and teenage years when so many of the others left."

Camellia could hear herself screaming not to give too much away. Jonas was too connected to her through the enhancements Whitney had given the two of them — and he was intelligent. She had no doubt he observed everything, from body language to every psychic emotional leak she gave off. She suspected that very little ever escaped him, and he was specifically tuned to her.

She desperately needed someone to talk to. To bounce her ideas off of. At the same time, she didn't want to know the answers. She couldn't shred that last piece of her heart. She just couldn't take it. She wanted to turn away from him, but she could feel his gaze on her, compelling her to continue. She needed to talk aloud. To say something to him. To give some explanation.

"Whitney did so many horrible things. I can't even begin to explain just how bad he could get. He tortured Flame over and over, making her sick, uncaring of whether she lived or died, as long as he could record her reactions." She was repeating herself. She

144

couldn't stop and Jonas didn't interrupt her. He just let her babble on. "We went on countless missions, but if one of us didn't come back, one of the other girls was punished. Later, as we got older, he infected us with a virus, and we needed the antidote in order to survive, so we had to return. If one of us escaped, he said he would kill one of the remaining girls."

Her throat closed. Her lungs seized. She couldn't breathe. It took discipline to force air through her body. It was really difficult not to look at him. She felt his reaction. Middlemist Red absorbed his emotions. Breathing in and out, accumulating his rage and letting it go into the soothing peace of the garden. That was Red, always finding a way to make things right when their world was filled with violence and rage.

She was sweating, little beads on her forehead. "I'm jumping around in my history here. Going back to when I was younger, before all of us banded together to try to get out all at once. I planned my escape. I just couldn't take it anymore. I knew it couldn't be while I was on a mission because I couldn't go with a virus in me. I was so careful. I studied the guards. He changed them often, and if we were on a regular military base, he made sure all the assigned guards were kept away from us. When I decided to make my move, we were on private property in an underground laboratory. He'd held us there for a while. We were brought to the surface to exercise and whenever we were needed to plan for missions. I'm extremely good at holding information in my mind, so I knew my way around the lab's maze of tunnels."

She doubted if she was giving him too much information about herself. He most likely had the same gifts she did. Whitney had enhanced him with fungi and Middlemist Red. He knew now about the mycelium, but not Red. Red's gifts would have allowed him to cope with the terrible amount of aggressive genetic coding Whitney had hardwired into Jonas. Without that, Jonas would probably already be dead or, worse, have gone insane.

"Camellia."

He said her name softly. Gently. The sound of his voice was like a piece of velvet cloth sliding over her skin in a long caress. Shockingly, when she'd closed her mind to him, when there was no bridge between them from Red or the mycelium, she felt the same brush of velvet in her mind.

"Just telling me this is hurting you. You don't have to tell me. I don't like you hurting. It isn't as necessary as I thought it was."

There was genuine truth in his voice, and she turned to meet the gold in his eyes. He meant every word. She'd worked to build up her protections, those walls she surrounded her heart and soul with. She didn't believe in anyone anymore. She couldn't afford to. She knew Jonas had been asking her to do just that, but now . . . he was aching for her.

Jonas had stumbled into her garden. Essentially, she needed to regard him as an enemy. He was a GhostWalker, another one of Whitney's creations. He didn't work for Whitney, she knew he didn't, but he was still a man who followed orders. Those orders could include acquiring her. She had secrets. She had skills. She could be useful.

Whitney had men in high places protecting him, and they still did deals with him. They wanted his experiments. If he wanted her back, there was no doubt in her mind those men would find a way to trade her.

Even with all that in mind, just looking at Jonas, into his eyes, crumbled her resolve all over again. She had a reason for not going down to the compound and letting the other women know she was there. She had a reason for refusing to be with him, even though she knew he needed her in the way she needed him. Her reason wasn't a trivial one. He had to understand that. She wasn't being selfish or emotional or afraid. Her reasons were deep and elemental, and there was no repairing the damage done.

"Thank you for saying that, Jonas," she acknowledged, "but I want you to know. Beverly found out I was missing from my bed, and she alerted the guards." Her stomach knotted when she told him, and she pressed her hand tight over it, because what if she was wrong? What if, all this time, she was wrong?

"They caught me just as I was leaving the tunnels. Whitney had all the girls assembled in their pajamas. They were crying and scared. He asked me if I remembered the consequences for trying to escape. He walked up and down the row of girls and told me to choose one of them. I told him to go to hell, but I was so terrified. I shook so bad I could barely stand. I didn't think he'd really do what he said. But he did. He took Ivy. I tried to attack him, but his soldiers held me back and they took her to another room. We all heard the gunshot. There was blood in the room, lots of it. He made me clean it up. We never saw her again."

She didn't realize she was crying again

until Red dipped her branches and used the blossoms to gently touch her face.

"Whitney asked me if I really thought Beverly loved me. He said I was stupid if I believed that. That she worked for him for money." She still remembered the sneer in his voice, the way he mocked her — all of them — for thinking anyone could ever care for them.

"Beverly denied telling the guards that I had escaped. She said it wasn't true, but he laughed and told her none of us would ever trust her again and he had no more use for her. He let her go. Told her to pack her bags. I was going to kill her. I planned to slip into her room and kill her for what she did, although I knew ultimately it was my responsibility that Ivy died, not hers." Camellia wiped at the tears on her face and straightened her shoulders. "Marigold stopped me. She said I would regret it later, and she was probably right. Mostly, I wanted to kill him and then myself. I've never been able to forgive myself."

"That was a huge break in trust," Jonas said. "Beverly was a mother figure to you for years."

Camellia nodded. He got it. "The only mother I ever knew."

5

Jonas studied Camellia's face. Her expression. The way she held herself. There was far more to the story than she was telling him. The betrayal of her nurse alone would have given her every reason not to trust anyone. To also carry the guilt for the death of one of her sisters . . . the burden had to be horrendous. As he well knew, that sort of guilt wasn't something you could just shrug off, no matter how many times someone told you it wasn't your fault.

He wanted to pull her into his arms and hold her, which was an entirely unusual response for him. He wasn't that man. He never thought he would be that man. He never thought he would or could be that man. He had the normal sexual urges of a man, maybe a little too much and too strong, but he had never wanted the emotional entanglements or physical closeness that came along with it. He wasn't a hugger. He wasn't a comforter. Yet looking at Camellia now and sensing her emotions more acutely than he'd ever felt another person's, that was all he wanted to do at the moment — just hold and comfort her.

"What happened after that, Camellia?" he coaxed, keeping his voice as gentle as he could. She was picking and choosing her words so carefully, he realized she was afraid she would give too much away. This was about trust. His little Camellia had trust issues, and with his unthinking reaction earlier, he'd played right into her biggest insecurity. If he was ever going to get anywhere with her, he had to understand exactly what he was facing. He wanted to brush his fingers over her soft face and remove the last of her tears to comfort her. He needed to do it but instinctively knew she wouldn't welcome his touch.

The Middlemist Red Camellia swept down, and this time, the branch moved against the breeze to brush her face gently. The rose-like petals stroked her skin along the exact path he had envisioned caressing her. That gave him pause. He was no longer connected to that network through Camellia, yet somehow that mysterious plant knew what he was thinking. Not only did it know what he was thinking, but it knew what he wanted to do — at least in connection with Camellia.

And it did it. The plant fucking did what he wanted to do. It was reading his mind and then acting on his need. That was plain mind-blowing.

"Whitney taunted me." Camellia shook her head. "All of us. He liked to pit us against one another. Eventually he split us up. Jonquille was put in this tiny little room because Whitney said she was too dangerous to be out any longer. Laurel was up in this attic where it was hot and the air quality was terrible. He did it on purpose because she had such trouble breathing, and he said her lungs should be better. She could barely stand up. I knew he wanted to keep us apart because he thought we were too close, too loyal to one another."

"Wouldn't that defeat his purpose of threatening you with another's death if you tried to escape?"

"He clearly didn't want to lose any more women, not when he could just poison us with the viruses and force us to return for the antidote. He began his campaign to undermine our trust in one another. Sowing little seeds of doubt, acting as if we told on one another. He even tried to convince me one of the girls had told the guards I wasn't in my bed that night, not Beverly."

"Had you told anyone you were going to try to escape?"

She shook her head. "I didn't want anyone to have to lie to him. He always found out and his punishments were terrible. I planned the entire thing by myself. I even made it look like I was in bed by putting rolled up blankets under the covers."

"Could anyone have seen you rolling the blankets and putting them in your bed?"

She hesitated. It was the first time she had. Her fingers twisted together in front of her until her knuckles turned white. Her gaze slid from his and flicked in the direction of the community. It was the tiniest of movements, but he caught it. Registered it. His gut clenched.

"It's entirely possible, but it would be difficult to believe one of my sisters would tell the guards. What would be her motivation? By that time, we all knew getting in good with Whitney wasn't a real possibility. He would never let us go. We weren't there for money or power, like Violet. So what would be the point?"

She sounded more as if she was trying to convince herself than him.

He nodded, but that knot in his gut had become a fist. "But he did manage to make you have a little doubt, and that made you feel guilty."

"I actually didn't have any doubts," she denied. "Not at all. I trusted in all the women. He separated us, but Marigold was a powerful telepath. I wasn't quite there yet with my skills, but I was building up to it and could help her out. At night, we'd talk to all of the others no matter where in the compound he was holding them. We kept those ties strong. He had no idea we could speak to one another that way. When he devised his idiotic breeding program, that was the last straw."

"And then the plan to have Marigold speak with Senator Freeman and ask for help failed," Jonas said.

She shrugged. "Clearly, it would have failed anyway. Violet had her own agenda, as did the senator and Whitney. Violet betrayed all of us. Fortunately, Norton's team helped us escape."

"But Marigold didn't follow the plan, and she didn't go with you."

Again, Camellia didn't meet his eyes and the Middlemist Red dipped low. Camellia shook her head. "No, she went with Ken Norton."

"That must have felt like a betrayal as well." Jonas could see those betrayals were stacking up.

"I suppose it did, but she had feelings for him. None of us knew what that felt like."

"But she knew you were still in jeopardy, and she didn't ask you to go with them," Jonas said, keeping his voice very low and gentle as he pointed out the obvious blow.

Her gaze jumped to his. She had hoped he wouldn't connect those dots. She nodded, sucking in the side of her lower lip, then biting down with her teeth.

"I would think that felt like an even bigger betrayal than Violet's, leaving you in the greenhouse and not having you leave with her and the team." He didn't even get a head nod. "When did you find out she had a twin sister, Camellia? When did you find out about Briony?"

His breath caught in his lungs, and that fist in his belly grew to outlandish proportions, dark and ugly, because the answer was already forming in his mind. Aggression sent adrenaline rushing through his veins, and the need to hunt and kill prey was a drive that shook him.

She moistened her lips. Took a breath. He felt the air in his own lungs, as if she'd given that to him, shared it with him.

"When I went down the mountain exploring. I thought she was Marigold at first, and

I was so happy to see her, but then her husband called out to her. He called her Briony. He said Mari needed her. I looked closer and Mari was looking out a window. I could see her face framed there. She waved and Briony waved back."

"She never mentioned Briony to you before that time?"

Camellia shook her head very slowly. "Not in twenty years of being together. All those late-night chats. Of declaring ourselves sisters. Best friends. Swearing that we had each other's backs and always would. I didn't know what to think, so I backed off and came to my garden. I find peace here. I can think clearly. I needed to figure out what I could trust after seeing that. You seem to know all about Briony. Maybe everyone does, just not the woman who grew up with Marigold and had her back for over twenty years."

Jonas realized that was the biggest wall of all. The steel one. The one sealing all the others. How could she trust anyone, least of all a man she barely knew? She'd just met him. He wanted her to go down to that compound with him and trust his team, a team that mixed regularly with Marigold's team. She'd experienced one betrayal after another. She wasn't suddenly going to take a giant leap of faith with a man she'd known for less than an hour. Truth be told, he wasn't a man to inspire a great leap of faith in the best of times. He was too hard and dangerous. She was sensitive to what he was. She saw right through that facade he put on for others.

That little seed of doubt Whitney had planted in her head, that one of the girls may have betrayed her instead of Beverly, had grown just a little bit more. He could see Camellia was struggling with her doubts. She didn't want to believe Marigold could ever do such a thing, and she obviously felt wretched for even considering it.

"I can see how it would hurt to have your closest friend keep such a secret." He swept his hand through his hair, a deliberate gesture on his part. He wanted her to see him as more human than he knew he really was. It wasn't as if he were a cyborg. Sometimes the pumped-up supersoldiers Whitney threw at them with armor plates in their bodies seemed more human than he was.

When he'd first seen Camellia, he'd thought, hoped — if only for just one fleeting moment — that he had a chance to fit in somewhere, with someone. She didn't have to be like him. It was more than enough for her to just see him and accept him. He couldn't quite accept himself, not after the horrible things he'd done or the equally horrible things he'd stopped himself from doing. Still, he wanted her to see the terrible truth of him and want him anyway. He'd blown his chance before he got started by inadvertently insulting her. Not accepting what she was.

"Don't," she said softly.

"Don't what?" He let his hand slip to the nape of his neck where his muscles were knotted. That wasn't feigned. He didn't want to give her up. On the other hand, he wasn't going to cause her further pain. He could feel it in her. The pain was very real and visceral. Tearing her up.

"Why do you despise who you are so much? You can't change it, Jonas. You know that. Lily must have tried. If she can't do it, and she's a genius, then you know you have to find a way to accept what you are and live with it. There must be really great things you can do. Like tapping into the mycelium network to sense danger before anyone else."

He sighed and leaned back in the chair, allowing blossoms of the Middlemist Red to work their magic on him. The petals were soft, the way he imagined Camellia's skin to be. "I'm not normally quite such a pessimist. It's just that the moment I laid eyes on you, we were connected, and I felt different. I liked the way I felt for the first time in years. Then I blew it and that feeling was gone. It's been difficult to pull myself together again."

He gave her honesty because she deserved it. Too many important people in her life had betrayed her trust. He didn't want to be one of them. She wasn't a threat to his team — or Marigold's team. At least not yet. He didn't know what her intentions were. She hadn't made up her mind about Mari, and he knew with certainty, unless she had proof that Mari had betrayed her, she would never condemn her.

Camellia sent him a little intriguing smile. "I doubt if I was the one that made you feel different, Jonas. This garden has a way of making you feel at peace."

He heard regret in her voice, and immediately there were alarms going off throughout his body. "You're making plans to leave, aren't you?"

"Sooner or later, if I stay, even if you never said one word about me, someone would come this far up exploring. The Nortons have been here a few times, and I managed to turn them away. It wasn't easy though, and I knew if more came, I would have to go. Once I went down there and realized the GhostWalkers actually had homes here, they weren't just vacationing or training, I knew it wasn't safe. I just kept procrastinating. I knew better, but I didn't want to leave my garden."

"I think you should reconsider. There's the threat we both feel, Camellia. That's real. Someone is out there, watching and waiting. I think they're after Ryland and Lily's son. I could be wrong. We have several other children to protect too — some Whitney would want even more than he wants young Daniel. These kids are special. Very talented. No one knows about them. Not Whitney, not other scientists. No one from the outside world. We protect them."

"And yet you suspect that someone already does know about them. How? Do you think someone in one of the compounds would sell you out?"

Jonas's first reaction was a solid *no.* The teams were tight. He would bet his life on his brothers and did quite often. They were the only people he fully trusted. Lily had a staff. They'd been with her since her childhood. She counted on them. Ryland and Kaden Montague, a GhostWalker nearly impossible to fool, believed the staff was loyal. There were others, nonteam members from both compounds, but they didn't see the children.

"Is it possible a computer is compromised?"

He shook his head. "There is no documentation on any of them. That was agreed upon. We don't put them in computers."

Camellia's eyebrow went up. She gave him a look of pure disbelief. "I can't believe Lily wouldn't document what her son is able to do. If you believe it, you're living in a dream world."

Jonas went very still the moment she said "dream world." Jeff Hollister was the man on their team able to dreamwalk. He wasn't the only one. Nico and Ryland could as well, but Jeff was very adept at it. Dreamwalking could be dangerous because one had to leave their body vulnerable when they left it. They could be killed in their dream or be so caught up in it they might not want to return to their body.

Jeff practiced dreamwalking often, with Lily overseeing him to watch out for any repercussions from his earlier strokes. Jonas's mind immediately began to build images of file cabinets and offices and documents stored away in the dream office they used. Was that possible? Anything was pos-

sible in a dream. Lily could be document-
ing each child's abilities and storing the
information inside a dream office where no
one would have access to it — unless they
knew what she was doing and sent out a
dreamwalker to discover it.

Was Jeff the target of the vague threat, not
Daniel or one of the other children?
Abruptly, Jonas stood, adrenaline pouring
through him once again.

"Tell me." Camellia rose as well, matching his movements as if they were chore-
graphed dancers. "What's wrong? What is
it?"

"I don't know yet. Just an idea. Something
you said."

"That Lily would document her son's
abilities. She wouldn't be able to help herself."

He stepped off the porch and paced out
into the garden with the swift, silent movements of the wolf in him. Already he was
blending into the very warm light gray mist
in the air that was weaving in and out of the
trees. Camellia paced right along beside
him, making no sound either.

"You're right about Lily," he said. "She
wouldn't be able to help herself. She's a
born scientist. But she would want a safe
place where no one would be able to find

the things she knows about her son — or any other child she studies. She would need to feel her hiding place was impenetrable."

Jonas looked down at the woman pacing beside him. She tilted her head to look up at him. Her eyes had gone pure silvery blue now. Light. The mist had nearly swallowed her, making her difficult to see, reminding him of how easy it would be to lose her in the garden. Once he lost sight of her, she would be like he was — a phantom — impossible to track.

"You have an idea of what she did."

In the mist, her voice was muted. He wanted their connection back. He wasn't certain how to establish it. He didn't understand how he'd first connected with her or how that connection had been severed. Deliberately, he thought about the mycelium linking all the trees in the forest together beneath the ground, creating an organic network to communicate. He was part of that system and so was Camellia.

"I'm not certain. It sounds bizarre, but then everything GhostWalkers can do can be considered bizarre. If she did what I suspect, I can't figure out how anyone would know."

He paced restlessly through the mist as he spoke, needing the physical activity to drain the sudden rush of adrenaline from his system. All the while, his mind continued to work on the problem of rejoining the mycelium network. He knew if he could reestablish that connection, he would find his way back to a closer emotional link with Camellia. Already he felt the whisper of her on his nerve endings. He was that close to reestablishing their severed link.

"I won't know if it's bizarre if you don't actually tell me what you're thinking," she pointed out.

"Have you heard of dreamwalking?"

She nodded. "I don't really know of anyone who can do it. I mean, I'm sure it can be done, because most psychic gifts that are speculated about turn out to be something others have the talent to do, but no one I know has admitted to dreamwalking."

"Suppose Lily knows someone who can dreamwalk, and they're powerful enough to bring her into their dream. She could potentially hide her data in the dream."

Jonas shared his theory while he concentrated on the organic threads that formed a vast infrastructure running beneath the ground. If those lines of communication could raise the alarm when a tree was under attack by insects or disease, the tree sending the warning to the other trees so they could arm themselves and be prepared, then he should be able to tap into that communication center. He could be a part of it. He *was* a part of it. That was how he knew when danger was coming his way. He opened himself up to it, welcoming the mycelium genes that Whitney had placed in his DNA, embracing them fully.

Heat blazed across his nerve endings as the connection flared to life. Alive. He felt so alive. Completely aware of her, just the way he'd been in the garden before he'd laid eyes on her. He'd known she was somewhere close to him, but he couldn't see her. He could feel her. His *body* could feel her even though he wasn't touching her.

He looked down at her and their eyes met. She was equally as aware of him. He gave her a slow smile. One that was genuine. He'd done it. He'd connected to that underground network — and to her. "You're so damn beautiful."

Her smile put more dark blue flecks in her eyes. She shook her head. "I'm not really beautiful, but I'm happy you think I am, but stay on track. You were worried there for a minute. And upset. Let me help you figure this out. Who were you worried about?"

She was very adept at reading him when

he knew there was no expression on his face. He wanted to touch her. Frame her face with his hands, but that would lead to other things. Color swept into her cheeks, and her thick, dark lashes fluttered and covered her cat eyes for a moment.

"You have to stop, Jonas."

"I can't pretend I don't think of those things. You put them in my head."

"I'm sure most women put them in your head. You're a very sexual man."

She wasn't fishing. She was stating a fact as she saw it. "I suppose some people might believe that, because I do have a very strong sex drive. Whitney loaded me with as many aggressive species as possible, very dominant and alpha, so yeah, physically, my body wants sex, but my brain is always at war."

She frowned at up at him. For some unknown reason, he found that particular expression adorable. And one he wanted to see often.

"What does that mean?"

"I don't like inane conversation. I don't like to pretend intimacy I don't feel, and I don't feel it with the women who are coming on to me."

"I can imagine women throw themselves at you all the time."

Again, he couldn't detect jealousy. She

was assessing the situation and stating facts as she saw them. He shrugged.

"When I want sex, I don't have trouble getting it. I'm no saint when I need relief, but I don't like to spend much time with someone I don't want to be around for any other reason."

"That makes sense. Quite a few male animals or reptiles Whitney chose for their fighting abilities or stealth, or for whatever reasons, were loners. They mated and left. You very well could have those tendencies."

"I don't seem to feel those same tendencies around you," he admitted. He figured he may as well just be up front with her. "I don't like to touch or be touched, and yet that's all I can think about when I'm close to you."

Camellia glanced up at him again and then looked away, stopping there in the middle of the garden. He stopped too, mirroring her immediately, knowing if he didn't, he could lose her in the mist.

"It's too dangerous." Her voice was low. Shaky. There was no hint of longing in the tone, or in her expression, but he felt the emotion running along his nerve endings.

"Why would it be dangerous, Camellia?" He kept his voice gentle, feeling as if he were dealing with a wild creature, one that would run at any moment.

She lifted her chin as if he'd issued a challenge to her. Her eyes met his without flinching. "We wouldn't be able to stop with one touch, Jonas."

Jonas's lungs seized up as fiery need engulfed him. It was all he could do not to jump her then and there. If not for years of practicing absolute control, he might not have succeeded. Jonas managed to suck in a shaky breath and slow the savage pounding of his heart. *Damn.* If just talking about touching her had this effect on him, he couldn't imagine what the real deal was going to do.

"I suppose that's true," he agreed, when he could speak again. "Would it really be such a bad thing?"

"It would be if we're supposed to figure out where a very real threat is coming from and who it's targeting."

He gave an exaggerated sigh. "I won't call you a coward, but I'm going to think it in my head. If I'm right about the dreamwalking nonsense, the most powerful dreamwalker I know is camped just down below in that circle of rocks being spied on by your wolf pack."

Jonas watched her closely, paying strict attention to the smallest inflections the mycelium conveyed to him. He wasn't a trusting man any more than she was a trusting woman, not when it came to the lives of his teammates. Jeff Hollister was a good man — one of the best — and he'd already been through hell. If, somehow, Jonas was being duped, and he couldn't conceive of how that was happening, he would protect Jeff with his life.

Camellia laughed softly. "We're a great pair, Jonas. Whitney knew what he was doing when he put us together. He didn't consider our backgrounds or any emotional baggage either of us would carry, did he?"

He shook his head, his gaze never once leaving her face. He wasn't a man to be distracted. He'd given her information that could harm his friend — a man he considered a brother. He couldn't feel even a whisper of a threat emanating from her. If anything, she was in total solidarity with him.

The laughter faded from Camellia's eyes. Her lips lost that sweet curve and her frown appeared, the one that told him she was thinking over something he'd said. She gave a little shake of her head. "If your friend is really guarding Lily's data on her son, how would anyone know? She wouldn't tell and neither would he. You didn't even know and you're his friend. No outsider would be in his dream, would they? Is it possible to spy in a dream?"

Jonas turned that idea over in his head. "I'm going to reach out to Jeff and ask him. He's our resident expert on what's possible in given talents. And then I'm going to take your hand."

She actually stepped back, nearly stumbled and would have fallen if a branch hadn't suddenly positioned itself under her bottom like a swing.

He grinned at her. "What a scaredy-cat. Hand-holding isn't the same as kissing."

Camellia gave him what she obviously considered to be a fierce scowl. He doubted if she could have intimidated a teddy bear with that look but refrained from saying so.

"Just ask him."

Jonas reached out. *Jeff, is it possible to send a spy into a dream?*

There was a long moment of silence. *It's possible to do anything in a dream. Anything at all. It's a dream. Why do you ask?*

Not only did he catch the wariness in Jeff's mind when he responded, he could feel his teammate's uneasiness. *I'm trying to figure out if you're the target of the threat I feel. Don't dreamwalk. Stay alert. How sick is Kyle?*

He's feeling a little better.

"Maybe I should have them move camp so Kyle isn't so sick. He could help protect Jeff."

Camellia shook her head. "They have more protection where they are. I can lessen the effects on both your friends, but if we want to keep everyone else out, we want the illusion and shields to stay strong."

Jonas considered the possibility that Jeff was the target of that threat. "If someone is trying to get to Jeff, wouldn't they do it in his dream? They wouldn't have to kill him in reality. If they killed him in his dream, then his body would die."

"What would be the point of actually killing him, Jonas? If the spy is looking to acquire information on Lily's child, they would need Jeff alive," Camellia pointed out.

She was right. Whoever wanted to know about Ryland and Lily's son needed Jeff alive. They needed Jeff to dreamwalk in order to get information from him. But who would have known to put a spy in Jeff's dream to give the data to Whitney, if he was the one to send someone after Jeff? Jonas was no closer to that answer. In any case, he could be completely off target. It was only one possibility.

A soft, low-pitched hoot, the notes long

and drawn out slowly over eight to ten seconds, slightly longer than Jonas knew a Great Gray owl would make to declare his territory, filled the night. Thirty seconds went by, and the male emitted the same call, letting all males know the territory was claimed and he would defend it. The owl was a distance away, yet he could be heard clearly, his low-pitched hoot traveling not only through the airwaves but along that communication center in the ground as well.

Jonas's gaze jumped to Camellia's. "You have this place wired."

She nodded. "That's why your friends are safer here."

She began to walk from him, her pace unhurried but all purpose. He followed, watching the way the mist curled around her body, making her look as if parts of her were dissolving right in front of him. At times, it appeared as if her body had been cut in half, her middle gone, and he could see through her. He wasn't shocked; he could hold his arm out and observe the same phenomenon in himself. The difference was, he was certain she knew why they could do it, but he didn't.

"What is the owl saying to you? You have a mated pair of Great Grays, don't you? The ghost owls. Phantoms. Like us. Nearly impossible to see if they don't want to be seen."

She nodded. "Yes, they come with me whenever I change locations. I tell them not to, but they don't pay attention. Blue and Gray." She sent him a little grin over her shoulder. "Really innovative names, right?"

He could see her having Great Gray owls. They flew low, just off the ground, no more than eighteen feet. They were silent, gliding mostly between perches. They preferred to sit on top of a broken tree stump and listen for prey with their acute hearing. They often flew just three feet above the ground with slow wingbeats, so silent even on the quietest nights they couldn't be detected as they hunted for prey.

These particular owls perched on tree stumps where the roots went deep into the forest floor and were connected into the information web that spread throughout the area. Their raptor talons dug deep into the tree trunks they sat on. If they had news to convey, they could relay it through that web running under the ground.

Jonas was not yet adept at understanding everything he was hearing. He knew the male bird had conveyed a message and Camellia had instantly reacted to it. She was heading toward a particular part of her garden. He didn't ask again what the owl had communicated. He did try to puzzle it out. He had to get skilled at reading the network, just as expert as she was.

"That threat we're both feeling is creeping a little closer to us," she said. "It's not close enough to worry about," she added when he reacted by lengthening his stride so he was breathing down her neck. Camellia was short, so that wasn't the easiest thing to do, but he knew it was intimidating as hell.

She sent him a quick look over her shoulder again, this time, her eyes looking like a cat's, a little wary, very feminine. "I would have told you immediately if your men were in trouble, Jonas." There was a low note in her voice, a soft hint of rebuke.

He wasn't going to apologize for needing to keep his brothers safe. "I told you, I have the same trust issues you do. You weren't happy to see me — or them. We were trespassing. After what you told me about how you were treated, I can't say that I blame you for how you feel about Ghost-Walkers or the program. On the other hand, that just makes it more likely that you'd do anything to protect yourself, including allow my men to be in harm's way to provide yourself with an opportunity to escape."

"It does, doesn't it?" She sounded

amused.

Jonas was tempted to reach out and grasp her shoulders to give her a little shake, but he didn't. He was afraid if he touched her, it would turn into something altogether different from the reprimand he had in mind. He had to make an effort to repress the sudden amusement welling up out of nowhere. Since the moment he'd set eyes on her, his emotions had been all over the place, bouncing from anger and suspicion to amazement, desire and humor. She did that to him. And damned if he didn't like it. Not that he would tell her that. She had way too many advantages as it was.

"Camellia." He forced a warning growl into his voice.

Her laughter bubbled over. The sound moved through the garden like bells on the wind. The exotic flowers blooming so explicably in this miraculous garden reacted, turning to follow her progress as she strode in the opposite direction of her home.

"Jonas. Seriously. Use your skills. And your logic. If I was going to throw you and your team members to the wolves, I wouldn't have told you what Gray was warning me about, now would I? And you can hear truth. If I tell you the men are safe but they aren't, you would know. If anyone has to worry, it's me."

"Why would you say that?"

"Because you know the moment you are out of my garden, I intend to run, and you don't intend to let me. You're the big bad wolf. Don't bother to deny it. I can read you like a book. You might think you're all badass and can hide your expression and body language from everyone, but you can't from me."

She halted abruptly in front of a little grotto. A narrow, shallow stream burbled across the bluish and gray pebbles making up the bed, sounding musical. A series of three tiny waterfalls stair-stepped artfully down the flat surfaces of three large, flat rocks, the water forming a zigzag pattern as it fell. At the base of the last stone, the water collected into a small pool before spilling over the sides into the stream. It was quite pretty, like everything else in the garden. Behind the little falls was a naturally formed cave, quite shallow, and lined with the same shiny bluish-gray river rocks that lined the stream and the pathway leading to her house.

The mist appeared almost lavender as it floated around the little grotto, stream and shallow pool. She stood very still, and once more, it was nearly impossible to see her, the mist making her nearly transparent. He had the urge to reach out and yank her to him, shackle her wrist with his long fingers and hold her to him.

"It isn't that I don't intend to let you run, Camellia. It's that I don't want you to go. That isn't the same thing. For the first time, I feel as if I have someone who actually sees the real me — all of me — and accepts what I am. There's freedom in that. I can talk to you. I'm attracted to you. I'd like you to stay and see where this takes us. Do I understand you wanting to get the hell out? You bet I do. On the other hand, if this threat is closer than I thought it was, I could use help determining what's going on, because I honestly don't have a clue, and I think you're better at puzzle-solving than I am."

He wasn't above appealing to her ego. He was strictly honest, not wanting her to ever catch him in a lie. He knew there would be times he might have to sidestep a question or finesse an answer, but he was determined to be as honest as possible, especially when it came to the personal stuff.

"You're also a hunter, Jonas," she pointed out. "Running makes me prey. You wouldn't be able to help yourself."

"I'd have to have a reason to come after

you, Camellia." He kept his voice low, trying not to sound like the killer he was.

She turned to face him, her hands on her hips, her head tilted back. She was so close, each breath drew the scent of her into his lungs. Camellia blossoms often didn't have scents. Neither did Camellia, the woman. Not unless she was like this, up close, so close they could have been touching. There was a subtlety to the fragrance of her skin. Feminine. Definitely exotic, something he couldn't quite pinpoint but that he knew he would always associate with her.

Camellia didn't lack courage. She looked him right in the eyes. "You do have reason to come after me, Jonas." Her long lashes swept down and then back up. "We have too many connections pulling us together. You're a hunter. You won't just sit around thinking about it."

"Neither will you." He made it a statement.

She sighed. "You're right. But I have too much to lose by sticking around. You don't." She shrugged, and there was the faintest hint of a smile curving her generous mouth. "It's possible I can lead you away from your team. If you choose to follow me, that's on you, not that I think you'll be able to find me, but you have a better chance than most."

He resisted the urge to take her face between his large hands and kiss that challenge away. "You can't play games with me and win."

"I wish it were a game and I wouldn't have to leave, Jonas. I don't feel I have a choice. Marigold is down there in that compound, and sooner or later, every one of the Ghost-Walkers are going to know I'm up here. Like you, they are going to start wondering why I haven't come down there to join them. I'm not willing to tell them, and I'm not willing to join them. That means I have to go. It isn't a game to me. It's difficult to leave and start all over again."

Truth rang in her voice, but there was also another note, something else he couldn't quite identify, not even when he was studying her face so carefully.

Camellia turned back toward the grotto, crouching down, her hand disappearing in the mist. "In the meantime, we have to get rid of this threat, regardless of who it's targeting. Gray indicated there are eight intruders coming this way from over the eastern side of the mountain. They shouldn't know that you're up here, but they may if your teammate Jeff is the target.

They will have known you got spooked and the three of you came up the mountain."

Jonas wondered just how she'd gotten that information from the owl. While puzzling that out, he simultaneously went back over her declaration about leaving. She wasn't trying to challenge him into following her, but she knew he would.

She pulled open what appeared to be a trapdoor built into the floor of the cave. The depression was shallow. Inside was a vest that she slipped over her head. Pulling a bow along with several quivers filled with arrows, she slung them expertly over her shoulder and added various small pots made of shriveled mushrooms. Even the tops to the pots looked as if they were made of the mushroom. The pots appeared to be sealed. She put them inside pockets in the vest. She added three knives to loops in the vest before turning back to him.

"Let's go. I don't want them to get this far. Your men will be safe where they are, and we can take most of the team out before they reach us. If we leave one alive, you can question him and find out who they're after."

6

When Camellia crouched down to open the trapdoor, Jonas stepped right behind her in order to see exactly what she was doing. The mist had grown thick, taking on a beautiful bluish-lavender tint that seemed to hide the woman very effectively, shrouding her movements, cloaking her in secrecy and mystery. Jonas was having none of it. She'd been right all along. There was no way he would ever let her go if she ran. The hunter in him was far too strong.

The more he realized he didn't know much about her, the more he *needed* to know. He loomed over her, using enhanced vision, grateful for his ability to see so well at night. He could see almost as well as an owl. One of Whitney's enhancements had been to give him a tapetum lucidum at the back of his retinas, essentially a mirror that reflected light back at the rods, allowing him to catch and amplify every bit of light. That should have made his sight blurry during the day, but Whitney had been prepared for that result by giving him the enhancement of eagle sight to call on during daylight hours.

He could see down into Camellia's neat little storage unit built into the ground. Thick grayish strands of tightly woven wood lined the walls and floor of the unit that despite being built into the floor of the grotto, showed no signs of water intrusion. The cache was surprisingly spacious and held numerous weapons as well as what looked like a go bag she could grab if she needed to leave in a hurry. He would have liked to see what was in that bag.

Camellia selected weapons and readied for battle with sure movements, as if she'd done so a million times, not even looking as she donned a vest and shoved knives into loops.

As she stood and turned around, he didn't step back, and she rose right into him, bringing them so close it would have been impossible to get more than a piece of paper between them. Her eyes went wide, lashes lifting, gaze meeting his in a kind of shock. Her eyes were even more beautiful up close than he had realized.

"This isn't good, Jonas," she whispered.

He felt that feathery voice running through his veins. Settling in his blood-stream. Something wasn't right and yet it was perfectly right. He ignored the quick shake of her head and settled his fist in the material of her vest, giving her plenty of time to step back away from him.

"Do you have any idea how lethal I am?" Camellia regarded him from under the veil of those dark lashes.

"Yeah, I know. You're like me. You know hundreds of ways to kill a man. I just saw you put knives in your vest. It doesn't matter. You think you have to save yourself, I'll understand, baby, I really will. You go right ahead, do whatever you think you have to do. I just don't have a choice here."

He drew her that last little bit closer so their bodies touched. He was careful not to crush her into him. Just letting her rest against him was enough. Feeling her close. Hearing her heartbeat accelerate. He cupped her chin, the first touch of her skin with his. His heart clenched hard in his chest. He had to suppress a groan. He never had reactions like this, but what he felt for her was visceral, tearing at his guts. A recognition, an electrical charge running through his veins, like scorching jabs of lightning that spread through his body to every cell, making him aware of her. Of him. Of them together.

His thumb slid over her lips. Velvet soft. Those generous lips. Did he dare kiss her? If he did, would he ever be free of her? He doubted he could be free of her now, even though he hadn't kissed her. Already they were tied together in some inexplicable way he didn't understand, and he didn't care how it had happened.

"Self-preservation," she whispered, her lips moving against his thumb.

The movement felt erotic. "Self-preservation seems overrated at the moment," he replied. "Don't you want to know what it would feel like?" He deliberately tempted her, his thumb stroking caresses along that sinful curve of her bottom lip. "Just once?"

Her tongue touched the pad of his thumb, a sexy little stroke that sent heat crashing down his spine and roiling in the pit of his stomach.

"Once wouldn't be enough, Jonas." Her breath turned ragged. She nuzzled his thumb.

"Babe." He meant it as a reprimand, but it came out an entreaty. He slid his free hand into the wealth of hair she had tumbling around her shoulders. It was thick and silky and sexy as hell. He was so far gone that the feel of the silken mass against his skin added to his nearly desperate need of her. "I'm going to kiss you."

"So stop talking about it and just do it," she advised. "Before I chicken out."

Jonas didn't need a second invitation. He'd waited for her consent, but now that she'd given it, he took advantage. His fist tightened in her hair, while his other hand cupped her chin, holding her still for him. He lowered his mouth to hers.

He was gentle, his lips coaxing hers, small little kisses. Tasting her. Discovering the flavor of tuberose and jasmine. Just a hint. Egyptian blood orange perhaps. He would need to taste more to know for certain. He kissed the corners of her mouth, feeling her texture. That satin. The perfection of those too-generous lips. He traced the seam with his tongue and then bit down very gently on the bottom lip. She gave a little gasp and he took advantage, sliding into the heat of her mouth, claiming her.

Her mouth was pure fire. Scorching hot. He stroked his tongue along hers, persuading her gently, hanging on to control with an effort. Kissing Camellia was something he was going to have to repeat often. He realized she had been right all along about this too. He was going to need to kiss her the way he needed air to breathe. Self-preservation be damned, they were both in trouble.

Her hands had come up to grip the front of his jacket, and then she did the unthinkable, sliding them up his chest and around his neck. That was so dangerous to both of them. It wasn't that he had allowed the kiss to get out of control. He contained the fire, not letting it run away with them, but both felt the flames licking through their veins, spreading that scorching heat and the urgent need to every cell in their bodies. It was a slow burn, but it was every bit as potent as a wildfire.

Her palms on his bare skin, right over the prominent veins in his neck, felt like two brands. He wouldn't have been shocked to find she'd burned her initials into either side of his neck. He doubted if he would have minded. Very reluctantly, he lifted his head, his gaze moving over her face, searching for signs of denial or doubt.

Her lashes lifted and her eyes had gone pure blue, sexy. A slow smile accentuated her lips. Drew attention to the ghost of a dimple she had on her left side. He couldn't stop from leaning down to brush his mouth over that small indentation.

"We could be in serious trouble, Jonas." Her hands slid from his neck and dropped to hang loosely at her sides.

He straightened and forced himself to let go of her. That took discipline, far more discipline than he wanted to admit. "I think it best if we just decide we're going to work it out, Camellia. It's smarter. Neither of us has to chase the other one all over the mountain."

Her eyebrow shot up. Amusement put color in her cheeks and poured more blue into her eyes. "You think I would come chasing after you if you took off on me?"

"Sure you would, now that you've had a taste of me."

She burst out laughing. He could get used to her laugh. He felt the vibration of it through his feet, in his veins, through the cells in his body. He looked around at the flowers that shouldn't have been alive there in that garden of paradise. They all reacted to her laughter. Leaves rustled, turning toward the sound, petals unfolded from closed flowers, all looking toward her. Camellia didn't even turn her head, as if she was so used to the phenomena that she didn't notice it.

"You know you're a miracle, woman." He spoke the truth as he saw it.

She sent him a smile, shook her head and pointed in the direction farther up the mountain.

Jonas shook his head. He indicated with his chin the direction Kyle and Jeff were camped. "We have to get my boys and have them come along. I'm not leaving them behind, Camellia. It's too risky."

She shrugged. "That's your call. I'd probably do the same if it was my team. You go get them, but I'm not waiting. I'm certain you can catch up."

Jonas had to hand it to her. Even with the intensity of their connection, he didn't feel even a whisper of her intent to run. She probably would too. He most likely had spooked her with that kiss. It might have been better to have gotten rough. She'd expected rough, not tender. Not gentle.

"It's best if we stay together. I'm not comfortable splitting up. Jeff's had strokes and Kyle's pretty sick." Deliberately, he played on her sympathy. She was compassionate, where he wasn't. He'd always have that one little advantage. He'd have to be careful not to use it too often.

"Strokes?" She echoed the word.

"I told you, we're Whitney's flawed team. He'd be happy to get us all back on his table for a redo, if he could. He's really angry that he paired Lily with Ryland and they had a son. Now that he has soldiers he considers perfect, he would rather one of them be with Lily."

Jonas turned and began walking down the mountain, moving through the garden, taking as much of it in as possible as he did so. He didn't look back to see if she followed. It was nerve-wracking, but it was a game of wits. She was either going to come with him, or he was going to hunt her.

They both were aware of the rules. He'd go after her if she ran from him. He had too many predatory species in him not to. If she asked, perhaps he could give her freedom. He was also fairly certain that if he bailed first, she would eventually track him, and he took comfort in that thought.

She made no sound. That made it damned difficult to keep moving in the direction of his two team members. Instead of looking for her, he observed the beauty of the garden.

"This place is spectacular." He poured genuine admiration into his voice. "If I didn't know better, I'd think you've been up here for years, but Mari hasn't been with Ken that long. Her twins are only a few months old. She got pregnant several months after Briony did."

He waited a few seconds for her to respond. When she didn't, his throat grew so tight he had to force the next words out. "She had a hell of a time with her pregnancy. Mari, I mean. We were really worried she was going to lose them."

When Camellia still didn't respond, he decided to try a different bait. He kept moving down the narrow trail, pausing every now and then to study a particular rare orchid that grew up one of the trees. "Is this a Pink Moth, Camellia? It's beautiful. How did you manage to get all of these rare plants?" He waited, counting his heartbeats. Hoping she would answer. Praying she hadn't gone off in the opposite direction, that she was every bit as enthralled with him as he was with her.

"Yes," she finally answered reluctantly. "Jonas. Stop walking. I don't want to meet your friends. I don't want them to see me or know about this place. I have to have more time."

Damn. The woman made him weak with relief, so much so that his knees had nearly buckled just because she'd chosen to follow him. He wasn't about to show her she had that kind of effect on him. He kept walking.

"You don't need more time, Camellia. You're either going to accept what's between us or you're not. I don't want to be alone anymore, Camellia. I don't want you to be alone. I can be the man who stands with you."

"Because Whitney did his famous pairing?" There was sarcasm in her voice, but also a small question, as if she were really asking him.

"Do you think it matters to me how I got you? I'm telling you how I really feel, babe. I want you to feel the same way."

"You think it's that easy? What's Ryland going to say? Especially when you came up this way investigating your hunch that there was a threat to the children."

She was right behind him. Close. Satisfaction sizzled through him. He knew how to find her now. He was locked into the network running beneath the ground, and that slight vibration singing through his veins and nerve endings belonged to her. He had her trail. She would never be able to hide herself from him again. Her psychic track lit his body up like fireworks on the Fourth of July.

"Rye's my friend, Camellia. He'll take one look and know you're it for me — that we belong. I'm not a man to cross. I give my allegiance to you; that means I fight for you. You belong to me, I protect you. It's that simple."

He felt her connect to him again, slide gently, tentatively, into his mind. After being separated from her, that psychic intimacy felt so right. A relief, as if after a long cold winter, spring had finally arrived. He didn't know how she managed to fill every dark, ugly crack and crevasse in his mind with something beautiful, as if she made memories of the two of them and inserted them where he had been ripped apart. Made him feel like he was no longer alone.

She saw the hunter. The killer. Yet that part of him didn't seem to bother her. She didn't cringe from it or throw herself out of his mind. She didn't shrink away. She stayed. He knew even his fellow teammates were leery of him. They had reason to be. They'd seen his mistakes and the results of them. More importantly, they'd seen what had happened with Oliver Borders, another team member, a decorated soldier. A friend. A man enhanced in the same way Jonas was enhanced, with all the same dominant and aggressive predators eating away with their killer instincts night and day. Oliver had never been quite as dominant or aggressive as Jonas was prior to the enhancements. Oliver was dead; Jonas was not.

"Don't think for a minute it will be

simple, Jonas, because it won't be," Camellia warned.

What did that mean? Was she saying she was all-in with him? He hoped to hell that was what she meant.

"Maybe it won't be, honey, but if it isn't, as long as we trust each other and stick together, talk it out, we'll come out on top." He poured conviction into his voice, willing her to believe him, to believe in them. The feedback coming from the mycelium network helped soothe the worst of his nerves. She was still with him, and he was no longer getting the feeling she was ready to bolt at the first opportunity.

He examined the input flooding his senses and realized that not only was the mycelium network beneath his feet going strong, but the other one was back too — the one she hadn't yet explained to him. That second network had reestablished its connection the moment Camellia entered his mind. Extremely strong and very personal, the mysterious second connection was the one that ran through his veins and spread to his cells with such fire. He felt the difference immediately. That pathway was growing stronger between them — growing stronger in him.

Whatever the second enhancement was,

clearly Whitney had given the enhancement to both Camellia and Jonas, along with the mycelium. Whatever it was, it worked in concert with the mycelium, amplifying the mycelium-fed awareness. Now that he was past his initial knee-jerk reaction, Jonas was grateful for both enhancements, because they more than doubled his ability to protect his teammates and their families. To protect his own family, as well.

"It has occurred to me that Marigold was the one who told Whitney I wasn't in my bed that night I tried to escape."

Camellia's voice was a thread of sound — so low Jonas barely heard. Mostly, he heard that shaken whisper of guilt in his mind and an echo of pain along his veins. Sorrow was a stroke of deep purplish black that ran up and down his nerve endings and drummed along his pulse.

It was difficult not to turn and take her into his arms, but both networks sparked, little flames hissing and dancing, throwing embers into the air, warning Jonas he would lose that tentative and very fragile hold he had with her. She had to tell him her own way. Talk to his broad back. Bounce the idea off of him rather than discuss it with him. She didn't need his input right at that moment — or his sympathy. That would only make her retreat. She didn't want to give in to emotion. She wanted to share her guilty secret — that she distrusted her best friend and sister of more than twenty years.

"She was in the same dormitory with me. I thought she'd gone to sleep, but she was a very light sleeper. I rolled blankets and stuffed them in my bed. Once, she turned over to face my bed. I stayed very still for several minutes until I was certain she was asleep again, not that I thought she would ever betray me. I didn't. We were very close."

She fell silent again as they made their way out of the garden. The mist beyond her garden borders was thinner and not quite as disorienting as it had been.

"When Whitney's soldiers dragged me back and he called all the girls and the nurses out into the yard, I noticed that Marigold was very agitated. She was pale and fought her guard until Whitney snapped at her. Then she went very still. She looked like she was terrified. That was part of the reason I was terrified. There was no one else who could have seen that I escaped unless one of the guards discovered me gone. It was either Marigold or Beverly."

"No one else shared your dormitory?" he couldn't help asking.

"Whitney had split us up to two per room

in that particular laboratory. Beverly still looked after our wing of the house. We were supposed to take a sleeping aid, all natural according to Whitney, but we knew it wasn't. It was another one of his concoctions, and neither Marigold nor I wanted to know what it would do, so we never took it. We flushed it. He knew, of course. He always knew."

"So you said you were all in the yard and he threatened you. What happened?" he prompted.

"I told him to punish me, it was my mistake, no one else's, but Whitney said we all had to learn the hard way. He told me I had to choose someone, that I should choose wisely because it was a permanent choice. I was looking at Marigold when he made his decree. Mari was shaking her head and pleading with him not to take any of the girls. The others were crying and begging Whitney and me not to choose one of them. She didn't do that. She pleaded with him not to take any of the other girls. Not herself. Looking back, it was as if she knew he wouldn't choose her. When I refused to pick anyone, Whitney had his soldiers take Ivy away. I went crazy fighting, but Marigold just sank to the ground and put her hands over her face. She doesn't do that. She doesn't give up like that. Marigold is a fighter through and through. Like me, even more than me, she would normally have fought to take Ivy back."

That sorrow hung so heavy in his mind and ran along his nerve endings, the purple growing deeper, darker by the second as he assessed the memories she'd shared with him. He replayed them over and over, analyzing them from every angle, trying to find a way to clear her friend's name. She needed him to say Marigold hadn't betrayed her and allowed Beverly to take the blame.

"I almost killed Beverly that night," she confessed in a small voice. "I came much closer than I told you. If Marigold was the one to betray me, I would have murdered an innocent woman."

"Marigold was the one who stopped you." He kept his voice matter-of-fact. He kept walking. Betrayal was one of the worst sins, no matter what form it took. That cut was always deep, and there was no taking it back. She'd had so many. Too many.

"Yes. I told her what I was going to do. I told her how much I hated Beverly and that she deserved to die."

"Did she know you could disappear into mist or the shadows?"

"No, I was still experimenting. I wasn't

certain how it worked, and I never told anyone what I could do until I could figure it out. Also, Whitney was already starting his breeding program, and I wasn't certain we'd gotten rid of all the surveillance equipment in our room."

"How did Marigold stop you from going after Beverly?"

"She kept telling me I would regret it later. That I didn't know for certain. That one of the guards could have discovered me gone. She kept pointing out how Beverly sounded like she was telling the truth when she denied reporting me missing."

"Would Mari have done that if she was guilty?"

They were getting close to the camp. Jonas slowed his pace.

"Yes. I think she would have. She wouldn't have wanted more innocent lives on her hands. She cared for Beverly too. At least I thought she did. She pointed out that the other girls sometimes came to visit us at night, which was true. She said she sometimes fell out of bed and the guards came running. That was true as well. I was so upset over being responsible for Ivy's death that I couldn't see straight. I remember being hysterical, crying, even fighting Marigold to get out of the room. The one thing she said that did stop me was that Whitney would know and that he would hold it over me for the rest of my life."

Jonas not only heard the pain in her voice, but he felt it. Deep sorrow. She felt that pain just as deeply as she had the day Whitney had his soldiers drag Ivy from the grounds to execute her. It didn't matter that Camellia hadn't pulled the trigger. In her mind, the sound of that gunshot ringing out had forever branded her as the one responsible for her sister's death. Sorrow and guilt spread to every cell until he felt so weighed down, he could barely take a step.

He shared that terrible, fateful moment with her and the aftermath, the days and nights of wanting to kill herself. Of plotting to kill Whitney. The guards were leery of her. The other women were kept away from her by Whitney's decree. Even Marigold was kept away. At night Marigold reached out to her, whispering telepathically, but Camellia lay curled up on her bed in the fetal position, unable to accept love and friendship from anyone when she felt she had murdered an innocent. Ivy hadn't known about Camellia's plans to escape, and yet Ivy, not Camellia, had paid the price for it.

Her life had become pure hell after that, Whitney taunting her, demanding to know why she thought Beverly would ever care for her. For any of the girls. Reminding her they were worthless — nothing. That Beverly wouldn't even be there if he weren't paying so well.

Jonas snarled, low and loud. The spine-chilling sound of a lethal predator issuing a challenge.

Camellia surprised him by moving up beside him and putting her hand on his arm. She just stood there, not speaking, her palm resting on his forearm. He hadn't even realized he'd stopped walking toward Jeff and Kyle. He knew they had to have heard the warning of the leopard, and they would know it was Jonas. It wasn't as if actual leopards inhabited the Lolo National Forest. He should probably double-time it down to them before they got worried and came looking. Still, he didn't move. This was the first time Camellia had voluntarily touched him other than when he'd kissed her.

"Whitney gets away with his bullshit because he has the backing of too many people in Washington." He made the statement in a low tone, leaning slightly so he could nuzzle the top of her head with his chin. Her soft hair caught in the rough bristles along his jaw. For some reason, he

200

liked that, feeling as if those strands bound them together.

"If it were just a few people in Washington, Jonas, he wouldn't get away with so much, but he has the backing of people much more powerful than that. He made certain of that before he ever started out."

Camellia didn't pull away from him. If anything, she leaned closer, as if she needed comfort. He took a chance and swept an arm around her. No one wanted to be alone. He had an entire team around him. Brothers he could count on, and yet he still often felt alone. She *was* alone. She didn't trust anyone for good reason. He knew it was only because of those two very strong and intimate networks they shared that he had a chance with her at all.

"You know a lot about him."

There was the briefest of hesitations, as if she didn't know what to do or say with him drawing her under his shoulder. She stood as if frozen, and then, very slowly, her body began to relax into his. He called that a huge triumph. Huge. He wasn't going to push his luck beyond that. He just wanted to give her a little bit of comfort.

"After what he did to Ivy, I tried to learn as much as I could. I was beginning to get the warnings from the mycelium, and I realized he had enhanced me with more than he had told me. That was one of the reasons he had watched me so closely and continued to ask me so many questions. I reviewed all the questions he asked me. I rarely forget anything. Once I realized I was tapping into the underground network, I remembered all the research I'd done on mycelium. I always thought it was very cool anyway. Then I compared it to the human brain and the way our brains work."

Jonas could see that she was very methodical. She took things one step at a time.

"After that, I looked into all the ways our bodies could possibly work the same as mycelium, so if I'm somehow picking up warnings, what sorts of information could it send me and how could I best utilize the entire network? Because mycelium is an enormous network. I have a good imagination, and I considered all the ways I could use such a vast network against Whitney. Listening in on his business meetings. Finding out where he would be so I could kill him. Little things like that."

She turned her face up to his, clearly expecting condemnation, but he had none to give her. If anything, he understood more than most would.

"You didn't tell anyone about the network,

not even Marigold." He brought the conversation full circle. He tried to think how he would feel if he discovered that Ryland or Jeff had completely betrayed him. Or withheld something vital, something as important as having a twin, from him for twenty years. Why would Marigold do such a thing? That didn't make sense. She had to have known she could trust Camellia.

Camellia shook her head. "By that time, there was this little tiny doubt in my mind. I didn't want it there, but Whitney had succeeded in planting that seed. Out of the blue, after taunting me about Beverly, he suddenly switched tactics and said maybe I was a fool for trusting all the other women. He would say it occasionally, implying there was someone who had their own agenda, just like Violet did."

She was looking down at the ground, wearing such an expression. As if merely voicing doubt about Marigold — or any of the other women — at Whitney's say-so was blasphemy.

"I swore to myself he would never get to me with his accusations. Marigold and I even discussed it at night with the other women. We used telepathic communication, but as my strength began to grow, I found myself afraid to use it. I didn't trust it.

Anything coming from Whitney was suspect, especially when he watched me so closely. So, at night, when we talked about our futures and the fears we had of Whitney's breeding program, it was easy enough to keep my doubts to myself. I didn't have to do much talking."

"But you listened to everyone else. The new networks helped you hear lies, didn't they?"

She nodded reluctantly. "Lies registered as a jarring note that jangled along the nerve endings when someone was talking. It could be a small jolt or a really big sizzling one, like a bolt of electricity running through me. Not at all pleasant. It was all new, so I was just learning what each reaction meant."

Jonas heard the note of reluctance that was still in her voice. Still in her mind. She didn't want to know if Marigold had been the one to betray Camellia when she was attempting to escape. Camellia had already accepted Beverly as the guilty party. She wanted that betrayal to be the damning one, the ultimate. If Mari had known about her twin and chosen to keep her existence a secret, eventually Camellia could come to accept that. But would she ever be able to forgive a betrayal that caused the death of a fellow sister?

Jonas sent a silent prayer to the universe that no one interrupted them. Camellia needed to get it all out. To let herself speak of her fears. She had to have one person she could talk to without fear of recrimination. He wanted to be that person for her.

Camellia sighed. "Marigold never brought up the subject of Ivy or Beverly, and when someone else did, she was very quiet as a rule. There was only one time . . ."

She fell quiet, swallowing hard. When she looked up at him, her eyes meeting his, she looked all woman, no sign of her cat. Her eyes had gone as liquid blue as the sea, making his heart ache. "Marigold said we knew who had betrayed us and we could never allow Whitney to drive a wedge between us. We had to stay strong together, that there was no sense in talking about it any longer. That was when she brought up the idea of talking to Senator Freeman and putting together an escape plan for all of us."

The wind tugged at their clothing, growing stronger. He felt that vague threat growing closer. Whatever — or whoever — was on the move. He had to talk with Jeff and Kyle and make a decision. Ryland and the others had to be warned. He didn't have a lot of information, but he knew for certain there was an actual threat. The team had to go on high alert. That meant getting the children under lockdown. Daniel was a handful, and if there was one thing the boy didn't like, it was to be restrained in any way. Jonas had hoped to know exactly what they were dealing with before he sent a report back to Ryland, but he couldn't wait. He couldn't risk something happening to him before he alerted the team and their families to the approaching threat.

Through the shared networks, Jonas examined the memory in Camellia's mind, noting every nuance, every inflection of Marigold's tone as she spoke to the other women about betrayal, trust and plans for escape. He did so dispassionately. He wasn't a man who ever made judgments about fellow GhostWalkers. Enhancements were difficult to live with. The things Whitney had done to them made it nearly impossible to get through a day at times.

Camellia's mind was a wonder. Each memory stored in vivid detail, down to the smallest aspect. Whether consciously or not, she had noted everything, from what the temperature was to the exact measurements of the room she was in. She had even counted the rotations per minute of the fan above her head.

Yeah, he was going to have to go with Camellia on this one — Marigold hadn't been telling the exact truth about something. She had successfully shut down the conversation about Ivy, Beverly and Whitney's intimation that someone else might have been the one to alert the guards to Camellia's absence. As she had volunteered to try to go out with her former unit to be on the protection team for Senator Freeman and Violet, she clearly believed she might be able to help all of them, including herself. That led him to the conclusion that she knew more about the night Ivy was killed than she let on. That didn't make her guilty. It only meant that, like Camellia, Jonas didn't altogether trust her.

"You don't believe her either, do you?" Camellia came right out and asked him.

"That's a tough one, honey. I don't know her. I'm not the kind of man to hang with the women from the other teams. In the old days, before the enhancements, I might have been considered a player, but not anymore. I make everyone nervous when I walk into a room. Whitney put too much of every predatory animal he could in me. Makes for an ugly mix. So I tend to keep to myself. I avoid trouble with the others that way."

Camellia spun around to look at him. "Wait a minute. When you say this, I'm getting a feeling that I don't like. *Your* team members accept you, and you don't make them nervous, right? Because you go on missions with them all the time and probably have saved their asses."

He tried not to smile. "Just as they've saved mine."

"So when you say you make everyone nervous when you walk in a room, you aren't really talking about Team Two members either, are you? Because they're enhanced as well. It's their women who don't know you," she clarified. "That's what you're saying, Jonas. Ken wouldn't like it if you disturbed her peace of mind, even though you're up here checking out a threat to her and her family."

His heart fluttered in his chest. She sounded outraged on his behalf. "Camellia." He said her name gently, wanting to kiss her again, just because she stood for him and she didn't know him. He might have deserved her championing him at one time in his life, but Whitney had changed him for all time. "Thank you. I wish I could live up to your good opinion of me."

"Aren't you up here checking out a threat to Marigold's family? It isn't just Lily and Ryland's family. You mentioned Briony and Jack. Marigold and Ken. I heard you. Right when we first were talking together. I wanted you to tell me everything you could about them. At the same time, I didn't want you to say anything more. I was confused and hurt. But I do know you were here for one reason. You felt a threat when no one else did, and you came to make certain the families with wives and children were safe."

"I suppose I can't deny that, Camellia. It's just that with a mixture of all the various enhancements Whitney stuck in me, I can become extremely aggressive. I don't like it, and I do my best to control it, but that doesn't mean I'm nice the majority of the time. I'm better outdoors."

She gestured toward the trail, retreating from his side, dropping a step behind him. "I think I am too. At least, after spending so much time on my own, I feel more at home outside with my plants."

Jonas knew she was telling him she wasn't going to accompany him back down to either fortress, not even to the one Team One had built. They were separate from Team Two, a distance away, although escape routes connected them. He didn't know how Ryland was going to feel about Camellia's refusal to introduce herself. He would just have to tell Ryland that the man would have to make a trip up the mountain if he wanted to meet her — that was assuming Jonas could convince her not to run.

With a sigh, he resumed walking down the mountain. "You'll like Jeff and Kyle." She would. He tried not to think too much about that. "Jeff Hollister and Kyle Forbes are two of the best men I know. Kyle helped me when I was at my absolute worst. Both men stood by me when others would have walked away."

They continued walking along that very narrow, almost nonexistent trail that wound through the trees. The fog was by turns either dense or thinner, depending on if the wind could penetrate the heavier brush.

"Where was the rest of your team? Weren't they supportive?"

He found himself with a ghost of a smile on his face. This woman. She didn't miss anything. "I'd gone off by myself. Something terrible had happened. Really bad. No one blamed me but me. It was well after we'd been broken out of the laboratory and I knew everyone was relatively safe. I had to think things over. I was a mess. Jeff was in bad shape. He had no business coming after me with Kyle, but he did. I didn't think anyone could find me. That damn Kyle, he's pretty crazy."

The affection and compassion that came

his way through the network made him clear his throat against a sudden welling of emotion. He'd thought he'd managed to conceal the deep affection he felt for the two men. But he hadn't considered that the highway of information connecting Camellia and himself worked both ways. Images and feelings had poured from Camellia to him, but apparently, she was on the receiving end as well. She had just as clear of a picture of him as he had of her. He didn't like that. She could see the worst in him. The jealousy. The way he wanted to hold her close to him. Keep her away from everyone else.

Her laughter bubbled up. That sound, like bells skipping over water, slid into him, suppressing the worst in the predators and somehow bringing out the better traits. Just like that, everything changed for him. He didn't feel jealous or possessive. Kyle and Jeff were part of his family. He considered Camellia his woman. Mate. His other half. Whatever anyone wanted to call it. Kyle and Jeff were his brothers. He wanted her to feel about them the way he did.

"You really are a miracle, Camellia." He felt compelled to point this out.

"I wish it were me," she answered.

They had reached the circle of rocks where he'd left Jeff and Kyle.

"Coming in," Jonas called.

Jonas felt Camellia reach out along the networks as they approached the boulders. He stayed very still, needing to see how she communicated. Also, he wanted to know who she communicated with. And what she had to say to them.

7

Blue, Gray, circle back and watch carefully in case I should need you. Camellia wanted to trust Jonas, but as much as she could feel and read his every thought, she couldn't quite bring herself to believe in anyone wholly.

She was well aware Jonas would know she was calling on the owls to watch over her. She considered disconnecting from him, but then she wouldn't be able to know what he was thinking or saying to his friends. The moment he sent them private messages, she would be gone. It wouldn't take much to distract him. She would have help.

"Camellia, stop."

Her gaze stayed on the ring of rocks. No one appeared in that circle. Her heart began to accelerate. "Where are they?"

"They knew I was returning and I wasn't alone," Jonas said.

Camellia cursed under her breath. She'd

been so caught up with telling Jonas her guilty thoughts about Marigold that she hadn't thought to consider what his friends might be doing. Immediately, she reached through the networks at her disposal, looking for them.

Both men gave off surprisingly low energy, as if they posed no threat to her, but she knew that wasn't true, not when she lifted her gaze toward the sturdiest of the trees a distance away. She used her vision enhancements, studying the trees, looking for a sniper, anything that might give away the fact that one or both of the men on Jonas's team had a rifle trained on her. It was unsettling that she couldn't spot either of them, especially when she began to get that tingling awareness that told her she was in someone's sights.

"Do you know where your friends are?" She wasn't going to play games with Jonas. Either they were partners, or they weren't. She switched her gaze to meet his.

"No. It's difficult to find either one of them when they don't want to be seen. They would have to move or make noise. I can reach them, but I would have to talk telepathically, and I don't want you to think I'm talking behind your back."

"Then include me." She made it a challenge.

He nodded. "I will, but it's possible they might think you're part of a team and I'm a hostage. I might have to kiss you to convince them you're not part of a larger conspiracy."

She sighed. "You will never make me believe you don't have a phrase or a word or code of some kind that allows your team to know you're safe or for them to spread out and eliminate any other threats to you. You would never have to kiss anyone."

He smiled at her, his eyes warming to a liquid antique gold. "That's the only way I'm going to convince them I'm safe, honey. I'd never kiss an enemy."

Jonas reached for her, keeping his movements slow, and telegraphing his intent the way he always did, giving her plenty of opportunity to retreat. She appreciated that he made it her choice whether or not to let him touch her. She hadn't been physically touched in so long, just the sensation was addicting.

Camellia felt as if she needed the feel of his fingers on her skin. Or the way he curled his fist into her vest and drew her to him in that strong, relentless pull. He made her feel less alone and so much a part of him. She needed that. She'd felt alone for too long. She also needed to know she had choices. She'd spent the majority of her life without freedom. Every single decision in her life had been made by Whitney. She would die before going back to that sort of captivity again, no matter who held the keys to her cage.

Jonas's hand was large, and his fist settled in the lapel of her vest, his knuckles brushing the thin material of her organic tee, sending a frisson of heat arcing through her body, snapping and sparking along all her nerve endings as if her electrical system were malfunctioning. It was impossible to look away from him, as much as she wanted to, as much as she knew she should be looking around to find his friends. She was trapped in his gaze.

Her heart beat too fast, and she knew they both heard and felt it, because they were connected to both networks. She still couldn't bring herself to drop from either network. That closeness gave her access to his mind. She didn't want to be alone. She liked feeling so close to him. She might tell herself it was easier to know he wasn't betraying her, but she knew it was more than that.

He pulled her up against him. She should have already accustomed herself to the feel of his body; the steel trap of her mind had already noted, analyzed and cataloged every tiny detail with immaculate precision, but each time he touched her, she felt the same wild flutter in her belly. A silly reaction she couldn't quite suppress. She wasn't sure she wanted to. He was built like a leopard, all roped muscle, his body dense and hard, and she found everything about him utterly thrilling. She wanted to breathe him in, lick him up, rub the entirety of her body all over the entirety of his.

His eyes blazed down into hers. Wholly focused. Intense. She couldn't look away. Captivated by that predator's stare. Had it only been that fierce, possessive gaze, she might have tried to break free, but there was too much warmth, something she'd had so little of — and she needed desperately. Then his lips were on hers and she couldn't think anymore. It was impossible with her brain melting. Every nerve ending in her body flared to life. Her veins flooded with adrenaline. Her panties were damp, her breasts ached. She'd never been so aware of being female in her life.

His mouth was pure fire. Addicting. The heat, scorching. Winding one leg around his thigh to get closer, blood pounded through her veins, thundered in her ears and settled wickedly in her sex as she pressed even closer to relieve the ache. Her bow and quiver of arrows dug deep into her shoulder, bringing her out of the foggy sex-induced euphoria.

Camellia pressed her forehead hard against Jonas's shoulder. "I can't breathe." Clearly, she couldn't think either. She was a sitting duck out in the open the way she was. She presented a great target, and kissing Jonas had made her forget all about the bullseye on her back.

Middlemist Red's network connected with the mycelium and began working to change the humidity there at the edge of the clearing. The abrupt shift in heat and air caused droplets to condense and merge and form clouds that weren't quite heavy enough to break open and rain. The clouds dropped lower and lower until they were dark and rolling along the ground, creating a fog bank that thickened and began to spread through the small clearing where the boulders were.

"Camellia?" Jonas's tone was low. A question. "You doing this?"

"I don't like feeling like I have a target on my forehead. Your friends are good, Jonas. They're hidden and I can't see them. If I can't see them, it's only fair they have a difficult time seeing me. I would feel so much better."

Jonas didn't release her, just kept her close to him as he studied the layers of grayish-lavender fog rolling through the trees. "You really managed to create that?"

"Not on my own," she conceded. She was a little reluctant to get into the way she'd done it. She knew Jonas thought somehow she'd managed to warm the ground through the mycelium network beneath them, which was partially true.

"This is how you created a rain forest right in the middle of a high-altitude forest where snow would otherwise be a problem." His eyes blazed down at her, so heated they looked liquefied, pure molten gold. He framed her face with both hands, bending his head to hers. "Woman, you have no idea just what a treasure you are, do you?"

She had no time to absorb his question. Or the fact that he truly meant it. His mouth once more descended on hers, and he swept her up in his fire. She opened her mouth, breathed in his heat and lost herself to the flames.

It was Jonas who lifted his head, looking over her shoulder, while she pressed her forehead hard into his chest. "The fog is so thick, it is difficult to see anything. If I put my arm out, even I can't see it."

"That's the point." The sound of her voice was muffled against his shirt but also by the fog. "If we move carefully, there is no way a sniper can find either of us."

"Can I do this, Camellia? Create a fog like this if my team were on a mission and we got in trouble? Would I be able to conceal them from snipers?"

She nodded, although she did so slowly. She knew sooner or later he was going to ask that question.

"Have I been able to all along?"

Camellia pulled her head back to look up at him. There was a note in his voice she didn't like. Guilt? Sorrow? It was nearly impossible to read his expression, but she felt the way his heart was troubled, and the burden of grief weighed heavily on him. It was impossible, as close as they were, not to share those feelings with him.

She chose her words carefully. "It took me a very long time to discover I was capable of changing the temperature in the air. I was experimenting with growing things and trying to change them slightly to develop the types of healing properties I needed or food or even weapons from plants. It was a lot of trial and error. Discovering how to change the air or ground temperature was an accidental by-product of everything in my experimentations. It happened in an enclosed structure the first few times. You would have had no way of knowing it could be done. Even though it happened to me, I didn't realize what it was at first."

He tipped her head up again toward him until her eyes met his. "Thank you."

"It's the truth."

"I know it is. I can feel that it is, and even hear it, but I could tell you were very careful in the way you wanted to present the facts to me. You're . . ." He broke off and once more brushed his lips over hers.

This time, his touch was featherlight. A butterfly's kiss. Gentle. Tender even. Stealing a piece of her heart.

"You two going to keep that up?" There was a wealth of amusement in the voice that came out of the fog.

Camellia stepped back immediately and turned to face the speaker. A slight breeze swept through the fog, thinning it enough so that they could see the newcomer. He was sitting on top of one of the boulders, looking relaxed, smiling. He appeared to be a little taller than Jonas if he stood. His thick sun-bleached blond hair hung around his head as if he were badly in need of a haircut, although on him it looked wildly appealing.

With his lean muscles and dark suntan, he looked more like a surfer out of one of the magazines she'd seen than a soldier. She knew not to be deceived. If he was with Jonas, he was every bit as enhanced and therefore dangerous, and she hadn't spotted him when she'd first looked for him. His energy was still so low she could barely feel his presence.

"Jeff," Jonas greeted immediately. "This is Camellia. Camellia, Jeff Hollister." He looked around. "Where's Kyle?"

"He's still moving a little slow. He'll be here in a few minutes," Jeff assured, that friendly smile still on his face. He was incredibly handsome and appealing in a charming way. There didn't appear to be any of the rough edges to Jeff that were in Jonas — until you really looked into his eyes.

His eyes were different, the color almost a crystal blue. He looked directly at her with his charming, open smile that warmed his expression but not his eyes. His eyes assessed her, taking in every single detail of her appearance. He didn't miss anything. She would bet anything she was looking at a man with an enormous IQ. Whitney wouldn't have missed that. He wouldn't have liked it either, not if Jeff had been declared more intelligent than he was. Whitney very well could have responded to that perceived threat by making this man's life much more difficult than Jeff would ever admit to his friends.

Camellia didn't want to feel empathy for the other members of Jonas's team. That would only draw her in even more, and she was already having a difficult time deciding whether or not to stay. She knew she shouldn't. She was already allowing herself to get too close to Jonas. To want to be with him when it was sheer madness. She forced a smile on her face to match surfer boy's, even though she knew he was lying about their friend Kyle. He wasn't being slow. He was trying to maneuver around to make certain he had a clear shot in case they needed one.

"So nice to meet you." *Liar, liar. Your good friend Kyle has a rifle on me right now. That's okay, I'm calling in my soldiers.*

That was just a little wicked of her, but she liked seeing the shock in Jonas's eyes and feeling the alarm spreading through his body.

She used the mycelium network, reaching out to the alpha wolf. *I have need of your eyes and ears. Of your nose. Is the pack close?*

The answering howl came immediately,

quite close, nearly on top of them. The sound was eerie, the call to hunt. It wasn't a mere summoning of the pack but the call of the alpha that he was already on his prey.

Oh, dear. I suspect Kyle could be surrounded. She batted her eyelashes at Jonas.

"That's not funny, Camellia," Jonas hissed. "He has a rifle. If he feels threatened, what do you think he's going to do?"

The smile left Jeff's face. "Who is being threatened? Kyle?" It was clear he reached out to the absent man. "He assures me he's fine."

"Did you think the wolves would actually give themselves away? They're ghosts in the forest, Jonas. Call your man off and I'll call off my wolves."

"Jeff, call Kyle in now," Jonas ordered. "Camellia is not a danger to any of us."

"I can see that by the ten thousand weapons she has on her," Jeff said, his voice dripping with sarcasm.

"In my defense, I would like to point out that Jonas has a few weapons of his own, as do you," Camellia said, indicating Jonas's jacket and belt. "I'm not even going to talk about what's in his boots — or yours, for that matter."

An owl flew just a few feet overhead with soft, slow wingbeats a distance from them.

It perched on a broken tree trunk inside the grove of trees from where Camellia and Jonas stood together. Immediately the Great Gray owl was lost in the fog and darkness of the forest. It was just that brief moment that the raptor had become visible, and then it was gone, as if it had never been.

"I suppose you're right, ma'am," Jeff agreed. "I'll call Kyle in, but I won't be happy if he loses his way in this fog or something happens to him."

"He's a GhostWalker," Camellia pointed out. "He won't lose his way."

"Although your little alternate trail has been sending GhostWalkers in a different direction for a while now, hasn't it?" Jonas asked.

Camellia shrugged. "I suppose. But only because there was a real trail there. The actual trail had forked. It was easy enough to redirect, make it appear as if the trail just went in one direction, not two."

"Then you embedded a warning system to keep any strays away," Jeff said.

"In case Whitney sent someone after me, yes," she admitted. "That was easy enough as well. I already had the system in place, a warning system set up for me, a way to send hikers or anyone else away from my home, so I just embedded a dread, and then if they continued, a slight illness. If anyone persisted beyond a certain point, the headache and illness would become more severe."

"Some people were obviously more susceptible than others," Jeff said. "Kyle's coming in. You make certain he's safe," he reiterated.

Camellia could feel the slightest vibrations along the mycelium network, indicating someone was approaching. He walked with deliberate steps, clearly trying to let her know he was coming. Jeff had evidently cautioned him to make a little noise because she was certain he wasn't the kind of man to give his presence away.

Let him through, she instructed the wolves.

The temperature changed subtly, and the breeze swept through once again, easing the fog so that it appeared to be just a thin veil of grayish lavender.

"Coming in," Kyle called out.

Camellia turned her back completely on Jonas to watch Kyle's approach. She knew both Gray and Blue were perched on dead tree trunks just a few feet apart, watching over her. They would fly at anyone with deadly talons and vicious hooked beaks. The wolves were close and would come to her aid. She went through the targets in her mind, practicing, going through each motion until she knew how she would make each kill in order to make her run should it be necessary.

The largest problem was she would have to kill Jonas first. The wolves or the owls wouldn't get to him in time. She would be responsible for that task. She would be the one to have to slit his throat or stab him through the heart or shoot him. She turned, pushing her forehead against Jonas's chest one last time before she stepped completely clear of him.

"Honey, do you think, connected the way we are, I don't know what you're thinking?"

She detested the way his voice was so gentle. She was going through the act of killing him in her mind, repeating it over and over after he had kissed her, and he could use that voice, look at her with such understanding in his eyes. Instinctively, she knew he didn't look at anyone else that way.

"I won't apologize for who I am or even what I am, Jonas," she said, lifting her chin. "Unlike you, I've come to terms with what Whitney did to me. I'll admit, I'm nowhere near as aggressive as you are. I can see that you have to fight your nature every minute, and that sucks. I wouldn't want to be you. I don't judge or condemn you the way you do yourself. I know what it feels like, if only

227

in a small way, to have a predatory instinct burn along my nerves, demanding I hunt prey when it runs from me. Rabbits, mice, voles, I've had to find a serene, peaceful place to go when I can feel that need rising in me. To have to deal with it every minute would be hell. But I will fight to stay free, and I'll do whatever I have to do to be free. Whitney is never getting me or a child of mine to experiment on. Nor will he get one of my plant creations."

The others heard her. She could tell they had enhanced hearing, just as both she and Jonas did. The two men exchanged a long look.

"Why would you think we would turn you over to Whitney?" the approaching man asked. "I'm Kyle Forbes, by the way. Whatever these two jokers told you about me is probably exaggerated or not true. I'm mostly a nice guy. Whatever you did to create this defense grid, by the way, is sensational."

He gave her a lopsided smile that genuinely lit his bright blue eyes. He looked to be around six feet tall or just under, with a medium build, but she could see from the way he moved and the muscles rippling beneath his clothing that his build was deceptive. The man was strong. His short dark hair spilled down onto his forehead, making his blue eyes seem even bluer.

"I'm a doctor, and I tried to figure out what was making me feel so sick, but I couldn't. Jeff wasn't as sick, although he got a headache. I couldn't figure out why he wasn't as ill as I was, and Jonas wasn't ill at all. Are you going to enlighten me? I really need to know. If you don't tell me, I might go insane just looping that shit in my head."

In spite of the circumstances, Camellia burst out laughing. "You might already be a little insane." She took a step toward him, but Jonas reached out and caught her wrist, anchoring her to him, holding her in the safety of the trees right at the edge of the clearing.

She glanced up at his set features. She felt the slightest of warnings moving from his nervous system to hers, yet other than that strange vague threat moving toward them, still very much in the distance, she couldn't find any danger directed at her.

"Answer Kyle's first question," Jeff suggested. "Why would you think we would have anything at all to do with Peter Whitney after what he did to us? Not only did he completely ruin and betray us, but he set us up to be murdered because we weren't his perfect soldiers. We're an embarrassment to him."

"He did pair you with his women. And he paired Lily, the one woman he still calls his daughter, with a member of your unit. I have to say, that doesn't sound like he wants you all dead," she replied, doing her best to keep the sarcasm out of her voice.

Jeff arched a brow and narrowed his eyes consideringly at her. "You have to know he thinks Ryland is inferior to Lily's intellect and wants to make her a widow. He'd like to pair her with someone else. Now that he has his near-perfect and perfect teams, he would also like to rid himself of the embarrassment of his mistakes, particularly Team One."

"Do you have proof of that? I escaped some time ago," Camellia admitted. "I haven't heard much after I left. I didn't dare try to contact anyone. It was too dangerous."

"Would you believe me?" Jeff challenged back.

Would she? She could hear lies. Middlemist Red could hear lies. Red had protected herself for centuries. "Depends on whether or not you tell me the truth. Try me and see."

"Whitney wants their son, and he'd like to pair Lily with someone else. Whitney has made three past attempts to acquire their son, and we know of at least two attempts he's made to pair Lily to one of his super-soldiers. And yes, we did find proof that Whitney has been trying to send Ryland and the rest of us on suicide missions as well."

Camellia turned that over in her mind. That would be like Whitney. He wouldn't just kill the soldiers outright. They were his creations, and he would want even their deaths to be useful. He would put them in highly dangerous situations in order to test them. To see if they measured up. He would want them to succeed, and yet he would also want them to fail so he could go forward with his agenda.

That's the reason it's important for you to learn to create the fog and to use the myce-lium network when you need it.

One of many reasons, Jonas said.

He pulled her closer to him. As always with her, in spite of his obvious strength, he was gentle, barely tugging, but he put enough pressure on her to force her to take the couple of steps to cover the distance between them. Immediately, his arm swept around her waist, locking her back to his front. That now-familiar sizzling sensation began along her nerve endings and moved to her veins, igniting a slow burn that spread through her body. He dipped his chin onto the top of her head and rubbed it so strands of her dark hair mixed with blond stubble, connecting them together.

Both Kyle and Jeff noted the way Jonas held her close to him, Jeff with a slight grin, Kyle with a lift of his eyebrow.

"My biggest fear is that Whitney will send someone after me," Camellia answered the question posed in the first place. "And he will. There's no question that he will. I've done my best to stay ahead of him and keep a warning system in place at all times so I have the ability to run. I'm prepared to fight if I need to do that. He underestimates women. I'll admit, I'm counting just a little bit on that. Jonas has warned me that he can track me through the tattoo on my ankle. I'll have to find a way to keep that from working, and I will."

"Is there a reason you don't want to throw in with us?" Kyle asked.

She shrugged, having anticipated that question and prepared her response. It was one thing to reveal her real reasons to Jonas, but she didn't want to talk about Marigold to anyone else. "I've been alone for so long now that I've become uncomfortable in the company of people. I also don't want to risk anyone giving me orders or performing more experiments on me."

Kyle frowned and then jerked his chin at Jonas. "Do you honestly believe the man standing behind you would allow anyone to perform experiments on you?"

Camellia hesitated. She knew these men could hear lies. Jonas was completely connected to her. Still, she didn't trust anyone completely. "I just met him. It's clear Whitney paired us, but I still just met Jonas. I want to spend time getting to know him before I make decisions that will change both of our lives. I would hope he would want the same thing." She didn't dare look up at him.

"I need to know how you made me so sick," Kyle said before Jeff or Jonas could say anything. "I really do. And why I'm the only one who reacted to what you did."

She didn't know how to answer him without telling him too much about herself and the underground network. Maybe it didn't matter so much. This was Jonas's team after all, and she really didn't believe they presented a danger to her.

Everything was happening so fast, but the connection between Jonas and her was so strong, it was as if they'd been together for years and she knew him intimately. She knew there were parts of him she couldn't quite see yet, just as he couldn't see all of her, but total transparency was close if they continued to spend time together. And there was no hiding his true character. He might be a natural predator, enhanced into an aggressive, dominating killing machine when necessary, but his protective traits shone through.

"There was an actual reason we came to get the two of you." Jonas intervened before she had a chance to decide how much to reveal about herself before she was comfortable. "The threat I felt, Camellia feels as well. And it's now gone from a vague feeling to a definite threat, meaning it is coming closer. We both thought it might be a good idea to go find it rather than wait for it to get to us."

Jeff, the smiling surfer with the deadly blue eyes, nodded. "Still not feeling it myself, Jonas, but you've never been wrong. We'll have to send word to Rye. Just in case. Wouldn't want to be taken prisoner or go down in a blaze of glory and have no one know where to start looking."

Camellia turned her head so she could look up at Jonas. "You're sending a message to your commanding officer?"

"To Ryland? Yes. We have to let him know there's a real threat to the others, and we're going to check it out and intercept it if necessary. Jeff and Kyle will come with us. We'll leave signs for our team so they can track us in case we don't make it back in a few days."

Jonas sent reassurance slipping along her nerve endings, a soft stroking caress she felt all the way to her toes. Camellia sighed. He was going to win a lot of arguments with that move.

"Fine, let's get moving then. I don't like traipsing around during the day. And don't leave any tracks. If you're going to leave anything for your team to find, do me a favor and wait until you're back on the main trail, and leave it there. Don't point them in the direction of my home."

"You heard the lady. Don't leave anything for our trackers to find until we're out of Camellia's territory," Jonas ordered.

Camellia stepped away from Jonas and immediately started to make her way back through the trees, avoiding a deer trail and the faint path that led to a hiking trail. There was a narrow stream running down the mountain about four hundred yards from the scattered trees, and she made for that, not looking over her shoulder to see if the men followed her. Once she got to the stream, she began to follow that narrow ribbon back up the mountain.

The stream widened in spots and appeared as no more than dark, swampy mud in others, but it snaked in and out of the rocks, climbing farther upward toward the straggly trees and brush. There was much less dense cover, more boulders and rocks, at this altitude. Jonas had moved into the lead position and Jeff was bringing up the rear as they hiked in silence through the rest of the night.

Camellia found it fascinating that she couldn't hear any of them breathing or stepping on twigs or debris as they moved in single file. Every few miles, one of the men would crouch down and leave a couple of stones arranged in a certain way. It was clear to her they were used to moving through rough terrain together at a fast pace. As dawn began to break, Jonas signaled a halt. No one made a sound.

She stayed very still, calling up the underground network, feeling for threats and listening for any chatter the trees, brush, wolves or owls might have passed on to the root system to give to her. *Jonas, a few miles ahead, there are several men just over the next rise.*

I feel them as well, he acknowledged, all business. *I'm going to make a bridge and include Jeff and Kyle so they can hear. Is that all right with you? We will still have our own individual way of connecting.*

She was well aware she could connect with him alone if she needed to, so she wasn't too concerned — and she would know if he was talking to them alone.

That would be best. Then there won't be a relay or the possibility of speaking aloud. If the men up ahead are Whitney's soldiers, they might be enhanced, which could include enhanced hearing.

Jonas passed on the information to the other two men. *We can hunker down here where we have more cover or proceed over this ridge to intercept. If we proceed, we have little cover, and we don't know what we're walking into. I suggest the three of you stay here and let me scout ahead and take a look.*

Let me send one of the owls. Gray or Blue can tell us how many we're facing, Camellia said. *They'll watch them and send us any information.*

She could feel Jonas's hesitation and knew he would prefer to observe whoever was giving off that feeling of a threat. As they had gotten closer to the group, the feeling had gone from vagueness to certainty. There was no doubt in Camellia's mind that whoever these people were, they had come with the idea of harming someone.

Camellia, Kyle said, the smallest reluctance in his voice, *do you access your owl's actual eyes when he's a distance from you?*

She frowned and turned her full attention to the man, really looking at him. He was uncomfortable asking her the question, and she could tell by both Jonas's and Jeff's reaction that neither one of them knew where he was going with it.

She shook her head. *I don't know what you mean exactly. The owls work independently of me. I have no way of accessing their vision. If I'm in the field, I can use my enhanced vision, if that's what you mean.*

Kyle shook his head. *No. I'm capable of tying myself to an animal or raptor and using their vision to see what they can see. It's very draining and I rarely do it, especially in a combat situation, because it would put those around me in jeopardy.*

Jonas and Jeff looked at one another. Jeff lifted his eyebrow and shrugged.

Will it upset Gray? Or harm him?

Kyle shook his head again. *I do my best to become part of the animal in spirit. I know that sounds hokey, but I don't know how else to explain it.*

Camellia was used to consulting with

Middlemist Red. The plant had lived a long life and seen many unusual things humans didn't understand or believe. Red had saved itself when it became apparent that people who feared what the species could do wanted to eradicate it. Red had vanished so completely but left behind a mystery that had been unsolved for centuries. Many guessed at the reasons Middlemist Red had vanished when once the plant had grown freely, but no one knew the reality.

Red had saved itself again when bombs were dropped, specifically targeting the plant's location, once again vanishing in the rubble only to turn up decades later. Humans thought of themselves as being first in the hierarchy, with animals perhaps second. No one considered plants might have intelligence. No one considered they might communicate, have weapons, poisons — have their own "soldiers." If anyone suspected such a thing possible, they would want to wipe out the "queen," just as they'd tried to do centuries earlier.

Camellia would never allow what she had discovered of Middlemist Red to ever fall into anyone else's hands. That was another reason she could never live with Jonas's team. It would be too dangerous to Red. The problem was, Jonas had Red running in his veins as well. Those same properties. Those same exact abilities. So many. Untapped. Unknown.

Is what Kyle suggests possible? I don't want Gray hurt or frightened. She asked the question only along the Middlemist Red network, knowing Jonas would feel that singing along his nerve endings. He would hear and see the images in his mind, and he would know she wasn't asking him. That couldn't be helped.

The answer came in the form of vibrations, a tuning of exact, beautiful notes. A dripping of chemicals into her bloodstream that lit up like a thousand candles. Those same notes and chemicals lit up in Jonas as well. His eyes met hers, filled with questions she couldn't answer. Or wouldn't. At least she had a reprieve until they were alone.

Is Kyle a good man? Are you certain he won't hurt Gray? She would much rather take a chance with her own life than with her owls. The owls had chosen to follow her, but she felt responsible for them. They were family to her, just as the wolves and Middlemist Red were. She would protect them, just as Jonas would protect his family.

There was a brief silence, and again there was that tuning of precise, beautiful notes in the form of vibrations that spread through their bodies like a symphony. The chemicals blossomed into heated light, glowing and hot.

What do you need me to do, Kyle? When I send him out, do I need to call him to us first?

It was difficult to look at Jonas when he knew she was keeping secrets from him. Not just little secrets — big ones. It wasn't as if they had fallen deeply in love with one another. They were connected on many levels, yes. She accepted that. She knew he was lonely and he found peace in her company. She calmed the savagery in him, and she was grateful that she did. The bottom line was, they hadn't met like normal people, hadn't had time to get to know one another and slowly fall in love.

Theirs was an explosive chemical reaction. There was no doubt about that. They also had a strong connective pull, not only because they were both so utterly alone in so many ways, but they were able to talk to one another and "see" each other. She knew Jonas was far more accepting of their pairing because he'd seen other pairings work. He wanted to have someone of his own. She had never believed it possible and had never seen pairings in action. The only pairing she had witnessed, that of Ken and Mari, seemed a terrible betrayal to her, and only because Marigold hadn't come for her when she knew Camellia was waiting in the greenhouse when all the girls had escaped. Mari had chosen Ken over Camellia to the point she hadn't even taken Camellia with them.

They were back to her trust issue. She doubted if she could ever overcome it enough to actually accept another human being into her life. Even Jonas. Maybe especially Jonas. And yet he might have her heart when no one else could ever come close to it again.

Call the owl close to us and let me see if he'll accept me, Kyle said. *If not, I'll take over one of the wild ones. I like yours because he's impossible to see when he doesn't want to be seen.*

She was especially proud that Kyle hadn't been able to spot Gray, even though he'd sensed the owl's presence, as Gray had flown slowly and silently past them to perch on the snag in the forest.

They're very good at staying concealed. I'm calling him close now. She did so, using the mycelium network, knowing both owls were waiting for her to contact them should there be need.

The male looked much larger than he

actually was due to the fact that he was tall and his plumage was very fluffy. Gray was patterned with brown-and-white mottling, streaks and barring across his wings and body, and he had white patches between his eyes and on his chin. His beak was yellow, and he had a large facial disk but no ear tufts. Camellia thought Gray was quite handsome.

The owl settled on the broken branch of the tree closest to them, where Camellia directed him. She wasn't in the least surprised that Blue followed her mate from a distance, ready to protect him should there be need.

Camellia stroked the owl through the mycelium network and let him know Kyle was her friend and ally — that he wanted to share the owl's vision in order to see the enemy coming to hurt her. If Gray objected, she would ask Kyle to use a different owl.

Gray's wings rose and fell in agitation just once. His feathers looked ruffled and she had to hide a smile. She'd definitely irritated him with the suggestion that Kyle use a different owl.

Do your thing, Kyle, but please stay connected to us if you can. She wanted to make certain the owl was safe at all times.

8

Jonas was amazed at how much information could be relayed when one spoke telepathically rather than aloud. He always had been. It was one of the reasons the team members had become so tightly knit. They learned so much about one another's true characters. You couldn't hide who you were when you spoke telepathically. Your mind was open and others could see you.

He had known Kyle Forbes for quite a few years. Jonas knew him to be a compassionate, caring doctor, an anesthesiologist, one able to get a vein on a patient when no one else could find one. He had many enhancements, most of which he didn't talk about. He stayed quiet for the most part but always carried his share of the workload.

Jonas knew Kyle had demons; they all did. He was enormously strong, and that strength had to come from somewhere. He was a genius with explosives, taking apart

244

and putting together bombs faster than anyone Jonas had ever seen. He had a talent for finding bombs, just knowing instinctively where they were. Like Jonas had the early warning system and no one questioned him, no one asked Kyle how he knew where the explosives were located, but they always believed him.

Never once had Kyle mentioned that he could access an animal's vision. Or a bird's. It was cool, but it was also a little freaky. Jonas remained very still, hunkering down in the grass, his back to Camellia's, waiting while Kyle silently seemed to connect with the Great Gray owl. Jeff prowled along their back trail, ensuring no one was coming up behind them, although Jonas was pretty certain Camellia had her wolves watching their backs.

The owl suddenly rose into the sky, using those slow, gentle beats of its wings, looking for all the world as if it were moving leisurely just a few feet from the ground, hunting for food. Then the bird was rising into the air, not by very much, maintaining the lower altitude but now winging its way toward the ridge.

Jonas immediately felt Camellia concentrating on the network running below the ground. He tried to puzzle out what she was doing. He knew the mushrooms above ground were the fruit, and below were the roots stretching from tree to tree, a great network much like a data network. He tried to see it that way. What message was she sending — or trying to send?

What are you doing? How can I help? He didn't want her to shut him out. He knew she was trying to do that, to use the opportunity to move away from him. To go back to doing things on her own. She'd made up her mind they couldn't have a future together. She didn't trust their instant connection. He shouldn't either. The difference was he straight up didn't care if Whitney had set some kind of trap. He believed Camellia and he could outwit the man if they stayed together.

She looked over her shoulder at him. Her blue eyes struck him again. Those jewel-toned eyes that were so blue they appeared a startling royal color.

I'm connecting with the mycelium network and asking it to bump the temperature of the ground up just a degree or two. There's compost in the ground above and below it, so it's easy enough to do. Once there's a temperature change even by a degree or two, I can bring in mist. It will be dawn soon. I don't want the owls to be spotted. They do hunt in the early morning hours, so it wouldn't be unusual if someone did spot them, except that this isn't their usual territory.

She thought she was chattering too much, that Jonas didn't need the entire explanation. It was guilt and deflection. Connected to her the way he was, Jonas found her thoughts all too easy to decipher. She didn't want to feel guilty, but she did. She didn't consider herself his partner, even though he'd made it clear to her that he was hers. Still, though she couldn't say it out loud, Camellia believed that if it came down to Ryland giving him an order to bring her in, Jonas would obey him.

Negative thoughts aren't going to help us, Camellia. Right now, we're in this together. We have to focus on the enemy. Tell me how to bring up the temperature.

He wasn't going to get into an argument with her. She had every right to be distrustful. The truth was, he didn't know what he'd do if Ryland gave him any kind of an order. He did know he wasn't a man to go AWOL, not without a very good reason, and if she ran, the only way to go with her would be to do just that.

You aren't the one bringing up the temperature exactly. The root system runs beneath the ground all the way from us over the top of the mountain, through the gorge, along the ridge and where they are. You have to feel it, Jonas. Not just the warning system. You're only listening to it for that reason. There are a million other things you can tap into it for if you allow yourself to be that sensitive.

Camellia had been able to create fog and mist several times. He'd seen her do it. If he could do the same thing for his team when they needed to escape, it would be an asset, but if there was even more he could do, he wanted to learn all of it.

There was a brief moment when Jonas struggled to let go of his ego. Camellia had been using the mycelium network for so long it was second nature to her. He had a difficult time believing plants could communicate as effectively as humans, just in a different way. It took a concentrated effort on his part to recall the many things he'd read about how the underground network worked.

Men have a difficult time with the word "sensitive." He made certain to send an edge of humor with his words so that it sang along her nerve endings when she felt his tentative movement joining with her on the mycelium network. He didn't want her to pull away. He followed her lead, trusting her to know what she was doing.

The two of them locked together within the root system, burned hotter, spreading the heat outward like rays of the sun. Carbon-rich materials reacted with nitrogen-rich materials. He could feel the nutrients spreading through the forest fast, the communication moving from tree to tree, bush to bush, plant to plant. With it, the temperature of the ground began to rise very subtly. Not by huge degrees. They didn't need huge degrees. They didn't need the temperature to go up fast. The ground carried the slight change in ground temperature over the ridge away from them.

Across from Jonas, Kyle dropped his head into his hands, fingers pressing into his temples. He looked so miserable it nearly yanked Jonas out of the network. He stayed because he had learned discipline over the years, able to keep his attention divided when he had to keep his enhancements under control, but he kept his gaze fixed on Kyle. Clearly, using the owl's eyes to see was taking a toll on him.

Gray made a pass over the resting area, Kyle reported. *They aren't camping, but they are resting. I've counted eight of them. They're in communication with others. All men. Gray is now on a perch just about a hundred feet from them.*

Jonas could hear the strain in his voice. There were beads of sweat rolling down Kyle's face. He felt, rather than saw, Camellia turn her head, then shift her body so she could keep her eyes on Kyle as well. He felt her uneasiness.

They're definitely scouts headed toward the compound, looking to acquire as much information as possible to send back to the troops following them. The troops appear to be four days behind. Possibly five.

Jonas's belly knotted. His eyes met Jeff's. This wasn't good. Troops? What did that mean? They needed to know who'd sent them. They were going to have to stop these men and question at least one of them. Where exactly were the troops? Why hadn't they been spotted by either Team One or Two? Four or five days out might be so many miles away even he couldn't feel them coming.

The leader is a short man with dark hair. He's wearing hiking clothing. Good boots. Dark plaid shirt and good jacket. They're traveling light, but they have appropriate gear for any weather. They know they could encounter anything this time of year and at this altitude. That's evident.

Kyle's voice was becoming more strained. His skin had a bluish tinge to it, as if he wasn't quite getting enough oxygen.

Red, if Kyle is touched or given nutrients would that harm him or disturb him?

Camellia posed the question, and Jonas knew that neither Jeff nor Kyle could hear her. Was she talking to the Middlemist Red? The plant? The one that had dipped its branches low and swept the blossoms along her face whenever he thought he wanted to touch her? Did she talk to the plant? She'd been alone for a very long time. She admitted she talked to them. But did she expect answers?

A low humming like a series of beautiful clear notes seemed to vibrate along his nerves, and then there was a spectacular burst of heat and light spreading through their bodies.

Some mushrooms have healing properties, Jonas. I can help Kyle.

There was the merest of hesitations, and Jonas knew instantly Camellia had nearly said something else, something of more importance. She had stopped herself, thinking she covered her tell by shifting her body. She rose to her knees to gain Kyle's attention.

Kyle, I'm coming over to you. I can help you feel better. Just keep your focus on Gray's vision and let me focus on helping you.

Jonas watched her closely. If she could use mushrooms or the mycelium root system for healing, then he needed to learn how. If there was another way she was helping, a way she wasn't willing to share with him, there had to be a reason for her reticence. He kept his mind open to hers and stayed as entrenched in the underground network as possible. This time, he stopped watching Kyle and kept his gaze fixed wholly on Camellia, needing to see and feel every single thing she did.

She approached Kyle carefully, almost the way she would a wild animal. He didn't look up but kept his hands over his face. Light was already streaking the sky, and Jonas suspected that even that small amount of light hurt Kyle's eyes. What he was doing was uncharted as far as Jonas knew. How Kyle had even discovered he was able to do such a thing was beyond Jonas.

Jonas found himself fascinated with Camellia. She didn't trust him — or Kyle or Jeff. Clearly, she had secrets she feared sharing with him. Most likely, those secrets had to do with enhancements Whitney had given to both of them. He had the feeling the Middlemist Red Camellia had also been used as an enhancement in both of them. That would account for the strange way the plant had acted with such awareness.

Camellia definitely considered it prudent to reveal as little as possible about her enhancements, yet she had such compassion in her for Kyle that she took the chance of revealing more to Jonas in order to help a fellow soldier. That only drew Jonas to her more.

He might have every dominant trait instilled and enhanced in him, but he also had quite a few others, and he looked for those in his friends and family. There were certain characteristics he knew he would need in a partner if he ever found one. He was too alpha, too aggressive. He would need a woman who would not only be able to put up with that side of him but also soften his harsher edges. He was highly intelligent and needed someone equally so. He needed a partner who would join him in guiding their children, nurturing them, teaching them.

Despite a lifetime filled with one-night stands, once Jonas settled in a relationship, he would demand absolute monogamy and give the same in return. Loyalty was too huge for him to settle for anything less. That also meant that once he chose a mate, he would mate for life.

Camellia possessed every trait he was looking for in a mate.

She had been willing to sacrifice herself for the other women she'd grown up with. They'd formed a family, and she'd been extremely loyal to those within that pack, so much so that she was willing to die for them. That meant she was capable of forming strong emotional attachments. Jonas knew she wouldn't love shallowly, or on the surface. Once she gave her heart to someone, she would completely surrender. And by that surrender, she'd make herself utterly vulnerable to the ones she loved. That was part of the reason she fought so hard to protect herself from emotional attachments. They opened her back up to the possibility of betrayal.

The leader and another one, presumably his second-in-command, have walked a distance away from the others and have come close to the broken tree stump where Gray is perched. The mist is much denser here. I doubt they can see him. He hasn't moved a feather.

The pain in Kyle's voice was so clear that Jeff signed to Jonas that it was time to bring him back. Jonas signed to wait another couple of minutes, to allow Camellia to see if she could aid Kyle. Jeff immediately turned his attention to Camellia as well.

She had slipped behind Kyle, her hands

going to his neck first and then sliding up to his temples. The pads of her fingers pressed on either side of his scalp. She didn't massage his temples so much as she simply pressed deep.

They are talking about Daniel and whether or not they should make a try for him or wait for the troops. They think it would be safer to extract him and his mother before the war starts. Since the plan is to wipe out everyone but Daniel and Lily, these assholes think it's best to snatch Lily and Daniel before everyone else gets here.

Jonas and Jeff once again exchanged a long, shocked look. They couldn't pull Kyle back yet. They would have to get as much information as possible. Who would send an army to kill both Team One and Two, including women and possibly any children in Team Two? It wouldn't be Whitney. He would never risk the babies he wanted so badly for his experiments. That really didn't make sense. Jonas hoped Camellia could aid Kyle before he burned himself out.

Switching his gaze back to her, Jonas assessed everything his body felt. There was definite heat along his nerve endings. When he concentrated on the flow of it, he could actually trace the warmth spreading out from a central location as if it were a network all its own. Even the pads of his fingers grew hotter — not uncomfortable, just capturing his attention, as if he should be doing something with them.

He felt he could extend that network inside him and make connections around him if he tried, but he wasn't certain how. There were so many outlets, so many wires sizzling with energy and life inside of him. He just had to know how to make that last connection to Kyle or Jeff or loop back to Camellia.

They decided to make a try for Daniel and Lily. They plan to gather information on the other compound and send back any weaknesses in their defenses.

In spite of the fact that Kyle had been using the owl's vision for a longer period of time, it seemed as if the pain was lessening.

Jonas kept his gaze fixed on Camellia's face. Her expression was soft. She looked perfectly serene crouched behind Kyle, her hands gentle on his skull, fingers pressed into his temples to ease the pain he was evidently experiencing. Outwardly, it was impossible to tell that she was doing anything out of the ordinary, but inside his body where their nerve endings seemed to be connected, he felt everything.

He suddenly realized he was looking in

the wrong place. The answer to the mystery of what she was doing was inside her mind. That lovely, sharp-witted, carefully guarded mind that was currently completely open to him.

He entered slowly, gently, careful not to disturb her. The activity and energy in her brain was astonishing. It was as if every cell was lit up and working overtime. He could see the neurons spread out like arteries, white-hot stars stretching in every direction, flashing and flickering on and off, so bright it almost hurt.

Jonas took a deep breath and forced himself to relax. He needed to connect completely with her, to tap into even one of those white-hot pathways. He did so, using that same gentle approach, sliding his sparking neurons against hers. Immediately, he felt an instant syncing in his own brain.

He became aware of her heartbeat. The rhythm steady. Strong. Powerful. More powerful than it should have been, he realized. He wasn't just hearing Camellia's heartbeat. The drumming was deep-rooted, as if the mycelium network had also joined them, bringing with it every tree and bush in the forest. Chemicals dripped through his veins. Through hers. Drained into their neurons and spread through their bodies to move out of their pores. He actually felt small beads of sweat, tiny droplets released into the ground where they were absorbed. Most rushed to his fingertips.

He shifted his gaze to Camellia's hands — to her fingertips where she pressed them into Kyle's temples. A single small bead of what appeared to be sweat slipped out from under one of Camellia's fingers to slide down the side of Kyle's face. Whatever it was that was moving through their veins, she was sharing it with Kyle.

Jonas tried to remember how the mycelium system worked to bring nutrition to the trees that needed it. He was aware the underground root system ensured the health of the forest, providing a means of communication. He knew that trees could warn other trees of disease or infestations via the underground network. Those warning messages could prompt the other trees in the forest to change their biochemistry, to increase the levels of toxins and repellents in their tissues to deter pests or produce airborne compounds that could lure natural enemies of a particular pest. The trees could also react to the messages in other ways.

The underground mycelium system provided nutrients to the trees in several different ways, threading through their roots or over them. Dying trees could pass resources such as nitrogen and phosphorus to neighboring healthy trees, giving them extra resources to combat any outbreak of disease.

In some way, the chemical Camellia was passing to Kyle was a healing or pain-relieving agent. There was no way for Jonas to directly examine the nature of the compound, but he knew it was moving through his own system and out his pores. That meant, like Camellia, he actually had the ability to produce that particular chemical. How? Even by examining Camellia's mind, he couldn't see the how of it. He could see the energy she used. He could see the way she called on the neurons in her body to spread the energy throughout her veins and muscles. He just couldn't see where the healing agent she delivered to Kyle came from.

The leader and his second-in-command are definitely enhanced. Kyle's voice broke into Jonas's thoughts and pulled his attention back to the problem of the threat. *The second-in-command is called Dex. He just went vertical about thirty feet and caught a branch, pulling himself into the tree. He's looking to view ahead. He did it easily. He's dressed much like the leader, jacket blue and green. Light pack just like leader.*

Kyle sounded much stronger. The pain was gone from his voice, and he lifted his head, dropping his hands away from his temples.

The leader is called Crawley. One of his men, a blond, short, with wide shoulders and abnormally long arms, just came up to him and told him he doesn't like the fog. They're having a discussion about it now.

Jonas immediately turned to Camellia. *Will they be able to figure out that it isn't normal fog?*

Camellia shook her head. *No, because it is real. The ground temperature is just a degree or two higher in spots. They won't be able to figure out the reason for that.*

Kyle smiled. *That's exactly what they're talking about now. The blond — Crawley called him Mott — just told Crawley that there was something strange about the ground, maybe some sort of geological hot spot to make the temperature higher than in other places.*

Camellia flashed an answering smile to Kyle. *That's good. If we need the cover of mist, we won't have to worry about them getting suspicious when we generate it. They won't consider it strange since they've already decided what could be causing it.*

Crawley's getting his team up, Jonas. They'll be coming our way soon, Kyle reported.

I'll need you in fighting shape, Kyle. How long of a recovery time will you need? Jonas asked.

I feel fine right now. Before, I was very sick and the pain was incredible. Whatever pressure point therapy Camellia used really helped. I'll have to learn it.

Jonas let Kyle's comment pass without remark. Now was not the time to discuss what Camellia had actually done to ease Kyle's pain.

We'll head back down the mountain and find a place where we can ambush them. I have to send word to Ryland to get our families ready for an all-out attack. Jonas was the strongest telepath. He would be able to project the farthest. *Camellia, if you combine your strength with mine, I think we can actually double the distance. I won't have to use any equipment that might risk tipping off the enemy.*

Camellia nodded. They were all on their feet, ready to move out. Jonas watched Kyle carefully for any signs of possible problems. There didn't appear to be any. He had pulled back from Gray but was ready to reconnect when he needed to.

We can't risk leaving any tracks. If they're

enhanced, they could easily spot our trail if we leave one, Jeff warned.

I'll make certain we're not leaving any evidence of our passing on the ground, Camellia volunteered.

Jonas realized that was yet another huge asset the underground network could provide his team once he knew how to use it. There would be no evidence of footprints or disturbed leaves on shrubbery.

For now, he let Camellia ensure that their small group left no crushed vegetation as they raced on the narrow game trail back down the steep side of the mountain, weaving in and out of the boulders and trees. He set a brutal pace, but he wasn't taking chances. They had to warn Ryland and prepare to deal with the eight enhanced scouts.

Camellia, have you been up this far before?

Yes.

Do you know the fastest way down the mountain to our compound? If you do, move into lead position and take over, Jonas instructed.

Camellia did so without hesitation. She stayed on the same course for another mile and then veered off the game trail, moving fast into a section of dense forest with heavy underbrush and no clear trail. It should have been impossible to hide the fact that they had passed through that way, but when Jonas glanced over his shoulder, the brush closed up behind them as if it had never been disturbed.

There's a ravine ahead. It's a jump of about thirty feet. Can all of you make it? Camellia didn't even pause in her pace.

No problem, Jonas answered for all of them.

She ran at the same ground-eating pace he had originally set, and when the gap loomed ahead, she launched herself. The three men followed, clearing the distance easily. She was already running down a steep rocky slope, trees on either side of her, a ribbon of water glimmering in the early morning sun as it tumbled down the mountainside.

Five miles later, she suddenly took an abrupt turn, and they were back on a narrow deer trail. Jonas was almost certain he recognized the area where they were. He had hiked up that same trail with Jeff and Kyle before running into Camellia's defenses. She had trimmed miles off their path.

We should be able to reach Ryland from here. We can stop in that little meadow just ahead, Jonas told her. *Kyle, while we're warning Rye, reach out again and try to connect with Gray. See if you can find out where they are exactly. Try to get an idea of their abilities.*

No problem, Kyle agreed.

The meadow was very small, really too small to qualify as a meadow, but there was an opening in the trees and the four sank down in the tall grass. Jeff immediately moved back to cover their back trail while Kyle reached out to the owl.

Jonas reached his hand out to Camellia. She hesitated before she allowed him to close his fingers around hers. Her hand felt very small and delicate next to his much larger, calloused one. Very gently, he ran his thumb along her inner wrist, over her pulse, staring down at her skin for a long time before he raised his gaze to hers.

She had incredibly blue eyes. Wary now. He didn't blame her. He would be if he were in her shoes. He took a deep breath and let it out. He hadn't realized the extent of the threat they would be facing. Or the magnitude of the gifts they both possessed.

Ryland's going to ask a lot of questions, Camellia, and I'll have to answer them. I'll do my best to leave you out of it as much as possible. The important thing right now is to let him know he's got an army coming to wipe out Team One and Two. Now is the time to make up your mind.

He glanced over at Kyle and then toward the forest where Jeff had disappeared. *You could get away clean right now, honey, before all hell breaks loose.*

Her blue eyes widened with shock.

He nodded his head. *I mean it. This is going to get ugly. Beyond that, I hadn't realized the extent of the abilities you have.*

We both have them, Jonas.

He nodded. *I realize that, but I have no idea how to access them the way you do. If Whitney found out, or hell, the government, you could be in real trouble. No one can find out. I want you with me. I do, Camellia.* He brought her knuckles to his mouth and rubbed them along his lips. *At the same time, you need to be safe. I believe my team will protect you, but you and I both know things happen. Look at what has happened with Daniel and Lily. There's a leak somewhere. I still have to track that down in order for Daniel, Lily and even Jeff to be safe if I'm right about what I think Jeff and Lily are doing.*

They sat in silence for a few moments. Jonas was aware of the early morning sunlight playing through the brightness of her dark hair so that it appeared glossy. Birds sang and flitted from branch to branch in constant motion. It was actually a beautiful morning, not one where he would ever have thought he was losing the one thing he knew he needed in his life to make it worthwhile.

I think I'll stick it out with you, Jonas, at least until after the threat is over. Then we can take the time to see if we're even compatible.

Jonas still had her hand pressed against his lips. He didn't realize air was caught in his lungs, and he hadn't taken a breath in some time. The pressure on his chest was tremendous. He barely comprehended what she'd said. He found himself just staring at her like an idiot.

Camellia? The burning in his lungs increased.

Take a breath, Jonas.

The gentle amusement filling his mind was tinged with something he couldn't quite identify but knew was good. Still. *As much as I want this, you with me, it isn't safe for you. The things you can do, Camellia, are unique and crazy valuable, and I can tell there's so much more.*

He knew there was more. He knew if one person found out who shouldn't, she would never be left alone. Never. As much as he wanted her for himself, he didn't want to risk her.

The bottom line is this, Jonas. I don't know for certain whether or not Marigold betrayed me that night when I tried to escape. I do know she didn't tell me about her twin sister, and I know she left me behind when we all escaped, but she's still my family. That means she's mine to protect. Lily is part of my family as well. I'm not going to run when they're in danger. I just can't do that. I'm not built that way.

Her response came as no surprise. She was loyal, and she was willing to sacrifice herself for those she loved. It didn't matter that Marigold had hurt her beyond reason or that she hadn't seen either Lily or Mari in a couple of years. They were important to her, and she would defend them with her life.

Jonas pressed his lips to her knuckles and then nipped the soft skin with his teeth. *I'm reaching out to Rye now. Feed me as much energy as you can. He's a good distance away. I'll tell him up front that you're helping me hold the bridge and can hear every word we say. Ryland will most likely have Kaden, one of our most powerful telepaths, doing the same on his end.*

Jonas didn't wait but reached out to Ryland. *Rye. We're all in trouble. I've got one of Lily's lost sisters with me, helping me connect*

267

with you over the distance. Don't have a lot of time. You need the details.

The response was slow to form, but several seconds later, his psychic energy spiked as two remote minds established contact with him. Ryland and Kaden together. They were strong when they twisted the path together, but the distance was long, and it took time to follow the trail back to him across such a distance.

Is everyone okay?

Yes. Camellia is with me. Jeff is watching our back trail. Kyle, at the moment, is keeping an eye on eight scouts tasked with kidnapping Daniel and Lily. A much larger force is coming behind them to wipe out the rest of our team and Team Two. They're enhanced, at least the eight scouts are. We've not seen the troops they report to yet. Our understanding is the main force is still four to five days out. The ones sent ahead are to acquire Lily and Daniel so they can't accidentally get harmed in the battle. Whoever these guys are, they don't appear to know much about Team Two or their children, only our team.

There was a long silence while presumably Ryland and Kaden talked over Jonas's intel.

We have a leak. Kaden's voice was grim.

We do, Jonas confirmed, equally as grim.

268

No estimate on the size of the army coming at us? Ryland asked.

Not at this time, but we hope to capture a couple of live scouts, Jonas said. *That's why I don't have a lot of time. We're going to ambush them and get as much information out of them as possible. I doubt Whitney would send an army after us, but you never know.*

Again, there was a long silence while Kaden and Ryland talked over what little Jonas was able to give them.

We can send you a couple more men, Jonas. If these soldiers are enhanced, there's only the three of you.

Four with Camellia. She's worth her weight in gold, Jonas corrected. *She's stood with us so far and intends to until the end. Says Lily is family and she protects family.*

You have to be certain about her, Kaden cautioned.

I'm as certain of her as you are of Tansy.

Jonas felt Camellia dig her fingers into his thigh, centering his attention back onto her. *What is it?*

Tansy. She whispered the name into his mind. *I remember her. We were all so little back then. She couldn't have been more than five when Whitney took her away. He said he found her a home with good parents. Is that true? Did she have good parents? A good life?*

Jonas kept possession of her hand and reached out with his free hand to touch her face gently. At that moment, it didn't matter that an army was coming at the two teams. She deserved to know about another one of her lost sisters.

Kaden? he prompted. *Kaden is married to Tansy, Camellia. He would know better than anyone else.*

She had a good childhood but was betrayed by her father. That hurt her very much. She will love catching up with you. Thank you for wanting to help defend her.

Jonas was very grateful Kaden took the time to give Camellia that brief explanation. *Don't send anyone to help us, Rye. If anything goes wrong, you'll need everyone there. Make certain Team Two is prepared to get everyone out. You should move Daniel and Lily. Have the Nortons get their children out.*

They can't. Let me correct that. Briony and her twins can go. Her boys are about five months younger than Daniel. Healthy boys. Briony's healthy. Marigold had major problems with her pregnancy and delivery. Her boys are only a few months old. I think they can travel, but she has an infection. From what I understand, it would be dangerous to move her. If we had to, we could, but we might have to make a stand, Ryland said.

There was no question that Team One would stand with Team Two. If they divided to send some of the men with women and children away from the compounds, the others would stay behind. Jonas felt the energizing sparks running along his veins and traveling through the neurons to spread heat and awareness through his body. Now he knew what it was. His woman approving of his teammates. Of him. Recognizing their loyalty to one another.

Kyle suddenly turned his head. *Those scouts are on the move, heading up the main trail, toward the top of the ridge. They're running silently. Gray flew low and no one noticed, although the one they called Mott turned his head for a moment, so he might have caught the movement. Maybe not though, because at the time, they were still in the fog. They're out of it now.*

Are they staying to the main trail? Camellia asked. *Did any of them appear suspicious when they crossed our trail? I wiped our tracks on the ground and through the brush and did my best with scent, but air is still the most difficult for me to manipulate.*

Kyle nodded. *They're on the main trail. None of them noticed any tracks, and two in particular seem to be looking, although just in general I think, not because they believe anyone was watching them. They have one "sniffer." He's always testing the air. They're coming up on the ravine. It's deep, but not very wide. Not like the gorge we jumped. Mostly rock. There's a large tree down, and they've stopped to maneuver it into position to use it as a bridge.*

Jonas relayed the information to Ryland and Kaden. They couldn't hear Kyle, and Jonas didn't necessarily want to try to explain how Kyle was getting the information.

Again, there was that brief silence before Ryland spoke. *These men are enhanced, and they didn't jump the ravine? How wide is the ravine?*

Sixteen feet, Jonas relayed. *The second-in-command leapt thirty feet vertical. Kyle saw him do it.*

When they let the tree trunk go, it smashed to pieces and fell into the ravine. Crawley just took off down into the ravine. He didn't even try to jump it or find another bridge, Kyle said. *The others have followed him down. The steep incline hasn't deterred them or slowed them by much.*

Do you recognize any of the soldiers? Kaden asked.

Jonas relayed the question to Kyle, who

replied in the negative. *None of them, Kaden. But we have to go. We need to find a place to intercept them. Once we have more information, we'll get it to you, but prepare for war. If you decide it's too dangerous to send Daniel and Lily away, stash them somewhere safe.*

Keep the team alive, Jonas, Ryland ordered.

Always.

9

The morning sun beamed down through the forest canopy, streaking rays to spotlight the dense fog that rolled along the ground in grayish-lavender clouds. The fog crept along the forest floor, barely covering the vegetation in some places and in others rising up to form thick banks of fog that were impossible to see through.

Crawley glanced back at the men running behind him. This side of the mountain was steep with ravines and thick, nearly impenetrable brush in places. They were keeping to a game trail that was barely discernible. The attack was orchestrated purposely from this side of the mountain because it would be unexpected. His men were stoic as he expected, even in the nasty and unexpected fog from hell.

The trail veered slightly and he glanced at his GPS again. He'd studied the maps given to him and this didn't feel right. He kept directions in his head easily. He never got lost, not in deserts or jungles. The GPS wasn't making sense. The trail continued to wind through a grove of trees and then was in the open for a moment. He felt a little better about that. When he pulled up the maps in his mind, he recalled a small clearing. Nothing was ever the same on the ground.

Dex moved up to join him, matching his pace so they ran side by side. "Something's off, Crawley. Really off. I think we should stop again and let Hound and Bear do their thing. We've got time."

Crawley shook his head. "I got word from Shaker. They're dropping the troops in earlier than we thought. They'll be here in four days, and we still don't have information on either of the two fortresses. Shaker says to get it for him. You know what that means. Four days isn't much time. We've got to get Lily and her kid out of the line of fire. Just sneak and peek, like we were ordered at the other fortress, and get the hell out."

Crawley knew he sounded grim, but he felt that way. Initially, he'd been sure they could get in and out of both fortresses, no problem. Surveil the fortresses, stage some sort of diversion so they could pop in and grab Lily and her kid, plus kill a few easy targets and disappear. But that initial confidence had evaporated, and his opinion of this mission had done a complete one-eighty. An inexplicable sense of dread had come over him. Like Dex, he had a bad feeling something was off; he just didn't know what it was.

They were out of the small clearing and back on the narrow, twisting path that went through the trees. The game trail was so narrow, it forced Dex to drop behind Crawley. The damn fog was rolling around like it was boiling up from a witch's cauldron, tumbling over and over like high waves at sea. There was no wind. Not even a breeze to move the dark lavender-tinged fog around.

Maybe Dex was right. He needed to make certain they were moving in the right direction. It would be easy to get lost. The map in his head said there was a lot more stone at this elevation and fewer trees. Had he veered off course by that much? Crawley was beginning to doubt himself again. He glanced down at his wrist and the GPS, trying to pinpoint where they were. He couldn't see the face of his watch clearly. The fog had penetrated the face of it, which was virtually impossible.

He blinked several times in an attempt to

clear his vision, then wiped the watch on his thigh, slowing the pace. He was really becoming disoriented. He wiped his eyes to clear them as well. Glancing over his shoulder at his men, he could see they were having as much trouble or more than he was. Lance, one of his trackers, actually staggered and nearly went down. If the other tracker, Dwayne, hadn't caught his arm to steady him, he would have fallen.

"We'll find a place to stop where the fog is at its lowest point and there's room for everyone to sit down. The sniffers can get ahead of us and see if they can ferret out any danger. If they can't, Snake, it will be your turn." He didn't like the idea of putting Snake in the field. Snake ended things in a permanent way. There would be no prisoner to interrogate if they came across someone, but better to protect his men than run into a problem.

He kept to the narrow trail but continued at a much slower pace, winding in and out of the thinning trees, grateful to see the rockier terrain he'd been expecting. A ribbon of water gleamed silver and blue to their right, winding in and out of the trees as well. He remembered that little stream, and satisfaction eased some of the tension in him. Eventually, the game trail widened enough to appear more like the original hiking trail he had seen on the map. Not that many hikers ever went up this way. That was why they'd chosen this entry point. Even the GhostWalkers seemed to have forgotten to be vigilant in the steep forest miles above them.

That made Crawley give a little sniff of contempt. He was sick of hearing about the GhostWalkers and how dangerous they were. The attack on them had to be planned so carefully because they were enhanced. Well, big deal — so was he. So were his men. He'd heard the first team, the one Lily and her kid were with, were nothing but fuckups. The second team might give them more trouble, but they had problems as well.

The path widened even more, just enough to tell him he was definitely back on the main trail. Unfortunately, the fog continued to roll along the ground, winding around the trees and small boulders, burning over his skin and then retreating to show the vines on the trees and strangely smooth rocks. The sun shone down on the rocks so that they glittered with veins of what looked an awful lot like gold. The area was wealthy in minerals and, some said, gold mines. Crawley had no idea how true that was, but he wouldn't mind stumbling across one of them.

Crawley slowed the pace even more so he could actually look at one of the larger rocks. He tried not to do more than glance, so none of the others could see what he was doing. If the rock actually contained a vein of gold, he would come back and mine that sucker. He'd be a millionaire from that alone. He didn't want to stop where any of the others on his team might spot the gleaming veins in the rock.

"This looks good, Crawley," Dex said. "We can send out the sniffers, see if they can pick up a scent."

"I think there's a place right up ahead, Dex," Crawley said without pausing. "A little more room for everyone to rest while Hound and Bear go out."

Dex didn't protest, and Crawley rounded two trees and found himself with a trio of fairly significant boulders on either side of him. The trail cut right through them. The fog rolled along the ground and crept up the sides of the rocks, making it difficult to see their shapes. He caught glimpses of them. The boulders were taller than they were wide, stretching upward like thick fingers pointing toward the sky.

Crawley felt uneasy, a kind of dread knotting his gut, but the sun shone down on the middle rock to his left, just as the gray-lavender fog parted. Once again, he caught sight of glittering color that dazzled his eyes. He turned his head to look to his right at the trio of boulders standing there like guardians of a gate. The vein of gold ran along two of the fingers. His heart pounded. He wouldn't need to work for a superior asshole who sent him out to fight rejects. He would have enough money to buy his own army of soldiers and bodyguards.

He hastened through the tall archway of boulders, leading his men through so they wouldn't notice the thick veins of gold running along the stones. There were trees that draped over the very large rocks, the canopy high above them. The sun beamed through the branches and the vines dangling from them. He'd only seen vines like that in rain forests. They were snakelike, some green and some banded.

The trail didn't widen as he'd hoped, it remained about the same. Dex could have run along beside him, but it would have been a tight fit. They were in some kind of corridor. He definitely didn't remember this from the map in his head.

Crawley slowed to a walk, suddenly concerned that he'd gotten off the main trail again. He didn't understand how he kept veering off course. He was best at directions, his brain always keeping him exactly where he meant to be. He felt very disoriented. He didn't remember the rocks at all, and he stumbled a little, the droplets of mist on his skin starting to burn.

"What the fuck?" He swiped at his exposed skin. What the hell was this? Some sort of acid rain–type fog? He looked back at his men. Like him, they were trying to cover their exposed skin. The fog created a weird sensation on skin. There were no blisters or burn marks, nothing to indicate in any way that there was an actual burn — only the impression of one.

"You might want to stop where you are and raise your hands over your heads." The voice came out of the mist. It was impossible to tell where it came from. The sound seemed to roll with the gray-lavender fog that was now up to their necks.

"Snake, hunt," Crawley ordered. Mist or not, it wouldn't matter. His number one killer would find their enemy and dispense with them in record time. Once given the order, Snake was relentless in his pursuit. He could kill in seconds.

His men went back-to-back. They couldn't see their enemy, even with their enhanced vision, not through the thick fog that continued to spin in giant waves as if alive. Crawley suddenly realized there was no sound either. He had excellent hearing. He should have heard breathing. Birds. Reptiles scuttling in the vegetation beneath their feet.

Because the silence was so intense, when the half-muffled grunt came through the fog, choked off, it sounded especially chilling and ominous. Fingers of fear crept down Crawley's spine.

"What was that?" Dex asked.

"Don't know." But Crawley was afraid he did know, even if he didn't believe it was possible. No one could get to Snake. He was too fast, too lethal. When he struck, he was like lightning. The toxin he injected worked to paralyze his victim so quickly they had no time to retaliate. He raised his voice just above a whisper. "Hound? Bear? What are you getting?"

The two members of his crew were known as "sniffers." Their sense of smell was so acute they could ferret out anything or anyone for miles. He and his men had come to depend on their abilities in tight situations such as this one. At no time did he stop looking around him with his enhanced vision, using everything he had in order to penetrate the bands of rolling fog.

"Nothing, Crawley." There was regret and even shame in Hound's reply. "I can't smell anything at all."

"Neither can I," Bear added. "This fog has layers to it that seem to confuse my ability to smell anything."

Crawley cursed under his breath. "Dex? Can you see through this shit? Because I can't." He hated to admit it, but it was the truth.

The disembodied voice came out of the rolling fog again. "Put down your weapons. There's no need for anyone else to get hurt. Any sign of aggression will earn retaliation."

"Mott, swing around and cover Dex from the other side. Cover fire," Crawley ordered. "Dex?"

At once, the others sprayed their automatic weapons in every direction. Dex went vertical, leaping high above the strange mist, whirling in a circle, his weapon spitting fire as he strained to find a target with his enhanced vision. He landed on a rock surface in a crouch. The moment he did, something tightened around his neck. He reached up with one hand, curling his fingers in the band.

Dex's heart jumped. He felt scales, as if a snake had dropped from one of the trees and wrapped itself around his neck. Every movement of his body tightened the coils. With effort, he didn't panic, gripping the band with his fingers and yanking hard to give himself room to breathe — except it didn't work. He dropped his gun and caught up his knife. Already he was gasping for air, choking, black spots beginning to waver in front of his eyes.

Bringing up the blade, he tried to saw through the snake's body as it coiled even tighter. His arm felt too heavy. The body of the snake felt more like a thick piece of wood. He felt his arm drop to his side. His eyesight failed. His lungs burned for air. He tried to call out to Crawley, even to use telepathy, but he couldn't remember how. Then his knees hit the rock and everything just faded away.

"Dex?" Crawley called out.

"He's gone," Hound said. "They got him."

Crawley realized Mott hadn't checked in. "Mott, you with us? Call out now."

There was absolute silence and Crawley's heart sank. He didn't need the others to tell him that Mott's body was somewhere in that disturbing fog.

"Put your weapons down." The order came again in a low, patient tone.

Crawley swore again under his breath. The mist was thick. If they couldn't see their

284

enemy, it was just as likely their enemy couldn't see them. *We're going to put the guns down, and when we do, drop to the ground and move backward in complete silence. We have to get out of these rocks.*

"We're putting our weapons down," Crawley agreed.

He removed the strap from around his neck and dipped low to place the automatic rifle on the ground in front of him, as did the rest of his men. On his signal, they went to their bellies, allowing the fog to close over their heads and swirl around their bodies as they began to crawl as fast as they dared back toward the opening between the boulders for the open trail.

Dwayne suddenly grunted, the sound loud in the hushed fog. Lance made a similar noise, much more guttural. In front of Crawley, Hound and Bear both stopped moving abruptly.

What the hell? Keep going.

Lance isn't moving. I shoved at him and he isn't responding. I think he's dead, Hound said. *I think Dwayne is too.*

Crawley waited a moment to see if either Lance or Dwayne would dispute Hound's statement. Neither moved or spoke. That dread in Crawley's gut had grown to real fear. Who the fuck were these fuckers, and how were they killing his men so damned easily? He was enhanced. His men were enhanced. None of this made any sense.

We have a better chance if we allow them to take us prisoner. As it is, we can't tell what we're facing. If they don't kill us outright, we can assess what we're up against and then hit them hard, Crawley decided. *Don't resist in any way. They're clearly playing for keeps.*

"We're going to stand up and surrender," Crawley said. "There are three of us left alive." He kept bitterness from his voice.

The men had not only been his responsibility but been his friends. He wasn't someone who chased after gold. His mind was normally clear, yet he'd been caught in some kind of hallucination fed by the fog, he was certain. Now he could think again. As he stood, he noticed the fog no longer had a lavender tinge to it. It still rolled and spun, but it appeared a normal gray and was thinning a bit.

"Walk out from the boulders and make certain you leave your weapons and all communication devices on the ground. If you're caught with a gun or knife or any means of communication to Shaker or anyone else on you, you aren't going to survive."

That voice, as always, didn't change tone. It was low, calm, patient and deliberate.

Crawley knew the bastard meant every word.

"Get rid of everything you have on you," he ordered aloud. *Remember you are a weapon. They don't know you're enhanced or that you've had extensive training.* He wanted to reassure his men they would be fine. He wasn't as certain as he professed, but he was their leader and wanted to keep his men sharp, alert and confident enough to seize whatever opportunity came their way.

He dumped his weapons, watch, every device he had and observed as Bear and Hound did the same. They locked their fingers behind their heads and walked out from the boulder corridor, stepping carefully around the bodies of Lance and Dwayne. He glanced at them quickly as he moved past. They both appeared to be covered in white and brown threads of some kind.

What the fuck was that shit? He wanted to examine the weapon or whatever had killed them much closer, but the fog, although thinning, moved in between them, and he had to keep walking.

Did you see their bodies? he asked his men.

I caught a glimpse, Bear said. *Looked like a fast-acting toxin of some kind. Dwayne had foam around his mouth and blisters on his skin where that plant touched him.*

It had been a plant. Crawley frowned, trying to digest that. How had a venomous plant erupted from the ground and covered both of his men, killing them? There weren't deadly plants that did that kind of thing, at least not in the Lolo National Forest.

Once clear of the boulders, Crawley found himself blinking in the early morning sunlight, free of the fog. He looked around him. The trail was a little wider than it had seemed leading to the boulders. There were more rocks than he remembered and fewer trees, the way it should have been at this altitude. Still, brush and trees, the forest beginning to emerge, meeting the rocks.

A man stepped out a distance from them. He waved toward some flatter rocks out in the open. "Sit down, Crawley," he invited. "I'm Jonas. Hound and Bear, take a seat beside him."

Crawley winced. He didn't like the fact that Jonas knew them all by name. They obeyed, although a little slowly, walking reluctantly to the very exposed rocks. They took a seat as ordered, all three of them searching the ground for any unusual plants that might suddenly attack.

Feel like I've got a target painted right between my eyes, Bear said.

Mine's on the back of my neck, Hound said.

Crawley felt the target in the area of his heart. He took a look around him using his enhanced vision, noting the trees in the distance. He was certain someone had a sniper rifle on them.

"Who are you, Jonas? What do you want with us?" He made certain to keep his voice just as calm. Just as even.

Jonas regarded him with unusually colored eyes. "You remember that team of misfit GhostWalkers? The really screwed-up one? The one you came here to scout so Shaker can bring his men in and wipe us all out? I'm one of them."

That news was like a punch in the gut. It was the last thing Crawley expected. All the data on Team One of the GhostWalkers said they were barely able to function. An impeccable source had been paid dearly for that information; at least, that was what Crawley's boss had told him. He had the sinking feeling that so-called impeccable source didn't know what they were talking about.

"I see." Crawley was noncommittal. He didn't want to give too much away. Clearly, Jonas or a member of his team had been watching and listening to them prior to the ambush. He couldn't very well deny his intentions, but he needed to find out just how much Jonas knew.

Jonas nodded. "Just so you're aware, I don't need all three of you. It would be best if you answer my questions. I know you're here to collect information on both teams and send it back to Shaker and his troops. You're also supposed to take Lily and her son to get them out of the line of fire. Who exactly sent you? Before you answer me, Crawley, I want you to know, I can hear lies. If you lie to me, Bear is going to die."

Shit, Crawley, Bear said. *There's no reason not to tell him. He's not bluffing.*

Crawley assessed the distance between Jonas and himself. He was fast. Very fast. They were out in the open, and he could cross that clearing and be on the man in an instant. If he got his hands on Jonas, he had no doubt he could kill him. Still, it seemed as if there might be more than one sniper pointing a weapon at them. If that was the case, Bear would be killed anyway. Possibly Hound. He would be too. It would all be for nothing other than the satisfaction of seeing Jonas die.

Crawley sighed. "I work security for a company called FreeAbrEnds. Most people just refer to the company as FAE."

Crawley could tell Jonas knew exactly what institution he was talking about. In a way, there was some satisfaction that his bosses weren't quite as anonymous as they thought they were. He knew they considered themselves so superior and entitled because they had enough money to buy the entire planet.

They didn't give a damn who appeared to lead a country, because they were the real power directing almost every country in the world. They started wars. They ended them. They created oil crises. They played God and toasted one another while they did it. Crawley worked for them because it was better to be on the side of the powerful people than to get crushed by them. He'd seen the results of getting crushed over and over.

"Why do they want Lily and her child?" Jonas asked.

Crawley suppressed his smirk. So, Mr. Know-It-All didn't really know as much as he pretended to. "Whitney is part of their inner circle, but he's also a huge patriot and doesn't always cooperate with their plans. Lily is his one vulnerability. He considers her the only one able to take his place. She's enhanced and so is her husband, Ryland, the child's father. So far, Whitney has no idea what Daniel, the boy, is able to do."

"The consortium wants Lily and Daniel,

mostly to bring Whitney in line. That's what you're saying."

Crawley nodded. "They're also curious to know what the child can actually do, if anything special, but they really want Whitney to do what they say every time, not just when he feels like it."

"And the purpose behind wiping out Teams One and Two?" Jonas asked.

Crawley studied the tone of voice. It sounded milder than ever. Soft. There was nothing soft about the man. His face was tough, hard angles and planes. His eyes were different, reminding Crawley of looking into a large predatory cat's eyes. Jonas didn't seem to blink. He just stared with an insane focus that made Crawley as uncomfortable as Snake made him feel. Snake was venomous. What the hell was Jonas?

"I honestly don't know," Crawley said, grateful he didn't. He had the feeling Jonas really could hear lies.

The wind shifted just a little, just enough that it should carry scents to his two sniffers. Crawley relaxed, some of the tension easing out of him. *Can you tell where the snipers are? Can you pinpoint their locations?*

Both men inhaled without seeming to do so.

Crawley tried to look harmless. "Do you

292

mind if we put our hands down? We removed all weapons."

"Before you put your hands down, I want each of you to tell me you left all your weapons and all communication devices behind in the rock corridor, starting with you, Crawley, then Bear, then Hound."

Crawley made a show of sighing to give his men time to sniff out the snipers. "I left all of my weapons and all communication devices behind in the rock corridor."

When Jonas indicated he could put his hands down, he did so. Bear followed his example and then Hound. Crawley was grateful they'd followed his orders to the letter. No one got shot.

I can't even smell Jonas and he's right in front of us. I have no idea what could be interfering with my sense of smell. We don't know for certain he's not alone, Crawley, but he could be.

Do you really want to take that chance, Hound?

"What do you plan to do with us?" Crawley asked.

"Turn you over to my team leader and let him figure it out."

It's a long way down the mountain, Crawley said with relief. *Cooperate.*

"Ryland might not be too happy with you

coming to kidnap his wife and son and providing the information to murder his team." Jonas indicated for them to stand. "You can start down the trail. Apparently, you already know the way. If you step off the path for any reason without first indicating to me that you have a reason, it will be the last step you ever take."

What do you think, Crawley? He's going to walk behind us. I haven't seen anyone else or even smelled them, Hound said.

Let's go down the mountain. It's the way we want to go anyway.

He could have part of his team coming up to meet him, Bear cautioned.

I thought of that. I think he's too arrogant for that. He wants to march us down to his crew and show off that he trapped us.

Crawley got up, taking his time, leading the way along the path that led down the mountain. Bear and Hound followed him. There was no more strange fog. Every now and then he caught glimpses of a silvery stream snaking down the mountain. The terrain grew less rocky and more forested as they dropped another thousand feet.

Lizards and rodents scurried out of their way, disturbing the vegetation on the ground. The wind picked up in the canopy and occasionally blew through the trees where the groves were more open. Birds sang to one another and flew from one branch to another. Squirrels raced up and down the tree branches, chattering nonstop.

Jonas made no sound as he walked. None. He was like a damned ghost. Crawley still felt the ominous sensation of having a target painted on the front of his chest right over his heart. A chill crept down his spine. He wanted to look back and see where Jonas was, but instead, he picked up the pace, trying to outrun the nerves he couldn't quite shake.

You two feel like you've got a sniper watching you?

Bear answered first. *It doesn't make any sense, Crawley. We've covered ground fairly quickly, but yeah, it's still there. The sniper would have to be moving with us.*

Same here, Hound said. *I've looked over my shoulder a couple of times because that guy doesn't make a sound. I thought for a minute he might have left us, but he's right behind us. Keeps his distance. No weapons in sight. He thinks he's safe from us.*

Keep walking. We have plenty of time. He can't be in the best of shape, not like we are. He might have set a sweet ambush, but that first team of GhostWalkers was considered defective for a reason, Crawley told them.

The more he thought about it, the more he was certain it was the truth. The people he worked for were brilliant, and they didn't make very many mistakes. They bought information all the time, and they paid premium prices for it. Those they paid knew if they screwed up, they didn't get a second chance. The consortium would send someone, an accident would happen and everyone would know not to try to cheat them again.

This Jonas was most likely going to be winded long before Crawley or his men were. They just had to bide their time. He increased his pace just a little more. Not wanting Jonas to protest but enough that it would wear him out faster. He was also becoming more convinced that Jonas was alone. If there were other team members — like the sniper they kept imagining — one of the sniffers would have smelled them by now. One of the birds would have reacted. A sound would have given them away. No one was that good in the forest.

Who knew? Maybe making people feel like they had a target on their backs was one of Jonas's enhancements.

Crawley sought his internal maps. They had made their way at least another two thousand feet at least down the mountain.

The sun had climbed higher. The trees were much closer together now, and the trail was narrow, no more than a deer path, forcing them to keep single file through the heavier brush.

He's closer, Crawley, Hound reported. *Within striking distance. I can take him. I know I can. I just need a little distraction.*

Crawley didn't make the mistake of glancing over his shoulder, although he wanted to. He had no idea how close Jonas actually was. *Hound, don't take chances. He could be setting you up.*

I don't think so. We're going downhill and you set the pace. He's traveling at a higher rate of speed. I don't think he's that aware yet, but he will be soon. It's now or never.

Crawley thought it over. If they could kill Jonas, they would have a chance to complete at least the scouting part of their mission. If they were lucky enough, they might even be able to grab Lily and her son.

All right, he agreed, albeit reluctantly. He'd prefer to kill the big bastard himself, but rather someone do it than no one.

Bear, I need you to stumble over the next obstacle in our path. Doesn't matter what it is, just make it look real. You don't have to go down either. Just stagger for a minute to draw his attention. I'll do the rest, Hound instructed.

On it, Bear confirmed.

Fallen tree, not big, just a little small thing we could easily step over, Crawley reported as he came up on it. That terrible dread was back, fingers of fear walking down his spine.

Bear glanced up at the canopy above him and caught the top of his foot on the thin sapling that had been uprooted. He appeared to trip, pitching forward toward Crawley, who was already some distance ahead, seemingly oblivious to the teammate behind him. Bear staggered and nearly went down, arms spreading wide in an effort to keep his balance.

Hound twisted around, going low, driving off the ground with the heels of his feet, rushing Jonas. Only Jonas wasn't there. Somehow, he'd disappeared, as if he'd become part of a tree trunk, only to suddenly emerge out of it and close a big, shockingly strong fist around Hound's throat. Something sharp and terrible ripped through Hound's flesh into his artery.

Hound had never felt anything like the force of that strike or the ferocity of the grip, as if a wild animal had him by the throat. He looked into the eyes of a merciless leopard, not a man. The eyes were yellow, focused wholly on him, a primitive force of nature, intelligent and cunning. Between the rapid blood loss, Jonas's intimidating hold, and the implacability in those cruel, ruthless eyes staring unwaveringly into his, Hound couldn't summon either the will or the strength to fight back.

Bear spun around to see Hound held in the air, his feet half a foot off the ground, blood spraying from his neck. He just hung there, staring in shock at the man killing him. Swearing, Bear put on a burst of speed, using his enhanced animal genetics.

No, stand down. Sit on the ground. Don't engage, Crawley ordered. *Bear, stand down.*

Bear was in full attack mode, the beast in him seeing red. He let that rage well up and consume him, filling him with the pure enhanced strength, adrenaline and aggression of the polar bear. Nothing could save the puny man killing his friend. Nothing. He was on Jonas fast. The distance was short, and he could run up to twenty-five miles an hour if he needed to for a brief period of time.

Jonas dropped Hound's body as if it were nothing but trash and whirled around to face Bear, his entire demeanor changing. Where before, he had appeared to resemble a leopard, his skin even appearing to take on a mottled leopard-like camouflage, now he seemed bigger, his skin darker, his eyes pitiless. It didn't matter. One blow from Bear would tear that fucker in half. One swipe of his fist. That was all it would take. Bear roared a challenge.

To Bear's astonishment, Jonas answered his challenge with a roar of his own, sounding so much like a grizzly it nearly stopped Bear midrush. The two slammed together, their bodies barreling into one another, fists flying as they grappled like two large bears in a dominance fight.

Bear expected to break bones with his enormous strength. He'd broken men's spines with one punch of his fist driving right through a body, but he didn't land a single blow on Jonas. The man was just too fast, freakishly fast, even for an enhanced. When Jonas smashed one of his fists into Bear's ribs, he felt the bones cave like sticks, leaving him gasping for air.

The two men circled one another, each assessing the other. Bear had always ended a fight fast with any opponent. He won with his sheer brute strength. Jonas never gave him an opening. Never took his eyes off him. He appeared to be an experienced fighter, battle-scarred and more than willing to kill. He wasn't enraged, he was methodical. Calculating.

300

Submit. Damn it, Bear, he's going to kill you. Never once had Crawley used that tone of desperation. He'd always had complete confidence in Bear's enormous strength. Bear knew instinctively his beast would never surrender, nor would this enemy accept or trust it. The three of them had already betrayed their word.

He'll kill me anyway. We didn't do what he said. Bear knew just by that admission that he was telling Crawley he couldn't win.

There was a brief silence. *Maneuver the son of a bitch closer to me. You have to be clever about it, Bear. Use your brain. Don't let the beast take over. We're in this together. I'm not letting him have you. I think he's alone. So far, no one else has shown up to help him out.*

Bear didn't think Jonas needed much help. He inched closer, and Jonas didn't back up like any other fighter might do. He glided to the side, mirroring Bear's footwork. That was when Bear realized the forest around them had fallen completely silent.

You hear that, Crawley? No birds. No rodents. Or reptiles. Everything in the forest is afraid of him.

Or they're afraid of you, Bear, Crawley hastened to say.

Bear knew better because, for the first

time since he'd been enhanced, he was scared. He could secretly admit it. He was facing a killing machine. Cold. Calculating. Cunning. Highly intelligent, trained and very experienced. He wasn't just scared; he was terrified. He had to go on the offensive before he couldn't think, only react. That would be a very bad place to be.

He rushed his enemy again, and Jonas gave no quarter, coming at him toe to toe, as if they were more bears than men. They swung punches, the force behind each individual blow enormous. He didn't dare take a hit from one of Jonas's massive fists, not when the man could punch with the force of a freight train. The most he could do was to try to follow Crawley's advice. Maybe with the two of them, they'd have a chance to bring the bastard down.

It wasn't easy to slip the punches, and Bear was an experienced fighter. Time slowed down, even though he knew it was only seconds that passed. He dodged and weaved and kept trying to use his superior size to push Jonas into moving back toward Crawley one step at a time. Just one small step. Maybe two. He was feeling desperate. Jonas was lightning fast, feinting one way and then striking another.

The kick came out of nowhere. The blow

was savage because Bear wasn't expecting it. He'd been concentrating on those fists with that blurring speed and power enough to break him in two. Jonas didn't need his hands when he had a kick like that — far, far more brutal than anything his fist could have delivered — and there was no doubt the fist would have broken his spine. Bear felt bones shatter. One lung collapsed instantly while the other began a slow crumpling. Every organ in his body turned to jelly, cells ripped apart by that jarring, vicious kick that destroyed him.

Jonas stepped back and just stood watching him with eyes that were ice cold and utterly detached. A rifle spat out a warning shot and then another. As Bear collapsed, slowly falling to his knees, he tried to find Crawley, sending up a little prayer the man hadn't been shot trying to get to him. Everything had happened so fast.

Crawley stood frozen several yards away, his hands locked behind his head, a stricken look on his face. Bear fell forward, his eyes, nose and mouth suddenly buried in a thick layer of leaves and dirt. Sounds dimmed. Receded altogether. The world went black.

10

Jonas trudged along the path, allowing Jeff and Kyle to stay between Crawley and him as they continued down the mountain toward their homes. He was connected to Camellia on three levels — through Whitney's pairing, the mycelium underground network, which was very powerful and allowed them to share feelings very easily, and another network, one even more powerful. He suspected it was the Middlemist Red Camellia.

He tried to puzzle out how that would work. Those nerve endings. He saw her work on Kyle and take away his pain. He'd thought it was the mycelium running underground and through them, but he knew it was so much more. They were bound on a molecular level, through nerve endings and even in their brains.

He deliberately hadn't disconnected from either of the two networks that connected them together when he became his true self. Telling Camellia was different than showing her the effects of the various predatory animals and reptiles Whitney had thought it would be a good idea to shove into him. Whitney had blended and mixed those violent traits until he had the most aggressive male he could possibly come up with. He had purposely enhanced an already dominant personality into something Jonas had to fight night and day.

The truth was, Jonas was afraid to face Camellia. He'd all but told her to leave while she could when they'd first contacted Ryland. When she'd been brave enough to stay, he'd shown her the worst in him deliberately. Why had he done that? He wanted her. The longer he was with her, the more he knew she was right for him. So, what was he doing deliberately pushing her away from him? He knew she'd have to know the worst, but not immediately.

The raging testosterone in him from so many mixes of predators kept the heat banding in front of his eyes and the need for violence coursing through his body. The pathways from his brain to his nerves spread the demand as if not his life but his teammate's lives and Camellia's life were at stake. His mind looped over and over, determined to tell him to take out the last threat — the one he knew was the worst.

Crawley was hiding something. He'd come there to take Lily and Daniel. He would have sent information back to his troops to allow them to murder every other man, woman and child in the two compounds. And there was Camellia. She was close. Beautiful Camellia with her deadly traps. If Crawley discovered that Camellia had set the traps for his men and him, he would do anything to retaliate against her.

Jonas knew men like Crawley. They never stopped once they decided on a course. He might pretend he was cooperating, but he was already thinking of a way to avenge his friends. Like Jonas, he felt responsible for them. That threat had to be eliminated, no matter what Ryland and Kaden had commanded.

The threatening growls rumbled in his chest, but he kept them to himself. He wanted Crawley to give him any excuse at all to challenge him. At the same time, he kept a distance between himself and his teammates, knowing from experience that even his friends could trigger the terrible need for violence raging in his system. If they didn't need him to help keep a watchful eye on Crawley, he would have run up and down the mountain paths in order to try to drain off some of the worst of the need to kill.

Every neuron in his body felt inflamed, pushed in the wrong direction as if his blood had reversed itself and spread through his body like a disease rather than something good. Now that he'd had a taste of what good with Camellia felt like, the adrenaline and hostility of the predators in his system seemed so much worse. The inflammation triggered more need for violence, a reaction that started in his brain — at least he thought it did.

He'd studied aggression in animals to see if he could better combat it, but so far, nothing worked but staying away from others. Running. Physical motion. Fighting. But when he fought, that just fed the level of aggression, and he couldn't bring it under control. He had to channel the terrible rages combined with cunning into another outlet in order to keep from harming anyone. He would leave his team and go off to scout on his own. That was always the safest choice.

Jonas felt her first, a movement along those star-patterned cells, the neurons that spread out to send messages along every pathway. She stroked caresses over the inflamed nerve endings, settling them in the correct direction with a delicate touch.

His breath hissed out of his lungs, a long slow burn of awareness. Now, the fierce violent rage in him mixed with other much more potent chemicals that added to his hyperalertness. He saw every detail of Crawley as he moved ahead of them. He was a great distance away, with Jeff and Kyle between them, running interference, but it didn't matter.

Jonas watched with the eyes of an eagle, noting the fluid way Crawley moved. He wasn't in the least defeated. He was thinking every minute, taking stock of their surroundings, sizing up Jeff, the man closest to him, trying not to appear as if he was doing so. Jonas paid attention to Crawley's hands, the way his arms swung free and loose as he walked, but his hands curled into fists, and then he'd open his fingers, spreading them wide, flexing them. He seemed to keep the same pace, but he increased it just a little bit every few miles. Jonas knew what he was doing. He thought, because they were the first men Whitney had experimented on, that meant they would be out of shape.

No one quite understood that by using the term "screwed up," the phrase didn't mean the soldiers in Team One weren't as intelligent or didn't have the same training.

It meant Whitney hadn't yet known what he was doing. He left brains wide open without filters. He gave them too many animal and reptile traits without realizing what would happen. He just threw everything together, believing more was better. He had enhanced their physical abilities as well as their psychic ones without telling them what was in them or what to expect, leaving them to discover, over time, what would come out. When they had no idea, they weren't prepared when a trait abruptly manifested.

Jonas had learned over time to turn inward when there was anything new. He would examine whatever was happening and try to get on top of it before it escaped. Right now, Camellia's touch on the neurons in his body produced a multitude of sensations in him. The drive to claim her was overwhelming, yet at the same time, that caressing motion began to, one by one, soothe those cells all going in the reverse direction, back to flowing correctly.

Crawley increased the pace just a little more, and this time, he stepped off the path, quickly correcting, but not before he had twisted the leaves on several bushes as he passed them. The second time it happened, he snapped a small twig so that it hung down along with the bruised leaves. Behind him, the leaves and fragile limbs of the bush slowly sprang back into perfect health. Crawley didn't see that at first. Not until his third misstep off the trail and his glance back with satisfaction.

He stopped abruptly, bending down, hands on his knees, as if taking in air, his eyes on the repaired bush. He lifted his gaze to Jeff, then Kyle, finally to Jonas, all the while judging the distance. Wondering what his chances were.

Jonas could smell the anger and fear. The need to attack. Adrenaline surged all over again. Jonas wanted Crawley to take the chance. The man didn't. Instead, he straightened slowly and took a long, suspicious look around.

"Keep walking," Jeff ordered, his tone bored.

"Who else is with us?" Crawley asked. "Because someone is. Maybe more than one."

"Does it matter?" Jeff countered. "Get moving."

Crawley cursed under his breath and turned back to start down the mountain. This time, he didn't walk fast. Jonas knew he was calculating the distance and hoping he could stall until nightfall.

Tell him to pick up the pace, Jeff.

"Get a move on, Crawley. You were more than happy to set a fast pace. Double-time it," Jeff ordered.

Crawley glanced back at Jonas. He seemed to know who was giving the orders, and he was holding himself in check by a thread. He didn't argue but did as Jeff instructed.

Jonas struggled to shake off the need to attack the man. It always took far too long to come down from the mix of animal and human predatory traits. It didn't help that Crawley continued to trigger his instincts by his aggression toward them and determination to escape and kill them. Or that Camellia was too close to the man.

"Jonas?"

That voice of hers was enough to soothe any nerve ending — or light it on fire. Camellia just appeared out of the last remnants of the mist, looking beautiful. Her hair was dark, a deep chestnut, now that the sun shone down on it. He could see a reddish hue moving through the glossy shine. Ignoring the others, she came straight to his side.

Catching Crawley looking back at her, Jonas could barely hold back a snarl of challenge and the surge of aggression accompanying it. He wanted to rush the prisoner and take him out for just daring to see her.

"I thought we agreed that you would

311

remain hidden." He snapped it at her, refusing to look away from Crawley, even though the man was intelligent enough to know he was in danger.

Jeff and Kyle both felt the swelling tension as well. Kyle kept walking without acknowledging there could be a problem. Jeff threw Jonas a quick assessing glance over his shoulder but didn't slow down.

Jonas took a deep breath. *It takes time for the . . . adrenaline to work its way out of my system. Until it does, I can be unstable. I feel especially protective of you, Camellia. I can be dangerous in this state.*

Her palm brushed his arm and then slid down to his hand. *Perhaps you are, Jonas, but not to me.* She spoke with absolute confidence.

Her touch sent little sparks jumping along his nerve endings and spreading through his body. He nearly jerked away from her. He felt like a wild animal, cornered, snarling and reacting with teeth and claws, and yet wanting to keep her close to him, at the same time needing to push her away to save her — or to save himself. To save what little was left of his honor.

You don't know the first thing about me, Camellia. He should have pushed her away. At least let go of her hand, but instead, he locked his fingers around hers.

What makes you think I can't see inside you the way you do me, Jonas? We're locked together by the networks, by our neural pathways. It would be impossible not to see you in ways others can't.

You can't see the things I've done.

Or had to do, she corrected gently. *Perhaps not, but I can see who you are, just as you can see who I am. Are you changing your mind about what you want? If you are, you need to say so now, Jonas. I'm taking a huge chance on you. Risking everything.*

She was. She had no reason to believe in him. He hadn't given her a reason to trust him. He'd given her the opportunity to leave, yet she'd stayed. He wanted her to stay for him. Not for Marigold. Or Lily. He was that selfish. He wanted her to stay for him and yet he was pushing her away.

I don't want you to leave, Camellia, I don't. I just don't trust what I am anymore. If you really can see inside of me, you can see what a fucked-up mess I am. I can barely control myself in certain situations. I never want to put you in danger, and that could happen.

She laughed softly, the sound that mysteriously cleared out more of the deep aggression in him. He wasn't sure how she did it, but those clear notes danced along his nerve

313

endings, sparkling in tune to her humor. He could see the notes playing in her neurons just as they were in his.

Jonas, think about it for a minute. What am I made up of? What do I do? What can I do? To be a true partnership, we both have to bring something of equal value to the table, right? When we were outnumbered by these enhanced soldiers, I could set the traps, and you could take them down. That meant we both contributed something of equal value.

She was right. She had set the ultimate in traps. Her rolling fog was extraordinary, especially in the way she could plant subtle suggestions that preyed on the unwary.

We have a continuing partnership in the field, Jonas. Clearly, we can use our network for aiding our soldiers in a battle. We can bridge communication and help run opera-tions. We can aid in healing. We can develop weapons using toxic plant materials.

He hadn't considered the ability to com-municate with not only their team but all the teams if they needed to do so. She was right. They could, using the mycelium network. As for developing weapons, he would need to talk to her about that.

A personal relationship is even more of a partnership, Jonas. We have to be compat-ible. Whitney may be a complete ass, but he was also a genius. He had to have known you had a certain personality when he enhanced you, the same way he knew I did. The idea was that two people worked well together. We made up for each other's shortcomings, so to speak.

That was true. Whitney's original plan had been that exactly, before he threw that out the window and decided he was going to produce superbeings. He didn't care about the pairings after that. He just wanted babies. In the beginning, though, he had created couples he thought would work well together.

Crawley's pace was a ground-eating jog. They were covering distance at a good clip. The man had long legs, and he was making good use of his ability to move. The pace didn't seem to bother Camellia with her shorter legs. She kept up without even breathing hard. So, aside from being compatible in the field and the obvious physical chemistry between them, what did she bring to him and he to her in the relationship department?

Camellia had created what had amounted to a rain forest at a high elevation where there should be snow. It was a little slice of paradise. When Jonas had entered, he had expected the enemy to be there. He should have been coiled like a snake, ready to strike. Instead, he'd felt peace and serenity, as he'd never experienced it before. She'd brought that to him. Just the way she had come to him, so confident when he was a snarling, brutal beast, ready to rip and tear anything in his path, managing to somehow find a way to soothe him when nothing or no one else could have. Could she be right?

Was it possible Camellia held the key to taming the violent mix of animal and reptile genetics in him? He couldn't conceive of anything doing that, yet in a short time she had managed to turn those neurons from moving in the wrong direction. Observing them through her eyes, he could see they were like a river flowing in the opposite way it was meant to go. With gentle brushes, she had coaxed the tide to reverse itself. Within a short period of time, the adrenaline was diluting and he could feel himself settling.

We're getting closer to the compound, Jonas. Jeff's voice startled Jonas, breaking into his introspection. Jeff used the pathway that included Kyle and Camellia as well. *It's now or never for Camellia. If she goes in with us, do you two have a plan if Ryland gets insistent about her? He could. He's going to be really upset that anyone is coming after Lily and Daniel. Kyle and I talked it over. We'll back your play. Camellia is no threat to Lily or Daniel, but Ryland may not see it that way. Or he may feel the need to talk to General Ranier about her and her abilities. That wouldn't be a good thing in our opinion, Jonas.*

Jonas couldn't help the affection welling up for Jeff and Kyle. They were good men. Good friends. They'd always had his back, no matter how bad things had gotten for him — and they'd gotten bad.

Camellia moved a little closer to him. He realized she wasn't aware she did it, or of the small positive chemical reaction she had to the admission Jeff made that he and Kyle had discussed the eventuality of Ryland's reactions to her accompanying them to the compound. Every protective trait he had kicked in tenfold.

She didn't feel as if she were going to take off on him though. She jogged beside him, head up, determination in her mind.

I plan to throw you and Lily under the bus to divert his attention away from Camellia, Jonas said truthfully. *That's after I kick your ass for being an idiot. I was going to do it without anyone around to spare you the humiliation, but then we ran into these jokers.*

There was a small silence. He could feel Jeff's rising alarm and Kyle's puzzlement.

What's he done now, Jonas? You might as

317

well confess, Jeff, Kyle said. *I'll find out eventually. If I have to patch you up after one of Jonas's beatdowns, I should know why he's kicking your ass.*

Again, there was a silence. Jonas kept his gaze fixed on Crawley. The man was pulling his bullshit move again, stepping off the trail to hit a bush, hoping to leave evidence of his passing. Camellia simply repaired the damage to the plant, sending the necessary nutrients ahead of her. She did so as if she were on automatic pilot. Crawley kept glancing over his shoulder, trying to catch one of them in the act. Every now and then, his gaze dropped on her. It was brief, but Jonas didn't like the speculation there before the man would turn his head and renew his efforts to pick up his pace.

Jonas knew there was no way for Crawley to know that Camellia had been the one to repair the damages to the plants, but he certainly was wondering if she was the one to have done so. If Crawley was in any way connected to Whitney, the man was going to have to die, no matter what Ryland said. Jonas didn't dare leave him alive. That was the problem with taking prisoners. There was always the possibility that they could escape or smuggle word out to someone. Whitney had enough money to buy a country, let alone bribe people.

You know there's a traitor in the compound, Jeff. Someone is aware of Daniel's abilities.

We don't know that, Jeff denied. *Crawley could have been sent up here to get him in order to discover what his abilities are.*

Whoever is behind this has a plant in our compound. They know his abilities, Jonas reiterated.

That isn't possible, Kyle denied. *The only people who ever see what Daniel can do are members of our team. No one else. We don't make those kinds of mistakes, and neither does Daniel. He knows better. He might be a toddler, but he's highly intelligent. He doesn't show off, and he doesn't ever show what he can do, not even if we go visit the Nortons and their sons.*

There was another long silence. Jonas waited to see if Jeff would confess to Kyle. He didn't. Jonas didn't really expect him to. He sighed. *Does Ryland know, or is Lily keeping secrets from him?*

Damn it, Jonas. We aren't doing this. We can't do this. The harsh denial exploded in their minds.

Jonas jogged down the mountain for a quarter of a mile before he replied. They were in very familiar territory now. He knew eyes were on them. *I wasn't the dumbass agreeing to do it, Jeff. That was you. And you know someone else knows. If I figured it out, someone else has. That someone is the traitor. We have to stop them before they deliver Daniel and Lily into enemy hands. Or you. At first I thought this asshole and his men were coming for you. There might be another team, for all I know, coming for you. You don't agree to this kind of shit without talking it over with us.*

They all felt Jeff sigh. *Talking things over means it isn't a secret, Jonas.*

Is it a secret from our commander? Jonas pushed. He needed to know how much trouble Jeff was going to be in.

I don't know. I figured Lily would tell him. Daniel is his son. It never occurred to me she would go behind his back, but he was never with us. I still thought he knew. Now that you're all over me about this, I'm getting a little worried.

Would either of you like to fill me in? Kyle prompted. *We're getting close, and I don't want to get blindsided if you're really going to talk to Ryland about something to do with Jeff.*

I don't have a choice. Jonas felt he didn't. *Jeff, you have to talk to him. We both do. You know there's a traitor. Someone reached out to make all this happen.*

Camellia didn't say anything at all, but

Jonas felt her moving in his mind. Gently. She didn't feel invasive at all. More like she belonged. That was a little disconcerting. He had things he didn't necessarily want to share with her yet. He knew he would. He just needed to figure out a way to put them in context. He didn't flinch away from her quiet inspection because he didn't want her to disconnect from him like she had before.

He switched to their private pathway. *Tell me what you're looking for, Camellia.*

What is it that Jeff did? I can tell that you're very upset. Much more than he realizes, or even than you do. You're worried for his safety.

Jeff is a dreamwalker. We talked about that particular talent. If Lily decided to use Jeff's talent to store her information on Daniel in files in Jeff's dreams and someone found out about it, he could be killed in the dream and the files taken.

She didn't reply immediately. She thought it over the way she did everything. Carefully looking at it from every angle. *It would be highly unlikely for anyone to stumble into Jeff's dream. As the chances would be so unreasonable to even think about, you're right — a traitor would have to know. So how would they know? If only Lily and Jeff were aware of the data being stored in his dreams, who would have the opportunity of discovering that information? It would have to start with discovery.*

Jonas loved the way Camellia's mind worked. She always went straight to the heart of the problem. Who would have that opportunity? Jeff hadn't told any of his teammates. Even if someone had tried to plant a listening device, the rooms were swept for bugs several times a day. They'd learned that lesson when Sam, a fellow GhostWalker, had first met his wife, Azami.

Crawley began to slow down. The buildings were coming into sight. Jeff moved up behind him but stayed a safe distance away.

"You've got two rifles trained on you, Crawley," he said. "You don't want to start being stupid at this late date. The welcoming committee has gone all out for you."

The "war room" was large, given that it held the long table where the entire team could be seated, as well as two smaller tables where they often built their models of enemy sites. Jonas, Camellia, Jeff and Kyle faced Ryland Miller and Kaden Montague. Kaden was the team's second-in-command. Of the two men, Kaden was definitely the most formidable. Ryland was diplomatic; Kaden got the job done fast if diplomacy failed.

"Crawley's secured. He was stripped down and searched as you suggested. All kinds of weapons and more devices to call home than one can imagine. We employed jammers to make certain he couldn't be tracked," Kaden volunteered.

Jonas didn't like the way Ryland remained silent, his gaze settling on Camellia. He also wasn't thrilled that Lily wasn't present. That wasn't a good sign. He knew she would have wanted to see Camellia after all the time apart. She had made it her life's work to find all the girls she'd been raised with.

"He's enhanced," Jonas said, although he was certain no one needed that reminder. "We left a few dead bodies up on the mountain. They'll have to be retrieved. His men were also enhanced."

Kaden nodded. "How many are coming for us?"

Jonas shook his head. "I don't have that information. That's why Crawley's still alive. I went up the mountain, clueless to what I'd run into, but I felt a threat. These men were after Lily and Daniel. I got thinking about that and why they would specifically be targeting Daniel and Lily when we've been so careful to keep Daniel under wraps."

"Whitney has always wanted her back,"

Ryland said, speaking for the first time, his tone dismissive. "Everyone knows he thinks I'm not good enough for her."

"Whitney didn't send these men. And they know nothing whatsoever about the Nortons. Whitney knows about the Nortons and their twins. He would never chance endangering them. These men were sent by someone else. Someone infiltrated this compound and acquired the information on Daniel. They didn't have the same access to Team Two and the Norton twins. They heard nothing extraordinary about them. Nor did they see anything. There was no order given to save them, unless there was a chance before the killing started. The troops coming are to wipe out everyone left behind."

There was a shocked silence.

"Even the women?" Kaden asked.

Jonas nodded.

Ryland looked for confirmation to Jeff and Kyle as if he couldn't believe what he was hearing. They both nodded as well.

"That doesn't make any sense," Ryland stated. He stood up, all flowing energy, and paced across the room to the window. "Why would anyone want to wipe out both teams and murder the women as well? Who would do that?"

"Crawley says he works for a banking

conglomerate."

Ryland spun around. "Banking conglomerate? As in Jacob Abrams? He's always been one of Whitney's biggest supporters. He's funded Whitney, allowed him to continue his experiments, given him sanctuary all over the world. Why would he suddenly turn on him?"

Jonas didn't have an answer for that. "Jacob Abrams heads the conglomerate. I do know that much. I know he wants Daniel and Lily. It's possible, even probable, he wants them to keep Whitney in line. Whitney is more of a patriot than Abrams is, and he doesn't always cooperate, at least that was what little I got out of Crawley. The bottom line is Abrams has more money than even Whitney, and he bought someone who comes here. Someone we trust. Someone who is able to get close to Lily."

Ryland leaned against the wall and crossed his arms over his chest, leveling his gaze at Jonas. Ryland Miller had steel-gray eyes, and when he turned them on anyone with his piercing stare, it felt as if he cut right to the heart.

"Talk to me, Jonas."

"I believe that someone figured out that Lily stored files she created on Daniel's abilities in a dream she created with Jeff."

Ryland went very still, a merciless predator in the room with them. His gaze switched from Jonas to Jeff. "I have the ability to dreamwalk. Why would my wife go to Jeff instead of me, Jonas?"

That tone was so low, it was barely heard. Every predatory animal instinct in Jonas reacted to that danger, his own aggression responding to match the rising threat in Ryland.

Immediately the sparks shot through his body, neurons altering, spreading, once again reversing the natural flow so that the need for a hot, violent response burst through him.

Camellia slipped her hand into his, her thumb sliding over the inside of his palm, that caress stroking along those same nerve endings inside his body. He let her take the lead in soothing him, even though he shifted his body so that he could slightly cover her smaller one. He didn't like that he was sitting and Ryland was standing, giving his commander the advantage in a fight.

"I would imagine that you had forbidden any documentation of your son's psychic or physical abilities. I say that because that would be what I would do under the circumstances," Jonas answered honestly. He had known this wasn't going to be easy. Ryland adored Lily. If she had actually documented Daniel's abilities without the consent of her husband, there would be hell to pay. All of them knew that.

"Jeff?" Ryland's tone was mild, but there was nothing mild about the way his very muscular body positioned itself as he turned to face the younger man.

Kaden stood up, a flowing of his tall, heavily muscled frame. He moved casually, partially placing his body between the leader of their team and those seated at the table. Jonas took the opportunity to rise as well, stretching, as if he'd been sitting for too long. He tugged on Camellia's hand, taking her with him, all but putting her in a corner so she was protected on three sides, with him standing in front of her.

"Jeff?" Ryland said again. "Last time I ask you."

"Lily came to me a few months ago, Cap," Jeff said. "It didn't occur to me that you weren't aware of what we were doing. I wasn't about to deny her. She's Lily."

"What exactly was it that you two were doing?" Ryland demanded.

Jeff didn't hesitate to give a report. "Once a week we got together in a dream state. She would dictate her notes on Daniel and file them in her office in the dream. I would ensure she was safe in the dream. Then we would come back."

"Who guarded your bodies while you were in the dream state?"

"We were locked in the psych room together. We both had messages to send to a guardian if we didn't report back in half an hour. Lily had one that would go to you, and I had one that would go to Jonas. We never ran into trouble, nor did I feel it was likely we would."

"You were taking a chance with Lily's life."

"I was following Lily's directive, which I thought was your directive," Jeff corrected.

"In all those weeks, or months, you never once asked me," Ryland pointed out.

That was the flaw in Jeff's reasoning. Jonas knew it. Kyle knew it. Camellia knew it as well. Jonas felt both Kyle and Camellia holding their breath. Waiting.

Jeff sighed. "I realized after a few weeks that it was possible you weren't aware, Cap. I asked Lily several times, but she refused to give me a definitive answer. When I told her I was uncomfortable continuing and couldn't without talking to you, she reminded me . . . ." He broke off, shaking his head, clearly hesitant to tell Ryland what his wife had said.

Ryland's gray eyes appeared to burn

through Jeff to the point Jonas took two steps in Jeff's direction. When he did, Ryland held up his hand. "Don't you move."

Jonas halted. "I'm sorry, Cap. I didn't realize I was interfering."

Ryland continued looking at Jeff, clearly expecting him to continue.

"Lily reminded me that she saved my life when I had brain bleeds from the stroke that paralyzed the right side of my body. She pointed out that she was the one who hadn't given up on me and that she worked with me every day and found the right people to help me."

"My wife guilted you into keeping something important about my son from me, even though you knew I didn't want it done," Ryland stated. His tone was back to that soft, threatening predatory sound.

Once again, the predatory as well as protective instincts in Jonas were triggered. He knew this was getting nowhere. Ryland was furious with Lily and Jeff, and Jonas couldn't blame him. The bottom line was, they still had a traitor to ferret out.

Kaden's sigh was deliberately overly loud. "It sounds like Jeff was stuck between a rock and a hard place. Loyalty to you and Lily. All of us feel that to both of you. If we're loyal to one, we're being loyal to both. I can't imagine being put in that position."

"Whoever was paid to betray your team had to be someone who only had access to this team, Jonas," Camellia said, using a very soft, speculative voice. "The person had to know Jeff very well. And Lily too. The person had to know their movements in the household. You know it isn't a member of your team, but it has to be someone who is around Jeff and Lily. Someone they both trust."

She spoke as if she were thinking aloud. Jonas knew she was directing Ryland's attention away from Jeff, just as Kaden had done, but he didn't have to like it. Ryland immediately turned those steel eyes on her. Camellia didn't look at him or appear to notice. She frowned, her small teeth biting into her lower lip, long lashes veiling her blue eyes. "There has to be someone, Jeff."

Ryland's gaze moved from Camellia back to Jeff. Jeff pushed his chair back and unfolded his frame. At one time, he'd been a champion surfer. He still moved with that grace and balance in spite of the stroke he'd suffered, leaving him with a slight weakness on his right side even after all the hard therapy he'd put in. He worked out hard, trained even harder, determined to be an asset to his team and never slow them down. He began pacing, his sun-bleached hair falling around his face as he went from one end of the room to the other.

"I'm still in therapy for my legs and arm," he said aloud to himself more than the others. "Lily comes in to oversee what Lydia is doing most of the time."

Ryland lifted his gaze to Kyle and nodded his head. Kyle used his phone to text someone. Jonas would bet his last dollar it was Flame, Gator's wife. Raul "Gator" Fontenot was a member of their team, and Iris "Flame" Johnson, now Fontenot, knew her way around a computer. If she was coming after you with her keyboard, there was nowhere to hide.

"That's Brandon Adams's assistant," Jeff continued, muttering under his breath. "I'm such a great case with my brain, you know."

"What does that mean?" Kaden interrupted before Ryland could.

Jeff scowled at him, not liking his train of thought to be intruded on. "Brandon Adams was the brain surgeon who saved my life. He's a good friend of Lily's. He's followed up to make certain I don't continue to have problems, which I sometimes did in the past before Lily taught me to develop shields."

"They aren't doing a study on you to present in some medical journal, are they?" Ryland snapped. "I'll strangle that woman."

"Not that I'm aware of," Jeff said. "But now that you mention it, I'd better ask. He sends his assistant, Lydia Fenamore, to oversee my therapies because there are multiple therapies for brain injuries. She actually studied molecular and cellular biology as well as brain biology at MIT before she decided she was really interested in the workings of the brain and she transferred to another school."

Ryland flicked his gaze once again toward Kyle.

She's the mole, Camellia said. *Without a doubt, she's going to be the one the banker paid to find out whatever she could. She's intelligent, she's with him often, she's interested in the things he is. She built up a relationship long before she ever betrayed him.*

Why her?

Camellia was silent for a moment. Her blue gaze met his. There was pain there. *I know what it feels like. What it tastes like. He knows it's her. When he said her name, it was there. She did something to give herself away. He didn't realize it until just this moment, but he knows. It hurts. Deep down. It really hurts. It's going to hurt Lily as well.*

Lily had hurt Ryland. Really hurt him. In some ways, what she'd done was a betrayal. Jonas wrapped his arm around Camellia's waist and drew her to his side. Betrayal seemed to be all around them. How was he ever going to persuade her that relationships were good? That family really did have one another's backs? At the moment, they weren't giving her the best examples.

11

"You really have no desire to see Marigold Norton?" Kaden asked, handing Camellia a bottle of water as they walked down the hall toward the dining room. "I would have thought she would be the first person you would want to see."

Camellia sent him a small smile. She knew a gentle interrogation when she heard one. Kaden was doing his best to sound friendly, but no matter how he put things, he was still asking pointed questions. Kyle kept pace beside her, refusing to get checked out by a medic. He claimed he didn't need one.

Ryland had insisted Jonas go with him to interrogate Crawley. She wouldn't want to be in Crawley's shoes when Ryland and Jonas confronted him.

"No, I'm quite content to stay here with Jonas for the moment. I've been up for twenty-four hours and I need to rest. When he gets back, he said we'd go to his home

334

and get some sleep. I'll be very grateful to do that."

"He didn't say how the two of you met."

"I would have thought that was obvious." She sent Kaden another small smile when he opened the dining room door for her. She glanced at Kyle. He reached over her head and held the door after Kaden opened it.

The dining room had several tables and chairs set up in it. A buffet counter with food warmers separated the kitchen from the dining room. The low pass-through window that spanned the length of the buffet made it easy for the cook to fill the warmers when food was prepared. To the left of the warmers were plates and utensils. To the right were bins to place the dirty dishes in.

"Kyle. You leave and come back with a beautiful woman," a tall man with reddish-colored hair called out from where he was seated at one of the tables. He shook his head. "Only you."

"Ian McGillicuddy, this is Camellia Mist, Jonas's woman," Kyle said. "Letting you know up front, he's staking his claim and he's serious about her."

Ian raised one eyebrow. "When that man decides to make a move, he doesn't mess around. Pleased to meet you, ma'am." He half rose from his seat to give her a little bow.

Up close, Camellia could see he was extremely tall and he had freckles that didn't make him look boyish, even though they should have. His emerald eyes were gorgeous. They moved over her, not with a man's interest, but with speculation and judgment, as if he were wondering if she was good enough for his friend. She quite liked him for that appraisal.

"Please call me Camellia."

The man sitting beside him stood up, sliding his chair back. "I'm Tucker Addison, Camellia. It's nice to meet the lady who managed to conquer Jonas."

Tucker Addison was a very imposing man with dark bronze skin, black eyes, military cropped hair and roped muscles that rippled beneath his tight tee when he moved. In spite of being a giant of a man, he had a gentle smile.

"I'm not sure I can actually claim I conquered him," Camellia denied. "But we do work fairly well together. The man can take down the enemy fast."

There was one woman in the room. She had unusual platinum and gold hair that she wore long. Her eyes were blue but had a silvery sheen to them. She wore faded jeans, a blue T-shirt and thin gloves. Camellia found her vaguely familiar, as if she should know her. She rarely forgot anyone, and she reached into her memory to find a picture of the woman.

Kaden guided Camellia away from the men and toward the table where the woman waited. Camellia, for some reason, felt a warning in Kyle's hand on her back.

What is it? They'd established their own connection. She wasn't worried that Kaden might overhear them, although she could tell he was unusually good at telepathy.

Before Kyle could answer, they were already at the table, and the woman stood, her smile genuine, one of welcome.

"Camellia, this is my wife, Tansy," Kaden said. "She was with you when she was a child, but Whitney put her up for adoption when she was five."

Camellia immediately pulled up the memory of that little girl, with her mop of white hair and her inability to be touched or to touch anyone without severe repercussions. She looked happy and healthy.

Be very careful, Camellia, Kyle cautioned. *She has the ability to read people's secrets if she touches you, or anything you've handled.*

"Tansy." Camellia smiled at her, a genuine

smile of happiness. "It's so good to know you're alive and well. I'd love to know how you and Kaden found one another." She sank into the chair opposite Tansy, across the table from her, well aware that if she ate anything, touching the silverware would leave her vulnerable.

Kaden frowned at her and then Kyle, who seated himself next to Camellia. "Are you two talking together? I don't actually feel the energy the way I would if GhostWalkers were talking on a private path . . ." He broke off abruptly.

Camellia wanted to know what would tip him off. She'd never once had anyone aware when she communicated telepathically with another. If she did so in a battle situation, she needed to know she could communicate with her team of soldiers without detection every time. If Kaden was aware of the private conversations between Kyle and her, then she had to fix the problem.

"What are you feeling?" She didn't have to push curiosity into her voice.

"Neither of you answered the question," Kaden said.

Kyle frowned at him. "What's going on, Kaden? I thought we were bringing Camellia here to meet Tansy and grab something to eat. Neither of us has had anything

338

to eat all day. We're both tired and hungry, and I'm out of sorts. I used enhanced vision for prolonged amounts of time, and if it wasn't for Camellia, I don't think I would have made it down the mountain."

Tansy leaned into her husband when he put his hand on her thigh beneath the table. "Are you feeling better now, Kyle?"

"I don't even have a headache, Tansy," Kyle admitted.

Tansy flashed a smile at Camellia. "Do you have healing abilities?"

"Some. I'm not great at it. Not trained. I'd like to learn more. I dabble a bit in the use of plants, and I'm getting better at using them. I know a bit about pressure points. I just don't have enough experience and it can be frustrating. I see someone hurting and I want to help them, but I'm just not certain how," Camellia admitted. "Sometimes it comes naturally, but often I just feel helpless."

Tansy nodded. "I know how that can feel, at least I used to. I have so many more resources now. You will too, now that you're here with us. I found that asking questions or just reading books helps me. There are so many of us here that have experienced similar things. Out in the world, our problems are very rare, but here, in this closed environment, many of us suffer the same kinds of complications. We can talk about the issues and usually find a way to resolve them."

Camellia didn't have the heart to tell her she hadn't made up her mind if she was going to live there with Jonas. Hopefully, Jonas would want to live apart from the others. With her. In her little garden of paradise. They would know if he was needed.

She knew that hope was a pipe dream. He was a soldier and he had to train with his team. He had to leave at a moment's notice. He wouldn't want to be that far away from his fellow GhostWalkers. She wasn't certain, after being alone for so long, that she could be around so many people day in and day out. Already she felt as if she could barely breathe.

"It would be nice to learn how to improve my abilities when I know I can do better. I have been working on growing plants that aid in healing. I'm good with plants," Camellia added. "They've always been a passion for me."

"I love photography," Tansy confessed. "When Kaden has the time to go with me, I go to various places and try to photograph wildlife. I especially love cougars, and I've gotten some great shots of them."

"She's being modest," Kaden said. "She's renowned for her photographs. Some of them are displayed in galleries. Others have been published in *National Geographic* magazine." He brought her gloved fingers up to his mouth and, at the last moment, turned her palm over so he could place a kiss on the bare skin of her wrist. Evidently, his touch didn't bother Tansy.

"I'm getting myself food," Kyle announced. "Come with me, Camellia. You must be starving." He stood up and put a hand on the back of her chair to pull it out for her.

Camellia rose as well. She really wanted to find out how Kaden knew they spoke with one another telepathically. It was important if she was going to help them in the coming battle. She slipped her hand onto the crook of Kyle's arm as they crossed the floor together to get to the buffet.

"How did he know?"

"Kaden is a scary son of a bitch," Kyle said. "Never underestimate him. Never. He can be charming when he wants to be, but you can bet Ryland and Kaden want to know where you came from and why Jonas has accepted you so fast. Jonas doesn't accept anyone. Hell, he hasn't accepted half of Team Two, and we've known them for

341

several years now."

Camellia laughed. "Jonas isn't that bad."

Kyle took a plate from the stack and handed it to her. "He's exactly that bad. Worse. And Kaden is right up there with him. The rest of us look normal compared to them. Jonas fights his demons all the time. All of us know it and we respect that about him. He's loyal to us and our families, and he'd protect us with his life. Suddenly, you're in the mix. He's made it clear that you're to be taken in and accepted by all of us and that you're under his protection as well. That's not something he does or that we take lightly."

Camellia looked over the range of food, most of which she hadn't ever eaten. She took salad and a small bit of what looked like cheesy potatoes.

Kyle lifted one eyebrow at her. "That's it? That's the extent of what you're eating?"

"I don't even know what half of this is." She whispered her confession. "I haven't been around this much food *ever*, Kyle. Don't embarrass me."

"I won't. But you're missing out."

"I'll try the desserts," she offered.

He laughed. "You're probably saving your appetite for desserts."

She thought she'd overdone the amount

of food as it was, but she didn't want to look like she wasn't going to eat what they provided for everyone. She sat down again across from Tansy, noticing that Tansy was eating salad as well.

"Kaden tells me someone has sent troops to wipe us out," Tansy said.

She sounded so matter-of-fact that Camellia nearly choked on the water she was drinking. She nodded when she could manage to speak. "That's what Kyle overheard Crawley speaking to someone else about. I thought maybe the teams would send the women and children away."

"There were two minds about that," Kaden said. "First off, some of us worry that whoever is plotting against us is expecting that move and is ready for it. And secondly, it isn't safe to move Marigold right now. She's been in a health crisis ever since she got pregnant, and it's only worsened since she gave birth."

Camellia's heart clenched to the point of pain. She pressed her hand to her chest. Marigold might not have told her about having a twin. She might have committed any number of sins, but they'd been sisters for many years, always having one another's backs. "Exactly what kind of health crisis?"

Kaden's blue eyes darkened almost to

black. "She bleeds internally, I think. Lily would have to explain it. I don't think she clots properly. Something called von Willebrand disease. In any case, jarring her right now by taking her over the road when it's a pitted mess could cause her to hemorrhage. I'm probably not explaining this right. I'm not a doc, but she's not in very good condition and hasn't been for a long time, from what I understand."

Camellia swung her head almost accusingly to look at Kyle. "Is he right about Mari?"

Kyle nodded. "Yeah. Her twin, Briony, doesn't have the same disease, so no one even considered it. It doesn't run in their family and isn't genetic. Our best doctors here have come up with a theory, but that's all it is. Marigold was given the original Zenith that Whitney developed when she went out on a mission."

Camellia knew all about that mission. Marigold had been given Zenith when she went with her former unit to try to talk to Violet and Senator Ed Freeman to see if they would help the women escape Whitney's breeding program.

"No one on Team Two knew she'd been given Zenith until it had been in her system for far too long and she was bleeding out.

She crashed completely. Lily and Ken saved her life, but it took a toll on her body. She has struggled ever since, and her pregnancy made things worse. She has had numerous transfusions since then. When the doctors discussed her case, we did consider long-term side effects of Zenith, but no one thought about her acquiring von Willebrand disease."

"What exactly is it?"

"It's basically the lack of a protein needed for clotting. That's simplifying things, but you get the gist," Kyle answered. "Sometimes someone with cancer or lupus or autoimmune disease can acquire von Willebrand's, but as a rule, it's inherited. That's why we didn't catch it even though the signs were there."

"What can be done for her?" Camellia asked.

Kyle looked across the table at Kaden, who leaned toward them and nodded. Kyle shrugged. "The other teams have a couple of good healers and doctors. We're holding out hope that they might come through with a way to help her. Ken and Jack have asked for someone to come as soon as possible. This particular disease isn't curable, but there are ways to help live with it. Her problem is severe and very complicated. We believe the way it developed and is presenting is the result of her body's interaction with Zenith."

Camellia's bloodstream felt as if it were on fire. The sudden onslaught of antioxidants rushing through her system, spreading to her cells, snapping every neuron and looking for her pores, for an outlet, shook her. She forced air through her lungs. Kept her head down to prevent the others at the table from seeing the change coming over her face. In her eyes. Her entire body began to shiver, and she couldn't stop it.

"I'm going to have to go outside for a few minutes, Kyle." She wasn't certain she could make it to the exit. She was that unsteady.

Her body felt apart from her, fighting her will, desperate to get to someone in danger. She hadn't examined Marigold, but instinctively she knew. Red knew. The part of her that was Red knew. If she went outside and connected with the mycelium that spread underground, it would possibly tell her even more about Marigold's condition — and she needed to know. She needed to know more than she needed to take her next breath.

She felt a gentle stirring in her mind. Jonas moved through the chaos, the twisting, urgent streams of her healer's drive demanding she find Marigold immediately. She found it shocking that Jonas, who had disconnected himself from her entirely so that she wouldn't be subjected to any part of the interrogation of their prisoner should he resist questioning, could so easily slip into her mind. More, that he would find her when she was so disoriented. How had he known she needed him?

I need to get outside where I can breathe. Where are you?

I'm still with Crawley. Is Kyle with you? I can send Jeff.

Kyle was helping her get to her feet, his hand under her elbow, then his arm slipping around her waist.

The moment we leave this table, Kyle cautioned, *Tansy is going to take off her gloves and try to read everything there is to know about you that she can.*

Camellia could barely focus on Kaden as Kyle gave the warning. She wanted to see his reaction when they were using telepathy. Her eyes were already seeing through a healer's vision. It was difficult to make him out. Her hands hurt, the pads of her fingers felt wet. She knew the extremely potent antioxidants Marigold needed were rushing through her bloodstream, desperate for her

347

to deliver the much-needed gift to a "family member."

Don't worry, Kyle. She tried to reassure him, but her mind was focused on healing, not on saving herself. It was difficult to know which path she was using to speak with him on.

Kaden rose instantly. "What's wrong? Kyle, I want to know what's wrong with her." The question wasn't coming from a friend. That was a demand from an officer.

"She needs to get outside," Kyle said. "I don't know what's happening to her." His voice rang with honesty because it was the truth.

Camellia, take a deep breath for me. Do it now.

Kyle's arm was a band around her waist. Kaden moved up to the other side of her to walk her to the door that exited out into a garden protected on three sides by the building. Tansy stayed behind. Camellia heard Jonas's command clearly and tried to obey him.

Something's really wrong, Jonas. My reaction has never been this strong. I don't know if it's because Marigold's condition is so bad, but even so, she's a long way away from me, and the distance alone should protect me. She knew she sounded desperate. She felt desperate. The chemicals in her body weren't letting up; they were growing thicker, stronger, raging through her, demanding she use her skills, her abilities and Red to heal where others couldn't.

You were tied together for over twenty years, Jonas pointed out calmly. *Do what I say, honey, just take a breath.*

Camellia felt dizzy, her eyes going from clear vision to a heated, almost strobing light. She kept her head down and struggled to draw air into her burning lungs. *Jonas.* She whispered his name like a talisman. Reaching for him. Trying to understand what was happening to her. She'd had instances of needing to heal something, or someone, but never such an overwhelming, overpowering urge. Every cell in her body felt transformed, armed with weapons to take down the enemy.

Unable to process what she was doing in real time, she stumbled just before she reached the door. Kaden wrapped his arm around her waist to help Kyle lift her off her feet even as he thrust the door open with one strong arm. The moment that solid arm completely encircled her back, she realized what was wrong — what had been wrong all along. She wasn't feeling Marigold, so far away.

It's Kaden, Jonas. Something is wrong with him. Really wrong with him.

Thankfully, they were outside and the fresh air hit her face. She kicked off her shoes and let her toes sink into the grass, pressed the soles of her feet into it as well, allowing the ground cover to soothe her. At once, she connected with the mycelium running beneath the ground. She sagged to the ground, and the two men let her, coming down beside her.

"You have to tell me what's going on, Camellia," Kyle said. "I've sent for Jonas."

She choked back her first reply and then indicated Kaden with a wave of her hand. She still couldn't see straight. The palms of her hands were damp.

"I don't know what that means," Kyle said.

"He's sick," she hissed just as Jonas cautioned her against answering.

She didn't look at either man as she rocked herself back and forth, burying her palms in the grass, digging her fingers into the ground to give back as much of the nutrients as she could. She didn't want to waste the life-giving gift.

There was a short silence. The wind blew cooling air through her hair and touched the beads of sweat forming on her forehead.

I'm coming to you, Jonas said. There was determination in his voice.

She could tell he wasn't finished questioning Crawley and that Ryland and whoever else was with him protested his decision, but he left anyway and started toward her.

"Kyle, go back inside," Kaden commanded. "You can wait with my wife."

"I have orders to stay with Camellia. If I leave her for any reason, Jonas will cut out my heart. I gave my word she'd be safe with me."

"I'm giving you a direct order," Kaden said. "That gives you no choice, so Jonas won't be cutting out your heart. I give you my word, she's safe with me. Go."

I'm sorry, Camellia, I have no choice here, not without directly defying a commanding officer's order. Kaden outranks me. We don't usually pull rank on one another, so he's serious.

"If you two have something to say, you can include me in the conversation," Kaden snapped.

Camellia made every effort to focus on Kaden, but she couldn't see him as anything but someone in need of healing.

I've got this, Jonas assured. *I know what you're looking for.*

It's all right, Kyle, go. Jonas is close. Deliberately, she used telepathic communication one more time in order to give Jonas the opportunity to discover how Kaden realized they were talking when there shouldn't have been any rise in energy.

Jonas was close. She could feel him moving fast toward her. She'd come to rely on herself, but it felt good to know that when she was disoriented and surrounded by strangers, she could count on Jonas. He was a strong wall of energy, a force all his own.

Kyle nodded and, after shooting Kaden a dark frown, went back into the dining room, leaving her alone with the battle-scarred stranger.

"We can't stay out here in the open when I talk to you," Kaden said. "We have to be somewhere private."

"Don't touch her," Jonas said, striding up, coming at them right from the front of the U-shaped garden. "You'll make the symptoms worse, Kaden."

Two blurry figures followed Jonas, but Camellia didn't try to make them out. She closed her eyes and buried her face in his shoulder when he swept her up. Everything about him was familiar — too welcome. She didn't question it then, not when she needed him.

"Follow me." Kaden sounded terse.

Abrupt. Not at all happy to see Jonas. "I didn't realize this was going to turn into a circus, Ryland. My health is private."

"What Camellia knows, I do," Jonas said. "I didn't have time to fill either one of you in on how that works between us. It has to do with our connection and the way Whitney paired us. It isn't her fault or mine."

Is she a psychic surgeon? Ryland asked. *It would be a miracle for us to have one. Even a psychic healer would be a miracle, and we'd take that.*

Camellia noted that Ryland spoke telepathically, so there was no way anyone could overhear them. He directed the question to Jonas but included her in the conversation along with Kaden and the other man trailing behind them.

She was shocked at the ferocious surge of reactive energy rushing through Jonas's veins. Every aggressive animal trait he had roared to life. She felt the hot testosterone-laced adrenaline spread like a wildfire through his body.

You dare to ask me this when, right at this moment, Tansy, who just pretended to welcome her and act as though she wanted to be her friend, is examining her silverware in order to discover everything about her she can? That's a betrayal by the way. Because it sure

353

as fuck isn't welcoming or friendship.

They were in another building now, striding down a hall. Camellia kept her face buried against Jonas's shoulder. His rage filled the hallway and had to be felt by the three men accompanying them. She could feel their uneasiness. Their rising guilt.

Jonas, we couldn't just accept a stranger into our midst with the stakes so high. We knew nothing about her, Ryland said.

What you're telling me is that my word isn't good enough. I told you I was connected to her, and I had already made certain she was safe before I ever took the chance of bringing her here. Jeff and Kyle did as well. You clearly don't trust me either, despite all I've done for this team. If it weren't for me sensing a warning no one else felt, we wouldn't have known these men were on the way.

Jonas, calm down, Ryland said. *You would have demanded we be even more careful of any stranger coming into our midst under any circumstances, and you know it. You're having a predatory reaction. I understand completely wanting to protect her, but we have to protect every single person here.*

Camellia felt Jonas take a deep breath. She didn't feel a reverse in the wildly aggressive chemicals and electrical impulses rushing through his system. Jonas kicked open the door to a room as Kaden twisted the knob and stepped back. He set Camellia on her feet to the right of the door up against the wall, his larger body shielding her from the others. The moment the door was closed he spoke aloud.

"What is it you'd like to know, Kaden?" There was pure challenge in his voice.

Camellia got the hint. These men were no longer dealing with her or their teammate, the man under their command. They were dealing with Jonas, the extremely dangerous predator. She was certain she could calm him down, but she wasn't altogether positive she wanted to. In a way, she found him magnificent. No one had ever stuck up for her before. Even under the circumstances, the feeling was exhilarating.

"How did she know I was ill?" Kaden asked.

"You sat at the table with her in a closed environment. She listened to all of you talking about Mari and thought she was reacting to what she was hearing, but the healer in her was reacting to whatever is wrong with you. You put your arm around her and she really reacted. Whatever your problem is has to be an immediate threat to you, or she wouldn't have had such a severe reaction."

Camellia leaned her forehead against Jonas's back and breathed deep in an effort to push the healer back. Now that there was a little distance between Kaden and her, she had some respite. Jonas's neurons snapping and rushing with heated aggression helped to push the terrible need further down so she could think again.

"Do you even want me to take a look at you, Kaden?" Camellia asked. "It's not like I'm this great gifted healer. I wish I could say I was. I just know I need to try when I'm close to you. I didn't mean to give anything away that I shouldn't have." She did feel bad about making a scene.

"It would be interesting to see what you think can be done," Kaden agreed. "If anything."

"Would you take off your shirt and lie down on the cot? I presume we came in here for that purpose. Jonas, you're going to have to actually move in order for me to get a look at him." Camellia pressed on his ribs in an effort to get Jonas to take a step forward so she could get around him.

"Tell me what you want me to do to help you."

"Go to the other side of the cot and stay connected to me. I imagine when I touch him again, the need to heal him will hit me just as hard as it did before. I want to share that with you so I can sort out what needs to be done." She was all business, moving into position on Kaden's right side, ignoring the skeptical expression on his face.

She glanced over her shoulder at Ryland. He had come up behind her to watch.

The other man moved in on Jonas's side. He flashed a sexy grin at her. "Raul Fontenot, ma'am. Mostly, they call me Gator around here."

Camellia switched her attention back to Kaden. He lay on the cot, eyes fixed on her face, as if he could see right through her. She ignored everyone else in the room, took a deep cleansing breath, and lay the pads of her fingers very lightly on the bare skin of his wrist right over his pulse. The jolt was hard, hitting her like a fist. She accepted the blow, mostly because she'd been expecting it this time.

She didn't fight the instantaneous flood of Red's nutrients and antioxidants, of all the weapons she provided to fight off infection while Camellia took care of the festering wound in Kaden's body. Camellia followed the thin trail of yellow invading his system back to the source. The sounds in the room receded until they were a distant blur. She could hear only Kaden's heartbeat combined with Jonas's and hers. The three of them settled into a steadier rhythm.

"Can you see it, Jonas?" she murmured aloud. "Metal. An unusual bullet with a very small cavity embedded in it, pushed up against his spine. You can see the original position, but it shifted recently. Looks like whatever was placed in that cavity is leaking out. I see traces of the poison. Can you see those drops? They're moving through his entire body."

"The tiny orange dots?"

She nodded. "Very, very small. We have to clear those drops first. It's imperative to get all of them. They're in his bloodstream — think blood poisoning — but even with intravenous antibiotics, you aren't going to stop that attack. This is some kind of chemical warfare."

"How do you clear the drops, Camellia?" Jonas asked.

She didn't reply but showed him, using starlike neurons as transports to send an army into battle. She was fast, the captain of so many ships, directing each of them as if they were at war, spinning and fighting, blasting away inside the veins and coming at the drops from every direction.

"Baby, I've never seen anything like this. You're a fucking miracle," Jonas whispered, sounding in awe.

Camellia barely registered his voice. "You can learn this too." She wasn't thinking when she said it, no longer aware they weren't alone in the room, but concentrating on making certain she ferreted out every last drop of poison in Kaden's system. "Nothing can be left behind," she murmured aloud. "My vision is getting blurry. Jonas, go back through the veins, study every organ, especially his heart and lungs, and then look at his brain. I need to look at the positioning of the bullet."

Someone wiped her eyes and she could see again. She blinked rapidly and went back to the bullet. "This is at a bad angle. It can't be left like this." She bit down on her lip. "This isn't in a good place, Jonas. Unless it's removed, he's not going to be walking for much longer, six months at the most. But trying to take it out could paralyze him just as easily."

"Can you do anything about it?" Jonas asked.

Camellia studied the position of the bullet from every angle. "It's tight. I can try to insert a few drops of liquid to see if that will float it out where I can get at it, but I'm only going to try if Kaden wants me to. It's your decision, Kaden, but you have to

359

make up your mind fast. I'm tiring."

She was. She had no idea how long it had taken her to battle the chemicals that had been released into Kaden's system, but she could already feel her body wanting to shut down. "As it is, I'll need a bit of rest before I make an attempt." She had to sit down soon or she was going to fall on her face.

"I'm talking to Tansy about it. I'd like you to try. I can't believe you got the poison out of my system. I can feel that it's gone. She's on her way and would like to be with me if that's all right with you."

Camellia shrugged. She didn't know who was in the room once she began working on someone. The healer in her blocked everyone else out for the most part.

"You're certain, Kaden?" Ryland asked. "If something goes wrong, there's no taking this back."

"I'm certain. Her touch feels delicate, but when she's working inside me, she's a powerhouse, Rye. I know there isn't any of the chemical left. Doctors said I'd be dead in a few days, a couple of weeks at the most, from the poison. If that didn't get me, the bullet was going to. It still will, unless a psychic surgeon gets here in time. With a war going on, I doubt that's going to happen."

"Jonas, I'm going to sit down for a while. Are you finished searching?"

"Yeah, babe. I'm with you."

It was Ryland who wrapped his arm around her waist and helped Camellia to a chair just as the door opened and Tansy came in, followed by a woman of average height with sable-colored hair and deep blue eyes.

Tansy went straight to the cot to take Kaden's hand. The woman looked around the room with a slight frown, and then her gaze came back to land on Ryland and Camellia.

"Ryland? What's going on in here?"

12

Jonas turned at the sound of that feminine
voice. Before he could ask how many more
were going to be joining them, Ryland
glanced up with a slight scowl on his face.

"Lily, what are doing in here? Tansy?
Didn't Kaden make it clear this was a
closed meeting?"

Jonas had never heard Ryland speak to his
wife in that particular voice before. Never.
Cold as ice. He didn't sound like a husband.
He sounded like a commanding officer, and
a very pissed-off one at that.

"Rye." Lily not only looked but sounded
hurt. "I followed Tansy. It isn't her fault.
Clearly, something was happening with
Kaden and I was afraid for her. He is my
patient. Who is this woman? What is she doing in here?"

"You'll be briefed when I see fit to brief
you," Ryland said. "Right now, you need to
leave."

"When you see fit to brief me? On my own patient?" Lily poured outrage into her voice.

Jonas could see she was genuinely shocked at Ryland's response. She looked around the room, taking in everyone, her gaze resting on Camellia, who looked pale and worn. Ryland stood, looking menacing, filling the room with anger.

"Yes, Lily, this is a military matter. Just like the soldiers coming up the mountain to kidnap you and Daniel and wipe the rest of our team and Team Two out. Do you want to know why they're coming? Why they would come?"

Jonas winced. Ryland's voice was very low, never a good sign with him. He could infuse more fury into his tone than anyone could by raising their voice. He stalked her across the room, looking so menacing Lily actually backed away from him.

"Because you decided you didn't have to listen to your husband and could do whatever the hell you wanted to do with our son. So now I've got a prisoner I've got to interrogate. Do you have any idea what that means? When one interrogates a prisoner quickly? One that refuses to give up information we need fast? Perhaps I should have you observe."

Jonas's heart nearly stopped beating. He'd

never seen Ryland like this. Never. They'd lost men. They'd been hunted. They'd been trapped in cages with men drugging them, taking them to hospitals and murdering members of their team, and still, Jonas had never seen Ryland like this. He didn't know whether or not to intervene. He could feel the absolute shock of the other men in the room as well.

He feels absolutely betrayed by her. He can't conceive of what she's done and the consequences to all of you, Camellia observed. *Or the consequences to their relationship.*

Jonas felt her understanding of what Ryland was feeling. She knew betrayal intimately. Once trust was broken, how did one get it back? Jonas looked at his commanding officer. He'd known him for years. He followed him because he believed in him. There were few men better than Ryland Miller.

Ryland was a simple man in that he was utterly loyal when it came to those he loved — just as Jonas was. Jonas had no idea what he'd do if Camellia had gone behind his back when they'd both agreed on a way to keep their child safe and done just the opposite. Wring her neck?

"I don't think you would like the way we

364

get information, Lily, but then right now, your opinion doesn't matter very much to me one way or the other. As for this woman, she's doing her best to save Kaden because we don't have time to wait for a psychic surgeon because there is an army on the way to wipe us out."

Lily shook her head. "That can't be true."

"I assure you, it's all true," Ryland said. "Especially the part where you betrayed your husband." Ryland's voice had dropped even lower. His eyes had gone almost pure silver, fixed on his wife.

Jonas moved to get into a better position to intercept just in case. Gator did as well. Ryland ignored both of them.

Lily put a defensive hand to her throat. "Ryland, no, it isn't like that."

"It's exactly like that. There isn't a way to put a spin on it, Lily. We had a discussion, we both agreed and you went behind my back anyway. You figured you could outsmart everyone, but you didn't. There was a traitor planted in our home. Your good friend, Dr. Adams's assistant, Lydia Fenamore, was paid to build up your trust and observe everything she could, including mapping what parts of Jeff's brain were active and when."

Lily kept shaking her head.

"You figured you would use Jeff instead of me because you thought I would never agree to what you were doing. You went behind my back, and you endangered our son and every man, woman and child on this team, as well as those on Team Two, through your own recklessness. You've gotten to be so arrogant, thinking you're above everyone else with your enormous IQ. Who does that remind you of, Lily?"

She winced visibly, as if he'd struck her. Tansy gasped. Jonas wanted to hold up his hand and stop Ryland. There were some things you couldn't take back. Implying Lily was like Whitney might be one of them. Lily was as white as a sheet.

"I don't have time to discuss this with you right now." Ryland was merciless. "You have to leave. Kaden has opted to allow Camellia to try to remove the bullet. She's already managed to remove all of the poison from his body."

Lily's gaze jumped to Camellia. "You're a healer?"

Ryland took her arm. "You are to leave now, or I'll have Gator escort you to your room and lock you in, Lily. If you think I'm in any way joking, think again. You put not only our entire team and their families at risk but Team Two and their families as well.

I have very little time to put together a battle plan. I don't even know how many I'm up against. This isn't one of Whitney's supersoldiers' experimental attacks to see what they can do. It's all-out war."

He led her to the door, ignoring the tears in her eyes. Lily went out and Ryland closed the door on her. Jonas handed Camellia a bottle of water. He didn't know what to say. Apparently, no one else did either. There was a long silence. Ryland paced back and forth like a wild animal in the small confines of the room. Jonas hadn't noticed that the room was all that small until Ryland began to act like a caged tiger.

Gator stepped all the way to the back of the room, his eyes meeting Jonas's in the shadows. There was pain there. Jonas felt it too. No one wanted to see Ryland and Lily at odds, especially now, when everything was going to hell fast.

"Do you really think you can get the bullet, Camellia?" Tansy asked, her voice hushed, even in the silence of the room.

Camellia leaned her head against the wall and took a drink of water. "It's in a very difficult spot. I can see why the doctor was reluctant to attempt surgery. I do think it might be possible to float it out of there. Once I do, I would have to break it up into small enough pieces for his body to get rid of it. Or find a way to break the bullet down altogether. That might be possible as well. I won't know until I study it."

"Are you a psychic surgeon?" Kaden asked bluntly.

"I don't even know what that is, exactly," Camellia admitted. "I know when I'm near someone ill, I feel as if I have to help them. I didn't have the ability when I was in the labs with Whitney. It may have been just developing, but it wasn't strong, not like now. I had no idea it had gotten so strong. I've been alone so much, avoiding people so he couldn't track me, that I really haven't had much experience healing humans. Animals, yes. Humans, no."

"Kaden," Tansy whispered, her voice a protest.

"I'm not going to wait for death, Tansy."

"If we wait, you have time for a psychic surgeon to get here."

"Not anymore. There's a battle coming, or have you forgotten? I trust her, baby. She got rid of the poison in me when no one else could have done that," Kaden said.

"I couldn't read anything on the silverware, Kaden," Tansy whispered. "Nothing at all. That makes no sense and I don't like it."

Jonas heard. They all heard. He exchanged a smile with Camellia.

How did you manage that?

You don't leave prints or impressions behind either, do you? she countered.

He was careful not to; that's why he didn't. He didn't leave tracks. He wore thin gloves in order not to leave behind fingerprints. He looked down at his hands. His hands were rough. Scarred. Unlike Camellia, his body was a road map, and that included his palms. He looked closer, turning his hands over. Was there a thin film over his skin? Barely there? Barely noticeable. It was unseen to the human eye. He looked at it with a bird's vision. His palms and the pads of his fingers appeared to be shiny, definitely covered in a very thin film.

Jonas rubbed his hands on his thighs. He'd never noticed the phenomenon before. When he looked at the material along his thigh, it was dry. His palms still appeared shiny. *What is it? Is this something from the mycelium network that I don't know about?*

Camellia smiled up at him and took another sip of water. She shook her head slowly. *You always look annoyed when you discover the tremendous gifts you've been given, Jonas.*

He raised an eyebrow at her. *Do I?* He

knew he did. This was something new. Something good, but another something new.

You know you do. I'm really tired. Let's finish this. We can talk when we're alone.

"We still have to talk to Crawley," Jonas said to remind her he would still have to finish interrogating the prisoner after they finished with Kaden. "Camellia, are you ready to try this?"

She nodded and took his hand. "Don't worry, Tansy. If I don't think it can be done, I won't even attempt it. I don't want to be the one to cause him harm."

She avoided looking at Tansy. Jonas knew why. She might say she understood why Tansy sat across the table from her, smiling and offering friendship while planning to uncover every secret Camellia had the entire time. That hurt whether Camellia wanted to admit it or not. He just wanted to catch his woman up and take her out of there. Ryland's hurt was raw and unrelenting, and it was bleeding into all of them, including the sadness that pervaded the room.

Jonas tightened his hand around Camellia's. Already he could feel their connection. It felt as if they even shared the same blood rushing through their veins. Hot. Alive. He looked down at the top of her head. All that silky hair. Thick. Wild. So Camellia. She tilted her head back so that her eyes met his just for a moment, and he could see the mischief there. That look was for him alone, and his heart clenched.

In spite of the tension in the room, he grinned at her. "You got this."

"*We* do," she corrected.

They took up positions on either side of Kaden's cot. Jonas chose the side Tansy was currently occupying. She still retained possession of her husband's hand, but Jonas forced her to move farther down toward his hips. Ryland stood by Kaden's head, one hand on his shoulder, more, Jonas thought, to steady himself than Kaden. Gator stood beside Camellia to aid her if she needed it. He had a bottle of water close as well as a cloth.

Camellia laid her palm on the bare skin of Kaden's ribs, and this time, Jonas followed suit. He wasn't prepared for the rush of heat that seemed to be generated not just from Camellia but from inside of him as well. Those billions of star-shaped neurons inside of him looking like starships spread out, flooding his system with fast-moving chemicals that snapped and flashed red, filling him with energy and vitality.

He was used to his vision patterns changing from animal to bird to human, but now, his vision was morphing into something else, something he'd never experienced before. He nearly yanked his hands away from Kaden. He was so closely connected to Camellia, he could see the same sparkling red liquid moving in her veins, see the same vision changed in her gaze. She accepted it so calmly, so easily, that he breathed away his instinctive resistance and just let the change take control.

That was the most difficult thing of all for him, giving up control. He was, out of necessity, the most controlled person there was. He had to be. And he knew, were it not for Camellia, he would have stepped away.

She was steady, her gaze fixed on Kaden's body, and when he followed suit, he found himself looking past the flesh right inside to the organs. This time, however, it wasn't through her eyes but through his own.

"The bullet is turned at such an odd angle, Kaden," Camellia said softly. "It's lodged sideways and tipped slightly. Part of it is embedded under the organ, where it's impossible to see. That's the tricky part. I don't know if that part is shredded or intact. I'm going to push a little natural liquid antibiotic all around the bullet and see if I can loosen it and float it out of there very gently. You have to let me know if anything hurts or changes the way it feels in any way at all."

Jonas wanted to see her face, the concentration there, as much as he wanted to watch the procedure. She was magnificent. *Insanely* so. She had control of the fluid moving through every vein. Every synapse. Coming in from every direction. From her. From him. Like the floodgates of a dam. All moving into Kaden. Nutrients. Vitamins. Antioxidants. The body's natural antibiotics.

How are the fluids being delivered?

Our hands. The pads of your fingers. Of mine. I need to concentrate.

"What are you saying to him?" Kaden asked.

"You're very sensitive to the slightest rise in energy," Camellia observed. "I need to concentrate; that's what I was telling him." There was the littlest bite to her voice that warned everyone in the room to back off and leave her alone while she worked.

Gator reached over with the cloth, distracting Jonas so that he looked up, blinking to clear his vision. Tiny beads of what appeared to be sweat dotted her forehead. Jonas wasn't certain it was sweat. The healer in her was strong, and she called various elements in the blood she manipulated. She kept her gaze fixed on the bullet, maneuvering the fluid around it in an effort to float it with extraordinary gentleness.

The bullet actually lifted minutely, and Jonas's breath hitched. She began to work it gradually, almost indiscernibly, back and forth. The movement was so subtle that, at first, Jonas wasn't certain she was actually doing anything but waiting to see if the damaged bullet responded to the fluid.

He stared at the projectile, willing it to move, so that when it appeared to wiggle the tiniest bit, he was certain he was simply seeing things. More fluid trickled around the breached cavity, tipping it upward just a little. The fluid leaked under the organ where the bullet was hidden.

Kaden didn't make a sound, nor did he shift position, but Camellia's gaze jumped to his face. "Talk to me, Kaden. Did that hurt?" Her voice was low. Calm. Steady.

Jonas felt the small rush of adrenaline pouring into her system, belying that soothing tone.

"No. But I felt something, almost like a scratch. It didn't hurt. It was a little uncomfortable because it was unexpected. It's moving, isn't it?"

"I don't want you to move around," Camellia said. "The tip is still embedded where I can't quite get to it. I'm trying to work it out. You're being very patient with me."

How much time had gone by? Jonas didn't know. It didn't seem like very long, but when he made himself actually look at the others in the room through his own vision, he realized Camellia had been working patiently at moving the bullet for well over an hour. She was pale. Swaying on her feet. She had a look of utter determination on her face.

"It moved," Kaden said decisively. "Can you yank it out?"

Camellia's soft laughter eased some of the tension in the room and relaxed the knots in Jonas's shoulders. "It doesn't quite work like that."

The smile faded from her lips, and a look of absolute concentration took over her expression again as her gaze dropped to Kaden's body. Jonas followed the trajectory of her eyes. He could see the fluid around the bullet getting a little thicker so that the metal seemed to float upward. Once again, it moved gently, barely, a tiny seesaw back and forth. Every fifth or so movement, there would be a gentle tug on the bullet, and then the back and forth would start again.

When Camellia had started, the bullet had been mostly hidden by the liver, but Jonas was certain he could see much more of it now.

"Camellia." He breathed her name in awe. "You're backing it out of there."

She didn't reply, didn't look at him, but a brief, triumphant smile flirted with her mouth. "Shh. Don't jinx me. I have to go slow."

More liquid surrounded the bullet, lifting it so it appeared to float, yet it was still anchored. Just the very tip, Jonas was certain. Like Kaden, he wanted to yank it free. There was just no way to do it. Two more times, she patiently did the seesaw motion back and forth and tugged, and suddenly, the bullet slid free into the liquid and floated right into one of the many long tubes that rushed toward Kaden's heart.

Jonas's own heart jumped, and he swore, unaware he did so aloud. Evidently, Camellia had anticipated the arc of the bullet because when it dropped into the fast-moving bloodstream, she was ready in her neuron-fueled starship, calmly blasting the projectile with Kaden's antibodies. With more than his own antibodies. With tiny little clumps of red missiles that Jonas couldn't identify but were very effective.

Each missile hit the target as if she were playing a video game. The bullet shattered again and again until it broke into such small pieces, she could no longer shoot them with the missiles.

Middlemist Red? Jonas couldn't help asking.

Camellia didn't reply but switched from blasting the pieces to using another liquid. This was a distinct pink, much like the color of the Middlemist Red blossom. It shot through Kaden's veins and arteries, overtaking what was left of the bullet. The liquid slowed. Gelled. Sat there devouring those tiny pieces until there was nothing left, not even specks.

"Put your hands directly over that spot just below his heart, Jonas," Camellia instructed.

She sounded utterly weary. Jonas did what she asked, moving his hands from Kaden's ribs to where he knew that gel had consumed the pieces of bullet. Heat spread through his veins. Through Camellia's. Through Kaden's veins and arteries. The gel liquefied and moved through Kaden's system, was absorbed by his tissues, dissipating until nothing was left, leaving no sign behind.

Camellia let out her breath slowly and

sagged. "I believe you are free from that bullet, Kaden. Do me a favor and don't get shot again anytime soon."

Gator caught her before she fell on the floor. "Don't crash on us, woman. Sit down."

Camellia just sat right on the floor. "I think I'm done for the night."

She looked it. Jonas wanted to scoop her up and take her to his home. He couldn't be in two places at one time, and now everyone knew she could heal. The thought roused his aggressive instincts, and he wanted to snarl. Where there was one traitor, there might be another.

"How do you feel, Kaden?" Tansy asked.

"Good. Very good. It doesn't even feel as though I've had anything wrong with me." Kaden sat up and looked down at Camellia. "You really did it. You removed the poison and you got rid of the bullet."

Tansy put a restraining hand on his shoulder. "Wait a minute before you start moving around, Kaden." She looked anxiously to Camellia. "Is it safe for him to just get up and start doing everything he did before? Could the metal lodge somewhere else?"

Jonas answered for Camellia. "It's gone. Dissolved. He's perfectly fine. It's as though that bullet was never there in the first place.

All the damage the chemicals did to his body were repaired."

He swept a hand through his hair and reached down for her. "You ready to get some fresh air before I find a place for you to sleep?"

"Out of curiosity," Ryland said, "you don't happen to have a small amount of that poison they had in that breached cavity, do you? Or know what was in it or what it was? Kaden was shot when we were sent into the field that first year after Whitney enhanced us. It was one of several missions we had gone on, and all of us were struggling. Kaden was one of the steadiest of all of us, and he's an anchor, drawing away all the psychic energy so the others could perform. If they use the same poison again, I'd like to be prepared."

"I'm sorry, I have no idea what it was," Camellia said. "I might be able to figure out the compound given a little time if that would help."

"You think you may be able to figure out the compound given a little time?" he echoed. His eyes met Jonas's over her head. "She's really amazing, isn't she?"

How, Camellia?

Not me. I have no idea what it was. I said I might be able to figure it out. I might have help. I'm tired, Jonas.

Jonas couldn't help the grin. "She is. Come on, baby." He tugged her hand until she was on her feet, swaying just a little bit until he steadied her with his arm around her waist.

"Thank you, Camellia," Kaden said. "You saved my life. I won't forget it."

"It's kind of a compulsion," Camellia explained as Jonas opened the door and stepped out into the hallway with her.

Ryland, Gator, Kaden and Tansy followed behind them. Lily sat on the floor across from the door, knees drawn up. She looked completely devastated. "Ryland . . ."

Ryland ignored her, striding down the hall, back toward the interior of the compound. Over his shoulder, he snapped a command at Jonas. "I'll expect you to join me, Jonas." He didn't wait to hear Jonas's reply. Gator went with Ryland, matching his commander's quick, angry strides.

Kyle waited, back to the wall, a short distance away from Lily. "I take it everything is okay with Kaden?"

Jonas nodded. "Thanks for sticking around, Kyle. I appreciate it. Kaden's fine."

"I think I'll stay here for a few minutes," Camellia said. "You go do whatever you need to, and Kyle can take me to your house when I'm ready to go."

Jonas studied the compassion on her face and then looked at the misery on Lily's. *I don't think there's a way to fix this right now, honey. They'll work it out.*

I know they will.

Jonas could see he wasn't going to get anywhere by arguing with her. He brushed a kiss along her forehead and followed Ryland and Gator down the hall.

Camellia watched Jonas — her lifeline — go. She stood there a moment, wondering what she was doing. She hadn't seen Lily since she was a child. She doubted if Lily even remembered her. Lily, no doubt, was embarrassed that Camellia, a virtual stranger, had heard what Ryland had accused her of. Still, Camellia couldn't force herself to walk away.

Behind her, Kaden and Tansy were talking in low voices, Kaden's hands moving over Tansy's in reassurance. Now that Kaden was actually on his feet and proving to his wife that he really was okay, she was weeping softly, and he was comforting her. Camellia glanced up at Kyle. He looked down at his phone, reading the text message there and shaking his head.

Taking a deep breath, Camellia walked over to Lily. "Would you mind if I sat with you for a few minutes? We weren't formally introduced. My name is Camellia Mist, and I actually was raised with you for a few years when we were children."

Lily removed her hands from her face just briefly, lifting tear-drenched eyes filled with complete desolation to Camellia. She nodded slightly before lowering her gaze and resting her forehead on her knees.

Camellia accepted the invitation and slid down, sitting beside her, with her knees up and back to the wall. The simple gesture of solidarity brought back memories from her childhood when the children were allowed a few precious minutes together. Whitney didn't like them to gather together too long because he thought they conspired against him. They hadn't so much at first, not until they realized that he was the one causing all their pain.

When they were allowed to be together, they would sit with their backs to the wall, facing the windows and vents, paying attention to the cameras to see if the red eye was on, telling them they were being recorded. They'd keep their knees drawn up and speak softly, covering their mouths. Often, they'd sit close, thighs touching just to have some kind of human contact. Most of them wanted to be close to Lily, Flame or Camellia. All three were powerful anchors and drew away psychic energy, allowing the others respite from the constant pain they experienced without the filters to their brains.

"Ryland's a good man," Lily said. "The best. You have no idea how good of a man he is and how hard he's worked to save his men." She lifted her head and dashed at her tears. "We don't fight. We just don't. He's so good to me. To everyone. He thinks about everyone before himself." She put her head down again. "I never once thought what this would look like from his point of view. Not once. How selfish of me is that?"

Camellia wanted to comfort Lily. She was a ferocious warrior, yet there was also a deeply compassionate side of her that had always been there. She was driven to fix things, make them right, so the people around her didn't suffer. At the same time, her strongest sympathies, in this particular instance, lay with Ryland. Lily had gone behind his back, not the other way around.

Tamping down her instincts to soothe and comfort, Camellia remained silent. Lily needed to talk and Camellia needed to understand. There was no question that Lily loved Ryland fiercely, so how could she have betrayed him the way she had?

Camellia knew there was always more than one side to a story. Perhaps Lily could shed light on her reasoning and make Camellia understand her actions. Because maybe that understanding would enable Camellia to forgive Marigold. She desperately wanted to be able to forgive Marigold's betrayal, and yet the hurt ran so deep, the break in trust so devastating, she just couldn't even face the idea of speaking with her. Now she'd learned Marigold had a life-threatening illness, and there was no way Camellia could stay away if she could possibly help her. That didn't mean she could forgive her.

"I sat here the whole time you were healing Kaden, trying to defend my actions, trying to be angry with Rye for not considering everything we've been through, all the times we've shared, and giving me a break. But then I realized, none of those good times stacked up against a violation of trust. He considers what I did as a betrayal of our marriage. Of everything we are together. I have been sitting here, imagining how I'd feel if I were in his place — if he were the one who went behind my back to someone else and did exactly what we both agreed not to do."

She pressed a shaky hand to her mouth to

muffle a sob. Her eyes briefly met Camellia's before she lowered her spiky, wet lashes to cover her pain. "I didn't mean it that way, but that's what I did. Now there's a war coming, and everyone I love could be killed. I've jeopardized not just our team and their families but all of Team Two as well. I don't see how Ryland can possibly forgive me. I didn't just endanger our teams. I destroyed the most important thing in the world to me: my marriage to Ryland. My family."

Camellia listened to the heartbreaking sobs, the compulsion to comfort her nearly overwhelming. It was just that she didn't know how to go about it. She hesitated to touch Lily, not just because they were essentially strangers but because, except for Jonas, Camellia hadn't really touched another human being in years.

"Why did you do it, Lily?" she finally asked. "It seems so out of character for you to go against anything you and your husband decide together."

Lily cried for a couple more minutes but struggled to get her weeping under control. "I know Ryland thinks I did it because I'm a scientist and wanted to have a record of anything Daniel might do because he's different. Everyone will probably think that."

Camellia had to admit she thought it. It was a logical conclusion. Lily was a scientist. Information was extremely important to her.

Lily rubbed her cheek back and forth on her drawn-up knees. "Daniel's my first child. He might be my only child for all I know. I wanted all those things every mother has with that first child. All the cherished photographs and videos of his firsts. The first steps. His first words. What he eats and doesn't eat. That was what was important to me. I tried to tell Ryland, but he didn't understand the difference between first steps and our son being Daniel."

Lily's eyes went liquid again. "Just because he's different, doesn't mean I don't want to have those special moments recorded or remembered, written down or photographed. It isn't fair that as a mother, I shouldn't have them like any other mother. I won't remember every little detail when I'm older. I want albums to look through when I'm seventy and eighty. I want to go through them with his future wife. I *didn't* record anything scientific. I won't say it wasn't tempting, but I'd promised Ryland. I just wanted what every other mother had."

Camellia found that heartbreaking.

Lily waved her hand in the air. "Listen to

me. I'm still defending myself and my position."

"I asked why you did it and you gave me your answer," Camellia said. She was a little shocked that she could actually understand why Lily had decided to do what she had. "But, and I'm just asking, if Ryland is a dreamwalker, why didn't you insist he listen to you and let you record everything with him? There wouldn't have been a chance that anyone would know if it was just the two of you."

"We argued over Daniel's safety, and in the end, I agreed with him completely. I did. What Ryland said made sense to me at first. But then there were so many darling moments that I knew I could never get back. I brought the subject up and Rye got angry with me. He said he was not putting our son in jeopardy, that he wasn't a science experiment. I kept trying to explain and he just wouldn't hear me. He compared me to Whitney. That really hurt. I was being a mother, not a scientist. So I went to Jeff."

Camellia realized Lily had reached out to Jeff when she was hurt by Ryland's thoughtless accusation — the one thing he said that had cut her deep. Instead of confronting her husband as she should have, she'd kept that hurt to herself and chosen a course of action she couldn't take back.

Camellia pressed her lips together. She wasn't the best at communication. She barely knew how to act around people. If Lily and Ryland, who clearly loved one another, could get to this point — so far apart — that a betrayal of this magnitude could take place, what chance could she possibly have with Jonas? They both had so many issues.

On the other hand, she and Jonas shared connections no one else had. They had the obvious pairing Whitney set up, just like the one he had clearly set up between Lily and Ryland. That had worked for a long time for the other couple. In addition to that, however, Camellia and Jonas had the underground mycelium network. They could communicate easily, feel what the other felt and know one another's thoughts. They also would know what the other needed as far as mental and physical health. Most important, they were connected through Middlemist Red.

Middlemist Red was inherently sensitive. She lived in both of them. Granted, the dose Whitney had put in Camellia was far stronger than what he'd put in Jonas, but Red ran through both their veins. The connection between them was extremely strong because Red was so powerful. The plant had the ability to hide, which gave them that ability. Jonas had tapped into it often. He just hadn't realized why he could disappear into shadows, mist and fog, not any more than he had comprehended that his early warning system came from the mycelium running beneath the ground.

"Ryland will never forgive me, and I can't blame him," Lily said. "And if anyone dies, I won't be able to forgive myself. I've considered leaving Daniel here and hiking up the mountain to find this army coming at us and turn myself over to them. Maybe they'd turn back and be satisfied with just me."

"You know better than that," Camellia said, alarm spreading through her. Lily not only sounded desperate; she felt it as well. She was liable to do anything when she felt so hopeless and guilty. "The man Ryland and Jonas are questioning was sent to kidnap you and Daniel. The ones coming up the mountain aren't here for you or your son. They plan on killing everyone they find here and at the other compound. That includes the women and children."

Lily's breath hitched audibly. "Marigold can't be moved. We could try it, but if she starts hemorrhaging again, it could kill her.

We've tried all kinds of medication, and nothing has worked so far. The road isn't smooth, and airlifting her is out of the question."

She ran shaking hands through her hair and stared with despair at Camellia. "Why would these men want to kill us all to begin with? Surely Whitney didn't order it."

"No, it doesn't appear as if he did. Some bank conglomerate that wants to force Whitney to do their bidding. He's too much of a patriot for them. According to Jonas, these people think Whitney will cooperate with them if they have you and Daniel."

"They're wrong. He would never sell out his country. He's completely insane in so many ways, Camellia. He believes he should be able to go to any country, including the United States, and take female children that he claims no one wants. He buys them, so in his mind, he owns them. To him, those children are worthless until he gives them greatness and purpose by experimenting on them."

"Why is it that so much of the world thinks females are mostly useless?" Camellia asked, suddenly feeling so tired she just wanted to slide down the wall and go to sleep.

"I haven't been able to figure that out,"

Lily said. "Not when so many women have made such amazing contributions to the world. Of course, as far as Peter Whitney is concerned, the only valuable contribution any female can make is what he deems necessary." There was bitterness in her voice. She looked at Camellia. "I believed him for years, you know. Looking back, I remember you and Flame both warning me that he was lying to all of us. I don't know how he managed to keep me so blind to the differences in how he treated all of you compared to me."

"Sometimes it's really hard to face the truth." A part of Camellia had always known Marigold wasn't telling the truth about the night of Camellia's disastrous escape attempt, but she'd refused to acknowledge her suspicions. She loved Marigold like a sibling, and she'd clung so desperately to that familiar bond. It was so much easier to lie to herself than consider the horrific possibility that Marigold didn't love her the way she loved Marigold. Or that Marigold didn't feel that same loyalty toward her.

Lily nodded. "I should have made Ryland understand how important it was to me to capture the memories of our son growing up. Things that have nothing to do with science. I shouldn't have let his words hurt me to the point of trying to hurt him back. That's what it was, I was striking out at him for his refusal to listen to me and the horrible things he accused me of, and then I just let it get too far. I was afraid to tell him what I'd done."

"You know you have to have this conversation with him, Lily," Camellia said as gently as she could. "He's angry right now, and he's hurt, but you two have to talk to each other. You have to do it for your son and for the two of you. If you tell him the truth, everything you told me, he still may be angry for a while, but he'll forgive you. If he's everything you've said he is, then he'll forgive you."

Camellia hoped what she said was the truth. She was fading fast. Really fast. "I'm sorry, Lily, but I'm so tired. I need to find a place to sleep. In spite of the circumstances, it was really good to see you. I hope we meet up sometime again." She had no idea what she was planning to do or where she would be staying, so she wasn't going to commit.

She glanced up at Kyle, who immediately came over to help her off the floor. Only then did she realize Kaden and Tansy were close, most likely waiting to ensure that Lily was taken care of. Camellia was too tired to do much more than lift a hand in a wave before following Kyle down the hall and through the maze that led to the outside parking lot.

13

Jonas had a sprawling cabin on the very outskirts of the fortified compound Team One had built together. Each of the men had their own home, mostly because they required alone time, but the main building at the center was easy to defend. The homes had escape routes leading to the fortified building as well as to the roads, the surrounding forests, the vehicles and all forms of transportation.

Jonas's cabin was one and a half stories with extremely high ceilings. Each log was meticulously scribed to lock into place with another. That was no small undertaking. Kyle told her they'd all helped. They'd used wood that was naturally dried. The forest was old, and trees would stand for up to five years after dying. Jonas had an affinity for the trees in the forest, and he seemed to be able to find the right logs for the cabin. By using the naturally dried wood, it made the cabin sturdy and extremely stable. There was no moisture to dry out so that the wood would shrink, causing structural problems. Kyle explained the process to her as he gave her a quick tour of the house.

There was no doubt that Jonas lived there. His presence permeated every room. There was masculine strength throughout. The flagstone flooring was cut from giant pieces, while the floor-to-ceiling fireplace was made of smaller pieces of flagstone. Huge windows everywhere provided breathtaking views of the mountains and forests, bringing the outside indoors. The bathrooms were modern, and everything was very clean. Given Jonas's constant effort to stay calm and in control, the immaculate, well-ordered tidiness of his home didn't surprise her.

After showering, washing her hair and pulling on fresh clothes from her backpack, Camellia wandered outside to the huge verandah. It was covered by a thick roof that would shade occupants from the morning sun. A very large lounge — big enough to be a bed — sprawled invitingly along the wall.

"I'm sleeping here, Kyle. Just tell him that."

Kyle gave her a salute and stepped off the porch.

"Thank you," she called after him. She honestly didn't know if he was going to stick around until Jonas came back, but it didn't matter. She was tired. Kyle could do whatever he needed to do.

Camellia curled up on the wide lounge, listening to the sound of the wind in the trees, her feet bare. If necessary, she could leap over the banister to bury the soles of her feet into the soil and hear what the land had to tell her. Gray and Blue were close by, each perched on top of a broken snag just inside the interior of the forest. It gave her comfort to know they were close.

Several small shrubs near the entrance to the house spread their branches invitingly toward her. She recognized those leaves. There were no blooms on them yet, but she recognized the shrubs instantly. Jonas hadn't planted her, but Middlemist Red was close to him, watching over him. He just didn't know it yet. She drifted off, smiling at the thought that there were so many things that Jonas didn't know yet. And they were good things.

She woke sometime later to find him smiling down at her. He looked tired, the lines in his face cut deep. As a rule, Red was antiaging, and in spite of the many types of animals and reptiles Jonas had to deal with, the plant kept him looking on the younger side. Camellia cupped the side of his face gently.

"It was a hard night for you, wasn't it?"

He shrugged and sat on the lounge, nudging her over as he bent to remove his boots. "Just another night. I could use some sleep. Why aren't you inside?"

"I like the night." She turned so she was sitting and waited for him to lie down and put his head in her lap. She could feel the raging headache pounding in his skull. She massaged his temples. "How much time do we have before we have to leave?"

"How did you know?"

She gave him a faint smile. "I knew we only had a couple of days anyway before the conglomerate sent their army. They aren't going to be happy we eliminated their scouts, so they'll probably move up their timeline. Of course we'll have to go back out."

He closed his eyes. "You don't have to go, Camellia. It might be safer if you stay here. Or if you go to the garden and weave your illusions."

"Maybe," she mused. "And maybe we already had these discussions, Jonas. Go to

397

sleep. If we're going back on the trail soon, you need to be fresh."

He caught her hand and brought her palm to his mouth, pressing a kiss to the center. "We have a day or so, more time than I originally thought we'd have, but Ryland wants us to take out their leaders, who are apparently the only enhanced members of their army."

"That makes sense, but you can't do it tonight. Just rest for now. You need it."

"You do realize I'm falling in love with you."

"You haven't seen my bad side yet."

He opened his eyes and looked at her. "You have a bad side?"

Camellia bit her lower lip and nodded slowly. "I do, Jonas. I'm very, very sorry, but I do. I wish I was that sweet, compassionate woman you envision in your head, but I'm not."

He didn't laugh at her, and she was grateful. She wanted him to know the truth of her. Yes, she could be very compassionate and empathetic, but she had other traits in her as well. Just as Whitney had enhanced Jonas, he had enhanced her. She was already a fighter.

"When I heard about Marigold and her illness, I thought the same thing you did —

that the healer in me needed to help her — but I was reacting to Kaden's illness, not hers."

She made the confession in a little rush. She wanted to get it out so he could go to sleep. Her fingers continued to massage his scalp through his thick hair. His eyes closed again, giving her a good view of his long, thick lashes, lashes no man should have without them making him look somewhat feminine. That just didn't happen with Jonas. He had an unrelenting harshness about his face that kept him looking far too rough to be anything but what he was — a dangerous predator.

"How does this make you think you have a bad side?"

That soft drowsy note coupled with his rough growl kicked her heart rate into overdrive and sent feminine hormones raging. She did her best to counter. Both of them were exhausted, and she knew if she committed to him physically, she would try to keep their relationship focused on sex so she wouldn't have to let him in any deeper. Or maybe it would be just the opposite. She didn't know. She only knew that Jonas was already getting past her many defenses, and the idea of becoming completely vulnerable to him was frightening if she thought too much about it.

With a little sigh, she leaned her head against the back of the lounge and closed her eyes as she continued to massage his scalp. His hair was thick and soft, almost like the pelt of an animal. She knew his hair probably grew wild due to the enhancements Whitney had done on him.

The lounge was comfortable, built for a large man and wider than most couches. The sound of the wind blowing through the trees coupled with the scent of Jonas surrounding her made Camellia feel secure in a way she hadn't for a long time. Not that she hadn't felt safe with Middlemist Red and the underground mycelium network, as well as her sentries, the owls and wolves. It was the camaraderie of having another human close to her — connected to her. She had missed being touched. She'd forgotten what that felt like, the tactile experience. She couldn't get enough of just having her fingers in Jonas's thick hair. Rubbing his scalp. Easing the ache she knew was there. She liked being able to do that for him.

Jonas reached up and ran his finger down Camellia's bare arm. He didn't think he'd ever get over how soft her skin was. He'd never get enough of touching her. He didn't open his eyes, just inhaled her and took her into his lungs. He loved the way she smelled. So subtle. To him, that faint fragrance was an aphrodisiac. But more than that, she smelled like home.

There was beauty to Camellia that she didn't see in herself at all. Whitney had told her how useless she was. The one person she believed in, the one person she'd dared to love as family, had betrayed her. That made her feel as though she was nothing. A throwaway, just as Whitney had told her she was. Jonas knew better. Camellia was . . . extraordinary. A miracle.

He had no idea how he'd gotten lucky enough to have any chance with her at all, but he was determined to proceed carefully, choosing his way as if walking through a minefield, because he knew her value. He wasn't going to chance losing her. He'd given her the opportunity to walk away from him twice. He'd done that for her. There had been a part of him that was well aware of how she might be treated when they arrived at the compound. He didn't want that for her. She'd stayed. She'd chosen him. That meant he needed to always give her his best.

"Jonas," Camellia murmured his name softly. Almost a groan. "Stop. I'm not that wonderful. See me. The real me. Don't put me on a pedestal. I need to be a real person to you, not some saint I can't possibly live up to."

Her fingers worked magic in his scalp and in his mind, helping to push the night's work to a distance. Interrogations were brutal, especially with someone like Crawley. He'd been arrogant, determined to resist. So certain he was better than they were. Smarter. They couldn't possibly break him.

First, Jeff could get into anyone's head. That was just ugly right there. Jonas could physically break anyone, and that was as vicious as it got. Then there was Gator with his sound that cut through a body and turned insides to mush, literally. Put all three together and Crawley told them everything he knew. None of it had been good, but they knew what they were facing. Jonas was going to have to live with what they'd done to try to save their families, and it wouldn't sit easy with him.

"I don't want a saint, Camellia. I'm so far from a saint it's not funny. A saint wouldn't be able to be in the same room with me."

They'd had this discussion before. He knew it was important to her, or she wouldn't keep bringing it up. He wasn't going to dismiss her concerns, even though he knew they weren't valid. He did see her. The problem was she didn't see herself the way she really was. That was true of so many people. Perhaps even him. He tried to turn the spotlight on himself and be realistic, but it was always possible he missed the mark.

"Look what's in my mind. See me, Jonas. I don't want to have to tell you. Not tonight when the night is so beautiful."

Her voice shook just a little, but her fingers were steady, never wavering. She didn't need to make her confession aloud to him. He saw, in her mind, what she considered her worst shame. She shared it with him. She didn't want him to come to her, to accept her as a partner, without realizing she held grudges and she could be ruthless.

Jonas wanted to smile. Ruthless. His little Camellia thought herself ruthless. She could be when she needed to, and that was a good thing. She would defend their children. Their home. Herself. She wasn't afraid to go after an enemy. She wouldn't wince or argue when he did what needed to be done. She would go into battle with him and create the best illusions and never falter when he killed inside those illusions. So yeah, he supposed that she could call herself ruthless if she wanted. Those things might earn her that title in someone's book. Not his. But someone's.

He searched further to see what she was really trying to show him about herself, although he was certain he already knew. This confession was about Marigold. About betrayal.

Camellia had been exhausted after staying up all night — running, jogging, running more — to get the prisoner to the compound. Then she'd healed Kaden. That had taken more hours. She had nothing left and desperately needed sleep. Instead of taking care of her own needs, she'd gone straight to Lily, a woman she really didn't know and shouldn't have cared about. But she had cared. She cared enough to sit with her and let her talk.

She hadn't condemned Lily for her actions as most people would have. Lily had brought the GhostWalkers to the brink of a war. She had placed her marriage in jeopardy. She'd risked her son. There was that ugly word: "betrayal." Camellia knew all about it, and yet she had sat with Lily on the floor in a hallway and listened to her side of things and tried to comfort her.

"Jonas." Camellia wailed his name and tugged his hair.

He had a lot of hair, so she got a fistful. She didn't hurt him though. She was too conscious that his head was pounding — that sharp spikes had been jammed deep into his brain, and his blood roared and thundered in his ears. She'd been pulling those spikes out one by one with her firm massage.

He laughed softly because Camellia was a badass when it was necessary, but she wasn't at all what she thought she was. "I'm getting there, honey. Give me a chance. I can't help it if you do mostly good things."

He casually caught her fist, pried her fingers open and brought her hand to his mouth. He'd planned on just kissing her knuckles, but he was very oral. He was leopard. Wolf. A lot of other things that demanded he pull each one of her fingers into his mouth and use his tongue to commit the shape and texture of her delicate digits to his memory. The pads of her fingers, the shape of each finger, her thumb, her knuckles. Skin like satin. Where were the calluses she should have? He felt strength in her hands each time she touched him, yet right at that moment, her fingers felt so fine and fragile, as if he could snap each bone in two with one quick bite of his teeth.

Reluctantly, he went back to his first idea and planted a kiss on each knuckle before returning her hand to her. Her fingers settled back on his scalp, pressing deep. Moving to his temples, down to the nape of his neck, following the worst of the knots.

"You're making my head feel better. Thank you, Camellia. I can't tell you how much I appreciate it." No one had done that for him before. He couldn't remember feeling as if he had a home once he'd lost his parents.

"Keep looking, Jonas. You need to see me."

It was there, when she was sitting on the floor with Lily, talking with her about Ryland and realizing there was such a huge break in trust. Lily had her reasons. She was hurt over something Ryland said to her. Lily wanted to be a mother, not a scientist. In her mind, she somehow made the excuse that her decision made sense and was okay when it wasn't. Still, Jonas saw into Camellia. She wanted Ryland to forgive Lily. She felt everything that had come before in their relationship should count for more than one bad choice.

His Camellia was soft inside when she thought she was hard. She had tried to develop a hard shell around that softness to protect herself because the hurt of betrayal had been horrific. She didn't want to go through that kind of emotional pain ever again. She didn't see that she was protecting herself, she only saw that she didn't want to look at Marigold. She didn't want to go see her.

Camellia took that as if she were refusing to heal Marigold because she couldn't forgive her betrayal. Jonas knew better. If his woman laid eyes on Marigold, her resolve would fold immediately. He knew it would. He saw inside her where she was vulnerable. He opened his eyes and looked up at her. She was watching him, waiting for his judgment. She really didn't see herself at all.

The moment their eyes met, his body reacted. It wasn't just his cock; his heart went crazy, a wild peculiar sensation that was almost painful. It felt as though the actual organ just melted, dissolved right there in his chest. His gut somersaulted. She was branded deep, stamped right into his bones. Into his heart. It was the strangest feeling, thrilling and terrifying all at once.

"You never have to worry, Camellia. Not when you're with me. I do see inside you. Right into that sweet place where you're so damn soft. Anyone wants to hurt you, they'll have to come through me."

He had to close his eyes because the feeling he had for her was too intense, too overwhelming.

"My father loved my mother and me. Really loved us," he murmured. He didn't know why he told her. Maybe because the wind was blowing so softly across his face, feeling like a caress. Or because her fingers were still massaging when she should have been too tired to make the effort. He reached up and caught her wrist, bringing their clasped hands to his heart.

"I grew up in the circus. Did I tell you that? It wasn't a huge circus, but everyone was very talented. We were like a huge family."

"That sounds amazing, Jonas. Every child's secret dream. Is that where you got your unbelievable balance and reflexes?"

"Yes. My parents started working with me when I was a toddler. We had a high-wire act, as well as a knife-throwing act. Also, a combination of the two."

"Dangerous."

"It would have been if we didn't know what we were doing, but we practiced day and night. We never took unnecessary risks. My father was a big believer in hard work and never showing off. So we worked hard and we didn't show off. He was head of the family and we followed his lead. He said something, it was law, not because he ruled with an iron fist but because he'd earned our respect."

Camellia's free hand was back in his hair, smoothing it from his forehead in little caresses that felt unbelievably like true caring. He could get used to this. The two of them. Having her close while he drifted off to sleep.

"I bet you looked really cute in a leotard. Was yours glittery and spangly?"

The teasing note would have gotten her retaliation of a very sexual nature any other time, but he was going slow with her. Giving her time to get used to their relationship. He wasn't certain how much more time he could give her, but she was safe for the next fifteen minutes at least.

"I look great in a leotard. Especially the glittery kind."

"I'll just bet you do. At least the ladies would think so."

They had. He wasn't going to admit that to her or lie about it either. He found himself smiling. "I'll get one just for you. There must be one of the beams I can walk on to show you the act."

"Do you still remember it?"

"I watched my parents practically from

409

the time I was born and then participated around the age of three and up in one way or another. Yeah, honey, I remember. I practice with knives daily. It's a habit."

"That's because you're bloodthirsty, not because you want to run away and join the circus again." She laughed, the sound melodic, adding to the music made by the rustling of the leaves in the trees.

He rubbed the pad of his thumb back and forth across the back of her hand. He had a large hand, much larger than hers, and he managed to cover a lot of her skin. "They rarely fought. Not often. They were passionate and always together, always touching and kissing. He'd suddenly just swing her up into the air, and she'd laugh and I'd laugh. He used to carry me around on his shoulders. He'd tell me that when he was an old man, I'd be carrying him."

"That sounds so lovely, Jonas."

"It was. I was lucky. I can't ever remember my father striking me, and he was a really protective man. Off-the-charts protective. He could get angry and violent very fast with outsiders if they messed with any of our people. If there was ever any kind of fight, the moment he came on the scene, it was over. No one wanted to fight him."

He rubbed her fingers over his chest. Over

his heart. "That's just some of what Whitney saw in me. What he enhanced in me. The protective trait. The violent trait."

"What happened to your parents, Jonas? Where are they?"

He had known she would ask and that he would tell her. He hadn't expected it to hurt as much as it did. He was a grown man. He'd distanced himself from it a long time ago, and yet now, just thinking about it, putting it into words for her, bringing the images back into his mind, it hurt like hell. It hurt the way it had in the days and weeks after he'd lost them.

"We all helped one another out. That was just the way it was. One of the big rigs had broken down, and my dad and I were helping fix the engine. We were a distance from where the others had stopped. Mom had parked our camper up about half a mile from us in some shade. It was hot as hell. Someone had told us there was a little stream with a swimming hole large enough for us to cool off in. A few of the kids were hiking through the trees just past Mom's camper to look for the stream."

His gut clenched hard. He could still hear his mother's screams. First there had been silence broken occasionally by his father's voice asking for a tool. Then the screams of sheer terror — of agony. Jonas would never forget that sound for as long as he lived. Sometimes he awoke hearing those screams echo through whatever room he was in.

"She screamed. My mother. She screamed like the world was coming to an end. My father took off running so fast I couldn't keep up with him. I remember seeing birds lifting off the branches of trees, startled by the sound of her screaming. Then the kids were screaming, the ones who had gone looking for the swimming hole. There was so much noise coming at me from all directions. Adults were running from the other cars and rigs toward our camper."

Camellia's hand had gone very still, but it was buried in his hair. He could feel her trembling, as if she knew what he was about to tell her. His mouth had gone dry. His throat ached. Felt raw. His eyes burned with unshed tears.

"Honey," she whispered softly. "I'm here with you." Her fingers trailed briefly over his face. So gentle. Almost tender. It was nothing less than a caress. "You aren't alone."

"I got there, but I didn't see anyone. Not my father or mother. But then the camper sort of rocked. I heard a grunt. Then another. A sob, not my mother's, but a man's.

I opened the camper door. There was blood everywhere. Soaking into the floor. On the walls, the curtains. Splattered all over the chairs and up the sides of the counters. I could even see splashes on the windows. The table was smashed right down the middle, and the seats around it were crushed."

At first her hands were still, then the one in his hair smoothed back strands from his forehead very gently, almost tenderly. Her breath hitched in her throat. "Your mother?"

"I could just see part of her nude body covered in blood lying under the smashed dining table. My father had gone insane. He beat her assailant to death with his fists. The man still had a gun in one hand and a knife in the other, but my father just ripped him to shreds. He was like a wild beast, and no one could tame him, not even me. He was so wild with grief that when I tried to get into the camper to go to Mom, he turned on me. The others pulled me out. Then the cops were there."

His face felt damp. He used the edge of her hand to brush down his face to clear it, then put her hand in his mouth, sucking at the fleshy part where he'd dragged it over his cheekbone.

"To be fair, the cops didn't know who

413

killed my mother. We were all shouting at once. The kids were crying. The animals were roaring and acting up. The heat was unbearable. My dad had the gun and the knife, and there was blood all over him. He paced back and forth like a wild beast, and then would go to my mother and lift her into his arms."

"How terrible for all of you."

Camellia was crying, weeping for him and his parents. His soft woman. He knew her. Knew the inside of her.

"The cops ordered him to put the weapons down and to come out with his hands up. He wouldn't. He wouldn't leave her. I truly think he was insane right then, unable to hear anything any of us said. I tried to get to him, but the cops and my circus family wouldn't let me near the camper. He suddenly turned toward them, the gun in his hand. I know he wouldn't have shot them, but they opened fire and he went down. I lost them both that day. He crawled to her. He had one arm around her waist and his head on her heart when they went in. She'd been stabbed over forty times."

"Do they know who the man was and why he killed her?"

Jonas found her hand smoothing his temples and caressing his hair, something he wanted to drift off to sleep with for the rest of his life.

"Later, the kids told the cops that one of the young girls, Betsy — she was eight — was being dragged by her hair through the trees from the swimming hole to a car. Mom intercepted them and got Betsy free. She told her to run. Betsy ran, but she saw the man pull a gun on Mom. He walked Mom to the camper. Betsy ran to get her parents, but they were a good distance away. They were the ones who called the cops."

Camellia was quiet for a long time. "I'm so sorry, Jonas. Your mother was a heroine, saving a child."

"Yes, she was. She did the right thing and it got her killed. My father rushed to save her and it got him killed. I lost them both because they did the right thing. They acted heroic."

"Would you have had them act differently?"

He sighed. "No."

"You're just like them, Jonas. You would go up the mountain and take on the army in order to stop them from coming here to take Lily and Daniel. That's the kind of man you are because you come from them."

"I have nightmares," he confessed. "Even now."

"That's the kind of trauma that stays with you. The good thing is, you also have so many wonderful memories that horrible man can never take from you."

"He managed to overshadow the good memories for a very long time." He rubbed his thumb along her knuckles. "He still does," he admitted.

"Then we'll have to make it a priority to see that he doesn't. I'll ask you to tell me something you did with your parents as often as I can. I didn't have parents, so you'll have to share yours with me. That way, I'll get to know them."

He liked the sound of that. If she got to know his parents, she could tell stories to their children. He wanted his parents to be alive to his children. He had photographs and videos stored. So much memorabilia from the circus. So many happy memories. He thought about that and what Lily had told Camellia. Kyle had given him the gist of the conversation, and he'd replayed it, looking into Camellia's mind through their connection, on his way to his home. He had judged Lily harshly, and yet he wanted those very things for his children — the photographs and videos that would keep his parents alive for them.

"That sounds fair, honey." He let himself

fall asleep, feeling happier and more at peace than he had since his parents died. Camellia might not realize it yet, but her declaration meant she had decided to stay with him.

14

Jonas lifted Camellia into his arms, liking the way she turned into his body, her arms sliding around his neck. Kicking the front door closed behind him, he strode through his house straight to the master bedroom.

He'd had two erotic dreams the short while they'd been on the verandah. Two. He rarely had even one dream at night, let alone two of them. But apparently Camellia turned him on whether he was awake or not.

Both dreams had ripped him from sleep, his body on fire — a painful, heavy, brutal desire that had turned his cock to absolute steel. He'd never been so full or so hard. The zipper of his jeans was the only thing holding the roaring beast back, and he knew that second dream was going to be the death of him if he didn't take control of the situation.

He had slipped into the house and showered, making it short, the hot water striking his skin so that he felt every drop sizzling through to his bones. It was an odd reaction — again, one he'd never had before. He found himself fisting his cock, desperate for relief, but it quickly became apparent he damn well wasn't getting any that way. Frustrated, and so hard it was painful, he returned to the bedroom where his woman stood near the bed.

"You smell good." Camellia rubbed her face in his neck like a cat. "I had dreams about you last night."

Locked behind his rigid zipper, his cock pulsed and jerked, his heartbeat pounding through the blood already forcing the denim into a desperate bulge. "What kind of dreams?" His voice was so hoarse he barely recognized it. Lowering her bare feet to the floor, he caught the hem of her shirt. "Arms up."

She obeyed without hesitation.

Jonas dragged the shirt over her head, balled the material into his fist and tossed it into the corner of the room. His breath caught in his throat as he looked down at her. He knew she had curves under her clothes, her breasts were beautiful to him. Staggering. Round and jutting out, her nipples taut perfection.

"Woman, you are the sexiest thing I've

ever laid eyes on." He bent his head and took her left breast into his mouth while his hands dropped to the waist of her leggings. He just wanted one taste to see how she reacted to his possession.

Her arms cradled his head, her entire body shivering. He caught her nipple gently between his teeth, bit down for a brief moment and then sucked the sting away before pulling his head back to pay attention to her leggings. Little goosebumps rose on her skin. He liked that her endorphins responded that fast to his touch.

"Need to get rid of these. Get them off you."

Her breathing had gone ragged and she nodded. "The material feels like it's almost burning my skin."

He knew the feeling. That was the way the water in the shower had felt when it touched him. He was that desperate for her. The drive to be with her was all-consuming. "Tell me about your dreams," he demanded again as he peeled the leggings down over her hips.

He crouched as he took the fabric down the length of her legs to her ankles. Camellia placed a hand on his shoulder and lifted one leg so he could tug until he pulled the cloth free. As her foot touched the floor, she lifted the other leg as he braced her. Before she could put her foot back to the floor, he caught her leg behind the knee and lifted it over his shoulder.

"Jonas." His name only. A breathless, broken cry.

"What did you dream, Camellia? Was my cock stretching your lips? The weight of it on your tongue? Did you struggle to take all of me into your pretty mouth? Was that what you dreamt?"

He ran his tongue up the inside of her thigh from her knee to her hot, weeping opening. Her scent was intoxicating. He'd dreamt of feasting on her. Devouring her until she screamed his name, until she never once thought of leaving him.

"Yes," she whispered her reply, one hand fisting in his hair, the other palm anchoring her on the wall to keep herself upright.

He dragged his tongue up her other thigh, just to the very edge of that slit, tasting her this time, those spicy drops that caused scorching heat to rush through both of them.

"Were you kneeling in front of me? Did you have your clothes on?" He didn't wait for her answer. The heady fragrance of her was driving him insane, calling to him. He caught her bottom in his hands and pulled her into him, lifting his head to drive his tongue deep to collect her spice.

A low, keening wail escaped. Fire sizzled through his veins; sparks arced over his skin and down his spine. Her taste fed the brutal need in him to claim her.

Tell me. I want to know exactly what you dreamt.

His hunger grew with every drop he consumed. He wanted to devour her. She bucked against his mouth, and he transferred his hold to her hip, clamping down to hold her in place, and used his other hand to explore.

I can't possibly talk. I can't think.

Show me.

She pushed the vision into his mind of her kneeling in front of him, totally nude, her knees wide so he could see the evidence of her desire for him glistening between her legs. Her nipples were erect, her breasts heavy and round. She had a woman's body, feminine and alluring. Her rib cage was narrow, emphasizing the roundness of her curved hips. The tiny curls covering her mound were the same glossy dark chestnut as her abundance of hair.

Her hands were small, but as they stroked up the inside of his thighs, they left electric charges running through his veins, lighting up every nerve ending in his body. The breath left his body as she cupped his balls and then leaned forward to lick up his shaft.

Camellia let out a small sob and placed both palms flat on the wall, her hips jerking helplessly as he devoured her. "Jonas, please."

He could feel her coiling tighter and tighter. *You have to be ready, honey.*

I'm ready. I'm so ready. I can't wait.

In his mind, her mouth engulfed the head of his cock and his vision blurred. He was beyond ready too. He had never thought it possible he could lose control, especially when she wasn't touching him, but he feared it might happen. He pulled back, wiped his jaw along the insides of her thigh.

Jonas lifted her easily in his arms. All that satin skin moving against his skin. Hotter than hell. Softer than velvet. He had no idea what he'd ever done to deserve her. He planted a knee on the bed and laid her right in the middle of it. Shedding his jeans was imperative. His cock had suffered enough, so full and aching, caged behind the material until he felt rubbed raw.

"Hurry."

He blanketed her body, that soft, feminine body that was all curves and felt like heaven under him. It was his intention to go slow, but he found it impossible. Her body was too tight, too scorching hot. Trying to inch his way inside was both heaven and hell. She dug her fingernails into his shoulders and then caught at his hips.

Jonas eased one of her knees up and guided her leg around his hip. "Relax, Camellia. You're more than ready for me. You want this."

"I do. I do want you. I want us. I have from the moment I first laid eyes on you." Her breath came in ragged pants. She rubbed her palm along his rib cage as if to soothe both of them, but there was no soothing either of them, not when he was using a steady pressure to find his way into her tight, silken heat.

She was beyond every expectation he'd imagined. When he was finally able to bury himself all the way inside her, when they were wearing the same skin, sharing their bodies, he could barely breathe. Fire streaked through him, through her, through their veins. Nerve endings lit up. Rockets went off.

He was careful for the first two orgasms he gave, but then Jonas began to move without inhibition, forgetting to worry about control. Letting himself take her the way he needed, hard and fast, his body a frenzy of brutal strokes. The friction sent waves of fire down his spine, rushing up his thighs, centering in his groin. He didn't want the feeling to ever end.

He caught her hips, fingers biting deep, and drove into all that scorching heat. He felt her body coiling around his. Biting down viciously. Heaven and hell. Then she was crying out his name as her body clamped down viciously on his, strangling his cock, milking ropes of seed from him. He emptied himself into her with hard, fierce jerks of his cock until there was nothing left, and he collapsed over the top of her, burying his face in her neck, fighting just to breathe.

Jonas had no idea how long he lay there before he was able to kiss her behind her ear and roll off of her so he wouldn't suffocate her. "Can you breathe?"

"I think so."

"Give me a minute, and I'll get a washcloth and glass of water. I don't think I can move yet."

She laughed softly. "I think you wore us both out. Who knew it would be like that with us?"

"I knew." He had known. He turned his head. "You should have known too."

That little laugh of hers came again,

galvanizing him into action. He rolled off the bed and procured the water and a warm washcloth, handing the glass to her but handling the washcloth duty himself, which made her laugh again. He loved that laugh. She stayed on the bed after drinking the water, with just the sheet over her. Personally, he didn't see the need for that, so he removed it.

"Are you aware that the plants you have growing right off your front porch are very rare camellias?" she asked, turning her head to look at him.

She looked sated lying on her stomach, her lashes at half mast, her features soft. Jonas slid his hand possessively from the nape of her neck down her spine to the curve of her bottom. He knew he would never take it for granted that she was in his bed.

He shook his head. It wasn't that he doubted her. She obviously knew her plants, but even though he only had a very basic knowledge of camellias, and he knew there was a wide variety, his home was at a high altitude, and every winter, there was deep snow to contend with.

"I haven't done any landscaping yet. There shouldn't be anything growing close to the house. The winters are harsh, and I need to really study which plants will thrive at this elevation. I also want to make certain I have protection around the house — ground cover, but nothing that will impede my view from the windows."

"Nevertheless, you have quite a few shrubs growing, and they are camellias. Rare ones. I thought you planted them." She turned her face back to the pillow. "I'm getting hungry. Do you have groceries here, or do you always eat at the main compound?"

"I keep groceries here. I have a little greenhouse out back. I like fresh vegetables. Ian makes fun of me all the time, but he raids my greenhouse."

She turned back to look at him. "He makes fun of you for growing veggies?"

"Mostly because I put in the greenhouse before the house was finished. And I slept in it a few times."

Her eyebrow shot up.

He laughed. "Okay, quite a few times. The greenhouse was the warmest place I had at the time, and there was food inside. Ian caught on after a while. He has this really cool ability to see through walls, so he always knew when the tomatoes were ripe or the cucumbers were ready. I locked my greenhouse on multiple occasions. Darned if my best produce wasn't stolen anyway. I put cameras in there, didn't tell a single soul, mostly because I suspected he was the culprit. He's big too. You've seen him. It's not like he can hide that easily."

Camellia reached out and gently ran her finger down his face. That little caress was light. He normally avoided anyone touching him, always feeling like a cat with its fur rubbed the wrong way, but with her, it was just the opposite. She managed to make him feel cared for with just a single brush of her finger.

"Did the camera catch him?" Her hand dropped away.

Jonas resisted capturing her wrist and bringing her fingers back to his face. He didn't want to appear obsessed with her, although he was afraid it might be too late. "Not exactly. The camera was trained on the door. The door never opened. I realized later that the positioning of the camera was a big mistake, but it took a long time for me to wrap my head around the fact that Ian might have bigger secrets than any of us knew. I don't know why, since all of us have them. Why shouldn't he? It's just that he always appears so easygoing."

"Does he? He didn't seem easygoing to me," Camellia objected. She rolled over, sat up and looked around his bedroom. "Where did you throw my clothes?"

"Do you need clothes?"

"I object to cooking without them and I'm hungry. But keep talking about Ian and the greenhouse. Was it really Ian stealing your produce?"

"Don't like the idea of you covering up," Jonas disapproved. He was up immediately though, catching up her shirt where he'd tossed it into the corner. "I can get one of my tees, Camellia. I should have taken more care with your clothes. This is wrinkled. We can hang it in the shower and the steam will take care of it."

"Thanks, that sounds good." She took the leggings from him and the clean T-shirt he pulled from one of the built-in drawers. "Get back to Ian and the greenhouse. You have me intrigued."

"He especially loves fresh berries. I grow them at one end of the greenhouse. He's always going after the berries."

Jonas pulled on his jeans and turned to watch her slide off the bed. She moved with fluid grace, the curves of her body so sexy beneath his thin tee. There was no hiding her breasts or hips even with his large tee. It might be long, but it clung to her very feminine shape. He held out his hand to her.

As a young child, he had observed his father constantly putting his arm around his mother. Around her waist. Draping his arm around her shoulders. Coming up behind her and locking both arms around her, high, just under her breasts. He held her hand every chance he got. He would lean in for a kiss. Sometimes the kiss would be just a brush of their lips. Other times he would really kiss her, pulling her tight against his body. He danced with her in their kitchen. By the campfire. After they practiced their act together.

Jonas had loved watching them together. He had never been like other children, finding the way his parents were together "gross." Maybe it was because his father taught him that expressing love for his mother was a good thing. Healthy and right. His father was open about loving his mother and loving him. He always told Jonas that the physical side of love was as important as the emotional, and not to neglect his woman. To show her she was loved in every way.

Jonas had never felt the need to be continually touching a woman. He'd never wanted to wake up next to one or go to sleep beside one — until now. Now, everything was different. He didn't want Camellia out of his

sight. For the first time, he truly understood why his father always wanted to touch his mother, why he wanted to be with her. It wasn't about controlling her or possessing her. It was about loving her and feeling driven to keep her safe.

"Tell me Ian didn't steal your berries? That's kind of sacrilegious." His woman was laughing her contagious laugh, so clearly she didn't consider Ian's sins too sacrilegious.

"He stole them," Jonas confirmed. "Every time the berries got ripe, he'd know because he could look right through the walls and see them. He never once came through the door. Eventually, I caught a glimpse of something moving in the greenhouse and realized I had the camera in the wrong place, and I added a second one on the berries."

Jonas loved the wide-open spaces of his home, the high ceilings and the banks of windows. Once out of the master bedroom, one room flowed straight into the next. The kitchen was large so he could move around when he was in it.

He liked cooking for his friends. That was another trait he'd gotten from his circus family. They'd often eaten together. Both his mother and father had prepared meals, and it was clear they'd enjoyed it. They always included Jonas when they were prepping, cooking or grilling. Because his parents made it fun, he'd always perceived cooking as enjoyable. It was one of the few things that he found soothing. Whitney had taken that from him, but he could still cook for a couple of his friends at a time, and he made the most of it.

He began pulling out his skillets and bowls to make omelets. "I saw Ian come through the wall. Actually come *through* it. It was like something out of a movie. I could see it took a toll on him. It wasn't easy and he had to go through without clothing. One arm appeared to be very twisted and misshapen. He sat on the floor for nearly an hour, shaking. It was stupid of him to do it without someone watching over him."

He knew his tone was perfect. No anxiety whatsoever. His expression was the same, completely deadpan. Unreadable. With anyone else, it would have worked, but Camellia was so connected to him, she saw inside his head. She knew Ian had terrified him with what he was doing.

"Did you confront him?"

Jonas pulled open the door to the refrigerator so he wouldn't have to look at her. "That was my first thought. I realized after

I got over my initial shock that he was just like the rest of us. He was practicing in what he considered a safe place without anyone around in order to perfect a new ability he'd discovered. He didn't want anyone knowing until he could control it."

He pulled out the ingredients he needed for the omelets. "You can choose what you want in yours, and I'll throw it together."

"But it was so dangerous, Jonas."

He nodded. "Yeah. I did take precautions. I made a point of trying to track his movements more closely. That way, I'd know if he was on his way here. I also put in a silent alarm so I'd know when he was trying his skills if I missed him before he got here. When I was leaving for a few days, I wasn't too worried because we'd be a few men down, and he'd have too many assignments to use the opportunity to get into the greenhouse."

Camellia tilted her head to look up at him. "You always think the worst of yourself, but just the fact that you were so careful of Ian's feelings and gave him the room to practice his skills in a relatively safe environment while you looked after him shows what kind of man you are."

"Since I've decided I want you to always see me as heroic and wonderful, I'll let you think that." He sent her a quick grin. "Although if I'm being strictly truthful with you, my actions fall under my need to protect family, which Ian is to me."

She watched as he chopped vegetables, the knife flashing fast as he made short work of the variety she'd indicated she liked.

"You really are fast with that thing." She seemed fascinated. "I can barely see the blade."

He lifted the knife and indicated the target on the wall across the room. "Sometimes I get distracted."

Camellia made her way across the room to look up at the target. "Um, Jonas, it looks to me as if you never hit anywhere but the exact center."

"That's the idea."

"That's no fun. In fact, I would say it's far too easy if you're always hitting the same exact spot. Muscle memory and all that sort of thing." There was a hint of challenge in her voice.

He looked up from where he was pouring the eggs into an omelet pan. "What does that mean?" Her eyes were sparkling with mischief, and his belly reacted, doing a hard clench and then a long drop. She got to him every single time.

She shrugged. "Just that it seems like it

might be easy to hit the exact same place on the target if you're always aiming for it every time you're in the kitchen. That omelet looks delicious."

"You're changing the subject on purpose."

Her laughter was inviting as she wandered over to the bay of windows and looked out. "You have more shrubs out here as well, Jonas. They're growing right under the window."

He glanced out the window and frowned. He'd never planted any landscaping, no flowers or shrubbery. He'd wanted the ground clean so he could see enemies coming at him. But she was right, there were plants growing up just outside the bank of kitchen windows. They weren't small either. It appeared they'd been growing for some time.

He pushed her omelet onto a plate and flipped his, which was cooking in a separate pan. "I think maybe someone in the team, most likely Ian, is playing a prank on me. I was here before I left to go up the mountain only a few days ago, looking right out these very same windows, and there were no shrubs. If there were, they were barely peeking through the soil, not even enough for me to notice them."

"Mmm. That must be it." Camellia collected her plate and silverware and sat down at the table. While he finished cooking his omelet, she stared out the window at the glossy leaves. A tiny smile curled the edges of her mouth. "They are beautiful, aren't they? Look at all the buds on them."

He growled at her. He'd perfected the growl, thanks to the animals Whitney saw fit to include in his enhancements. He was pleased to see goosebumps rising on her skin. She lifted her chin at him, and her eyes showed her laughter, but she couldn't hide her response to his aggression. She liked it.

He set his plate on the table and sat down across from her. "Why do I think you know far more than you're telling me?"

Her eyebrow went up. "Why would you think I would know about the landscaping on your property when I've never been here before?"

There was that little enigmatic smile again, the one that told him she knew exactly what he was talking about. She liked teasing him, and he liked her teasing just a little too much.

Camellia took her first bite of omelet. "Mmm. This is really good."

"One of my many talents." He grinned and took his own large bite. Cheesy, savory goodness melted on his tongue, reminding him of how long it had been since he'd eaten. He tucked into his meal and didn't stop until his plate was clean.

Leaning back in his chair, he eyed Camellia across the table. "It's time you give me the rundown on what you did for Kaden, Camellia. That wasn't the same as a psychic healer, at least not according to any of the explanations I've ever heard. You used the same method healing him that you did when you helped Kyle when he was using the eyes of the owl to spy on Crawley and his men, didn't you?"

She nodded slowly, finishing off her omelet. She pushed the empty plate toward the middle of the table and took a drink of water before she sank back in the chair. "I don't have a psychic healing talent the way Ryland expected me to. Or you for that matter. That isn't the way my gift works. You have a bit of talent yourself, Jonas. You just haven't discovered or developed it yet. Didn't you feel it when you were connected to me when I was working on Kaden?"

"Yes." There was no denying it. He had. "But whatever gift I have is nothing compared to yours. Even if I worked at it day and night, I'd never come close to your ability. It's possible, since Whitney paired us, that my talent is more of a support system

437

for yours."

Her brows came together in that little frown he found far too adorable. Adorable. What the hell kind of word was that for a man like him? It suited that look though — and her. She could melt him so easily. Her dark lashes fluttered, went down, covering her blue eyes, and then lifted so he found himself drowning there. Small white teeth bit at the side of her lower lip for a moment.

"That's a possibility I never considered, Jonas. Are you sure your healing gift isn't the same? Maybe you just need to practice more."

"Think about it, honey. I know you were caught up in what you were doing, but did it feel as if I could have actually saved Kaden without you?"

More frowning and biting on her lip. The long lashes veiled her eyes while she replayed the healing session in her mind. Jonas was right there with her, but he kept his distance. She fascinated him the way she remembered every detail. He was able to see more clearly how the various elements in the bloodstream had rushed to Kaden's defense. She had marshaled Kaden's body's natural defenses but also used others. Where had she gotten them?

She hadn't just manufactured them out of thin air.

"You're using abilities given to you from Middlemist Red," he guessed. "The properties she has in her. Whitney suspected all along she possessed far more benefits than oils to be used for skin care or antiaging. Does she give you the ability to create the mist and the illusions in it?"

Camellia nodded. "Yes."

"She's the reason we can hide in the mist."

"Absolutely."

Jonas drummed his fingers on the table. "Do you know why Middlemist Red disappeared all at once when she used to be so plentiful in China?"

Again, Camellia nodded slowly. "Plants communicate with one another, and Red is extremely advanced. She uses the mycelium network to reach out to trees and plants for miles, not to take over the world, as some came to suspect, but to ensure the health of the plants. Humans became suspicious and she caught wind of a conspiracy to burn the camellias down. To prevent that, she had them all disappear."

"How?"

"She took them underground. Just as she did in England when the Nazi bombs blew out the windows to the conservatory and let in the freezing cold air. She took all the rare camellias underground with her, where they could stay warmer and survive."

Jonas sat back in his chair and regarded his woman. "That is one scary plant, Camellia. I can see why people would fear her. Do you think Whitney had any idea of what he was actually dealing with?"

"Not a chance. He doesn't like anyone smarter than he is. Can you imagine if he thought a plant was more intelligent? He sure wouldn't have taken a chance putting Red in our DNA."

"What do you think he was hoping for?" Jonas asked. "Anti-aging?"

"I think he believed she might have some healing properties, but nothing nearly as advanced as she does. He may have suspected she had some ability to communicate as well, but he had no idea of her true abilities. He had theories, but he changed them all the time. He wanted to know how she survived when other plants died out."

"Longevity then?"

Camellia shrugged. "Whitney was big on experimenting with anything he thought might help his soldiers survive when the enemy couldn't. He put Middlemist Red in me when I was very young. When nothing happened, he operated a second time when

I was around ten. I remember being very ill. After that, he watched me like I was an insect under a microscope. He brought me to his office once a week and into the greenhouse — or as he referred to it, the hothouse — at least once a week. I think he thought the plant would react to me or I would to the plant."

"You felt nothing?"

"I felt her gathering power. She doesn't feel rage in the way we do. She feels disgust."

"What does she do when she feels this disgust?" Jonas couldn't help the wariness creeping into his voice. He was used to being at the top of the food chain. But now, he had the feeling he wasn't quite as high up as he had envisioned himself.

Camellia stood up and stretched, raising her arms above her head before reaching for her plate to take it to the sink. He suspected she was buying herself time before she answered him. He would know if she lied to him — or even deflected.

"Camellia?"

She turned to face him, leaning against the sink. "I just told you what she did when she was disgusted. You weren't listening — or you didn't want to hear. You do it too. So do I. We both have Middlemist Red in us. I might have more of her, but you have far more natural aggression in you than I do. She allows you to draw on that when you gather power."

Jonas pushed back his chair and paced away from her. She stated it so softly, almost gently — matter-of-factly, as if a plant gathering power didn't mean anything — but it did, and they both knew it. Middlemist Red was a weapon. Pure and simple. He kept his breathing under control as he paced, trying to keep his thoughts from going to places Camellia would be upset with him for going.

She watched his agitated motion with a slight frown on her face. "Honey, why would you think this is any different than you or me being disgusted with an evil person doing evil things and reacting to it? You accept that a leopard retaliates against something or someone hunting it. Or that a wolf pack does. You utilize the strengths of those animals. You admire the cunning intelligence of them. Why is it so much more difficult for you to accept that Red might react to Whitney's evil?"

Jonas had to think about that. Why was it so much more upsetting? He looked out the kitchen window at the plants that hadn't been there before. They could effectively block his sight if an enemy was coming. Even as he thought it, the branches parted to show him a clear, unobstructed view. Just as the plant had reacted to his thoughts when he'd been in Camellia's garden, the ones outside his kitchen reacted to his. How was that even possible?

"I can understand how Whitney managed to insert animal DNA into us, Camellia, but plant? I don't know. I'm not a science expert like a couple of the others. Some of it, like the communications network, I can get that even on some small level. I get the healing maybe because I can visualize it. But the way the plants react when I'm thinking . . ." He trailed off, shaking his head.

"We're connected to them." She sighed and shoved both hands through her hair. "When I first escaped, I didn't want Whitney to ever be able to take me back to his laboratories. Not ever. I wasn't going into his breeding program. No child of mine was going to have to go through what I did. No son was going to grow up a soldier the way he wanted him to be. And no daughter of mine was going to be used for his purposes. I knew, sooner or later, he'd find me. That was inevitable. I moved often to buy myself time, but also so I could get stronger."

There was something in her voice that warned him. Jonas stopped moving and went very still, nearly fading into the wall behind him. He kept his gaze fixed on her expressive face. There was so much passion there. So much determination. His woman. Camellia. Little did Whitney know the warrior he'd created. The man had been so certain women were inferior. All along he had evidence to the contrary, but he refused to see it because he was so certain of his preconceived beliefs.

"I always loved gardening. Always. I also loved ecology and botany. I studied mycology. I found all the subjects so fascinating. I had no idea why, and all the other girls thought I was a little crazy. They kept asking me how that was going to benefit me. It made no sense to them, because I excelled at tracking and using just about any kind of weapon. The point I'm making is this: all those studies came in handy when I found myself alone and in need of figuring out how I was going to defeat Whitney when he sent a team of his supersoldiers against me."

"Not sure what mycology is, but how did botany, gardening and ecology studies help you plan to escape Whitney's soldiers?"

"Mycology is the study of fungi. The various properties, genetic and biochemical, and the uses for healing or eating. Or just the opposite, the dangers for toxicity or even death. Botany is the study of plants. Ecology is pretty much what it sounds like, the relationships between living organisms."

She was telling him something right there, and it was very important. She looked at him in a way that said his little Camellia was as lethal as they came. He loved her even more for that.

"Are you telling me that you developed your own army of plants?"

"Not exactly an army. There are plants all over the world that possess all kinds of ways of protecting themselves or striking back at their enemies, whether insect, mammal, reptile or human. But no, I didn't utilize any of those because I didn't have them at my disposal, nor would I have had the necessary time to mutate them. Instead, I decided to develop weapons."

Jonas folded his arms across his chest. She was quite small in comparison to his larger frame, but she was no less dangerous. Everyone, him included, had underestimated her. "You're really amazing, Camellia. Keep talking. What exactly did you develop, and how?"

"Some types of mushrooms are already toxic, but they take a bit of time to work and have to be ingested in most cases for the subject to actually die. That wasn't going to help me in a fight. I had to figure Whitney would send a five-man team after me. That's if I was lucky. So I had to plan to face a minimum of ten of his enhanced soldiers. I would have to ensure they would go down fast and stay down. Shoving a toxic mushroom down their throats wasn't going to work."

Jonas found himself smiling at the image she pushed into his mind. He could see her leaping into the air, wrapping her legs around a startled soldier's waist as she shoved a mushroom into his mouth.

"The only man whose waist you're going to wrap your legs around is mine."

She rolled her beautiful eyes. "I should have known that would be your reaction. You're supposed to laugh, not growl. You sound like a bear."

"I have bear in me," he acknowledged.

"I did notice that."

He grinned, then directed the conversation back on topic. "Tell me what you developed."

"I needed a much more toxic mushroom, one that would kill them just by breathing in its spores. Only I couldn't have spores that would wind up creating more of the mushrooms that might kill innocent people. It was quite a difficult problem to figure out. Whatever I developed couldn't ever reproduce. Once it was used, even the tiniest pieces of it had to dissolve so there were no traces left. If, for any reason, the body of a downed supersoldier was taken back to Whitney, I couldn't afford to have him know what killed that soldier."

Jonas admired her even more. "You solved the problem?"

"After a lot of work. Red helped me. At least, having quite a bit of Red's properties in me helped. That and my ability to use the communication systems from Red and the underground network."

"You're telling me you have lethal weapons we can use against this coming army to help even the odds."

"Exactly. If we can lay traps for them, we can stop them before they reach the compound, Jonas. The weapons will help. I can lay them out for you, and you can decide whether you want to talk to Ryland about them or not."

"That's generous of you, Camellia, when you know how dangerous it could be. If word were to get out about your talents, you could be in a world of hurt."

"I don't think Ryland or your team wants

anyone to know about me," Camellia said.

Jonas agreed with her. He also wasn't a man many crossed, and he'd made it known he didn't want anyone talking about her. Kaden had made it clear as well. Team One needed a healer. Kaden hoped to convince Camellia to stay.

Camellia reached for her plate and carried it to the sink. "The omelet was delicious. You really are a good cook. I might just stick around for the food."

"Tell the truth, you're sticking around for the sex."

Color rushed up under her skin, but Camellia didn't look away from him. "Well, yes, I suppose I have to admit you've got some skill there as well."

"*Some* skill?" he repeated, pouring warning into his voice.

"Oh dear, is that what I said?"

"I guess I'm going to have to teach you the difference between some skill and master skills. As you're a novice, your ignorance on the subject can be overlooked. We'll get on to those lessons here very soon."

She nodded. "I think that's a good thing. I wouldn't want to make any mistakes. Although I did want to talk to you about your knife skills. It is for your safety. That's important. We could make it interesting by placing small wagers on the outcome."

Her eyes met his, and there was definitely a sensual teasing light there.

"What do you have in mind? And bear in mind, I grew up throwing knives in the circus."

She nodded solemnly. "I have taken that into consideration, but you like to hit the center of the target. We aren't going to do that. We'll call other spots on the target for each other to hit. I think that's fair. No money, by the way. The bet has to be more inventive than that."

Jonas considered the look in her eyes. "If I win, I get to have you at my mercy for as long as I want for the rest of the day. I like to play, honey, and I can keep at it for hours."

"I see." She rubbed her lower lip. "That sounds . . . interesting. If I win, you have to teach me how to give you a proper blow job. The mind-blowing kind. In light of what you just said, it might take me a little while before I get the hang of it."

Jonas groaned and pressed his fingers to the corners of his eyes. He'd never thrown a game in his life. Win or lose, he supposed either way he was going to come out on top, but her bet sounded very promising. Still, he couldn't cheat. That just wasn't in him.

"I think you have a bit of the Tasmanian Devil in you, Camellia Mist," he accused.

She laughed. "You think?"

15

Jonas woke on alert, his warning system flaring to life. The sun had already climbed into the sky, telling him it was midmorning. Camellia was on her side, and he was curled protectively around her, his arm draped possessively around her waist.

"Wake up, honey. We're about to have company. You've got enough time to wash your face." He sat up and immediately tugged her up with him, glancing out the long bank of windows. He hadn't pulled the privacy screens, and he could see into the forest.

A Great Gray owl skimmed about three feet off the ground, flying silently past with soft, slow wingbeats. Jonas paused at the bathroom door, watching its progress into the forest before following Camellia inside.

There was no wasted motion in anything Camellia did. He couldn't help but admire the fluid way she moved and found himself

451

smiling as she struggled to braid her hair. The wild mass refused to be tamed no matter how hard she tried to gather the silky strands and twine them together.

He stepped up behind her and took the dark fall of waves and curls and braided it for her, his gaze on hers in the mirror. "I believe our company are members of Team Two, honey. We haven't even had our coffee yet. Do you want to go into the kitchen and make that for us while I talk to them first?"

Gossip traveled fast, especially when it came to something as huge as a healer in their midst.

Teams Three and Four had both psychic healers and doctors. One and Two didn't have a psychic healer and they desperately needed one. He had made it clear that no one was to talk about Camellia. Ryland had made it clear. He was certain Kaden had decreed it as well. Jeff and Kyle and Gator had all been in the room with them. So had Tansy.

Damn it.

There was no doubt in his mind that Tansy was the one who'd blabbed.

"You need a better sense of humor." Her voice was very soft. She leaned her body against his after he looped the little tie at the end of her braid.

"I have a sense of humor."

"You need a better one. Or maybe you're all snarly and grumpy in the morning because you didn't get much sleep. We had a great day yesterday and a really good night together. We're not going to let them spoil this."

He wrapped his arms around her waist and rubbed his chin on top of her head. "All of those things could be true, but I'm admitting to none of them. Did the owl warn you? Is that why you're already so prepared?"

"He warned you too. You just weren't listening."

The trace of amusement in her voice and the dancing mischief in her eyes sent heat rushing through his veins and happiness spreading through him. "I listen. I think he just likes you more than me. He didn't even look at me."

Her laughter bubbled up, just like he knew it would. He couldn't help himself. He leaned down and tasted the temptation of that smooth skin on the side of her neck just below her earlobe. He loved the way she smelled. The fragrance was so subtle. One had to be very close to catch it. His lips wandered to her ear, and then his teeth caught her earlobe and tugged. Her breath hitched but she didn't pull away. Her eyes met his in the mirror, darkened with desire, with something else he hadn't expected to ever see from a woman.

The connection between them was growing stronger, deepening into something far more intense than he ever thought possible. The burn of physical lust was stronger than ever.

"They're here, Camellia. What do you want to do?" Jonas pressed a kiss to her neck, right over her pulse.

She raised her chin. "Let's go see what they want, but I'd rather talk to them outside on the porch. I always feel safer outdoors."

He felt the same way. They stepped outside, and he closed the screen behind him. For the first time, he felt a small ripple of unease move through her. He recognized Jack Norton and his wife, Briony. With them was the leader of Team Two, Logan Maxwell. Jack was one of those men you never wanted coming after you. He just didn't have any stop in him, not ever. And Jack was willing to take orders from Logan, so what did that say about him?

Jonas reached for Camellia's hand, his larger one completely enveloping hers. To hell with what anyone thought. He wasn't going to let her face this alone. "Jack, Logan, Briony." He stated their names immediately so his woman would know who she was dealing with. "Good to see you. We were sleeping and haven't had time to make coffee, so I can't offer much in the way of refreshments." Deliberately, he glanced at his watch. "We were going back out into the field soon. No one gave us the heads-up that you were coming to see us."

That wasn't subtle at all. He didn't mean it to be. He always gave Team Two the courtesy of letting them know he was coming to see them before he showed up. There was an unspoken rule between the teams that they let one another know if they were visiting. That way, men arriving in their territory didn't set off alarms. Team Two had set them off, and his men would already have known it, even before Jonas.

Kyle and Jeff would be on their way, but they wouldn't be the only ones. He knew Nicolas Trevane, a highly decorated sniper who never missed his target, was somewhere watching them right now. If Jonas needed to, he could pinpoint his location. Nico wasn't the only one covering his back. Ian McGillicuddy would either be sitting up in the trees as well or lying out somewhere not that far from them, utterly unseen, rifle steady as a rock. Jonas knew his brothers had him covered.

You told me that Ryland would send Lily and Daniel to be taken care of by Team Two, and yet you're so distrustful of them. In fact, your team plans to have all the women going there to have these men guard them. Now you're practically ready to shoot them down when they haven't done anything but want to talk. That doesn't make any sense at all, Jonas.

"I tried texting," Jack said smoothly. "You know how spotty our system is out here."

Jonas waved his hand toward the chairs scattered around the verandah. "We've got some time. This is Camellia Mist, my woman." He made the claim deliberately, letting them know they would be dealing with him. "Honey, Jack Norton, his wife, Briony, and the leader of Team Two, Logan Maxwell."

Camellia had a point. The two teams had always been friendly. More than friends. They'd counted on each other. Why was he suddenly feeling so protective? Was it just because of Camellia? Or had the other team done something to set his radar off?

Camellia moved closer to Jonas, right under his shoulder, tucking her front against his side like she belonged there. She gave the visitors a small smile, the one that didn't reach her wary eyes. "It's nice to meet you." Her voice was whisper soft, her tone just as leery as the look in her eyes.

Are they your friends or enemies, Jonas? I don't know how I'm supposed to act.

She went with Jonas to the lounge again and sank down beside him, her thigh tight against his, keeping her gaze from Briony by concentrating on Logan. Jonas was so tuned to her, he felt the connection flowing from his veins to hers, a deep purple lighting up like sparks along the edges of the flow. He wasn't certain what that meant, but he knew it was all about her mood.

He caught flickers of trepidation. The verge of anger, carefully controlled. He caught glimpses of pink surfacing in the midst of the purple as it flowed through their veins and spread through the neural pathways and cells throughout their bodies. That bright pink was all Camellia. The heart and soul of her in spite of trepidation and anger. He kept possession of her hand, his thumb rubbing soothingly along her inner wrist.

"What can we do for you, Logan?" Jonas decided he might as well get right to the point. Keeping the conversation centered on the commander of Team Two and acting as if he thought their visit was official business would make it just a little harder for them to make their request.

Logan glanced briefly at Jack, then back to Camellia. "Tansy told Briony what your woman did for Kaden. Both Jack and I talked to Kaden. I will say, Camellia, Kaden was reluctant to speak about it and wasn't happy with his wife for calling Briony. He said what happened was a private thing between the two of you, and until you gave him permission to talk to me, he didn't feel he had the right to confirm or deny anything Tansy said. In fact, she was in deep shit for saying anything at all."

A long silence followed Logan's statement. Jonas lifted an eyebrow. "I'm not certain what you want. That doesn't tell us anything other than Tansy is a damn gossip. First she disrespects Camellia and then she has the balls to gossip about her."

Briony lifted her head. "Don't, Jonas. Tansy's trying to save my sister's life." She looked directly at Camellia with tears swimming in her eyes. "I know something terrible happened between you and Marigold. She told me even if you could help her, you wouldn't come. That what she did was unforgivable. Maybe it is. Maybe whatever she did was so terrible no one could forgive her. But she has two beautiful sons and a husband who need her. I need her. I'm begging you, no matter what she did to you, if you can help her, please do it."

Jonas kept his gaze fixed on Logan. "You know this is bullshit, right? That you let them come here and put Camellia in this position. It's blackmail any way you look at it. Emotional blackmail. If she doesn't go with you, she'll look like the worst person on the face of the earth. If she does and can't help Mari any more than the doctors and specialists you've brought in to try haven't been able to do, you can accuse her of not really trying because she's holding a grudge. Nice setup. But it isn't going to work because I'm not allowing you to trap her like that."

His fury was rising to such a point that the starship neurons were reversing and edging with a darker purple, spreading like a virus through his veins to hers.

"Fucking Tansy doesn't know anything about Camellia. You all can talk to Ryland if you want information."

Jonas. Don't be upset.

Camellia's presence in his mind was like fresh air moving through him, blowing away some of his fury. Those chemicals of dark purple running in the opposite direction along with the electrical charges sparking

459

along the long arms coming off the neurons calmed somewhat from the flow of a single vein of reddish pink.

From somewhere in the distance, a wolf howled and another answered. Logan raised an eyebrow. "Friends of yours, Jonas?"

"Actually," Camellia answered before Jonas could, "they're my friends."

Jack Norton leaned toward her, but he kept his wary gaze fixed on Jonas. "Briony may have stated her plea entirely wrong, Jonas, but do you really believe we came here with the intention of setting your woman up? You know me. You know Logan. Do you honestly believe we would do something like that?" His voice was pitched low. Very calm. "I'm not a man who goes around explaining myself, but I understand the need to protect your woman."

He turned his head and for the first time deliberately looked away from Jonas. It was a move that made him vulnerable to attack, and they both knew it.

"Camellia, I'm sorry if our coming here upset or hurt you in any way. We don't know what happened between you and Marigold. We don't even know what occurred between you and Kaden Montague. Our teams have been desperate for a healer, not just for Mari but for all of us. I'm going to tell you straight up, I'm the worst spokesman our team could possibly send to you, but Briony needed to come here. She was desperate and I couldn't say no to her, even though I felt it wasn't the best idea for either of you."

Camellia's fingers tightened in Jonas's. "I don't make any claims to be a psychic healer, not in the way I've heard all of you, including Jonas, describe. Briony, if you ask your sister, she'll tell you, I couldn't have healed a cut when we were children. Sadly, I don't have that type of broad talent. I wish I did."

"But you did help Kaden," Logan persisted.

Camellia inclined her head. Her fingers inside Jonas's hand curled into a tight fist. "His problem was very specific."

"His problem was life-threatening and would have killed him," Logan stated. "Will you at least take a look at Mari for us and tell us if you think you can help her? She has a clotting disorder that is extreme. We believe it was brought on by too much exposure to first-generation Zenith. If you can't help her, it's no different than every doctor who has assessed her condition so far."

It's up to you, Camellia. I can get you out of it. Tell them you'll do it when we get back from going up the mountain. Anything at all. You tell me what you want to do.

Jonas waited. He hated that she was put in this position. He felt as though almost from the moment they'd met, he'd put her in one precarious situation after another.

You haven't put me in any situation I didn't choose to be in, Jonas.

He knew the moment she'd made up her mind to go to the other compound. The silky brilliant pink liquid raced through his veins, soothing the dark purple and turning the ruffled edges back the correct way so that the fluid flowed in the direction it was meant to, easing the tension from his body.

Camellia sighed. "I don't know how much time I have or if I can actually help you, but it won't hurt to take a look." *I prefer that you're with me, but if you have to leave now, I'll catch up.*

Like hell I'm going to leave you. "We can run up the mountain later if we have to, Camellia. I know you're nearly as fast as I am. Let's get this done if we're going to do it."

Briony gave a little hiccup as her husband and Logan instantly came to their feet, clearly not wanting to give Camellia or Jonas time to back out of her decision.

I don't feel any animosity or danger coming

462

from these people, Jonas. They feel nothing but friendship toward you.

Jonas sent Kyle a look that meant he'd better make the right choice. "You coming?"

Kyle nodded. "Jeff and I brought a truck. Room for you and Camellia. We can follow Logan, but we've got to move. We don't want to get too far behind schedule."

Jonas followed him down the stairs, signaling to Nicolas and Ian they were good and were going with Team Two willingly.

"Honey, you really didn't have to do this," Jonas said as they traveled along the rocky trail. The roads never held up for long. Every winter, the snow tore up every road they'd created, so there were bumps and holes until they fixed them.

"She has children." Camellia leaned her head against Jonas's shoulder and closed her eyes.

Jonas was okay with that. "Camellia brought up a very good point. Our team is willing to send our women and children to Team Two to guard for us, and yet we're acting like they're the enemy. We've got snipers on them, and every time I'm near them, I want to rip into them."

Kyle tapped the steering wheel and glanced at Jeff. "Yeah, she's got a point. I can't help but get a little tense around them too, but I don't have any idea why or when it started happening."

"Gotta agree," Jeff said. "Weird acting like we trust them, but not really trusting them. As far as I know, they haven't done anything to earn our distrust."

Jonas slid his palm over Camellia's thigh. "And this thing with Ryland and Lily. Rye said things to Lily that one of us might say because we're idiots with women, but Ryland isn't. He not only compared her to Whitney once, but he did it twice."

Kyle and Jeff both gasped. "No way," Jeff protested. "No way would he do that."

"Something isn't right," Jonas concluded.

Camellia kept her eyes closed. "Someone's found a way to drive a wedge between everyone. I have no idea how, but your team seems to be infected by it. Team Two isn't."

There was silence in the truck. Jonas sighed first. "Ryland is planning to move our families to Team Two's compound for safety. The troops coming at us aren't enhanced. They're mercs hired by the conglomeration. Only those leading them are. Since my woman is probably right about her suspicions, and something may have been done to try to turn us against each other, I'm going to text Ryland about the possibility and suggest in the nicest way possible that the situation between he and Lily may have developed because of this very thing."

Jeff drew in his breath. "Could get you killed, bro."

"You might rethink that last part," Kyle added.

"Rye wanted an advance force to take out the enhanced leaders before the troops ever made it to the compound." Jonas shrugged, trying to sound casual as he sent off a text. "He might never get the chance to yell at me."

"By advance force, you mean you, Kyle, Jeff and me?" Camellia asked with a faint grin.

"A couple of others might come with us," Jonas agreed. "Then we'll face the larger force with both teams."

"That will take some coordination on the battlefield," Kyle said. "Signals are spotty at best on the mountain. You know that, Jonas. No matter how well we work on the equipment, we just don't always get what we want. Not everyone is telepathic on both teams. Bridging for everyone takes tremendous energy, and sometimes that fails."

"Jonas and I can handle communication for everyone," Camellia said without opening her eyes.

We can? Everyone? Even Team Two? He was going to have to sit the woman down and find out exactly what they could do. Clearly, he was missing out on the application of great skills. *All of them?*

Her soft laughter bubbled up. Got to him. Got to Kyle and Jeff too. Both men looked at her. Kyle nearly ran off the road.

"How can you do that?" Jeff asked. "I'm not doubting you, Camellia. I wouldn't doubt you if you said you could walk on water. You can't, can you?"

"I haven't tried. It never occurred to me that I might not sink." Amusement permeated her voice, inviting all of them to share in her laughter.

Jonas found heat blossoming between them. Joy spreading when he hadn't known joy since his parents had died. In the middle of a mess, Camellia still found a way to share humor. The mood in the truck lightened considerably. He realized several times, when the nearly uncontrollable enhancements had overtaken him, what used to take him hours of isolation to suppress, she had handled with seeming ease. That realization sobered him.

There was so much to love about Camellia. Jonas was like his father, an intensely passionate man who would give himself completely to one woman. He would be loyal and ferociously protective of her and their family. Whitney had amplified those traits so much more, enhancing them to the point of borderline obsessive. If his father had been so out of control that he hadn't stopped to think about the son who would need him after the loss of his mother, what would Jonas ever do if he lost Camellia under similar circumstances? In the past, he'd already proven he could be a monster.

Stop. Camellia's warmth slid into his mind. *The species Whitney made a part of you aren't all bad. They have wonderful traits, Jonas, and you never give the good traits a thought.*

Jonas dropped his hand over hers and pressed her palm into the muscle of his thigh. He'd just been thinking how Camellia didn't see herself the way she was, persisting in believing she was so tough and unforgiving, yet they were on their way to see Marigold, the woman who had hurt her the most in the world.

Jonas knew without a shadow of a doubt that Camellia would help her if she could. He'd known they would be going to her aid sooner or later. He had wanted to spare Camellia the pain of seeing Mari, but he knew he couldn't. Camellia would go because

Marigold was suffering and needed her. He saw that loyalty and compassion in her so clearly, yet she didn't. Was she seeing something in him that he didn't?

He closed his fingers around hers, caging her hand in, wishing they had more time to be alone together. He needed to disclose everything to her. The longer they were together and the more he knew her character, the surer he was that they were meant to be together and that they had been even before Whitney paired them. *Before.*

After. He heard her muffled laughter. At first he thought it was aloud, but then he realized she'd laughed only for him. In his mind.

You don't have all the facts.

Just pushing the statement into her mind sounded melodramatic. She tilted her head up, her eyes meeting his. All that intense blue looking at him. The laughter faded, and he was looking at something else altogether. Another emotion he hadn't seen in a woman's eyes ever when she looked at him. His stomach dropped away. She had the ability to tear out his heart.

"Coming up on the house now, Jonas," Kyle announced.

Jonas brought her hand to his mouth, kissing her knuckles. "Long fall, honey," he

468

murmured, conceding. If love was a battle, he'd lost that war before it had ever started.

Her gaze softened even more. He didn't have to explain anything to her. She understood him probably better than he understood himself.

Kyle circled around and parked the truck, nose out, behind Jack Norton's truck, making certain he had plenty of room to exit quickly. Jonas made no move to get out of the back seat with Camellia until both Jeff and Kyle were out and waiting for them.

"Stay close to me, Camellia. Don't let them lead you away for any reason," he cautioned as he helped her from the vehicle.

"I thought you trusted one another. We just talked about this. You said they've always been your friends, Jonas," she reminded.

Jonas slung his arm around her neck and leaned down to put his lips close to her ear. "We do. I did," he corrected. "Until this. I don't want any of them to report you or what you can do to anyone above them. I like Logan, but I don't know how independent he chooses to be from his commander. I don't want to take chances with you."

Camellia nodded. "I get it, Jonas. I'll be very careful."

They started up the steps to the house

where Logan, Jack and Briony waited.

Marigold betrayed you once, Camellia. You have to expect her to again. Whatever she remembers or can understand about what you do to help her, she will relate to her team.

Jonas saw her blink rapidly, those dark lashes that were very feathery, long and curved up at the ends. He hated reminding her, but he knew the moment she saw Marigold in a vulnerable state, that soft spot inside her would kick in, and she would go all out to aid her. He needed her to be cautious while she did so.

Logan stepped aside to allow them through the door. Jack and Briony led the way.

Jeff went in first. *Ken's in the house, but no one else. Not even the children.*

Ken is Marigold's husband, Jonas reminded Camellia. They followed Jeff, with Kyle behind them.

Marigold was sitting up in a very large bed, her dark chocolate gaze fixed on the door. She had platinum-and-gold hair just like her sister, Briony. It was cut short, whereas before, she had worn it longer. Her face was thinner, her skin pale, almost gray. She had always been a confident soldier, running missions by the time she was twelve. Now, she looked anything but confident.

Jonas knew all about her. He'd made it his business to know after the things Camellia told him. He'd asked Gator to have Flame — Gator's wife and a talented woman on the computer — gather everything she could on Marigold and send it to his phone as soon as possible. He'd read every word. The woman was a soldier, no doubt about it, even if she didn't look like one now.

Marigold was reputed to be an excellent sniper. But at the moment, her hands shook, and she twisted her fingers together until Ken Norton, who sat on the edge of the bed, put his large hand over both of hers to cover the anxious motion. Mari could telepathically control machinery, so she was strong mentally. She looked on the verge of tears, a woman worn down by months if not years of struggle.

"She came, Mari," Briony said softly. "Hopefully, she can help. She's just going to take a look and see."

"Cami." Marigold breathed her nickname more than spoke it. "I never thought you would come after what I did."

Camellia waved her hand as if dismissing the past. She walked briskly across the room, extending her hand to Ken. "I'm Camellia Mist. We just missed meeting one another a few years back. Thank you for what you did. Getting us out of that hellish place. I certainly hope I can help. Let me take a look. I'll need to put my hands on you, Mari. Jonas will have to as well. Does it hurt to be touched?"

There were bruises all over Marigold's skin. Marigold hadn't taken her eyes from Camellia. She shook her head. "It doesn't matter. Do whatever you have to do. I can't even hold my babies anymore, Cami. I can't hold them when they cry. I can't feed them." Tears welled up. "I promised I wouldn't cry if you came. I don't want to put pressure on you. No one has been able to help. If this is my punishment for what happened to Ivy . . ."

"Stop it, Mari," Camellia said decisively. "Whitney is responsible for what happened to Ivy. Not you. Not me. Whitney."

Jonas knew that long fall just got longer. He loved her. There was no getting around it. Loving someone was grounded in who they were. Their character. The traits that made them who they were. He admired and respected Camellia Mist the more he spent time with her, not just in her mind, where he could see how she thought, but in the way she conducted herself and the way she dealt with other people.

"They've tried all the therapies available for von Willebrand disease," Ken volunteered. "None of them have worked. They diagnosed her with VWD type 3, said it was rare and they couldn't cure it." He pushed a hand through his hair. "Lily has stuck with us, doing everything she could. She was the one who sent word to the other teams, asking them to send us one of their healers. When Tansy called Briony and said there was a chance you might be able to help, we grabbed at it with both hands."

Camellia nodded as if she understood. "I won't know until I see what's going on. Please don't think I'm a miracle worker, because I'm not. Jonas, you'll need to stand on the other side of the bed. Kyle? I'll need a bottle of water and a cloth of some kind. Jeff, you might need the same for Jonas. The rest of you, this might take some time if I can help. If I can't, I should know fairly quickly."

Jack gathered the things she requested and gave them to Kyle and Jeff. Camellia took a deep breath and looked across the bed at Jonas. For the first time, he realized she hadn't once really met Marigold's eyes.

Are you all right, baby?

473

Don't be nice to me. I can't fall apart. This is much more difficult than I expected. She looks as if she's at death's door. It's bad, Jonas. Whatever is happening inside her body, it's bad. All this time, I've been just miles away, holding a grudge, and she's been dying slowly, inch by inch.

He clenched his teeth. She was ashamed and feeling guilty, not hurt and angry at Marigold. He should have known that would be her reaction when Mari was so ill. Camellia had that enormous soft spot he needed to protect.

I'm looking at death, we both are. I had so much to say to her. If I had just let go of the hurt and come down the mountain, I would have been able to talk to her. Say things. Tell her I love her. That nothing else really matters.

She made his heart hurt. She also made him so damn proud.

All right, honey, let's get this done. She isn't going to die. Take a breath and let's go see what Whitney did with his crap drug. Deliberately, he brought up their nemesis to steady her.

Camellia squared her shoulders and nodded at him. "All right, Mari, why don't you lie down and get comfortable. We'll both just rest our hands very gently on your arms. Hopefully that won't hurt you."

Ken stood up to help his wife lie back down. He was very gentle, but it was obvious, even with his hands touching her around her waist, shifting her down along the mattress with care, it still hurt her. She was stoic, looking up into Ken's eyes and doing her best to smile at him, but there was pain etched on her face, whether she knew it or not. Stark love was on Ken's scarred face, so much love that just seeing it made Jonas feel like he'd intruded on something profoundly intimate. He quickly glanced away and fixed his gaze on Camellia.

He hoped to God Camellia would be able to help Marigold. Because if she couldn't, there was no doubt in his mind that Mari was going to die. Ken was well aware of it. Jack and Briony knew it too. As did Logan and probably all of Team Two. It was no wonder Briony had made her impassioned plea. Camellia was their last-ditch effort. Tansy had called Briony in spite of Kaden's directive not to because she knew Marigold was dying.

Jonas wasn't certain anymore that things were all black or white. Lines were blurred. Each of the women had done things none of them would have chosen to do because it went against what the men considered right. The women made their decisions partially based on compassion. Hell, maybe wholly based on compassion.

Jonas. I need you with me.

Camellia's soft call yanked his full attention back to her. She was afraid of what she was going to find. He nodded his head, and Camellia placed her palms very lightly on Marigold's skin. Jonas didn't need to put his hands on the woman. Camellia's body's reaction was so strong he felt the explosion of chemicals bursting through her. A million neurons reacted to what felt like an arch-enemy as she connected Mari's body to hers through the pads of her fingers and the pores of her skin. The jolt was so strong, she staggered, her body unable to stand with the amount of adrenaline and weapons it was marshaling to fight off the molecular warfare taking place in Mari's body. Already Camellia's body was forming the necessary antioxidants and proteins Marigold lacked in her cells in order to provide normal clotting.

Kyle caught her around the waist and stood behind her, allowing her to lean against him. Briony gasped and covered her mouth. To the side of Jonas, Jeff waved his hand toward the door, clearly signaling to

Briony to leave the room if she couldn't be quiet. Camellia required every bit of concentration she could possibly muster. There couldn't be any distractions. Jack put his arms around Briony to steady her and leaned against the wall. Only then did Jonas put his hands on their patient.

He was more prepared for what he saw after the jolt he felt when Camellia had connected with Mari. His vision changed dramatically, just as it did when he called on the eyes of an eagle or a wolf. This time, his healer vision was sharper than it had been with Kaden. The heat was still white-hot and silvery when he looked at Mari's body, but he guessed that allowed him to penetrate through skin to see organs inside.

His hands didn't possess the surface sensitivity Camellia's did, but his pores in the pads of his fingers and palms wept clear liquid into Mari's pores, and the moment that happened, his veins and arteries, already connected with Camellia, were attached to Marigold's. There was blood everywhere there shouldn't be. Her internal organs dripped blood like leaky faucets.

Jonas marveled at the vast network of star-shaped neurons pulsing with energy and information throughout her body. There were so many of them, galaxies of them.

Somewhere around eighty-six billion, Camellia murmured absently. Her eyes were pure silver, the blue gone. *Look for something that seems off in color. It wouldn't be in her blood. It's going to be hiding in her bone marrow, where the blood is made.*

Everything looked off in color to him. Her bone marrow? What the hell was Camellia talking about? He turned his peculiar vision to Marigold's marrow to inspect it, not that he'd ever looked at anyone's bone marrow. He wasn't a doctor. He had no aspirations to be a doctor.

Think of the bone marrow as a factory, Jonas. We need red blood cells, white blood cells, platelets and plasma. The bone marrow is where that's produced. Something is going wrong with Marigold's platelets, with the clotting process. If she developed von Willebrand's disease from prolonged use of Zenith, then the damage would have to be in the bone marrow.

She was musing aloud, like she did. Well, not aloud, only to him, but she was talking to herself really, puzzling it out, trying to figure out what was wrong. He remained silent, allowing her to use him as a sounding board. He couldn't help her, but he did begin scanning the bone marrow in the hopes of seeing something that might be an

478

odd color. He didn't hold out much hope he would, considering that it all looked odd to him, but he kept looking, determined to try to be of some help.

Jonas, look at this mess. It's like an army is attacking her. Or a bomb went off. This isn't cancer. It's a reaction to the Zenith. You can see where it starts, and then it just grows.

"Where's it getting its nutrition to grow to this extent?" She definitely was talking to herself, not realizing she was speaking aloud. "What's feeding you?"

Jonas glanced up toward their audience and shook his head quickly, warning them not to speak or move. Camellia was on the verge of discovery. He felt it. There was a peculiar sizzling along his veins, like the tingle in the air before lightning struck. Marigold didn't move a muscle, but he knew she was also aware that Camellia was on the cusp of a momentous discovery.

"That doesn't matter right now, Camellia, does it?" Camellia chided herself, still speaking aloud. "We have to find the source. It's here somewhere."

Then she was back internally again, turning that silver gaze onto the mass of red spongy-looking cells at the core of Mari's bones, inspecting them carefully, looking to see if she could catch a glimpse of the damage Zenith had left behind. *Marigold always had a strong immune system in the past, Jonas. Von Willebrand disease is caused by a deficiency in von Willebrand factor, which is a large protein made up of multiple subunits.*

Jonas was in awe of the way her mind worked. She was figuring it out, putting the pieces of the puzzle together at a rapid rate when he would have been back on step one. He did feel the need to help her though. He could also see the sparking on the edges of Mari's neurons, as if those starships were revving their engines, eager to join in the fight for Marigold's life.

"The VWF is needed to bind to clotting factor eight in the blood. That's what protects it from being broken down. You have to have that. It's also needed to help the platelets bind to the inside of injured blood vessels." Camellia frowned as she stared down at Mari's body.

There's no binding going on that I can see.

Exactly. She has little to almost no VWF to bind to clotting factor eight, which she desperately needs. She's bleeding into her joints, her stomach, everywhere, because she can't form a clot.

Jonas didn't like the sound of that. Or her tone. Camellia sounded tired already and discouraged. When he looked at Marigold, he found her condition overwhelming, and he didn't know her. He couldn't imagine what it must be like for Camellia when the woman meant something to her.

Baby, look at me. Right now. Look at me. See me, nothing else. Not Mari, only me.

Camellia reluctantly lifted her gaze to his. Her eyes were pure silver beneath those long dark lashes.

One small section at a time. Only one piece. Don't try to look at her like a whole. You're letting the fact that you know her get to you. I'm right here with you. You can do this. He poured absolute confidence into his voice because, in spite of the mess that was Marigold's insides, he believed in Camellia's abilities.

Her tongue touched her upper lip, and then she gave him a faint smile and nodded. Once more, she turned her attention to Mari's bone marrow. *All right. We've got this. Red, we've got so much work to do.*

Once again, Jonas wanted to ask questions, but he remained silent. Whitney certainly must have given Camellia a healthy dose of the plant. He knew he had to have some of the plant in him as well in order to connect with her on such a molecular level, but it was nothing to the extent of what Camellia had. She was extraordinary at what

481

she was doing.

She concentrated on bone marrow in the spine first. She had that little frown on her face, and she began by immediately targeting a tiny cell that he had barely noticed among all the other cells. It was a putrid green color, and it seemed to be attached to nearly every cell that he could see. He thought it belonged because there were so many of them. Nests of them.

What is that?

I believe Zenith left this behind, and it's multiplied in her.

He knew she wasn't paying attention to him. Camellia was wholly consumed by what she was doing. Now that he knew those green cells shouldn't be there, he studied them. They looked to be an invasive species, so tiny, a leech attaching itself to feed. She took out the nests first, destroying them with electrical pulses she sent from the starships — the neurons with the widespread arms reaching throughout Marigold's body.

I can help with that. Jonas had seen her wield the neurons before.

He might not be good at too much of the healing, but he'd played video games, and he could shoot electrical charges into the larger targets and take them out. The larger targets were tiny, but not like those single cells, attached to the bumpy ones Mari obviously needed. He wasn't going to take a chance on destroying those. He'd leave them to Camellia to finesse with her superior skills.

That will save us time.

She didn't ask him if he thought he really could destroy the cells without harming Marigold. She acted like she was certain he could help her. She didn't even look to see what he was doing when she began going after the single cells attached to the bumpy-looking cells.

What are those?

This is a lymphocyte, the rounder one that looks as if it has multiple cells inside is a neutrophil, and the third one that's shaped kind of like a kidney bean is a monocyte. Basically, they're white blood cells and are necessary to the immune system. They fight bacteria, viruses, fungi, anything invading our systems. This leechy thing is cutting off all aid to Mari's system before she has a chance to even try to fight it.

Jonas concentrated on destroying the nests of green cells trying to hide among the field of red, white and yellow cells. The nests were so tiny that he had to really search for them. He learned to look with that veil of silver that was so foreign to him. He couldn't think of anything but sending electrical pulses along the neuron's long spike and out to the synapse. He could see the jump provided by Red increasing the pulse as it leapt to the next neuron and sizzled down the extended arm jumping from synapse to neuron until he guided his missile straight into the center of the putrid green nest. He had no idea of time going by, his complete concentration on the electrical pulses and the flood of chemicals fighting to save Marigold.

"Her temperature is going to begin to elevate," Camellia informed the others in her distant voice. "You'll need to be prepared to get it down. That's her body trying to fight again."

There was movement in the room around them, but Jonas didn't look up from his work, now determined to ferret out every single one of the enemy camps. That was how he looked at those nests. The ones attaching themselves to the red and white blood cells or platelets were assassins sneaking and attacking under cover of darkness. He and his woman would find and destroy them. Every single one. But as he was discovering for himself, the effort took tremendous energy.

Camellia staggered back and would have collapsed on the floor if Kyle hadn't caught her. He eased her down, handing her the water bottle. She took it with shaking hands and held it to her mouth. Some of the water spilled, and Kyle helped her hold it. There was silence while he wiped what appeared to be beads of sweat from her face.

Jonas sat on the floor, his back to the wall, his eyes on his woman, nearly as shaky as she was. "We have a long way to go, don't we?" he asked softly.

She nodded and leaned her head back, closing her eyes wearily. "We have to get into every bit of bone marrow producing active blood cells. This stuff is horribly invasive and something is feeding it. It reproduces very fast."

"What is it?" Logan asked. "Was Lily right? Did this happen because of prolonged exposure to Zenith?"

Camellia sighed. "I don't know for certain. I'll try to get her a sample of what Mari's been dealing with. She might be able to tell from that, but right now, I just want to sleep for a few minutes."

Jonas wished he was sitting next to her. "Marigold's bone marrow is compromised," he explained so Camellia didn't have to make the effort. "There's some sort of green stuff attacking her healthy blood cells. That means we've got to check all of her marrow, in every bone. So far, we've only managed to clear the spine."

Jack and Briony looked at one another, both frowning. "How does that make sense? Her bone marrow was checked," Jack said. "They came back and told us she had a clotting problem, but no one said she had any kind of alien cell in her marrow."

"I don't know what to tell you, Jack," Jonas said. His arms ached as if he'd fought a battle holding a cannon. It was strange to feel so utterly worn out when he hadn't actually used physical strength. "The invasion was very real and quite enormous." He closed his eyes as well, raising the bottle of water Jeff had handed him to his mouth. "I will say it looked to me like that green stuff was hiding. Maybe they couldn't see it."

Green stuff? Camellia's voice slid into his mind. Gentle. Teasing. *So scientific of you.*

You're good for me. Because all he wanted to do was smile.

Her hand came up, fingers pressing against her lips to hide her smile, but when she lifted those long lashes and looked at him, her eyes held pure laughter. *I know.* She was teasing him. That long fall was getting longer. Dropping deeper. He was in it

486

for the long haul. All the way.

Whitney paired us. Then he dosed both of us with Middlemist. And to top it off, he added the underground network, the fungus.

Um, first, she prefers to be called Red. And she's always first. She has a bit of an ego for a good reason. Never put the underground network on top of her. She might short-circuit you for a while. And yes, he did pair us as well.

We're connected three ways. He stated it with great satisfaction.

I suppose you could say that, not that I know why you're puffing out your chest and getting all macho about it.

It means you can't run off. I can find you anywhere.

She was silent for a long time, but her silvery-blue eyes drifted over his face carefully, examining every inch of it. *I don't expect you to ever give me a reason to run off. The others on your team maybe. Those above you in rank, but never you.*

He liked the quiet confidence in her voice. He glanced down at his watch. They were already past the time they should have started up the mountain to intercept the army coming at them.

I can't do this successfully without you. This time there was a hint of panic in her voice.

You can, but you don't have to. I'm staying with you. It isn't like this army is going to get here before we get to them. He poured honesty into his tone.

"Jonas, she's beginning to run a fever," Ken said.

"That was expected," Jonas admitted. "Camellia warned you that might happen. Keep cooling her off with a cool cloth and ice. Kyle's here, he can advise you if it starts to climb too high."

Briony wrung her hands together. "Do you think you can stop this? At least keep her alive?"

Jonas wasn't certain the way Mari had been living was worth it. He wouldn't want to live out his days suffering the way Marigold had been. If they couldn't stop what was going on with her, then what was the point of her being alive? He didn't ask that question of Briony. He figured she wouldn't welcome it.

"I don't know, Briony. If it can be done, Camellia will do it, but it isn't an easy task. In fact, it's downright daunting. Whatever this crap is, it looks like an alien invasion. If the rest of her bones are like her spine, I don't see how whoever read the bone marrow scan could have missed it. There were hundreds of nests of this stuff. Granted, the ones we took out were tiny, but there were so many. Practically every cell had one of the little leechlike invaders attached to it. Anyhow, getting them off without damaging the cells is no small feat. It takes time, and we don't know how fast these things replicate. It's also tiring."

"And you have to be somewhere," Logan said. "After, can we take you to the top of the mountain by helicopter? Would that help save time?"

Jonas considered it. "Depends on where their scouts are. As soon as we're done here, Logan, we'll clean up, eat and rest while I find out where their advanced scouts are, and then we'll see if we can get away with a helicopter ride."

Logan nodded. "Sounds good to me."

Camellia's eyes were wide open, looking into Jonas's. "Let's get it done then, Jonas."

Kyle stood and reached a hand down to her to help her up. "This time, loop me in so I know what you're doing."

She tilted her head back to look at him. "You got it."

"I'm all for that," Jeff said.

She nodded.

Jonas liked that she was coming to accept his friends, the ones he considered family.

16

"You up for this, Cami?" Kyle asked, nudging her. "I'm thinking you should use a blue fog, with purple undertones. Make it really eerie. Night's beginning to set in. Can you add in flickering lights, like fireflies only bigger?"

"Fireflies?" Jeff gave a snort of derision. "You have no imagination, Kyle. Dragons, Camellia. Think really big, like dragons. Fire-breathing dragons. The dragons don't have to be big, just the concept of them, coming out of the fog and raining fire on the bastards. I'd like that." He smirked at Kyle and folded his arms across his beefy chest.

They were like two little boys trying to outdo one another. "You two. I'm only supposed to be spreading a fog across the mountain slowly, not trapping anyone in it. The scouts can get through the lines right now. We're going after the leaders. That means we have to sneak into their lines. The fog bank will help with that."

"Not *we*," Jonas said decisively. "You're staying here, Camellia. You're running everything from our command post right here."

She made a face at him behind his back. "You certainly can sound bossy when you want to. You didn't say anything about leaving me behind when we talked about our partnership."

Jonas raised an eyebrow. "I'm certain I did."

He sounded way too innocent, so much so that both Jeff and Kyle burst out laughing. Camellia didn't smile; she just continued to look at him. She refused to be charmed by him. It didn't matter how tough and strong he looked sitting on her porch in her garden. Or that, surrounded by Middlemist Red Camellias all in bloom, he managed to look more rugged than ever, which just made him more appealing. His bossy attitude certainly didn't make him appealing.

Jonas shrugged. "Need you here, honey. This is the perfect command post."

"Then you stay here, and I'll go with Kyle and Jeff and find the leaders of these soldiers. Gray and Blue respond to me best. I

491

can understand their peculiar language. I'm used to the way they communicate. The same with the wolves."

She didn't take her gaze from Jonas's, not even when she heard Jeff give a little snort of pure derision. She was going to kick him hard in the shins the first chance she got. Whose side was he on, anyway?

"Beautiful place you have here, Camellia," Kyle said.

She was beginning to understand he was the peacemaker. He was subtle about it, but he wanted them to get along. He also didn't want her to go with them, not if he knew she'd be safer right there in the garden.

"Camellia, it doesn't make sense for you to go."

Jonas used his most gentle voice when she was certain he wanted to just order her to stay behind.

"I can understand that you would want me to set up a command post when we're going to have to take on their army, Jonas, but not now when you're sneaking behind enemy lines and need my help to cover all of you. Hiding me away in the garden doesn't make sense, and you know it. You're just doing it to keep me safe."

Camellia knew he couldn't deny it. She shared his mind most of the time. It was virtually impossible for him to hide his motivation from her.

Jonas sighed. "You're killing me, Camellia. The advance scouts are out in front of the troops. We have to allow them to get past us. If we don't, the leaders are going to be even more alert than they already are. They lost all of their forward enhanced scouts sent to kidnap Lily and Daniel. That means we'll have enemies in front of us and behind us."

She stepped closer to him, seeing his very real fear for her in his eyes. Feeling it in his mind. All he could hear in that moment was his mother's screams. He ran and ran to get to her, just as he had in his nightmares, over and over throughout the years, and he never managed to make it in time.

He framed her face with his hands. "I can't lose you, Camellia. I can't." His voice was raw with emotion. He didn't seem to mind that Kyle and Jeff heard him or could see the stark love that was so plain carved deep into his expression.

Camellia's heart clenched hard in her chest. He was putting his emotions out there for her to see. For his friends to see. She was always so closed off. Always so afraid of getting hurt again and yet Jonas, who had suffered every bit as much as she had, was so willing to put himself out there again.

She brushed his lips with her fingertips, trying to find the right words to make him understand. "We're so much stronger when we're together, Jonas. You aren't thinking straight. If you stash me somewhere you think is safe, all you're going to do is second-guess yourself. You know you will. You're going to think you should have kept me right with you."

She could see that wasn't enough to convince him. In her mind she chose an image of vines twisting together for strength. The roots of trees connecting underground and forming a strong system nearly impossible to defeat. *Baby,* she whispered softly, for him alone. *We need to be together. The two of us. Just the way we were when we healed Kaden and Marigold.*

Jonas pushed his forehead against hers with a soft groan of defeat. His hands slipped to her arms, fingers tightening there. "What am I going to do with you, Camellia?"

Keep believing in us for both of us. She couldn't say it out loud the way she wanted to. Not with Kyle and Jeff right there. Maybe not ever. She raised her gaze to his, wanting him to see what was in her heart.

She did love him already. She couldn't admit it to him. She barely could admit it to herself. She hadn't even shared it with Red, although she was certain Red knew.

I can do that, he whispered back in her mind.

"Are you two finished with your argument?" Jeff asked. "Because it was really lame as arguments go. Jonas, you disappoint me. You're supposed to be all badass alpha. She bats her eyelashes a couple of times, and you just fall at her feet. What kind of example are you?"

Kyle nodded solemnly. "Ordinarily, I pay Jeff no mind. He's basically a lunatic. In this case, I have to agree with him, Jonas. Even if you were ultimately going to give in, you should have held out a little longer."

Branches of the Middlemist Red Camellia shivered and rustled all around them. One branch behind Jeff reared back and then rushed forward as if a heavy wind pushed it straight at the back of his head, where the blossoms slapped him. Kyle was treated to the same smack from the bright pink flowers. Petals sailed through the air, flying all around them.

"What the hell," Jeff said, slapping at the branch. It was too fast, snapping back into place and waving in the breeze as innocently as ever. He regarded the towering shrub with suspicion. "What exactly was that, Camellia? Did you put some kind of spell on that plant? Some hex? Illusions don't smack you in the back of the head."

"Don't be such a baby, Jeff," she replied, giving a little sniff of pure disdain. "I'm sure the wind gusted a little. Didn't you feel it? How could I have possibly caused the branches to move like that? I was — er — *occupied* with other much more important things."

"Like what?" Jeff demanded.

"Looking into Jonas's beautiful eyes. Don't you think he has the most beautiful eyes in the entire world?" She poured dreamy into her tone. It was really difficult not to laugh when Jeff and Kyle exchanged a disgusted look.

"Pull your head out of your . . ." Jeff started, then stopped abruptly when Jonas made a single growly sound. "Out of the clouds," Jeff corrected. "Are you even monitoring when those scouts are getting close? We have to alert our brothers in the field."

"We need to know if the advance scouts are enhanced," Jonas said, sobering instantly now that they were talking about their mission. "Crawley said the leaders of the battalion were enhanced. He claimed he didn't know about the scouts, and no amount of questioning changed that answer."

Camellia froze, one hand on Jonas's face. "You just used the word 'battalion.' That implies a far different number than 'troops,' Jonas. When were you going to tell me you were facing a hundred to two hundred men rather than ten to twenty men? At the most, I thought forty."

Jonas looked down at his hands and then back up at her face. "It didn't occur to me these people would send a battalion after us, Camellia. Not once did I think that. I said 'troops' because I thought 'troops.' I considered the same numbers as you. It's possible that's where you got those numbers, right out of my head. When we questioned Crawley, we found we were facing at least a hundred men, possibly two hundred, all mercenaries Abrams and his banker friends hired. Abrams is a billionaire. He's got so much money it's sick. He and his friends — and all of them went to school with Whitney — formed a conglomerate together. They're probably one of the most influential conglomerates in the world. They buy and sell governments. Take down presidents. I mean that in the true sense of the word. They have such a sense of entitlement by this time, they think they're unstoppable."

"They sound worse than organized crime," Camellia said.

"That's because they are," Kyle agreed.

Jeff nodded. "These people have no problem hiring contract killers or sending soldiers on missions to be killed if it suits their agenda. They would trade lives in a heartbeat, wipe out entire villages or even a city of people in order to achieve their goal. They've done it before. They'll do it again."

"Sending a battalion to murder every man, woman and child of Teams One and Two is absolutely nothing to them. They want to rid the world of all GhostWalkers deemed flawed and, at the same time, teach Whitney a lesson. With Lily and Daniel in their possession, they'll have something to bring him in line," Jonas said.

"They sure don't know Whitney if they believe that," Camellia said.

"And they don't understand GhostWalkers either," Jonas said. "Because these assholes have no loyalty, they don't understand it. They think because Teams Three and Four aren't flawed in the ways we are, they won't care what happens to us. They couldn't be more wrong. If the conglomerate succeeds in taking us out, Teams Three and Four will hunt them to the ends of the earth. Once you're a target of a Ghost-Walker, it doesn't end until you're dead."

"What Whitney, the conglomerate or the other GhostWalkers are or are not going to do isn't the point, Jonas." She scowled at him. "The bottom line is you, Kyle and Jeff were *knowingly* planning — just the three of you — to sneak into the enemy camp, find the enhanced leaders of the battalion alone and kill them right under the noses of hundreds of armed men. And you want me to stay here, hiding, too far away to help you the best way I can, while you three put yourselves in that kind of danger?" Camellia couldn't help feeling a little outraged. She wanted to shove Jonas right off the porch.

The towering shrubs around her home rustled and quivered in response to her emotions, branches shaking. At first the shuddering was no more than a slight shiver, but the motion increased in strength as she became more agitated. She paced away from Jonas and the other two Ghost-Walkers, stepping off the porch to walk back and forth on the small path between the plants. The branches dipped so the blossoms brushed her face and hair as if to reassure her — or calm her — but she paid no attention.

"Honey, calm down for a minute and just listen to me," Jonas said.

She held up her hand without looking at him. "Not a good time to talk to me right now. I did listen to you. That was before I realized you were deliberately putting yourself in danger. A few troops, okay, I knew you could handle it, but this isn't even reasonable, and you know it. All of you know it. Right now, if any of you speak to me, I'm going to zap you so hard with an electrical charge you will think you were sitting in the electric chair, so don't talk to me until I calm down."

The three men looked at each other. Jeff raised his eyebrow at Jonas. "Can she really do that, bro? Because if she can, you'd better think twice about marrying that woman. She's got a nasty little temper, and you're about as mean as they come. That combo is going to get you in more trouble than you can possibly handle."

Kyle stepped closer and lowered his voice. "I really like her, Jonas. And I thought for sure she was your match. You've got to have someone who can handle you. I never thought there was a woman alive who could do it, but I have to agree with Jeff. Camellia not only can handle you, but I think she can seriously kick your ass. Do you even have any idea what she's capable of?"

"She's capable of hearing you, I know that much," Jonas assured. "So if you don't want to get zapped, stop acting crazy. I like my woman feisty. She has every right to be upset at me. I should have come clean with how many soldiers we might run into. Crawley gave that up and I didn't tell her. I told her we'd be partners, that means keeping her in the loop."

"You were protecting her. We have the right to protect our women," Jeff decreed, raising his voice to the normal range and glaring at the back of Camellia's head.

The moment the words were finished coming out of his mouth, she raised one hand over her head, fingers poised in the classic sign, flipping him off. At the same time, just briefly, fireflies danced in the night, sparking little lights all around Jeff's body. They never seemed to actually land on him, but he winced and then jumped to one side and then the other.

"Cut it out, you little monster."

Camellia turned around slowly, looking very innocent — too innocent. "Are you addressing me, Jeff? What are you accusing me of?"

"You know darn well what you did."

"Other than wanting to kick Jonas, which

I haven't done," she replied in a pious voice, "I have no idea what you're talking about."

Kyle burst out laughing. "You aren't going to win this one. None of us are." He held up his hands in surrender. "I had no idea there was a battalion either until Crawley let it slip in questioning. We're all guilty of wanting to protect you, Camellia. Maybe 'want' is not the right word. 'Need' might be better."

She tilted her chin at him. "Because you need a healer for the teams."

Kyle looked genuinely puzzled. "A healer for the teams?" he echoed, sounding as puzzled as he looked. "No, babe. Because it's you."

Jeff nodded. "Don't want to lose you any more than Jonas does. He might think you're the love of his life, but we know you are."

"Even though I can kick his ass?"

Jonas loved the amusement in her voice. That was his Camellia, her moods mercurial. Passionate. One minute hot with temper, the next full-on laughter. That was coming, he could feel it.

"He often needs his ass kicked," Jeff admitted.

Jonas's protest was lost before he could voice it. Camellia burst out laughing, the sound contagious. Beautiful. Impossible to resist.

A wolf howled in the distance. An owl screeched as if it missed its prey. That was their warning system, and they all sobered in an instant. It was time for the fog to start rolling in across the mountain. They would have to leave the safety of the garden. Jonas really hated taking Camellia with him, but at the same time, he knew she was right. If he didn't, his attention would be divided. He wouldn't stop worrying that he'd made the wrong decision.

She wrapped her hand around the thickest branch of the largest Middlemist Red Camellia shrub and stood there for a long moment, head bowed. Jonas went to her, both hands fitting on either side of hers, caging her in, opening his mind to hers.

At once, he felt the expansion of Camellia's reach across the forest. It wasn't confined to the garden and the plants there. She had tapped into the trees and brush, the flowers and shrubs, fern, fungi and even moss. All of those plants were connected through the underground network and the ruler of them — Red.

Camellia was very accepting and accepted. Nothing in the forest network questioned her presence because she was no threat to them. Jonas buried his mind in hers. Once connected to her, their shared Middlemist Red properties allowed the neurons in their bodies to sync up so that he could see the way the nutrients moved from her to him and him to her — shared so all their nerve endings lit up as the process took place.

The liquid energy from Camellia was an interesting deep shade of pink, not red but a brilliant pink, while his was a dark purple. The two distinct streams of nutrients moved together, flowing in the proper direction because for once, he wasn't raging. They moved together in harmony, stretching beyond the human body to find the veins of the mycelium beneath the ground.

I need warmth from the surface to cool rapidly and one hundred percent humidity to be achieved. The skies are clear tonight, and there is little to no wind. Red will have to have the plants help with that. I can't do it. They have to.

Jonas remained silent. Camellia was confident she would receive help from the plants. They were her army. She had talked about weapons she'd developed. He should have asked more questions. He'd been thrown by the idea of floras as intelligent beings capable of protecting themselves. He hadn't conceived that a plant might be just as capable of feeling emotions such as rage at betrayal or feeling loyalty, which Red clearly had in abundance for Camellia.

Camellia leaned her body into his, lifting her face toward him. He didn't hesitate. Jonas took her mouth, his tongue tasting hers and then pushing deep, looking for the fire between them. It rose fast and hot, a scorching burn that refused to smolder but leapt into flames immediately. Both let go of the branch they held and wrapped their arms around each other. Jonas pulled her in tight against his body while he kissed her.

She fit so easily with him. He inhaled, drawing her into his lungs as he lifted his head. He found it so interesting that the majority of the time, it was impossible to catch her scent, especially since he had such an acute sense of smell. She sometimes exuded a subtle fragrance, but not when she was about to go into the field. When it was time for battle, her scent completely disappeared, just like now.

I can't find your scent at all. Is that Red protecting you?

She nodded slowly, her blue eyes looking up at him. *That's one of the many things that help us disappear. You can't be tracked through scent either. Haven't you noticed?*

He had been told by his team that even

those with acute senses of smell couldn't detect him at times. Yeah, he'd wondered, but he certainly hadn't suspected a plant protecting him.

The four of them left the garden together. As they did, Jonas made certain to remove all traces that might lead Abrams's scouts to Camellia's garden. As he did so, grass and dirt pushed up behind where they walked. Little tendrils of fog began to rise along the trail and snake among the trees.

A wolf howled, this one sounding a little closer than before. Somewhere in the distance, another answered the call and then a third. A good minute passed. A fourth howled. Once they got on the main trail, Camellia and the three GhostWalkers began to run in single file, Jonas in front, Jeff bringing up the rear. The four waited nearly five minutes as they ran just in case the sentries had more information to deliver.

You'll want to let Logan's men know that there are four scouts heading their way. Three coming together although spread out. The fourth is hanging back, Camellia reported to the others. *They're running. We're running. They're about an hour from us.*

That puts them about two hours from Logan's men, Jeff calculated.

Jonas was well aware they only had an

hour before they would be sneaking past the enemy scouts. He tried not to notice that the fog was nowhere near what it needed to be. Darkness had fallen, but there was enough of a moon to reveal any tracks on the ground to an enhanced scout. It was only a matter of time before they could see things the teams didn't want them seeing. Jonas wasn't worried for Kyle, Jeff, Camellia or himself, but he didn't know the capabilities of the two men Team Two had sent to keep the enemy's forward scouts from reaching the compound.

He had met the two men, of course. Antonio Martinez was a man who tended to stay in the shadows, much like Jonas did. You rarely noticed him, if ever. No one spoke of him or drew attention to him.

Wait. Who? Camellia's voice was pure accusation. Her running faltered and she stepped off the trail, halting, both hands on her thighs, head down. *Antonio Martinez?*

The moment she stopped moving, they all froze. Jonas couldn't help the flash of hurt at her first feeling of betrayal. He stopped himself from reacting. Of course her mind would go there first. Antonio had been a guard at one of the laboratories she had been imprisoned in. He'd been there with Kane Cannon, a member of Team Three.

Both men had been assigned when Whitney was still in good standing with a number of power brokers in Washington.

"You know him?" Kyle asked.

"He was a guard at one of the facilities where I was a prisoner." Camellia kept her head down as if she were trying to catch her breath from running.

Jonas knew she wasn't having any trouble breathing. She was clearing her mind, pushing aside the first conclusion her brain had instinctively jumped to, which was that Jonas had betrayed her and was possibly selling her out to Whitney or to the government. She knew him. Believed in him. She was in his mind. Jonas kept his mouth shut and his thoughts ruthlessly corralled. He had to let her work it out, even if the time it took her to do it felt slow to him. She struggled with trust. He couldn't blame her for that.

He had grown up in a loving environment. His heart hadn't been battered and scarred by one betrayal after another. Just watching the way his team had handled her arrival gave him a little insight into what her life had been like. She was used to it. She'd been expecting betrayal and mistrust, and she'd been right. He had thought his endorsement of her would be enough, but it hadn't been. That had shocked him. It had been an insult. He tried not to allow her reaction to Antonio's name feel insulting to him.

Finally, Camellia lifted her head, her eyes so intensely blue they looked like two bruised cornflowers pressed into her face. "I'm sorry, honey. For a minute, all I could think about was Whitney's torture camps. At the facility Antonio guarded, Whitney was conducting all kinds of experiments. He tortured us under the pretense of learning what would break a soldier. He kept inserting more and more horrific genetic materials into us. At the same time, he would tell us he was enhancing our psychic abilities. Already some of the girls were far past their ability to cope without filters."

"Antonio wasn't guarding you," Jonas reminded as gently as possible. "He was sent there to guard the compound, just as other guards were. They had no idea what Whitney was doing."

She rubbed her temples, as if she had the beginnings of a headache. "Perhaps not at first, but it would have been impossible to ignore the screams of agony coming from his laboratory. It wasn't soundproof. That was one of Whitney's biggest beefs. Eventually, he demanded that anywhere he worked, he have the best security with his own handpicked soldiers, and everything was sound-proofed."

"That's because of the three soldiers testifying against him to a committee in Washington. Kane Cannon from Team Three. Malichai Fortunes from Team Four. And Antonio Martinez from Team Two. All three of those men were targeted after that. Sent time after time on suicide missions, often alone. If their team leaders hadn't sent backup without anyone knowing, all three would be dead. They risked their careers and their lives to try to save you women and get Whitney arrested and brought to trial."

"I should have asked you," Camellia conceded.

Jonas wrapped his arm around her shoulders and pulled her tight against his chest. He wondered how Ryland and Lily were going to fix their problem when trust had been broken between them. Trust was so fragile. Camellia was trying. He could feel her making every effort, but it was so difficult to overcome her past. And the two of them could share one another's mind. That should have made it even easier to trust one another.

"I understand, honey. You good now?" He

hated to rush her, but he could feel danger coming closer with every passing second. "We have to get a move on."

The fingers of fog were drifting up from the ground, darker in color than before. Taking on a purplish hue. Instead of fingers moving through the trees, the fog appeared as dark, spinning masses, growing in size, the threads clotting together as if magnetized until they became a bank of rolling clouds. The fog spread out and raced along the ground, low and so dense that the trees appeared to rise up out of the mists with no anchor to earth.

Camellia tilted her head in order to brush a kiss along the underside of Jonas's jaw. "Let's go. I'm good. Really. Who is the other man Team Two sent?"

Jonas took lead again, setting a faster pace in spite of the fact that the fog blotted out the trail. He used his connection to the mycelium under his feet to keep them on the right track, sharing his visualization with the others as he ran. Camellia's connection to them all telepathically was so strong that Jonas didn't have to think about it. He allowed her to do most of the heavy lifting of sharing their minds so he could keep them on track running.

The fog was growing thicker and darker,

roiling as if in cauldrons. He shouldn't have worried that the "weather" wouldn't cover Logan's men lying in wait for the scouts. Their orders were to trail the scouts and then take them once Jonas and his crew had killed the enhanced leaders of the battalion coming at them.

The second man is Trace Aikens. Like Antonio, he seems to disappear into the shadows when he doesn't want to be seen. He has a brother, Todd, also on Team Two. Trace is a deadly man, from what I understand. And incredibly fast. I imagine the reason Antonio and Trace were sent out on their own to handle the advance scouts was because Logan figured they wouldn't need help. Like us, Whitney considered Team Two flawed, although not nearly as severely as us. Jonas wanted Camellia to know the second team wasn't held in much higher regard by Whitney than his team.

Abrams thinks neither of our teams is worth much, Kyle added in his thoughts. *Whitney would lose his mind if he knew Abrams's consortium had hired mercenaries to kill the Nortons' babies. He's left them strictly alone, believing Jack and Ken would raise them to be the kind of GhostWalkers the country needs. Clearly, Whitney hasn't shared information with Abrams about the Norton twins having babies.*

But then, Jeff contributed, *Abrams isn't a patriot. He's all about power. He backed Whitney's genius because everything Whitney did turned to gold. Abrams didn't care if what Whitney did was legal or not. He didn't care if he experimented on children or put women into breeding programs. He especially didn't care if Whitney was creating babies in petri dishes and splicing nonhuman DNA into their genetic code just to see what would happen.*

Jonas took up the narrative on Abrams. *I don't know how true the rumors are, but Team Four supposedly shut down a very hot virus that had wiped out an entire remote village in Indonesia. That virus was developed by men working for Whitney. Those men took off with the virus, selling it to someone who had been paying them all along for information. Those people were traced to what we believe is part of Abrams's coalition.*

Following the trail through the trees laid out in his mind by the mycelium network was easy. It seemed almost as if LED lights were illuminating his way. He didn't have to use his eyes. The guidance system was so completely integrated through his mind and body, but he could clearly see the trail laid out in front of him, right down to every branch, loose rock and patch of uneven ground that lay in his path.

It took time for him to notice the trail smoothed itself out as he ran. One moment it dipped significantly just up ahead, and then it was straight as he raced over it. When Jeff, who was bringing up the rear, crossed it, the ground once more dipped.

You seeing what I'm seeing, Camellia? He ensured he asked her on their private communication path. There were some things he didn't think were best to share with Jeff and Kyle — not that he didn't trust them, but just as in the case with Lily and Jeff, secrets had a way of creeping out of closets.

The mycelium is helping us, Jonas. They know we're in a tight situation. Red is communicating with the network.

That didn't surprise him. She'd told him Red was going to help. The fog was gradually climbing to greater heights. It looked and felt very real, rising upward in churning masses, the bank so long and thick, mingling with what appeared to be clouds heavy with potential rain.

They climbed quickly to a higher elevation, and the heavy forest began to thin. Blue, Camellia's Great Gray owl, lifted off a snag, gliding low to the ground just in front of Jonas, effectively blocking him from continuing along the trail. He stopped instantly and signaled to the others to melt into the fog. The forward scouts were coming.

Camellia, you have to let Antonio and Trace know they're about an hour out, Jonas said. *They're on the main trail at this point, but that doesn't mean they'll stick to it. If they go off of it, you'll know, right?*

Yes. I'll wait to warn them until we know if these men are enhanced.

Jonas remained upright, frozen in place, hidden in the dark purple fog. Kyle was a few feet from him, lying prone in the vegetation, eyes locked on the trail. Jeff had gone up a tree. The fog hadn't quite covered him yet, but somehow, the clouds reached him. Jonas was certain that strange phenomenon was Camellia's doing. She manipulated weather to a degree using Middlemist Red. Camellia herself was nowhere to be seen. Like Jonas, she could simply disappear — even from him. He wasn't sure whether to be impressed or bothered by that. He decided to be impressed.

The first scout appeared on the trail within five minutes of Blue's warning. He was a short, stocky man with a natural, easy pace that told Jonas he was definitely enhanced. He turned his head this way and that as he jogged, only occasionally looking ahead at the trail through the fog. That also told Jonas he could see through the dense, roiling fog, something few could do.

One scout coming through the trees to the lead scout's right, Camellia reported. *The lead is obviously trying to direct him but isn't able to see the ground, because he's on the trail and this one is off of it. There's a lot of swearing going on.* There was amusement in her voice.

"Cut the crap, Simon," the one in the forest snarled. "Give me the trail and you take this route. I keep tripping over rocks and downed trees you didn't see. I'm going to break my neck."

"I'll break your neck, Jarvis, if you keep talking. Do you have any idea how far sound carries at night?" Simon demanded.

"Jarvis is right," a voice came from about a hundred yards from Jonas. "This sucks."

Jonas had smelled the sweat on the third man. He oozed a burnt-smelling venom. If he continued his course, he might just jog right over the top of Kyle. Jonas wouldn't allow that to happen.

He won't stay on that course, Camellia said with total confidence. *He will have to move around too many stumps and boulders. No dragons though, Jeff, I'm sorry. Not this time.*

I'll create those for you when I can get away with it.

Again, there was that little bit of laughter in her mind that she shared with the others, turning an otherwise tense situation into one they could find amusing.

"Stop being a whiner, Craig," Simon said, but he slowed down just as Craig tripped over a large rock.

Craig caught the front of his shin and stopped. "Simon, is anyone around us? Can you see them? Smell them? Because if no one's around, we would make much better time if all of us ran on the trail. When we get closer to the compound, we can spread out again."

"It makes sense," Jarvis agreed.

"Shaker won't like it," Simon said. "He gave very strict orders."

"Yeah, well, Shaker isn't here, is he?" Craig demanded. "Who's going to tell him? No one's here but the three of us."

"Parker's coming up behind us," Simon warned.

"True, but he can't read tracks in this pea soup. He won't be able to see his own hand in front of his face."

Already, without Simon's consent, the other two scouts were doing their best to make their way through the dense fog to the main trail. Camellia didn't make it easy on them, and the underground network aided her, continually throwing up obstacles for the two men to run into or trip over to make the threats in the fog seem very real. Once the advanced scouts were back on the main trail and running behind Simon, she left them to it.

Jonas and the others waited for the fourth man, Parker, the backup scout. Shaker had learned his lesson after losing his first scouting team. He wasn't taking chances with the others. Shaker was used to being enhanced and working with soldiers who were enhanced. They always had the advantage. The mercenaries Abrams had hired might be considered the best by many, but Shaker wouldn't think so. He needed information in order to feel safe bringing what he considered ordinary men against two teams of enhanced soldiers. He wanted to know how many he was up against. Jonas could understand that.

Parker came along at a fast run five minutes later, proving that, like Simon, he could see through the fog, although he didn't search his surroundings the way Simon had. He kept his gaze fixed on the trail.

He has more trouble seeing than Simon did, Jeff guessed.

He's looking for tracks, Jonas countered. *He's not worried about anyone waiting to jump him. He figures if that was going to happen, it would have happened to the others. He's looking to see who else has been here.* Jonas was suddenly very grateful for Red and the mycelium for covering their tracks so thoroughly. *Let Antonio and Trace know that in my opinion, Parker is the most lethal of the lot, Camellia.*

Don't anyone move yet, Camellia warned. *Parker is out of sight, but he's slowing his pace. I think he's going to backtrack.*

Jonas stiffened. *Why would he do that?*

There's no possible way he found any tracks, Jonas. He can't smell us or see us. Any of us, she assured. *It's most likely the way he operates.*

Jonas knew all about being careful. He often backtracked and then did it a second and third time, especially if he was uneasy. Parker was enhanced. He didn't need to smell or see an enemy. Sometimes it was a gut reaction telling them they were in trouble. Parker emerged through the fog, walking slow, this time looking left and then right. Up into the trees and then down along the ground. He stopped several times, his fist around his gun, clearly listening.

He nearly walked right up on Gray, who

suddenly flapped his wings and glided off, startling Parker more than he appeared to have startled the owl. Eventually, the man turned and jogged down the trail again. They waited in silence.

Camellia reached out to Antonio and Trace, giving them what little information they had on the four scouts and the approximate time they would be passing their location.

Will you be able to maneuver adequately in the fog? she asked them.

Yes, no problem, they replied.

Just let Red monitor them, and if they need help, she can let you know, Jonas decided. *We need to get on with our task and take out Abrams's private army.*

17

The cool breeze touched Camellia's face and ruffled her hair, helping her to breathe when she saw the extent of the army Jacob Abrams had sent to exterminate the Ghost-Walkers. Her fingers crept up to her lips and pressed there as she stared down from her vantage point and studied the crazy scene below. It seemed surreal. Jonas, Kyle and Jeff might not think it was any big thing, but that many men gathered in one place willing to murder men, women and even babies was just too much for her.

A part of Camellia wanted to start a battle with them right there. Send the fog with burning droplets in it. Embed illusions in it that would turn them against one another. Bring her plant-based weapons into play. Had she been on her own, she might have been so overcome with emotion that she would have done it, but she had to consider the safety of Jonas, Jeff and Kyle.

The clouds covered the moon for the moment, and she'd managed to keep the fog rolling through the valley so that as the army began its climb and they ran into more fog, it would be believable. Moving that many men with stealth wasn't easy. They didn't want to use vehicles. They had air support. Helicopters, two of them. She could see the helicopters were well armed, just as the army was well supplied.

Shaker had made it clear the helicopters were to stay back until he called for them. He was bringing the army in slowly so as not to tire them out or to tip off anyone at the compounds. He'd ordered the mercenaries to hang well back. Those men were farther down the mountain in the heavier groves of trees, most catching up on their sleep.

At the moment, Shaker leaned over a small table with six others, all observing a map, clearly showing where he wanted each of the other commanders to bring in their troops. Camellia thought that was a good thing. That meant they would divide this massive group into smaller, more manageable units, which meant the two Ghost-Walker teams had a better chance to take them out before they reached the compounds.

Both Blue and Gray are in place. They found natural resting places that won't raise suspicion if anyone spots them. Not that it was likely that anyone would. The fog she'd created was thinner and more blue-gray in color; it hung through the entire valley now. The owls blended into the fog-shrouded trees so perfectly, it was extremely difficult to spot them, even though they were very large birds.

Kyle made his move to connect with Gray. The owl had positioned himself where he could oversee Shaker's table. He was above it, close, hidden in a little grove of trees near the edge of the small clearing. The snag was taller than Gray normally would have perched on, but it gave him a good view of what the seven men were doing as they laid out their plan of attack. That meant Kyle could see everything he needed.

Camellia didn't like the fact that she was so far away from Kyle. He would be disoriented and have a migraine, at the very least, after using the owl's eyes to see what the men were doing. She had never tried healing anyone over that distance.

I have no doubt that you can do it, Jonas whispered, brushing a loving caress through her mind.

You can do anything, Jeff echoed.

523

Does Shaker look familiar to either of you? Jonas asked. *Kyle, really concentrate on his face and then on the man to the right of him. They have the same features. Similar height, even mannerisms. What do you think?*

Camellia had never seen either of the men before, and she waited for the verdict. Both Jeff and Kyle took their time studying the two men, comparing their features.

Definitely could be related, Jeff confirmed. *And you're right, they do look somewhat familiar, as if I've seen them somewhere, but I can't recall where.*

Maybe we trained with them? Went on a mission together? Kyle ventured.

I don't forget missions. Could have been early training, before GhostWalkers.

Jonas felt frustrated to Camellia, although his tone didn't sound it. He was getting some kind of bad feeling from the leader of these men.

We know they're here to kill everyone, Jonas, she reminded gently. *He is sending his army to murder every man, woman and child, even babies. Of course he would feel bad in some way to you. It looks to me like he's going to stay back here, safe in his command post, while everyone else takes the risks.*

Camellia poured her contempt into his mind even as she continued to build the density of the fog in the valley. Shaker had his mercenaries resting at four thousand feet. They still had another five thousand to climb, go over the summit and back down nearly four thousand feet to reach their destination.

He'll probably keep one of the helicopters back to make certain he has a quick escape as well, she added. *If he manages in my fog.*

Jonas mentally shook his head. *I wish I agreed with your assessment of him, honey. Shaker doesn't feel that way to me at all. He might seem arrogant and overconfident, but we probably do as well to other soldiers.*

Camellia remained silent. Jonas had been a soldier for a long time and had a great deal of experience. Others relied on him. Neither Kyle nor Jeff interrupted his train of thought either.

Doesn't this all seem excessive? Why would Abrams risk sending an army like this against the GhostWalkers just to bring Whitney in line? Abrams does everything he can to stay in the background, right? He doesn't want anyone to know about him and the rest of his little cockroaches running the world.

Camellia had to admit, she did think it was not only excessive, it was stupid. Abrams hadn't gotten as far as he was being a stupid man.

If two full teams of GhostWalkers and their families are murdered, including children, that kind of news is hard to keep under wraps. It's bound to surface. Do you believe the general is going to stay silent? Because I don't think so. Sam Johnson is his son and a member of our team. Adopted or not, he loves Sam. If Sam is murdered, the general is going to take that all the way to the top and keep screaming until someone pays.

You're onto something there, Jonas, Jeff agreed. *What about Azami, Sam's wife? Azami owns Samurai Communications along with her two brothers. If she dies with Sam, that would be worldwide news. If she doesn't, that will still be worldwide news because she would make certain it would be. Abrams wouldn't have a place to hide.*

Jonas was quiet for another moment. *See why none of this is adding up for me? Why would Abrams do this on such a massive scale? He had a spy in place he could have used to keep an eye on us and send him information for as long as needed. Even if he wanted to kidnap Lily and Daniel to keep Whitney in line, there were other ways to do it. Ryland and Lily go into town. Daniel goes into the yard and even into the forest. Why go after Team Two?*

Camellia had to admit Jonas was right.

Maybe Abrams thinks this can't be traced back to him.

He can't possibly think Whitney would let him get away with that. Even if he stayed silent about Lily and Daniel, he'd find a way to leak the information to the press just to get back at Abrams. Whitney is vindictive. Jonas was adamant. *Abrams has known him for years. He would know that.*

Camellia had studied Whitney for years. Jonas was certainly correct about his personality. He wouldn't hesitate to get back at Abrams by outing him to the press and every official at the White House. He would also make certain Azami's brothers knew exactly who was to blame. She had to agree with Jonas, this was not a wise decision on Abrams part, so what had prompted him to make it?

Kyle, let's see what they're up to, Jonas directed.

Kyle focused on the map on the table so all of them could see the way Shaker had the troops divided and coming at the compound from various sides. He indicated that two of the units were to skirt around the base of the mountain and come in from the east. They would have to double-time it in order to get into position quickly enough to be effective — and Shaker demanded they

527

be effective.

The enhanced leader of the troops was called Lowell. He had the fastest of the mercenaries and believed he could come at Team One's fortress from the eastern slope. He had thirty-three men under his command. All were fast runners and climbers. He seemed to have faith in his men, unlike Shaker.

Pops, as they referred to the oldest of the enhanced commanders — although he didn't look older than thirty — was to take the second group of soldiers around the base of the mountain to the west with equal speed. He also had thirty-three men under his command. They too were considered fast runners, particularly going uphill. He nodded when Shaker asked if his men could get to Team One's fortress in time to aid the others in defeating the GhostWalkers.

Camellia tried to keep focused on Shaker, but Jonas was moving carefully in the mist. She knew he was hidden, but she could see a shimmer now and then. She worried that if she could see him, the others at the table might look up with enhanced vision and catch a quick glimpse. Jonas's goal was the helicopter farthest from the group of enhanced commanders. The chopper was decked out with numerous weapons. The pilot and his copilot were nowhere in sight.

Jonas slipped around to the other side of the helicopter where Camellia couldn't see him, but she could still feel him through the underground connection. Then she couldn't. He had climbed into the helicopter. Her heart seemed to beat right into her throat.

What are you going to do? She did her best to keep the trepidation from her voice and pour confidence into his mind the way he always did for her.

Treat the weapons to a little bath with special acid a friend of mine cooked up. Then I'll go back outside and treat the main rotor blade and swash plate to the same.

The rotor blade? He was going outside the helicopter where any of the enhanced commanders might look up and see him. Maybe she really would have a heart attack.

Jonas's amusement echoed both Kyle's and Jeff's.

Laugh it up, boys, she said, but her attention was pulled back toward the table, where one of the enhanced commanders had shifted restlessly, glancing toward the grove of trees and then up into the heavier forest.

One of them is definitely feeling our presence. He doesn't know where the threat is coming from, but he knows one is close. Kyle?

Shaker referred to him as Gorman. No one move until he stops being paranoid.

Camellia dug her feet into the ground, getting an even firmer connection with the mycelium beneath the soil. It was spread wide, going from tree to tree, shrub to shrub, a conduit for communication that went up the mountain all the way along the trail to tell her exactly where Shaker's forward scouts were.

Suddenly, Gorman lifted his face toward the sky and issued a stuttering hoot that was answered from the interior of the forest. Gray let out a very distinctive primary call, one that declared in no uncertain terms he was proclaiming the territory as his, and he would defend his mate and nest from all other raptors.

Kyle, break off. Break off now, Camellia ordered. *Gray's going to attack.*

Gray was already in the air, flying straight at the large owl coming off the branch of a tree in the forest. The two combatants met in midair, Gray slashing viciously at the raptor's breast and eyes with his curved razor-sharp talons and his hooked beak. He was an experienced fighter and went in low and fast, like a heat-seeking missile. A formidable bird of prey, Gray didn't break off for more than a moment to turn and come back at his foe. The owl had dared to come into his territory, possibly to lay claim to his lady or kill any owlets Gray might have.

Gorman screamed and collapsed, one hand covering his eyes and the other his chest. Blood trickled from between his fingers. He hadn't retreated fast enough.

"Shit, Gorman, do you want me to shoot that thing?" another one of the enhanced commanders asked while the others all stared in shock.

Camellia wasn't certain she could call Gray back. He was in full defense of his territory and family mode. His instincts as a predator had taken him completely over.

"No, he's just defending his nest, Lewis. It's what they do. Look at him. He's the coolest. If I'd seen him, I would have chosen him, but he was so still until he actually moved, I didn't know he was anywhere close." There was real admiration in Gorman's voice.

Camellia could tell it didn't occur to him that anyone had used the owl to study them. He kept his hand over his eyes, peeking out through his fingers. She knew, being inside the owl's body, using its eyes when Gray struck, Gorman had been injured as well. He was lucky the owl hadn't torn out his eyes. Had he been any slower, he certainly could have lost them.

How can Gray claim this territory as his? He just got here. And he's serious, Jeff said.

Blue's with him, Camellia pointed out. *It's instinct to protect her.*

"Are you going to be able to see?" Shaker asked. "I need you to be able to carry out your orders." He might've sounded annoyed, but he was hovering over Gorman, snapping his fingers and pointing toward a duffel bag.

The man they'd identified as Lowell hurried over to it and returned with a first aid kit. It was Shaker who very gently attended Gorman's wounds.

"Yeah, Shaker," Gorman said. "I can carry out orders." He took the cold pack from his commander and pressed it to his eyes. "That owl is damn beautiful."

All of them turned to watch the raptors conducting their battle low to the ground, only a few yards from them. At times they seemed to get lost in the fog, but then they would break apart, go to ground hissing their challenge and once more lock beaks or talons, usually Gray as the aggressor.

"Let's get back to it, gentlemen," Shaker said, turning to the table with obvious regret.

I'm going to access Blue, Kyle said. *We*

need to see what they're doing.

She's not happy and wants to join her mate. Camellia soothed the female owl. *Let me talk to her first, Kyle. She knows Gray has helped you before.* It took a moment to get the female's cooperation.

Luckily, Gray had pinned the great horned owl down, and the two raptors were clicking beaks angrily, wings spread wide, Gray blanketing his opponent, making it nearly impossible to look away. That gave Camellia the necessary time to convince Blue to let Kyle use her vision to read the map and send the information to everyone.

She'll do it, Kyle, but she's reluctant. She wants to be watchful of Gray in case he needs aid. I promised her I would alert her if he does. If I indicate for you to remove yourself, do it fast.

I will. Kyle took over the female owl's vision and hearing quickly, before she could change her mind.

"Lewis, you're going to take your men straight up the trail and hit Team One's compound. Word is, they haven't had time to establish themselves there yet. Hit them hard and take out everyone. No prisoners. Kill them all," Shaker directed. "You should have very little trouble. The men we sent ahead should soften them up, if not kill quite a few. There aren't very many of them. Ten at most. Our numbers will overwhelm them. Some don't operate well in chaotic conditions."

I'd like to know where he heard that bullshit, Jeff said.

Apparently, we're known far and wide the world over, Kyle replied.

Jonas was just leaving the second helicopter, boots back on the ground after being on top of it and applying the acid to the main rotor blade and swash plate. Camellia was just grateful he was on the ground, where she could better monitor him. If he was spotted, Red and the underground network would help her protect him, she counted on that. She told herself if she was looking for him and she couldn't see him, neither could their enemies, but her anxiety was high.

The female owl flapped her wings, signaling her mood and drawing the attention of the seven men gathered around the table. Gorman removed the cold compress and peered into the dense blue-gray fog, spotting the female sitting atop the snag.

"That's the reason the male got so upset. His mate is there. He's not happy with another male anywhere close to her."

Blue called to Camellia, shaking her head,

trying to dislodge Kyle. She turned her head in Camellia's direction, looking up toward the rocks and trees above them rather than at the fight the two male owls carried on.

Kyle, break off right now. She can't handle the stress of so many things happening at once. Jonas is out of her sight. She believes I'm in danger. Her mate is fighting. Get out of there.

Kyle did as she said, retreating. Camellia assessed his condition. He hadn't been utilizing the raptor's vision and hearing long enough to have damaged anything. She could turn her attention to Blue. The owl called to her repeatedly as she would to an owlet in danger. That only increased Gray's ferocity.

Camellia sent soothing messages to Blue, trying to connect to her without giving a verbal call that a young owlet might make. To her dismay, Blue's head continued to go down and she spread her wings wide in the classic threat/aggression manner, clacking her beak. Her eyes were definitely searching the fog to find Camellia, as she turned her head this way and that.

Camellia, Shaker and his men are picking up that something's wrong, Jonas warned.

Camellia turned her attention back to the clearing. Shaker and the others were showing the same signs of uneasiness that Gorman had displayed earlier. His radar may have gone off first, but now all of them were looking around, casting wary, prolonged looks into the forest and then up toward Camellia's vantage point.

The two owls continued to circle each other on the ground only a few yards from them. Most people would have been fascinated with witnessing actual combat between two male owls, but the seven men stepped away from the table, even Gorman with his cold pack, and, facing outward, began to actively search for anyone that might be watching them.

The sudden surge of psychic energy was extremely strong, so much so that Gray, who had pinned the other owl and was using his wicked beak mercilessly, broke away. The moment Gray gave way, the losing owl took to the air to retreat. Gray shook himself, spread his wings and let out his challenge for any other intruder.

Blue left her position on the snag and flew low along the ground over the victor and then rose up just a few feet, climbing to avoid the men and table, although she flew directly above them. The men did turn their heads to follow her progress as she made her way into the blue-gray fog with her slow, easy flight. Her mate followed her until both disappeared.

Blue relayed the map as best she could to Camellia, embedding the lines and graphs into her mind. Gray followed suit. He was much more adept at it, used to working with her. She didn't try to decipher what the two phantom owls had given her; she would do that later. She sent them her thanks and urged them to go deeper into the forest, where the men wouldn't see them again.

Camellia turned her attention to the seven men. She didn't have the details of where the last two commanders were bringing their troops, but it didn't matter. It might be on the map the owls had provided. Right at the moment, she feared her boys were in trouble.

She caught a hand signal passing from Shaker to the man they called Lewis. Lewis nodded and began to move in the direction of trees. His trajectory would take him several yards from the tree where Jeff was sitting. She had covered Jeff by simply making him appear part of the tree, but that didn't mean one or more of the enhanced men couldn't see beyond her illusion.

Swearing under her breath, she watched Shaker give a slight jerk of his head to one of the unnamed men. This one was the one she'd been concerned about. He moved like he could really handle himself, not that all of them didn't seem capable. It was just that this particular man seemed to flow over the ground. When he turned his head to survey his surroundings, he was the only one who had looked up toward the rocks where she was concealed. He'd only flicked his gaze her way twice, but it made her uneasy. He was too aware.

While Shaker rolled up the map, he skirted around the table. He didn't take off running or jogging toward the forest interior; he walked with purpose, using a smooth, easy gait, almost like an animal.

"Angel," Shaker called.

The man walking with that smooth gait stopped and half turned to look back.

"You know where you're taking your men?"

Angel nodded. He turned back toward the forest without saying a word, but he looked up, straight at her where she was hidden in the fog. For some reason, that alarmed Camellia. The look on his face . . . Cunning? Like an animal?

Jeff, whatever you do, don't move. I'm going to build an illusion in the fog. It won't deceive these men, but it will hopefully distract them. The one called Gorman and the other one called Lewis are both on you. I don't have any idea yet how they know we're here.

Don't worry, babe, Jeff said, as calm as ever. *I'm watching them.*

Five of the six enhanced commanders each took off in a different direction. She could see them in the fog, and the underground network told her where they were, but she had no idea what they were up to or how they knew someone was watching them. She increased the thickness of the fog slowly, not adding to it all at once, but bringing it into the valley in increments so the buildup wouldn't be noticed.

The fog hid her boys effectively, but it also hid the enhanced commanders. Now she relied solely on the underground network to tell her where everyone was. Two of the commanders were running in the forest, one coming straight toward her, another circling around behind her. Two were making their way stealthily toward the grove Jeff was in. Shaker remained in the small clearing with another man, the one no one had identified as of yet. He was the one Jonas thought looked like Shaker. Two others circled around back behind the helicopters. None of it was good.

A prickle of awareness crept down her spine. The one called Angel was close to her. She smelled him, the faint traces of soap and sweat. She took her time separating the various scents. There was much more to him than human, just as there was much more to Jonas. He was a mixture of various reptiles and mammals, just as Jonas was. Whitney had a hand in creating these men for Abrams. Abrams used them for his own private protection.

They can't have too much actual field experience, Jonas. They have to be Abrams's private security.

It would explain their arrogance. They hadn't come up against anyone else enhanced. So what tipped them off? What warning system did Gorman and Angel possess that allowed them to know or at least guess that someone spied on them? Had Whitney given one of them the ability to tap into the underground network? Red would have alerted her if there was a connection there.

If he sent his entire enhanced security force here to get rid of us and we kill them, I doubt if Whitney is going to be inclined to replace them. I'm telling you, honey, something isn't right here.

The other two men, Pops and Lowell, were close to Jonas. Jonas was perfectly still, immersed in the midst of the fog, impossible to see when he was so much a part of the drops. Still, because the enhanced soldiers were so close to him, Camellia's heart drummed in her ears, a steady, rhythmical beat.

Slow your heart, baby, Jonas advised.

They can't possibly hear my heart. Camellia was confident that Red muffled the sound. She was hidden in the mist, impossible for Angel to find. No scent. No way for enhanced vision to see. So why was he so close?

Do you think the underground network connects him to us? she ventured. *Watch yourself. Pops and Lowell are coming around the helicopter, Pops to the right of you. The other to the left.*

I'm on it.

Her heart lurched again. *If you move, they'll know where you are. Shaker may be the boss, but it's Angel directing everyone right now. He's connected to the underground network. I know he is. He can't feel Jeff because Jeff isn't touching the ground. But he's in the tree and the tree is part of the network.*

Silence met her declaration. She was very aware Jonas would know what that meant. If Angel was plugged into the mycelium network, then Whitney very well could have gone a step further and paired the man with her. That would explain why he had locked on to her presence.

She was directing the others. Would he have felt their presence through her? She didn't think so. That didn't make sense. Something else was going on. All of them were in danger until they figured it out. She didn't want Jonas to overreact. She willed him to think calmly, not allow the animals in his genetic code to take over the way Gray's had the moment he saw a rival in his claimed territory.

That pulled her up short. Was that something Whitney or Abrams counted on? Was this a trap planned in advance if Jonas was leading a team against them? Even that didn't make sense. How could they count on Camellia and Jonas meeting? Her brain worked at a very fast speed, computing all the possibilities and discarding them just as fast. They couldn't. Unless . . .

That fucking Whitney and his gift to all of you, the tattoo on your ankle. Jonas filled in the blanks for her. *We weren't aware of it immediately and weren't able to start interfering with his ability to track each of you. But he was sophisticated in the way he placed his tracking devices on each of you. They aren't the same.*

542

Camellia took a deep breath and allowed herself to tap into Red completely. Red was aware of the six enhanced commanders and Shaker, as well as their movements in the fog. She did not confirm Angel was on the mycelium network. In fact, she rejected the idea of it. Camellia had been studying him and the way he was stalking her through the mist.

It would still be too much of a coincidence. They couldn't rely on us meeting, Jonas. This is something else altogether. They're all shifting positions. Guessing where you are, but they know you're there. They haven't alerted anyone else. Not the troops, not even the helicopter pilots. Don't you think that's strange?

They sent the helicopter pilots away earlier with the troops, Jonas told her.

Camellia considered what that meant, turning the information over and over in her mind. It didn't make sense for Shaker to give that order unless he didn't want the mercenaries to see what the enhanced men were doing. What was Shaker up to that he didn't want all those men to see?

She pulled the map up that the two owls had pushed into her head. Because Kyle had already used Gray's vision and hearing more than once, the owl knew how to assemble the lines and grids. Blue had followed her mate's example. They had taken a snapshot of the map from various angles as they flew overhead and sent it to her. It looked to Camellia as if Shaker was sending all six commanders and their troops to Team One's fortress for a hard strike from every direction, including air. He hadn't spared a single man for Team Two. At least not now. There was no doubt his intention was eventually taking them all out. Team Two would not be spared.

The breeze blew through the fog, creating a subtle movement, proving a distraction. The blue-gray mist swirled just a bit, where before it had been still, just hanging dense and impenetrable. Now there was a slight sound, like a musical note on the lower end of the scale, that added to the ominous feeling in the fog. She used every very real resource available to her when building illusions to make them more compelling. Oftentimes, people overlooked sounds in fog. Sound could be muffled or distorted, and it was often the cause of a feeling of fear.

She found it was difficult to remain absolutely still. Muscles became cramped. She wanted to rub her shivering arms. Right now, Angel had the advantage. He could move at will while she had to remain frozen in place. He didn't know exactly where she was, but the moment she so much as eased her weight from one side to another, he could spot her. Figuring out what was going on made it difficult to control her heart and lungs. She had to work at discipline. Jonas, Jeff and Kyle had a tremendous amount of experience with all the missions they ran. She had been living alone for so long, she hadn't practiced as much as she should have.

No way is this about me. They didn't come here knowing about me, or if they did, it was last-minute. This is about Team One and Ryland, Lily and Daniel. I'm not even certain this is about Abrams and Whitney having a beef. Did your team do something to Abrams?

Jonas would have to consider her speculation. Jeff and Kyle did as well. It was a fair question. They'd run countless missions, most covert operations. That was why they were called GhostWalkers. No one knew about them. They were sent in to get a job done when no one else could do it.

I honestly can't think of anything, but that doesn't mean we couldn't have, Jonas finally said. *Jeff? Kyle?*

We've pissed off just about everyone at some time, but we were always under orders,

Jonas. If Abrams was angry, you'd think he'd take it out on whoever sent us, Kyle ventured.

I have to agree with that, Jeff added. *Even if Abrams had his hand in all the dirty operations we were sent out to stop, we were plugging the hole in the dam, so to speak.*

Angel shifted his position, actively searching for her, moving back and forth in a grid. He had a powerful presence, much like Jonas. There was no doubt that he had the genetic code of several predators, and he was using them to try to get her scent. She had every confidence that Red would mask her from him, but just as he was searching for her location, the others were conducting a very thorough probe for Jonas, Jeff and Kyle.

Lewis just about stepped on me, Kyle whispered in their minds. *He was sniffing around just under the tree where Jeff is, and he circled back. Now he's crossing in a grid pattern with Gorman.*

It's Gorman you really have to watch out for, Camellia reminded him. *He's got built-in radar, even more so than the others.*

Jonas, Jeff said, *let's kill them now and get it over with.*

And what about Camellia? Angel's up there

546

with her. We don't have all the information we need as to why these bastards are coming at us. Abrams would just send another army. What's wrong with you?

Listen, Jonas, Camellia replied softly. *In the fog. Listen.*

All of them went very quiet. There was that low musical note, a repetition built into the breeze, almost like a rolling wave, coming and going. They were used to the mist now, used to Camellia's illusions. When they would have said something, she stopped them with a slight hiss in their minds.

Keep still. Keep listening. It isn't the breeze. It's a voice.

Camellia could hear the softest of voices. At first she hadn't realized it was anything but that low note rolling in the breeze. Muted. Just part of the reality of fog hanging in the clearing and cutting through the forest.

He's experienced. He knows exactly what he's doing. He's laying the foundation right now that it's cold and our muscles are cramped. We have to move. Our bodies can't take being so still. I've always been able to be still for hours, but all of a sudden I can't. We want to attack them. I can't make out everything he's saying yet, he's that good.

If he's that good, how come you can't

understand what he's saying? Kyle asked.

He repeats it over and over, Camellia explained. *The same dialogue and it gets in your head. Eventually you do what he says. I'm already feeling the need to move. Angel is close to me. He knows I'm here. The moment I move, he's bound to see me. Jeff just pushed to attack them. He's working on us.*

Jonas sighed. *Which one, Camellia, can you tell?*

I believe it's Shaker. I can barely see him. The fog is so thick now, and it doesn't move, so even with enhanced vision, I can't see his lips. It just feels like him to me.

She found it difficult to monitor the two men moving around the helicopters. They were climbing in and out of them, searching for Jonas. She tried not to panic, knowing the voice was working on her nerves. She had to trust Red to keep Jonas safe.

Jonas, what kinds of missions did you go on that might have brought the spotlight onto your team? she asked, because she needed the distraction of thinking of something besides Angel stalking her and those men so close to Jonas.

Mostly, we disrupted drug, gunrunning and trafficking operations.

Jonas sounded steady. Calm. Camellia was certain that Shaker knew Jonas had all kinds of predatory animals in his genetic code, and he would eventually begin to push challenges into his mind in order to get Jonas to react. Jonas was extremely protective. That was in his file. If Whitney knew that about him — and he did — he most likely would have shared the information with Abrams. Or would he have?

Although Abrams had money enough to buy information, he hacked his way into computers and bought spies. He probably knew more about the GhostWalkers than Whitney by now.

Do you think Abrams is involved in all of those things? He's an international banker. And a billionaire. Why would he need to be involved in anything illegal?

Power, Jonas answered instantly. *He needs it, and so do the others he formed his partnerships with. They rule the world, and that includes the underworld. No one does anything without their say-so. I guess that's supposed to include us.*

If that's so, he would have been the one ultimately behind your orders, Jonas. You would have just been carrying out what he wanted you to do.

They were back to square one. An army this size didn't make sense. The idea of wiping out two teams of GhostWalkers didn't make sense. None of it did.

18

"Camellia, I think we both know it's time to cut the crap. You're cold, and you need to move before your body begins to cramp. There's no need to stay locked in position. I just want to talk to you," Angel said.

Camellia's heart jumped and then began to pound. Angel had just taken off the gloves. She could answer or not.

Don't. Jonas's voice was sheer command.

What else is there to do? He knows I'm here. He doesn't know you are. They're guessing about you. I can throw my voice, mix it in the fog. It's possible I can find out why they're really here.

She wasn't going to let Jonas tell her what to do. She wasn't under his command, and in the end, she had to do what she thought was best. He was trying to protect her. That was all he was thinking about. They couldn't stay in a standoff forever. Shaker was aware of it. Jonas was either going to have to begin hunting in the fog or get out of there.

Jonas swore. *I will hunt them to the ends of the earth if anything happens to you. He'd better not put a hand on you.*

I'm confident he won't get the opportunity, Jonas.

"Camellia, there's no need to be afraid of me."

Angel's voice was smooth, like velvet. It played along her nerve endings. If she felt it, Jonas could as well. This could be a very dangerous situation. There was no doubt in her mind that Whitney had paired them. Jonas would have to trust her to handle the situation.

She threw her voice into the forest, well back away from the tree where Jeff was. "I'm not afraid of you, just a little shocked that you would be willing to kill women and children who haven't done any harm to you. To me, Whitney was the ultimate monster. I never considered anyone he experimented on, the way he did me, to be a monster, but clearly, that isn't true."

She poured contempt and distaste into her voice because she felt both. She wanted all of them to feel it. Let them know what someone who had been experimented on and enhanced thought of them. Her opinion most likely meant nothing to them, but they were going to get it just the same.

Angel was silent, and she knew he was communicating with his brothers. She was looking right at him. Like Jonas, he was able to keep his facial expression completely blank, but his eyes told her he hadn't liked her evaluation of him.

"I can see why you would think that, but you don't know the entire story, do you? Passing judgment without knowing everything is wrong."

She kept very still. He was still looking straight at her. She took great care to send her voice to the same place — the forest interior. "There are certain lines that aren't to be crossed, Angel. Terrorists cross them. When you decided to cross those lines, you put yourself on the same level. There isn't an excuse."

The mycelium network alerted her that there was movement in the forest. One of the men moved rapidly toward the interior.

Gorman is running along a deer path, Jeff reported. *I've got a visual on him.*

Don't move. Don't make a single movement, Camellia cautioned. *They're looking for me. I want to see what this man has to say for himself. There is no excuse for this behavior and he knows it. I can feel his discomfort and even guilt.*

553

She didn't ask Jonas if he could, that would be like rubbing salt in wounds. The fact that she could feel Angel's emotions would only make it worse for Jonas. She refrained from sending him soothing caresses, instead treating him with every confidence that he would believe she was his partner.

"Again, I can see why you would think that," Angel conceded. "Come out into the open. I'm not going to harm you."

"Why would I believe you when you came here with the express purpose of killing babies? Of killing women who did you no harm? They didn't, did they? Your leader just sent one of your men chasing my voice into the forest to find me. He won't. You know he won't, but still, he had to look." This time she threw her voice into a different part of the fog, one closer to Shaker, one on the opposite side of the clearing, away from where Kyle was lying so still.

"I can understand why you wouldn't trust me, but you aren't part of that team, unless you've hooked up with Jonas." There was accusation in Angel's voice.

She remained silent for a few moments. "Why would you think I would have anything at all to do with any member of a GhostWalker team?" She poured genuine puzzlement into her voice. She knew Shaker would be the one to analyze her tone. Why should they think that of her? It didn't actually make sense.

"I was just considering clearing out before Whitney sent his soldiers after me when all hell seemed to be breaking loose. Normally, I wouldn't get involved, but I'm not about to stand by and see innocent children killed to protect my freedom." All of that was the strict truth, and Shaker would hear that in her voice. "Quite frankly, I was spying on you to see what I could do in the way of sabotaging you."

"The owls are yours," Angel said.

That's how he found me. Blue gave me away for certain. Gorman was uneasy from the beginning, and when Blue got so upset, Angel and Gorman knew someone was here. Blue looked right at me, Camellia said.

"Yes, they go with me everywhere I go. Gray is very steady, but Blue can get upset. The fight for territory was disturbing to her, especially when all of you were here, and she knew I was . . . concerned." Deliberately, she hesitated before she described her own state of mind. "Clearly, I was affecting her."

This time, no one ran to try to get to her, but the two men who had made their way around the helicopters eased to the ground on their bellies. One — she believed it was Pops — used his hands to propel himself easily over the leaves and twigs without making any more noise than a lizard might. She couldn't see much of him in the dense fog, but the underground network mapped his progress for her. His enhancements allowed him to travel quickly without sounding like a human moving around.

They've got to have something else directing them, Kyle said. *Gorman was about to use the owl's vision, but suppose someone else is using an animal's hearing or sense of smell?*

Camellia hadn't thought of that. *Jonas, is that possible? Do you have anyone on your team that uses animals or reptiles like that?*

Not other than the way Kyle did. I haven't even heard a rumor of it, Jonas admitted.

"Whitney paired you with Jonas Harper. Are you aware of the pairing?"

Camellia had the feeling that soft, calm question was a trap. "Yes. He was hiking on the trail with two other men. I felt a tremendous pull toward him right away and knew Whitney had to have paired us. It was a very scary moment." She was careful to stick strictly to the truth. Their first meeting had been frightening.

"He has skills in the mountains. It took all of mine to make certain he couldn't find me." She had been hidden in the mist, just as she was now. "At the same time I became aware of him, he was aware of me. I hadn't expected to stumble across someone I was paired with."

"He's a monster beyond anything you could ever imagine, Camellia," Angel said. He leaned against a large downed tree trunk. "I know you're somewhere up here. They can look for you all they want down below, but you're here. I feel you close to me. You want to know why? Because Whitney paired us together. We belong. I can take care of you. Give you everything you want. A family. You always wanted a family. I studied everything about you."

"You don't know anything about me. I would never, under any circumstances, go back to Whitney or put myself into someone's hands that would kill children. I want children more than anything. For a man to ruthlessly come here with the idea of murdering innocents sickens me."

"I didn't come here for that reason," he denied.

"Angel," Shaker cautioned. "Let her show herself before you decide to give her information."

"Why would I do that when you have all the advantage?" Camellia asked. "There's seven of you and an entire army of mercenaries. I'm one person and a couple of raptors. The only advantage I have is to remain hidden from you." She kept her voice coming from across the small clearing from him, well aware of Pops scooting on his belly, trying to zero in on the sound.

"I'm going to tell you the truth about Jonas Harper and Ryland Miller, Camellia," Angel said. "The truth about why we're here."

Camellia heard the ring of honesty in his voice, but more importantly, she felt Jonas's sudden withdrawal. He didn't pull completely away from her, but he did retreat.

Camellia. Jonas whispered her name into her mind. Stroked a caress so intimate he turned her heart inside out. Something was terribly wrong. She felt it in his gathering tension.

Do you know what he's going to tell me?

I should have told you myself. I was going to tell you myself. I was waiting . . . He broke off and stroked another caress inside her mind.

When? When were you going to tell me?

I don't know, he answered honestly. *When you loved me so much, you wouldn't leave*

558

me no matter how ugly and vile you found out I was.

Her stomach dropped. She couldn't stay still. She just couldn't. Even Red couldn't save her if whatever Angel was going to tell her was that bad.

"Why are you here, Angel? Tell me your excuse to kill children."

"I'm telling you, we aren't here to kill children," Angel repeated.

"I would believe you, except the owls have excellent hearing. Shaker did give the order to kill everyone but Lily and Daniel, didn't you, Shaker? There really isn't any way to get around that."

Angel swore under his breath. "Jonas Harper murdered Shaker and Tusker's brother, Oliver. They told everyone he died in the cages, killed by Whitney's enemies, but that wasn't how it happened. No one even speaks of him now."

No doubt Tusker was the unknown man who looked so much like Shaker. He had to be the one able to use the animal sense of smell or hearing. Maybe both. Tusker was another name used for "elephant," and elephants had an exceptional sense of smell. She sent the slightest of breezes toward the meadow, just enough to move the fog around the two men. They stood back-to-back. Shaker's eyes scanned the rocks and trees repeatedly, covering Angel. His brother watched the helicopters, still uneasy that something was close to them, unseen in the dense fog.

Jeff and Kyle both had an instant reaction to his statement. Like Jonas, there was a partial withdrawal from her. They moved from the four-person telepathic communication they were using to a three-person one, leaving her out.

There was no doubt Angel told at least a partial truth. His voice rang with honesty. As much as she didn't want to, Camellia had to accept that he believed what he was telling her.

Jonas, who is Oliver?

Her question was met with silence. She didn't say anything. She was patient. Two could play the same game if need be. Finally, Jonas sighed, stroked another caress in her mind. She didn't want caresses. She wanted answers.

He's dead, Camellia.

That doesn't tell me anything.

Again, Jonas remained silent.

"Harper and Oliver were best friends, like brothers. They went through boot camp together. Trained together. Went through Army Rangers training together. Then applied for and were accepted into the Ghost-Walker program. Both were enhanced with practically the exact same genetic material."

"You can't know that." *He couldn't, could he?* she asked Jonas. *Was he? Was Oliver enhanced in the same way as you?*

Jonas's reply was terse. *Yes.*

"He talked to his brothers when things began to go wrong. He was worried about Jonas. Worried about himself. Worried someone was trying to kill the entire team. He had a strong protective instinct," Angel continued. He crossed his arms over his chest and stared straight at her. "You may as well just let me see you. I swear to you, if you don't want to come with me, I'll let you go."

"That's your word and not the others'."

"We speak for one another. We're in this together," Angel insisted. "You can't stay still that long. You have to trust someone."

Isn't that strange, Jonas? That's exactly what you said to me. I have to trust someone. Yet we're right in the middle of the enemy's camp, surrounded by them, and you, Jeff and Kyle went into your huddle, leaving me out. Was that so you could get your story straight? That doesn't feel like trust. That feels like betrayal.

Camellia, don't. I can't come to you. I can't

move. Not unless we decide to try to kill them all right here. Angel is on you, so that might be something we wait on until he backs off.

I am perfectly capable of taking care of myself. I've been doing it for a long time now.

"I gave up trusting anyone the night I was betrayed, and Whitney killed Ivy because I tried to escape. Just say what you have to say," she told Angel.

The men close to Jonas, Kyle and Jeff might've seemed as if they were looking for her, but she didn't think they were really serious about it. Like Angel, they believed her to be right where she was. How? What had given her away other than Blue? Blue may have given Angel her direction, but not her exact location.

Kyle and Jeff are worried about what you'll think of me if you hear Angel's account before I have a chance to tell you what happened, Jonas said. *I should have told you, Camellia, but this kind of thing isn't something you spring on someone you're trying to get to fall in love with you.*

Tusker watched the helicopters, believing someone was close to them. Lewis and Gorman were in the forest, knowing — *knowing* — someone was there. Kyle had nearly been stepped on. It wasn't owls. Gray would have told her. Lowell and Pops were on full alert.

Camellia had to figure out what they were using to find them. If Angel knew she wasn't alone, he wasn't buying into her story at all. He had to know Jonas was with her. Still, he believed what he was saying.

"At first, as they discovered the various enhancements weren't just psychic, they worked together to develop them. They found they were unusually fast. Enormously strong. The two of them shared information. They had friendly competitions, pitting their abilities against one another in order to develop their skills for missions."

So far, it all sounded sensible to her. As Angel told his story, she searched the fog for anything that might have given her and the others away to Tusker. She was certain he was the one communicating with a creature. If she could find a way to connect with him without his knowledge, she might be able to figure it out and stop the communication. That way, he wouldn't be able to hunt them. Right now, no matter what they did, Shaker's men might have the advantage.

Are you going to say something, Jonas?

What's there to say, Camellia? So far, he's doing an okay job of telling what it was like.

He wasn't there. You were. Hearing the story isn't the same as going through it.

Discovering each separate genetic tempera-
ment you have to deal with and learning to
use and control it.

Camellia waited for Jonas to say something, but he didn't. He allowed Angel to
tell his version. Jonas could be terribly stubborn, and right now, he was choosing to be
at his worst. She wasn't certain why. Kyle
and Jeff remained in the background, neither one adding to the conversation, just
listening to Angel give her the details.

She took her gaze from Angel and placed
it firmly on Tusker. His back was to her. He
seemed to be looking toward the helicopters,
but every now and then, he tipped his head
up slightly and looked toward the trees. She
followed his gaze upward. There was little
fog in the branches of the trees so high up,
and she could see the occasional flutter of
leaves as the breeze passed through. Insects
chased one another in the sky. There was
very little movement other than a lizard or
two skittering up the trunk of a tree.

"Something began to happen to their
friendship over time. It was subtle at first."

Angel's words were ominous enough to
pull her attention back to him. His mask of
calm began to disappear, to be replaced by
lines carved deep with anger. "Jonas can be
very jealous and controlling. He likes to be

the center of attention. The one in charge. Oliver went from being his best friend to a rival. Jonas didn't like that sometimes Oliver outran him or bested him in any way on a mission. There were troubling fights. Jonas began acting arrogant and talking to Oliver about how others without enhancements weren't worth much, and why should they risk their lives for them?"

The Jonas she knew could be jealous; maybe being the commander might make one think he was controlling. Definitely, he preferred being the man in charge, but he didn't seem to like to be the center of attention. She couldn't see him claiming that others without enhancements were less important or valuable. He was a protective man, and she couldn't see him ignoring those not enhanced.

Camellia waited in silence, but Jonas didn't defend himself. Jeff or Kyle didn't leap to his defense either.

"Go on." She didn't bother throwing her voice. She spoke directly to Angel, but she remained hidden in the mist.

Again, she turned her attention to Tusker below, studying him carefully. He turned his head to look over his shoulder toward her. When he did, there was a fluttering of wings in the trees, and bats wheeled and dipped, rushing to get the insects, especially night moths, from the sky.

Echolocation. She breathed the word into the minds of the three men. *We can't hear it, even with our superior hearing. But he can. Tusker. He must have tremendous hearing. Very acute. That's how he became aware of us. Or rather believes he's aware of us. Jeff is so still in the tree, he appears part of the tree to the bats. Kyle seems part of the ground. They can't locate Jonas.*

"I'm going to give you the short version, Camellia," Angel said, his voice harsher than it had been. "Team One was sent out on a mission. I wasn't there, but from what we understand, it was hell."

"Where did you get your information if you weren't there?" she interrupted, watching the bats. *Gray. Blue. I need you now.* She didn't want the owls to kill the bats, just drive them away as if they were too close to a nest.

"A very, very reliable source. From someone who was there," Angel assured her. Again, his voice rang with so much honesty that she swung her full attention back to him.

Immediately, he had Jonas's attention as well.

If what he says is true, someone betrayed

us, Kyle said. *Someone on our team.*

Her heart sank. She suddenly was tired and wished she was anywhere but where she was. She'd asked to come along. Jonas had given her every opportunity to stay in her beautiful garden where she was safe and protected. She wouldn't have met these men, and she wouldn't have heard what Angel had to say. She wouldn't feel hurt. Her hurt. Jonas's hurt. Was life just a series of betrayals? One after another? Was there no real loyalty?

That seems to be the name of the game all over the place, doesn't it? Camellia said. *You really can't trust anyone, can you?*

That's not necessarily true, honey, Jonas said. *Let's hear him out. And let's not lose sight of why they're here. Even if I did everything wrong and murdered their brother the way they think I did, it still doesn't give them a reason to wipe out men, women and children who had nothing to do with it.*

It was the first time he'd said anything that might be a rebuttal to the version of the story Angel was telling her.

I'm not about to forget why these men are here. She wouldn't. The idea that they had so callously decided that Marigold's twins could be murdered right along with Mari and her twin sister and nephews sickened her. What was wrong with them? No matter how charming Angel thought he was, she would always keep that purpose uppermost in her mind. There was no forgiveness for that.

"As the mission was being carried out, several of the team members were wounded. They were in a valley surrounded by heavy gunfire with the enemy above them."

She could smell the gunpowder and hear the heavy shells hitting all around them. Jeff and Kyle as well as Jonas were thrown back in time, remembering the tense moments when they all thought they wouldn't make it out.

Nico got to higher ground and gave us covering fire. I'm not sure any of us would have made it out alive without him, Jonas supplied. *It was chaotic with so many wounded and the enemy surrounding us.*

"The enemy had them pinned down. Oliver decided to make a run for it. He figured he could break through the enemy lines and get help for everyone. They were running out of ammo and desperately needed medical supplies. He went to the commanding officer, Ryland Miller, and told him his plan. If he succeeded, they would all be saved. If he didn't make it, only he would suffer the consequences. He was extremely fast. Their sniper could help him get through."

So far, he's right on the money, Jonas informed her.

They could have access to the report, Jeff said. *Ryland files a report with the general each time we come back from a mission. Someone could have hacked into the general's files.*

It's a possibility, Jonas agreed.

My leg is cramping, Jeff said.

Don't you move, Jonas snapped, the order clear. *The one in the clearing is definitely directing everyone, and he's got his ears on you. No one is killing you today, Jeff.*

That brought Camellia's gaze back to the bats. *Gray, Blue, run them out of here. Chase them far away.*

"Oliver was a hero that day. He broke through enemy lines and got the word back to his superiors that his team needed aid. Jonas couldn't take that he received all the attention from everyone. It was too much for him. When Oliver snuck back to his team, there in the valley, determined to help carry the wounded out, Jonas attacked him. The entire team witnessed it, including Miller."

Camellia felt the instant rejection from all three of the men sharing the telepathic communication with her.

That's bullshit, Kyle whispered. *That's not the way it happened.*

Hear him out, Jonas said. *Clearly, he believes what he's telling her.*

Camellia repeated the last phrase to herself. *Clearly, he believes what he's telling her.* Jonas had distanced himself from her, almost as if being close to her hurt. She didn't reach out to him along the familiar lines of connection. They were still there, still intact, but she didn't test them for strength.

In that moment, Camellia's relationship with him felt fragile. She didn't know the first thing about relationships. She could admit that. He knew far more than she did. If he thought pulling away from her when she needed them to stand strong together was the right course of action, so be it.

She needed to hold on to something, and that was going to have to be her own power. The character traits she'd come to rely on. She was strong when she needed to be. She could expertly use nearly any weapon. She had weapons no one knew about, not even Jonas. They'd talked about them, but he was really unaware of what they could do.

Regardless of what any of these men said or did, the decisions they came to, she would not allow them to harm Mari and her babies, Briony and her twins, Lily and young Daniel, or any other mother and child who happened to be in the compound above them.

"Don't stop there, Angel," she whispered.

"Whitney put so many aggressive animals' genetic matter into both Jonas and Oliver. Not just mammal, but reptile as well. The two were pumped up beyond belief. They came together like animals, Jonas roaring a challenge that could be heard throughout the valley. There were no guns. No knives. They went at each other bare-handed. Bare-knuckled. Beating each other's bodies. The way they hit should have smashed bones, but neither went down. Blood ran down their chests and necks as they circled one another, roaring like animals."

Overhead, the owls screamed a challenge and dove at the hoary bats, chasing them through the night sky. Gray sounded so feral Camellia nearly jumped out of her skin. She'd heard him countless times.

Jeff's telepathic gasp could be heard by all of them. At first she put it down to the owls relentlessly chasing the bats away from the small grove of trees, but his protest followed swiftly on the heels of Angel's commentary.

"Jonas went berserk. He attacked the

wounded, ripping open bandages and tearing at their wounds. He fed on the blood like a wolf and then howled for his pack to join him."

"Angel . . ." she protested.

Again, Jeff made a soft, telepathic protest while Jonas and Kyle remained silent. She knew Angel's account couldn't be accurate, but Middlemist Red was assessing his voice along with her, and Red was affirming what he said as strictly the truth. Jeff and Kyle weren't able to do anything but hear Angel's voice and assess it themselves, but Jonas would feel what Camellia was. He would know Red was making the same evaluation she was.

The tension and hostility, as well as grief, in Shaker and Tusker were palpable. The other men's emotions fed the need for violence into the darkness of the fog so the colors shifted slightly from blue-gray to a darker purplish gray. Or was that Jonas feeding the fog? Camellia felt the familiar flow between Jonas and her, the neurons suddenly flooding her body with adrenaline-laced chemicals.

Jonas was angry; there was no doubt about it. She would be too if she heard someone saying such things about her. Most people would never believe a story like that could be real, but she'd seen Whitney's experiments when they'd gone terribly wrong. She'd seen his soldiers going mad, foaming at the mouth, raging, throwing themselves at electric fences and taking a hail of bullets before going down.

"I'm not making this up, Camellia. A witness who was there told the story. I swear to you. Jonas killed Shaker and Tusker's brother. My friend." Angel's voice broke, and he pressed the heel of his hand to his forehead for a brief moment before he lifted his head and looked at her again. He would have been looking her in the eye had she been allowing him to actually see her.

"Oliver, as wounded and battered as he was, tried to stop him, but Jonas was too strong. They fought again. Jonas tore him from limb to limb. Do you have any idea how strong you have to be to rip off someone's arms? To break the bones so badly you can turn the arm the other direction? He smashed him. Stomped on him until his bones were crushed in his body."

"That couldn't have happened." She whispered the denial.

"Ask Ryland Miller. He was there. The entire team was there. No one tried to stop him. They all had guns. They could have shot him, but they didn't. Not one of them put a bullet in his head. They didn't even try."

That's not what happened, Jeff protested. *That was a nightmare. A persistent nightmare. How could this man know about a nightmare I had? My God, Jonas, this is on me.*

Camellia felt his intention or, more than likely, the underground network and Red did, as Jeff had one arm wrapped securely around the branch he was stretched out on.

Don't you dare move, Jeff, she snapped. *You'll give everyone away. This isn't on you any more than it's on anyone else.*

It's my nightmare. There's more. It's so ugly. I couldn't get it out of my head. I had it for months. I was afraid to go to sleep at night.

There was so much pain in Jeff's voice, Camellia closed her eyes, wanting to weep. She wanted to cry for all of them, Shaker, Tusker, Angel included.

This is on me, Jeff, not you. I'm the one who killed him. Jonas said it so quietly, Camellia nearly missed the confession.

"It's hard to kill a GhostWalker," Angel continued. "We don't just die like everyone thinks we should. Oliver suffered and Jonas wanted him to. He tore out his jugular. He's an animal, Camellia. A time bomb. They keep him because he's useful to them. And if they keep him after what he did, you have to wonder how many other time bombs they have on that team. Do you have any idea the havoc he could wreak on the main population? Or the rest of us for that matter."

Camellia took several deep, calming breaths, trying to sort through everything she'd learned and what they still needed to know. How much time did they have before Shaker gave the order to attack? She knew Gorman and Lewis had shifted their positions. The changes were subtle, but the underground network had sent their locations to her. She was concerned for Jonas. She didn't know what Pops or Lowell were up to, or Shaker and his brother.

"You took all this to Abrams, and he was so sympathetic he sent an army? He's a man who wants to hide in the shadows, Angel. He definitely believes himself superior. To you. To me. Probably to Whitney. Why would he ever agree to send mercenaries to help you wipe out Ryland Miller's team, even if he wanted Lily and Daniel?"

"Abrams is just like every other entitled asshole, Camellia," Angel said, his voice filled with contempt. "He does think he's superior. He gives orders, and everyone blindly obeys him. He doesn't even look at his security detail. They're beneath him, even though they're expected to take a bullet for him. It doesn't occur to him that any one of us would ever consider turning on him. Or that we would take his shit for a reason."

"A reason? I lived alone, giving up my need for a family in order to keep from having to take anyone's crap ever again. What would be your reason when you have so much power, Angel? Especially all of you combined?"

She was careful to keep her tone curious. She *was* curious. Even a little shocked. Angel seemed intelligent. Why would he follow Abrams when he wouldn't need to do so?

"Abrams has money and power. Not only that, Camellia, but he belongs to a small consortium that pretty much rules the world. They have a hand in influencing the world's markets. They can take down governments, all behind the scenes, of course. If we control Abrams, we have control of that."

Camellia's stomach did a hard somersault. "Shaker's voice."

Angel nodded. "Shaker takes a lot of shit from some of the others. We keep our circle tight so there's no chance of it getting out that Shaker controls Abrams. He only uses his ability when it's in our interests. We move pieces around on the board, making certain the GhostWalkers are protected when they would have been left wide open. That sort of thing. We tried to shut down some of Whitney's worst experiments. Abrams would be so angry at Whitney, not even realizing he was the one behind the orders." There was amusement in Angel's voice.

"Shaker persuaded Abrams to send you here with the mercenaries. Why would you give all that up for revenge? You know by coming here, you would lose everything. You could never go back."

"Jonas *murdered* Oliver and they did nothing," Shaker snapped, for the first time speaking directly to her. "I knew Oliver was unstable. When I heard he died, I accepted his death, but then this report came in, and it was disgusting to me that an entire team betrayed his trust. His best friend betrayed his trust. I'm his brother. Was I going to do the same? Not on your life."

"I get what you're saying. I do. If I believed this one report rather than talking to Ryland Miller myself and asking him questions, then I might be out for revenge . . ."

"Justice," Shaker said. "It isn't the same."

"Revenge if you're willing to murder in-

577

nocents, Shaker," Camellia pointed out. "What does killing children have to do with what you believe happened to your brother? I don't understand that at all."

"Ryland Miller has to suffer."

"Yet he'll be dead and his wife and child alive," Camellia said. "And what about Team Two? They had nothing at all to do with it. Why include them?"

"They'll hunt us," Angel answered. "You have to be with us, Camellia. This is your chance. You can't want to be with him, knowing what he did. Jonas Harper is a monster."

"You're going off one report that makes no sense. Those are men of honor, and yet not one of them behaved honorably, according to the story you just told. Before all of you throw away your lives like this, shouldn't you investigate what happened a little bit more? Don't you owe it to yourselves?" Camellia felt as if she was pleading for all of their lives. For their honor as well. "Angel, you and Shaker seem like good men. You have to know this isn't the right thing to do. At least take a little more time and make sure you're right."

Jeff groaned again. *How could they have gotten ahold of my nightmare? I didn't talk to a shrink about it. I didn't even talk to Lily about*

578

it, not even when she asked me.

I remember when you weren't sleeping, Kyle said. *I asked you about it.*

We talked, Jonas said. *You told me you were having nightmares and what they were about. You don't have any reason to feel as if any of this is your fault.*

You saved my life that day, Jonas. He was your friend. You loved him like a brother. If you hadn't been there, I'd be dead. I was the one who forced you to make a choice. Jeff's voice was filled with pain and regret.

Camellia found the entire exchange heart-breaking. She realized, in part, why Jonas hadn't explained more to her with the two men so close. The explanation was very personal to Jeff. He blamed himself. He was blaming himself even more now. She supposed it was human nature to take on guilt for things it was impossible to control.

No one forced me to make a choice, Jeff, Jonas said flatly. *I've never been forced to do anything in my life. My choices are my own, and I stand by them, even if they might be difficult to make.*

I was there that day, Kyle said. *We all were. Oliver would have killed a lot of us before he was through. He was out of his mind. If anyone was to blame, it was Whitney.*

"You need to choose whose side you're

on, Camellia," Angel hissed, his voice a thread of sound, as if he were hiding it from those below. "Choose now."

They'd run out of time. There was no more negotiating and no finding out more information. Shaker was going to make his move against Jonas.

19

Camellia couldn't help Jonas. She didn't know exactly where he was in the dense fog. Like her, he was capable of disappearing into it. Pops and Lowell, the two men hunting him, had climbed up onto one of the helicopters. She had the vague impression of each of them through the droplets of mist, but she couldn't let herself be distracted by trying to figure out what they were doing. Jeff, up in the tree, and Kyle, lying on the forest floor, were most at risk.

They're going to attack, she warned the others and turned her attention first to Angel. She wanted to be able to keep her entire focus on Jeff and Kyle and not worry whether Angel was going to attack her the moment she turned her back.

She called on the mycelium network, bringing her weapons close to the surface. Mushrooms began to push through the forest floor, shoving aside the dirt and leaves.

Rotting vegetation gave way to bright capped heads and subdued tanned ones. Several blackened cones pushed through the leaves to sit among the rocks and downed trunks. Little mushrooms sprouted on the living tree trunks as well as those that had fallen years earlier.

"Don't do this, Angel," Camellia pleaded. She let the fog drift around her. Let him catch glimpses of her. She sat on a flattened boulder, one hand planted firmly to give her the ability to push off.

"You're either with us or against us, Camellia," he reiterated. "Loyalty is everything." He leveled a gun at her. "Make your choice."

"Clearly, you made yours."

The jerk on his ankles was extremely hard, taking him to the ground and destroying his aim at the same time. His legs became completely tangled in thick fibers made of natural polymers created from the fungi running beneath the soil. The long ropes of fibrous material tightened the loops wrapped around his ankles and legs as more and more snaked out of the ground like the arms of an octopus. He tried to roll and, at the same time, squeezed off several hasty shots at her.

Camellia pushed off the boulder as Angel

went crashing to the soil. She leapt to the opposite side of the rock as leaves, twigs and even branches were thrown up into the air around the big man as the fibrous ropes took him to the ground. He continued to fire his weapon at her, the bullets skimming along the boulder just above her head and to either side of it, kicking up dirt and debris and shaving off splinters of rock.

Gray came out of the fog, a ferocious fury without mercy, claws a dark brown, tipped in black, razor-sharp, slashing first at Angel's eyes and then stabbing into the back of his head to puncture deep. Before Angel could raise his arm to shove the gun into the growling bird, Blue was on him, tearing the weapon from his hand and then raking at his eyes.

Camellia did her best to drown out the sound of Angel screaming in agony. She'd given him his chance.

"Angel?" Shaker yelled. "Camellia, I'm going to fuckin' kill you."

She ignored his threat. She wasn't supposed to defend herself? Just let Angel shoot her? These men were insane to think they could just kill people and no one would try to fight back.

She couldn't think about Shaker and his threats, or Jonas and who might be after him. Kyle was in immediate danger. The moment Angel had attacked her, it must have been on Shaker's orders. They no longer had the bats to give away locations in the dense fog, but Shaker's men knew they were there.

At Camellia's warning, Kyle rolled, the only thing that saved his life. Gorman pulled a spear from the sheath at his back, stabbing down at him viciously. Instead of going straight through his throat, it went through his shoulder and pinned him like an insect to the soil. Wisps of purplish-gray fog curled between Kyle and Gorman as blood spurted around the wound, blossoming on Kyle's jacket and then seeping to the ground beneath him.

Kyle went still as Gorman very slowly lowered himself into a crouch beside him. "You're not going anywhere, GhostWalker. I'm going to slice open your belly and see if your guts are as yellow as I think they are." From his boot, Gorman withdrew a knife and held it up for Kyle to see. "Wish your good friend Ryland was here to witness this. Maybe I should take a video and send it to him."

"Yeah, maybe you should," Kyle said. "You're such an upstanding guy." He couldn't move with the spear shoved through his shoulder, holding him in place.

Jeff put a rifle to his shoulder and squeezed the trigger, attempting to kill Gorman before he could finish Kyle off. Jeff was struck hard from behind, knocked from the branch and dropped thirty feet to the forest floor. He landed in a crouch, turning to face Lewis, who stood just a few feet from him, grinning like an ape.

Kyle, turn your head away, close your mouth and hold your breath. Camellia gave the order. *Don't take a breath until I say otherwise. You'll die if you do.*

I want to look him right in the eyes when he kills me.

He isn't going to kill you if you do what I say right now. You can't get any powder in your eyes, nose or mouth. Now, Kyle.

Do it, Kyle. Jonas snapped the command.

With visible reluctance, Kyle closed his eyes and turned away from Gorman. The moment he did, white fibers erupted from the ground to wrap around his head, covering his eyes, nose and mouth. Simultaneously, black cones erupted from the soil, rocketing straight at Gorman's face. The missiles struck their targets precisely, each eye, his nose, his mouth. The cones exploded, bursting open. A cloud of fine powder went everywhere, covering Gorman's face so that he had a mask of black powder completely coating his skin and scalp.

Gorman opened his mouth wider to yell, but the powder penetrated deeper and clogged more, preventing air from moving in either direction. Foam bubbled up around his lips as they turned a dark blue under the powder. There was no cough, no sound, other than a muffled choke, and then he slumped to the ground, the knife still gripped in his hand. His entire body went rigid. The powder began to dissolve in the wet mist as if it had never been.

Need to breathe soon, Camellia, Kyle said. *What the hell is going on?*

Already, the fibrous strands were falling away from Kyle's face. *Need to remove this fucking spear.*

"Gorman!" Shaker shouted. "Lewis, what's going on with Gorman?"

"I don't know, I can't see him," Lewis answered.

Shaker called out to Gorman a second time and then swore steadily.

The fog rolled and churned as the breeze turned into gusts of wind. Each time the bursts of air pushed through the mist, the dark purple drops spun, producing a low, swelling roar like the wave in an ocean that retreated and returned with each gust.

Don't look toward Gorman when you inhale, Camellia cautioned Kyle.

On my way to you, Jeff reassured Kyle. *Lewis is between us, trying to stare me down, thinking he's a silverback gorilla or something. I'm coming to help you as soon as I take care of Bobo here.*

I've got a spear through my shoulder. Can't move.

They were all aware Kyle was in agony. They could feel it through their shared connection with him. Camellia didn't want to think about Jonas attempting to reach Kyle with Pops, Lowell, Shaker and Tusker hunting him as well. She knew where they were. The underground network kept her informed of everyone's position.

Right now, Pops was scooting on his belly, slithering over the vegetation on the ground much like a lizard or, more likely given his size, a Komodo dragon. He had turned in a full circle to go back toward the helicopters, but he was a distance from them, moving toward the edge of the clearing where Tusker stood facing the helicopters. Lowell stepped off the helicopter he'd been standing on and circled around, coming toward the same exact spot.

Camellia's heart dropped. To her, they

resembled a pack of wolves circling prey, ready to tear him apart. *Jonas, I think they're on you. Get out of there.* He had to see what she was seeing. He was part of the underground network. Why wasn't he moving?

She started to rise to go to him.

Stay down! Shaker's on you, Camellia, Jonas snapped.

The bullet hit the rock just above her head, splintering off shards of granite. She had dipped her face down and covered her ears, but the sound was deafening. Splinters peppered the backs of her hands and arms. Two stuck in her scalp, up near her forehead, the blood immediately running down in little rivulets.

Damn it, Camellia. Don't you move.

She'd never heard Jonas use that particular voice before, but it froze her in place. She had no intention of moving, not with Shaker being so accurate with his gun and his intention. She didn't blame him. She'd killed Angel. Technically, she'd killed Gorman as well, although Shaker had no way of knowing she had been the one to actually kill him.

Don't you worry about Shaker being on me, Jonas, not with them all converging on you. That was the best she could do. She couldn't lift her head, not to get up and help, but she wasn't cowering behind a boulder waiting for Shaker's crew to kill Jonas, Kyle and Jeff if she could do anything to help.

She rolled over and crawled on her belly, wiping at the blood running down her face, depending on the underground network to keep any foliage from moving as she crept out from behind the shelter of the boulders to seek another spot. When she'd chosen her lookout perch to begin with, she'd scouted two other areas, discarding them as not being ideal. She didn't need ideal now, only a place where she could see what was happening and know whether or not she could help the crew below by joining them or staying where she was.

Kyle's pain jarred all of them. He gripped the spear in both hands, and her heart began to pound with alarm.

You're a damn doctor, Kyle, Jonas declared. *Leave it until one of us gets to you. It might be keeping you from bleeding out.*

I can't stand it, Jonas. It's got to come out. If I just lie here, they'll use me as bait to draw the two of you in. I won't have that.

Camellia took a deep breath. *It's Shaker, Kyle. He's burying his voice in the fog again. I almost stood up because of him. You're trying to remove the spear because of him. It's pos-*

sible I can find a way to plug off the hole and any damage it's done from here. You have to give me a few minutes to get to a safe place. Don't do anything until I can help you.

Damn it, Camellia, I can't worry about you and kill these bastards at the same time, Jonas said. *Stay put.*

Camellia didn't reply. She monitored the underground network as she moved in the dense fog toward her destination, a depression hidden in a small grove of trees ringed with several large rocks. The depression was to the right of the smallest of the trees between two of the rocks. As shelters went, it wasn't the best, but she could hide herself in the mist if she didn't move around.

I'll stay here, Jonas, for now. If I can help Kyle, I will, so he can move. That way, Shaker can't use him as bait. She tried to sound reassuring. *I'm in my second-choice location, so Shaker won't know where I am.*

She detested that Jonas was surrounded by Shaker, Tusker, Pops and Lowell. It didn't matter that Shaker was currently focused on trying to shoot her. She suspected he was a multitasker, and if he was, his brother had to be as well. She also felt Jonas's heavy guilt. He had loved Oliver. Whatever had happened, he had yet to come to terms with it. She worried that he might hesitate to kill Oliver's brothers, even in self-defense.

Lewis moved, his boots stomping on the vegetation deliberately as he approached Jeff. Leaves and twigs snapped and crackled beneath his weight. He began to sway slightly, his body seeming to disintegrate and rematerialize in the fog.

Those connected to Jeff were able to see Lewis and his mesmerizing effect. Camellia felt her heart lurch. There was something wrong. Shaker's voice continued to try to weave his spell on them. Pops scooted closer to where some of Tusker's bats had returned and found Jonas with their echolocation. Lowell had begun some odd movement, swinging *away* from Jonas at the last moment, which should have made her happy, but instead, it made Camellia so uneasy she wanted to leave her new location and rush down to help out.

Jeff suddenly launched himself skyward just as Lewis rushed him. The wicked-looking blade that had been concealed up against Lewis's wrist slashed upward toward Jeff's belly, but it missed him entirely. Jeff sliced with his own knife as he came down behind Lewis, the blade cutting deep, right through the jugular. Jeff kept going, jogging away from Lewis, heading toward Kyle along a narrow deer trail.

Keep your eyes on him, Camellia, Jeff warned.

I've got him, Camellia said.

She expected Lewis to go down, but he didn't. He clamped his hand over his neck, the blood pouring between his fingers. Turning his head toward Shaker, he let out an odd cry that was muffled in the fog. Shaker turned toward him, and as he did, she could see the absolute pain on his face. Shaker sent a single sound back into the fog. The note matched that same sound.

Camellia analyzed the way the musical note twisted and moved in the rolling fog as it rushed back to Lewis. Sound could do so many things, including kill. Shaker didn't kill with his voice. He could persuade with it. What else could he do? Was it even possible to repair a wound with sound? She doubted it, at least not the sort of fast-bleeding mortal wound Lewis had. Already, Lewis had dropped to his knees. That pain on Shaker's face had told the tale. He knew it was a lost cause, but he was willing to try.

"Shaker," Camellia whispered into the fog, "take your brothers and go home. This is so wrong. It's all wrong. There's no need for more deaths."

"I'll get to you soon enough," Shaker

whispered back.

There was no sense in trying to talk to him. He was so certain Jonas had murdered his brother and that Ryland and the rest of Team One had covered it up. Why they would do that made no sense, but then what Shaker was doing made no sense either.

Contact Team Two's men and tell them it's a go. Take out the advance scouts, Jonas ordered Camellia. *I had hoped we could get Shaker to call them back, but he isn't going to listen to us. We have to stop them before they get to the compound.*

Camellia tapped into the underground network and sent the green light to Team Two, who were waiting to take out the four enhanced scouts. She wished them good luck and then turned her attention to Lowell, who had turned away from where she thought Jonas had been.

Jonas, he's moving back toward Kyle and Jeff.

I'm on him. Jonas sounded completely confident.

She didn't understand how he could be so certain of himself. Shaker might not be able to disappear into the fog, but like them, he could use it, and he was adept at using it. Tusker could hear a whisper of sound. There was no hiding Jeff's movements from him. Jeff didn't care if they heard him. He wanted them to know he was going to protect Kyle.

Camellia turned her attention to Kyle's wound. The mycelium network pushed close to the surface, allowing Red to bring one of the flowering vines right over Kyle's shoulder where the spear had entered. Petals of a blossom pressed around the blade.

Hold very still and don't try to pull away even if it hurts more, Kyle. Camellia didn't see how it could hurt more.

Pops was easing closer. In the thick mist, there was no way for Jeff or Kyle to see him, but she made certain, through her connection with them, that she provided Pop's exact location. He was coming up behind Kyle's head, going in a wide circle so that he had already entered the forest and was out of the clearing. Unlike Lewis, he didn't make a sound. He was more like a giant lizard, at home on his belly, claws gripping the soil and moving him as quickly over a surface as if he were jogging on two feet. Pops was an unknown, and that was a little terrifying. She would have to trust Jonas and Jeff to keep him off of Kyle while she tried to prevent Kyle from bleeding out.

Camellia pushed everything out of her mind but the terrible penetrating wound in

Kyle's shoulder. The blood supply to the upper extremities was carried in the subclavian artery, which began near the heart and traveled under the clavicle bone. From there, it branched off into several smaller vessels and then continued on as the axillary artery.

Gorman had either known exactly what he was doing when he brought that spear down so hard on Kyle, or he'd been incredibly lucky when Kyle had rolled. The spear had gone down through the shoulder and come out the armpit. The tip was buried at least an inch deep in the soil. The moment she saw the blade had gone through his armpit Camellia knew, just as Kyle did, that the situation was bad.

She followed the path of the blade as it went through skin and muscle, through veins and finally, the axillary artery. She bit the side of her bottom lip hard. She'd never tried such a difficult task from a distance.

Get on it, Jonas said. *You can do it.* He knew Camellia could.

Jonas had complete faith in Camellia. She had brought them all together with the underground network, extending the communication to Jeff and Kyle. Right now, he would have to block her out of his mind because the things he would have to do to protect his brother GhostWalkers were the things that might be abhorrent to her. He would have to call on those traits that Whitney enhanced him with in order for all of them to survive. He understood that Shaker was far more dangerous than any of them had realized.

Shaker had penetrated Team One. He had undermined their trust in one another by using the spy Abrams had instilled in their midst. It had taken time for Jonas to work out how Shaker had managed to do it, but Camellia had given him the idea. Shaker's voice had become more beguiling over time. It was a slow influencer, but he'd had a couple of years to plan his revenge, and he had taken full advantage of every minute.

Shaker was using his voice now, trying to stop Jeff from rushing to Kyle's aid. Trying to persuade Kyle to pull the spear from his body. Trying to get Camellia to stand up and walk to him. The one thing he wasn't doing was working on getting Jonas to show himself. Shaker and his brother Tusker had something very special planned for the man they were certain had murdered their brother Oliver.

Pops had nearly reached Kyle, his head moving from side to side, held down low, eyes fixed on him. He was walking on hands and feet, body held low off the ground. He swayed from side to side as he walked. Like a lizard. A giant lizard.

He's venomous, a Komodo dragon, Jeff, Jonas warned. *He's going for Kyle's head. You can't afford to let him sink his teeth into either of you. Komodos have a powerful bite, and their venom will eventually make you bleed out.*

Kyle can't move, Jeff argued.

That's why I'm here, Jonas said.

He was risking his relationship with Camellia, but she either could accept him as he was, or she couldn't. He would never be free of what Whitney had done to him. He would always be that man — the one needing to protect those he considered family or too weak to protect themselves. That was part of who and what he was. It was one thing to talk about it, another to witness it.

Oliver's brothers knew him — had known him for years — and yet they hadn't reached out to him to ask him what had happened after their brother's death. Not once. They'd joined the GhostWalker program after Oliver and Jonas. Oliver had tried to talk them out of it, but neither of his brothers listened to him. They were intrigued with his abilities and ignored the toll it took on his sanity.

Apparently, they had both managed, through Whitney, to wash out of the program so they could be hired as private security for Abrams. The less demanding schedules of private security forces had clearly left them plenty of time to plot their revenge when they decided Jonas and Team One were guilty of murdering Oliver. They'd changed their appearance just enough that Jonas wouldn't recognize them immediately. Every step had been planned carefully, including the plan to murder the members of Team One and their families.

The fury welled up like a volcano and, with it, strength beyond any human. Shaker and Tusker had sacrificed good men. All those enhanced soldiers they'd sent in advance to kidnap Lily and Daniel, forcing Jonas and the others to kill them. The advance scouts Team Two would have to kill. Crawley and his team, whose only sin was being loyal to the wrong men. Angel, who had believed them so absolutely. Knowing that Gorman and Lewis and Angel were dead hadn't stopped Shaker. He still wouldn't stand down.

Jonas was aware of Camellia instructing Jeff to come up on Kyle's left side in order to get a better grip with both hands so, when she told him, he could draw the spear upward in increments. It would be excruciating for Kyle. Before Jeff started to extract the spear, Red dripped some other liquid into Kyle's veins in order to counteract the pain. Kyle's life was in their hands. Jonas was all about death.

Jonas found their ability to heal both fascinating and ironic. Camellia's healing gift in particular. Why had that bastard Whitney decided to pair Camellia, a woman who was all about life, with Jonas, who was all about death?

Pops suddenly rushed Kyle, coming at him in an explosive attack, much like the Komodo dragon. As he drove at Kyle's head, he opened his mouth wide, so wide his jaw appeared unhinged, exposing two rows of serrated teeth. Venom dripped between the teeth, telling Jonas the man would bite down and tear, allowing massive amounts of venom to infiltrate the wound. If Pop's venom was similar to a Komodo dragon's, it would contain over six hundred toxins and would prevent clotting. Pops wouldn't need to deliver a killing bite, only drip the venom into the open wounds and sit back and wait for the toxins to take effect.

Jonas intercepted the attack, coming out of the fog, ripping a thick branch from a tree as he raced past it. The branch was green, not at all brittle. He swung it with deadly accuracy, slamming the heavy limb into Pops's open mouth and smashing as many of the serrated teeth as possible, then using it as a battering ram, shoving the branch down his throat until a good two feet of bloody wood tore through the side of his neck. Pops died instantly, his eyes wide with shock and panic, his body toppling as far as the branch would allow.

Instantly, Jonas was gone again, disappearing into the fog, moving slowly with the droplets, circling back around Kyle to where Jeff was crouched beside him, doing his best to follow Camellia's instructions.

Jonas was becoming adept at reading the underground network now that he knew what it was. Tusker and Shaker had changed positions, utilizing the dense, covering fog to move covertly. Shaker was no longer in the clearing. He had disappeared that quickly, with no hint of his movement telegraphed over the mycelium network, which meant he wasn't touching the ground.

Tusker was close to Jeff and Kyle. A threat to them. Tusker should have known better.

They should have known better. But then, Jonas had known they would go at Kyle again. He was the bait after all. Kyle had known he would be used to bring Jeff, Jonas and possibly even Camellia straight to Shaker and his men. They wouldn't have to cast around in the fog. They would know right where to look.

He was beginning to know Shaker now. This was all about him. His enhancements. His ego. His cunning intelligence. Shaker had been enhanced *before* his brother had been killed. Oliver had tried to talk him out of it. Oliver had been adamant that his brothers not undergo the psychic or physical enhancements. He'd been extremely upset when he found out they'd gone ahead with their plans.

"You want me to be the one to have killed Oliver to let you off the hook, Shaker. You know you were like him. Like me. You can't control it, can you? The testosterone raging in your body making the demands to challenge any other male who won't do exactly what you say? You have to be alpha, and everyone had better do what you tell them."

He whispered into the fog, dispersing the thread of sound into those droplets so they wouldn't give away his location. He and Shaker were playing cat and mouse, and

Jonas refused to be the mouse.

Shaker was about to find out what a real alpha was.

Jonas had learned over time through trial and error — so many errors — that the way of the wolf alpha was the most effective for him. He tried to follow that lead, to not beat his chest, snarling and demanding. When rage became too much, he took himself away from anyone he loved until he had himself under control.

"Did you always need to be alpha? To force everyone around you to do what you said? I know you did to your brothers. Oliver's abilities made you jealous, didn't they, Shaker? You wanted them for yourself. You thought he couldn't handle them because he was weak." He kept projecting the whisper into the fog, all the while keeping track of Tusker.

Tusker moved with stealth, and the fog muffled any sound he might have made. Jonas didn't need to hear or see him, not with the underground network keeping track of him as surely as any GPS satellite could have. Tusker made his way around the dead body of Pops, pausing for one moment and then creeping around to come at Jeff from behind.

His movements, now that Jonas could

actually see Tusker rather than just monitor his progress via the underground network, reminded him of a bull elephant. Jonas instantly cataloged everything he knew about the animal and the way it behaved when attacking. It was one of the most dangerous and aggressive animals in the world when riled.

Head down, eyes on his target, Tusker's entire demeanor had changed. He looked larger and much more lethal. He was a handsome man, just as Oliver had been, but his facial features were somewhat distorted. Examining him closely, Jonas could see a thick patch of darker skin on his forehead that was worrisome because it made no sense. A similar thick patch had formed on his cheeks and along his jaws. Jonas had never seen such distortion, as if those patches were still growing and taking over Tusker's entire body — like armor.

That pulled him up short. Was it that? Was it armor? He only had seconds for his brain to analyze and figure out exactly what was covering Tusker's face and most likely his body under his clothes — clothes that suddenly looked entirely too snug in places, as if he were wearing a policeman's vest.

Pieces of the puzzle were beginning to fall into place, pieces that Jonas didn't have time to connect, not with Tusker suddenly charging Jeff's back as Jeff pulled at the spear in Kyle's shoulder. Jonas leapt over Kyle and Jeff, the balls of both feet striking Tusker precisely in the eyes, driving him back and away from his intended target.

Jonas was enormously strong, and he'd put not only his body weight behind the blow but every bit of his enhanced strength. He rocked Tusker, drove him back, but Tusker didn't go down. What he did do was trumpet a challenge, rage and pain all at the same time. Jonas had targeted the other man's eyes because that was now the only place on Tusker's face not protected by the thick patches of hardened, armor-like skin. Jonas was certain that armor would protect Tusker from feeling too much pain — possibly even block or deflect any bullet that hit where those patches grew thick.

Keeping his body between Tusker and his two fellow GhostWalkers, Jonas studied his opponent, searching for any area of vulnerability. Jonas had speed and he had strength. He might be more animal than man when he battled, all those predatory traits rushing to attack anyone who dared to threaten those he called family, but he also had a brain. And his father had taught him that, above all else, his brain was his greatest weapon.

Tusker rushed him, driving the heels of his boots into the ground as he ran, his eyes taking on a red glow even as they began to swell alarmingly. The man didn't have much time before he would lose his vision.

Jonas had practiced so many times with his throwing knives, they had practically become a part of his body, like his arms, his hands, his fingers. He drew the knives easily from the loops in his belt where they lay flat against his body, and he flung each of them into the air, one after the other. The blades flew like beautiful flashing wings, taking on a life of their own. Lethal. Deadly. True.

All six blades found their targets. Both eyes. The throat. The groin. The inside of Tusker's right thigh. His left armpit. Tusker continued forward for two more steps, plowing through the forest vegetation, and then he went to his knees, trumpeting a mournful note into the fog before going down face-first into the leaves.

Jonas wanted to roar with rage. For a moment, all he could see was banded heat, and all he could feel was that terrible self-loathing consuming him. So much senseless killing. Every death felt like murder.

For God's sake, Tusker was Oliver's brother. Why hadn't Shaker intervened or tried to help Tusker? For that matter, why hadn't he tried to help Lewis, or any of his men? More pieces of the puzzle were starting to click into place. Bile rose, and with it, that dark purple fury that threatened to consume him.

He could actually see the way the adrenaline-laced chemical rushed through his system, the neurons feeding his veins, taking the toxic neurotransmitter and spreading it through him fast. The chemical moved the opposite way it should, disturbing the cells and nerves to push the wrong way so blood flowed hot and fast, swirling in a hot, volcanic mess.

Through the dark purple, a single, bright pinkish-red vibration slipped in, the electrical pulse interrupting the way the chemical flow rushed, reversing it, soothing the bristling nerve endings until that hot, shocking rage was controllable. A part of him wanted to wrap his arms around Camellia, bury his face in her silky hair and just thank the universe for her. Another part wanted to rage to the universe that she had to experience the worst in him, see him so out of control that she needed to pull him back from a killing fury.

The ground trembled and then shook hard enough that the leaves on the trees shivered. Jeff swayed and then sat abruptly on the ground, the bloody spear out of Kyle's shoulder and now lying in the vegetation beside them. Jonas took a hasty look at Kyle's wound. Blood wasn't gushing. Leaking yes, spouting no. He took that as a good sign. Whatever Camellia was doing to repair the damage from the inside appeared to be working.

Jeff turned and faced outward, away from Kyle, preparing to defend him.

Stay with him, Jonas commanded. *I'm the one Shaker wants.*

Shaker was calling him out. The underground network told him Shaker was moving in a circular direction up toward Camellia — at least where he believed Camellia to be. She'd moved, but she wasn't that far from where she'd been. He was grateful she'd changed positions despite his orders. Even if Shaker couldn't pinpoint Camellia's exact location in the fog right at that moment, Jonas was taking no chances. Shaker had extraordinary enhancements, and some of them seemed to be directly tied to the weather.

Jonas moved to intercept, judging the distance as he went. He noticed that if he moved slowly, Shaker couldn't perceive any activity in the fog, but if he sped up, Shaker was instantly aware. The disturbance — not on the ground but among the droplets — told the man exactly where Jonas was. Jonas went still again and drifted away from where he'd been to give himself another starting point.

I can throw him off by stirring the drops here in various places, Camellia said. *If you don't come at him in a direct line, he shouldn't be able to detect exactly where you are.*

Jonas didn't like Camellia having to do anything that might in any way put her in danger. Who knew what enhancements Shaker had?

Don't be an arrogant ass, Jonas. We're partners, remember? Camellia didn't sound in the least soothing in that moment. She sounded more as if she needed soothing.

It's a good idea, he agreed, calling on his memories of studying the wolves. He often tried to apply the traits of the alpha to his own life. The alpha could be aggressive and savage when needed, but he was also protective and tender. He didn't rule his pack through intimidation but possessed a quiet self-confidence and self-assurance. He always led by example.

With all the aggression from the other animals and reptiles in him, Jonas had purposely chosen to study and model his behavior and control after the wolf, admiring the behavior. He had been born with many of the same characteristics, and Whitney had enhanced them. He was loyal. Protective. Faithful. Caring.

The fog pitched and rolled despite there being very little wind. Jonas recognized Camellia's hand in the disturbance. He didn't hesitate, quickly gliding as lightly as he could through the fog, first at an angular direction and then moving more in a circular one, but always making his way toward Shaker.

Camellia wasn't randomly disturbing the drops. She set routes toward Shaker from multiple directions as well, making it impossible for the man to determine where Jonas was coming from. All he would know was that Jonas was coming and he should be ready for the attack.

Jonas smelled Shaker before he could see him through the rolling purple-gray sheets of the fog. Oliver's brother was hunched over as he made his way stealthily up a deer path, past the boulders where Camellia had been concealed. Just beyond the boulders, Angel's body lay, his face torn by the owls, his feet and legs still wrapped in fibrous threads. His gun lay on the ground just inches from his hand. Shaker crouched there for a few minutes, studying the ground, clearly trying to figure out what happened. Then he turned his attention to tracking Camellia.

Jonas didn't move. There was no whisper of sound to alert him, yet Shaker suddenly whipped around, firing his gun in a covering pattern. The only thing that saved Jonas was the fibrous loops that caught at his ankles from underground and yanked him down. He rolled toward Shaker, not away, his most familiar knife in his hand. This wasn't a throwing knife but one his father had owned before him. A blade made to be used in close-quarters combat for self-defense — or to kill with.

He came up on Shaker fast, inserting his legs between Shaker's as he continued to roll, slamming his opponent to the ground in a scissor takedown. He did it hard and mean. The moment Shaker hit the soil, fibers erupted, curling around the man's gun, wrapping up the metal fast, over and over, and wrenching at it, ripping it from Shaker's fist. Simultaneously, as he rolled and took Shaker to the ground, Jonas came up on top of him, one hand reaching to pin Shaker's wrist that had held the gun, the other stabbing down three times with the knife. Each stab went deep. Jonas had no intention of allowing Shaker to ever get up, not when he was this close to Camellia.

He wanted answers, but he didn't want them at the expense of taking a chance with the one person who mattered the most in his world.

20

Jonas crouched beside Shaker, looking down at Oliver's oldest brother. This was the man Oliver had most looked up to. He wasn't dead yet, but he soon would be. Jonas had killed all three of the Borders brothers. Wiped out the entire family. For what? Once again, that volcanic rage in him welled up from all that testosterone he couldn't keep under control.

The aggression and hostility rose so fast, a brutal insanity that left him wanting to eviscerate Shaker for putting him in such a position. He wanted to hunt down Whitney, make it his life's work to find the doctor and tear him limb from limb, just as Jeff had dreamt he had done to Oliver.

And then Camellia was there. A warm, tranquil Middlemist pink presence inside him, spreading calm throughout him, body and soul, nerve by nerve, cell by cell. How did she manage to soothe the many beasts in him so easily, when he'd been unsuccessful at it even after years of meditation and practice? He didn't understand how she did it but, now especially, he was grateful. He only had a very short window to get any information from Shaker, if the man would talk to him at all.

"You know me, you know I would never murder Oliver like that, no matter the circumstances. I would have turned on an army before I would have turned on him. He was a mess. He was the one killing innocent people. He couldn't stop himself. Our team members were wounded. Some in bad shape. I pulled him off of them and yes, beat the holy shit out of him, but I stopped, Shaker. He was Oliver. He was my best friend. He begged me to kill him. I couldn't do it. I just couldn't, no matter how much he pleaded with me. In the end, he went after the others and fought me, giving me no choice. You don't have to believe me, but that's how it happened."

Jonas pressed hard at his pounding temples. The more the aggressive traits raged, the more his skull hammered afterward, until his brain felt swollen and too large for his head. He detested thinking about how Oliver died, and yet he rarely slept because if he did, he had nightmares of killing Oliver, reliving that day over and over. Then Jeff had come to him with nightmares, and sometimes the two had morphed together, making it impossible for him to close his eyes for any length of time.

"Hell, Jonas, does it matter?" Shaker whispered. "He's dead. Whitney killed all of us."

What did that mean? Jonas wanted to smash his fist in Shaker's face. Hell yes, it mattered how Oliver died. He wanted Shaker to admit he understood Oliver hadn't been murdered. Looking down at Shaker, he realized his face was distorted, his chest too thick. He hadn't rushed up the mountain to get to Camellia or charged in to save Tusker or Lewis.

He wasn't wearing shoes on his feet. They looked like claws, the toes curled, the nails thick and sharp. They weren't talons like a raptor or the claws of a cat. Shaker had been caught somewhere in between, his body fighting to be all things and succeeding at none of them. There was definitely something off about the shape of his head.

Camellia? Can you see him? He's lying flat on his back on the ground. Can you feel him? Tell me what's wrong with him, other than what I've done to him?

There was a small, telling silence. Yeah,

she knew. He felt her sorrow. Her compassion. His woman. Too good for his world of violence and twisted, fucked-up creatures Whitney created.

I'm one of those creatures, Jonas, Camellia reminded. *You persist in thinking of me as some kind of angel.*

That's because to me, you are. What did Whitney do to him?

What he asked for. He wanted to be stronger than you. Than Oliver. He wanted to be the best of the best. His internal organs are a mess. Everything is all mismatched. His heart, his lungs. Nothing fits right in his body, Jonas. It must have hurt just to breathe. His brain is too big for his skull.

"Shaker, why would you do this?" Jonas wanted to weep for him. For all of them. They'd all volunteered. Jonas thought he'd be useful. He'd be able to protect other soldiers. He'd do something good with his life. "Why would you send your men on a virtual suicide mission? None of this makes any sense to me. You're one of the most intelligent men I know. How did it come to this?" He spoke low in a soft, compelling voice.

He needed to know. If Shaker couldn't sort through it and come out on the other side, along with Oliver and Tusker, with all

615

those same aggressive traits, how the hell could he ever trust himself with Camellia? She was courageous and compassionate and far too good for a man like him — and that was without the enhancements Whitney had saddled him with. Why had Shaker ever decided to do something so stupid when he saw how Whitney had wrecked Oliver's and Jonas's lives?

Will you stop? You saved Jeff's life. And you saved Kyle's life. Why don't you think about that instead of the negative?

She didn't sound compassionate or sympathetic. His woman sounded exasperated. Even in the middle of what was one of arguably his worst moments, with his body still trying to overcome the aggression, she managed to make him love her even more.

Shaker shook his head weakly. "You can't let them live, Jonas. It's up to you now."

Jonas rubbed his forehead. His head was pounding, screaming at him. "Tusker was dying, wasn't he?" He was fairly certain Tusker hadn't been the only one. Shaker most likely had known he was dying as well.

"Yes." The admission was low. Muffled. "He didn't have long. We knew we didn't have much more time. None of us should have been alive." Shaker didn't open his eyes. "Abominations. All of us. You know,

616

Jonas. And none of us should have children. They know better. Lily, Ryland. You. All of you know better. It has to be stopped."

Jonas pressed his fingers to his pounding temples. How many times had those exact thoughts run through his own head? It wasn't as if he could condemn Shaker for thinking what he'd considered so many times.

"You planned to turn everyone against each other. Hopefully kill everyone off." Jonas made it a statement. "Somehow, you managed to plant your voice in with our team, didn't you?"

"It was the only way."

"You were never going to keep Lily and Daniel alive."

"No, they were going to have to die too." There was regret in Shaker's voice. He coughed. Little bubbles of blood formed around his lips. "I never wanted to kill children or women, Jonas, but Whitney left us no choice. You know I'm right. You have to know all of us are monsters, and eventually we're going to turn on the population."

"Call off the mercenaries, Shaker. I know you have a way to send them away. They have no chance against two teams of Ghost-Walkers. They'd be slaughtered. Send them away now and I'll consider what you're saying. It isn't as if I've never thought along those same lines myself."

"My watch. Underneath. Pop the button up. Sends fail-safe to each captain. They'll take the men and leave. They were told the possibilities. Money would be wired to their accounts."

Shaker was panting so hard it was nearly impossible for Jonas to assess whether or not he was telling the truth. *Camellia?*

I think he is. Red says yes.

Jonas took a chance. What else was there to do? He reached carefully. Even in his present state, Shaker could be very dangerous. Jeff had come up on the other side of Shaker, staying at a respectful distance but ready to back Jonas up. Shockingly, Kyle was on the move as well. Jonas knew through his connection with the underground.

Sit your ass down, Kyle. You want to ruin whatever the hell Camellia did to patch you up? I'm a little too busy to perform some sort of mouth-to-mouth crap on you, he ordered as he removed the watch from Shaker's wrist and popped up the fail-safe button.

When your woman decides to heal someone, Jonas, she does a thorough job.

For one moment, he thought about asking her to try to heal Shaker so he wouldn't

618

have to bear the responsibility of having murdered all three of the Borders brothers. He felt Camellia grow very still in his mind. Holding her breath. He wondered what she would do if he asked her. He knew it wouldn't be fair to her or Shaker.

"How did you get your voice into the compound, Shaker?"

The man coughed again. "Lydia is our cousin. I was going to let Oliver's death go, but then she found out how you murdered him. Told us Miller did nothing. That the entire team did nothing to save him. Knew then all of you were as fucked up as Tusker and me. Had to destroy everyone."

"Team Two?"

"Couldn't get her in no matter how hard she tried, even as a registered therapist." Shaker opened his eyes and stared straight into Jonas's. "You have to get rid of them, Jonas. I know it will be hard, but Whitney turned everyone in that first experiment into killers. You know he did. I couldn't get it done, but you can. You're strong enough. They trust you. Go back to your team and kill them all. Wipe them out. If you get the chance, do the same with Team Two."

Jonas stared down into Shaker's eyes. Already they seemed to be clouding over. This man had led his entire team of eighteen men to die all because a cousin had reported a dream, not realizing it was a dream. No one had checked it out. Not Lydia, who was supposed to be a professional but was taking money from Abrams to sell information to him. And not Shaker, who should have at least investigated before he decided to murder men, women and children.

Jonas sighed and nodded. "I'll do my best to make things right." That said nothing and everything. He hoped it would give Shaker peace as he slipped away.

Jonas held out his hand to Camellia on the path to the garden. Jeff and Kyle continued to take the trail leading down to the compound below them.

"You haven't said one word to me in all the time we've been hiking back, honey," he pointed out. "I asked Jeff and Kyle to go on without us so we can have a day or so alone before I have to report to Ryland. Pretending you aren't hurt or that you're not thinking of retreating and running the first opportunity you get isn't going to solve anything."

Camellia stared at his hand for a long time. He didn't move. He just stood there, holding it out to her, waiting. She raised her lashes, those long feathery lashes that helped conceal what she was thinking and feeling from him. But not so much anymore. He was becoming adept at reading her through their connection.

Jonas knew he would always need that extra help. Camellia had learned to internalize so much. She'd lived on her own a long time, learning to rely on herself. As a young child, a teen and a young woman, she'd learned not to trust easily. Already their relationship, as brief as time had given them, had been put to the test. He kept his gaze fixed on hers. His hand out to her, willing her to take it.

Camellia pressed her lips together and then bit down on the side of her lower lip. Very slowly, with great reluctance, she put her hand in his. The instant she did, he closed his fingers around hers, locking her smaller hand inside his. He wasn't dumb. He wasn't taking chances with the one woman who meant the world to him.

"Thank you, baby," Jonas said softly.

He continued walking along the winding path until they were in the thicker trees of the rain forest before he spoke again. He enjoyed just walking with her. Having it just be the two of them again. Birds were in constant motion. Lizards skittered under the vegetation on the forest floor, announcing their presence with rustling noises. Exotic flowers wound their way up tree trunks, giving off fragrant scents. Tree frogs in various shades of green, blue and red stared at them with large, curious eyes as they made their way to Camellia's house.

Tucked back into the grove of tall Middlemist Red Camellias, even the porch of Camellia's little house was difficult to see, but Jonas knew exactly where it was located, and he went that way. He walked them slowly through the trees and shrubbery, letting the beauty and peace of the garden sink into his system. This was Camellia's home. This was who she essentially was at her core. Beautiful. In complete harmony with nature. She didn't rage against fate. She just went with whatever fate threw at her.

"I should have told you about Oliver, Camellia," he said. "Right away. I just should have done it instead of putting it off. It wasn't because I didn't think you'd understand. It wasn't fair that you were thrown a curve ball the way you were, and I couldn't explain anything to you. I wanted to look at you face-to-face when I explained it, or at least be alone with you, not try to defend myself in the middle of Angel telling you about Jeff's nightmare."

He led her unerringly through the rain

forest of plants. As he did, the blossoms all around them dipped and stretched to reach her. Some touched her face or her wrists or forearms as they passed. He realized they were trying to tend the splinters of rock embedded in her scalp and arms. The underground network had sent word ahead that Camellia had been injured, and already the community was reaching out to give her whatever she needed to heal.

He tried to think back to all the times he'd been wounded on the various missions he'd been on. So many countries, so many environments. He hadn't thought about the plants touching him.

He remembered one time when he'd been lying on his belly in a sea of pain, shot to hell, thinking he wasn't going to make it, blacking out twice. The first time he woke, there were vines wrapped around him. He'd been semiconscious and thought one of the GhostWalkers had found him and covered him. He was in enemy territory and training had taken over. He hadn't made a sound, even when he slipped back under.

He woke a second time, far more aware. He knew where he was and that he was alone. He thought he had been the one to wrap the vines around him and build a blind. There wasn't so much as a single drop of blood on the leaves or ground to give him away. When the enemy got close to his blind, there were no tracks leading them to where he lay on the ground, covered by the vines. Looking back, he realized there had been a few flowers positioned exactly over the worst of his wounds.

Jonas shared his memories with Camellia. "All along, I had help and didn't know it."

Camellia nodded as they made their way up the stairs to the porch. Middlemist Red bordered either side, and the plant greeted them both by dipping her branches and running her blossoms along their arms.

Camellia smiled. "It's nice to be home, Red."

Jonas looked around him. "I love it here. I also love my home. We might have to compromise and divide our time between both places. We'd have a lot more privacy here. What do you think?"

She looked up at him with her blue eyes. He expected anything but what he saw. Amusement. He should have known. Camellia managed humor even in the worst moments. He appreciated that trait in her. She would need it with him.

"I think we'll need both places. One won't be enough. I'll need a retreat and so will you." She led him over to one of the chairs on her porch. "Sit down, Jonas. We may as well get this over with. Do you want anything to drink?"

He shook his head. "Over? By that you mean Oliver Borders? There is never going to be a way to get over Oliver Borders. Not for me."

"I heard what you told Shaker. In the end, I think he knew you told him the truth. That Oliver wanted you to kill him. That he needed you to."

Jonas turned his face away from her. He didn't sit down but rather walked to one of the porch's support posts and wrapped an arm around it, looking out toward the beautiful paradise his woman had created. The scene blurred, but he didn't wipe at his eyes. It wouldn't have mattered. Oliver's name was tattooed on his body right under the GhostWalker creed. Right where the things that mattered most to him were.

"Oliver and I both felt as if we were going insane. It wasn't just Oliver fighting for control every minute. He wasn't alone in that. Our heads were splitting, pounding until we wanted to scream. Our bodies felt as if they were being torn apart. We felt the need to fight over everything with everyone. Everything felt like a challenge. All that testosterone raging in our systems. We would go off together and try to sort through it, try to find a balance."

He pushed his forehead hard against the wood. Camellia ran her hand gently down his back, barely there but he felt it like a brand — deep. He didn't know if he deserved her — not when Oliver was dead. Not when he hadn't made it.

"It's impossible to tell someone else what it's like, that fight every minute of the day for sanity. For control. What it was like in those early days. The first weeks and months when we both tried so hard. Even now. It still scares me that the same thing could happen to me."

"You don't have to tell me, Jonas. You can show me."

"I would never want you to think less of him. He was a good man." His voice sounded hoarse to his own ears. He cleared his throat. "It isn't as if I was blameless, Camellia. I had trouble, just as Oliver did. During combat situations, it was especially difficult to turn off the various temperaments we were called on to use. All of ours came with a high price. At times, that price was a blinding rage, and we would have to get away from our own people. The cost of using what we could to protect our team and risking their lives at our own hands wasn't worth it to either of us, but it wasn't always our call."

Camellia laid her cheek against the small of his back and wrapped one arm around his waist, but she remained silent, allowing him to tell her in his own way. He let the story unfold in his mind so she could see just how difficult it had been for Oliver and him in those early days and how hard the two of them tried to get a handle on the enhancements Whitney had thought himself so clever for bestowing on them.

He wanted her to see the friendship between them and how they shared information. How they worked as a team, fighting through the painful revelations they learned about the various animal traits they now possessed. They studied each animal or reptile together, the good useful attributes they could draw out and develop, make stronger, and the ones that might lead to aggression and dissension on their team. They would discuss ways to suppress or rid themselves of the characteristics that posed a danger to their team.

No matter how hard they tried, the violent tendencies raged through both of them. At times, the aggression was useful, like when they were on missions, having to break through enemy lines or defend their team, but then they couldn't just easily put it all away when the mission was done. Oliver found it harder and harder to control himself. He smashed things in his room, tore up fences, went to bars and got into fights. More than once, Jonas had to stop him from killing civilians and regular soldiers.

"The last mission with Oliver was a bad one. We knew we were set up. We walked right into an ambush. I warned Ryland we couldn't go through the pass, but the men we were supposed to pull out were in that valley, and the only way in was through a narrow pass. There was steep rock rising on either side. I felt the danger. I could actually taste it in my mouth."

"The underground network was telling you to stay back."

He nodded and reached around him to take her arm and bring her to his side. Locking her against him with one arm, he stroked her silky hair with his free hand. He needed to touch her, to hear her heart beat close to him. He listened to the hum of bees, the steady drone of insects and the rustle of lizards and small rodents in the dried vegetation on the ground. The bright sound of water, as it ran over a series of rocks and fell into a shallow pool, brought a sense of harmony to the garden.

Jonas tried to ground himself in the blossoms and Camellia. He didn't want to remember that valley and that day and night of blood and violence that ended with the loss of his best friend.

"It wasn't that Ryland didn't believe me. It was that we couldn't find another way in. We were prepared for an ambush. Oliver and I went in first. It was overcast but still relatively clear, giving neither of us anything we could work with. I stayed to the shadows of the rock as much as I could. Oliver did the same."

Jonas wrapped her hair around his knuckles, the silk trapped inside his fist. "We were good at blending in with our surroundings, and we could go up the rock fast if needed. I eliminated seven of their assassins, but it wasn't enough."

Guilt weighed him down. Pressed on his shoulders, in his chest, pounded through his skull as it did every time he thought of that time. "Half the team went down in a hail of bullets, wounded, the moment they stepped into the mouth of the valley. I should have known where all the enemy were. They were too far above us, and I didn't have their locations."

"Jonas, you're taking on too much. You

know you are. How could you know where every single man would be lying in wait? That isn't even logical."

"It was my job."

"You had a partner. Where was Oliver? What was he doing while you were eliminating those lying in wait to kill your fellow team members?"

Jonas found himself uncomfortable. This was always the moment he hesitated when giving a report. He didn't put that shit on paper, nor did he talk to a shrink about it. He wasn't ever going to betray Oliver that way. Ryland and the others knew because they were wearing small recorders. He had destroyed every version he had but one. Ryland had insisted on keeping that one to protect Jonas. Jonas didn't give a damn about protection, but he did about Oliver's reputation and his legacy. As far as Jonas was concerned, Oliver had earned his hero status on the other hundreds of missions he'd run.

"He was having problems, Camellia. Sometimes the headaches are so severe, it's nearly impossible to think straight." He touched his temple where his head felt as if it had shrunk several sizes and his brain was trying to burst through his skull.

"Like it is for you right now?" she

prompted gently.

He despised admitting he had a migraine, but that was the truth. He'd had one since he'd started out after Shaker and his team. He'd known from the beginning he would be racking up the kills. He didn't want his woman to see him in that light. Not now. Not ever.

"It's pretty bad this time."

Instantly, Camellia reached up with her slender arms, sliding her palms up his chest, her hands going up his neck, her touch delicate as her fingers moved over his jaw. Her touch was light, but it was as if an electrical charge had rushed through his entire system, sparking every nerve ending to life. Blood thundered in his ears, rushing and receding like a never-ending tide, pounding through his temples to add to the mounting pressure in his skull.

Camellia's fingers slid over his temples, barely felt, a wispy brush like a passing butterfly's wing, leaving behind the need for more. The trail of her touch led straight to his hair. The pads of her fingers settled there, buried deep and began a slow rhythm, a fluttering dance, like the butterfly's gentle awakening. Pumping wings to dry them after emerging from the chrysalis. Each touch on his scalp brought relief to the pounding in his brain.

He became aware of the starships, those neurons with the outstretched arms, connecting with one another via synapses so that chemicals could flow to every part of his body, chemicals or electrical signals or both. Camellia sent a brilliant pink-red chemical flowing throughout his veins, carrying it to his brain. After the chemical, a series of electrical charges followed, flashing and igniting as they rushed to his brain. The little explosions should have made the migraine worse but instead seemed to knock it completely away.

For the first time all night and most of the day, he was able to take a full lungful of air. He dropped his chin on top of her head. "I don't know how you manage to do what you do, Camellia, but don't ever tell me you aren't my angel."

Her laughter was muffled against his chest. "Someday, I'm going to be really upset with you, and you'll see I'm no angel."

"I'll wait for that day. In the meantime, I'm just going to keep thinking of you as my personal angel."

He sighed, determined to finish telling her about Oliver so he wouldn't ever have to bring that day up again. He stepped back into the middle of her porch, tugging on her hand until both were standing where the Middlemist Red Camellias had the thickest and longest branches. The blossoms were spectacular. Red leaned toward them, the branches moving in a circular motion as if the huge tree-shrubs could surround them.

"Oliver went into crisis at the worst possible time. I had been keeping a close watch on him because I'd been worried for months. I knew the moment I took out the first assassin and saw the fight and smelled the blood that I was in for trouble with him. The battle was too much and tipped him over the edge."

Before he could put a hand to his roiling gut, her palm was already there, pressing over the exact spot where the well of rage was always pooled, waiting for the aggression to overflow. Now it was gone, responding to her touch.

"You were trying to keep him quiet. Fighting him off the dying men. Trying to reason with him."

She saw right into his mind.

He nodded. Oliver had gone into a fit of madness, foaming at the mouth, wanting to paint his body in the blood of the enemy. He seemed to be in a kind of fury, yet he refused to hunt, forcing Jonas to take the lead. Jonas could no longer trust Oliver at his back. Oliver had gone cunning and feral on him, not something entirely new — Jonas often had those traits spring to the forefront, but not quite like this. Oliver was off in a way that Jonas instinctively knew was dangerous to him.

Oliver watched Jonas as if he were an enemy. Oliver refused to make a single kill, yet as soon as Jonas did, Oliver would rush to the body and desecrate it in a manner that Jonas found reprehensible. Sickening. He found himself caught between needing to warn Ryland about Oliver's behavior and needing to protect his friend. In the end, he had tapped a code to Ryland and sent him a short recording. If Oliver managed to kill Jonas, it would take more than one of the GhostWalkers to destroy Oliver. They would need to know what they were dealing with.

Showing Oliver's sick insanity to Ryland — which meant showing it to Kaden as well — had felt like one of the biggest betrayals of his life. Jonas still sat in the dark thinking of whether or not it had been necessary to send an actual recording to Ryland. Would a simple warning have been good enough? He knew Ryland had saved the recording in order to protect him even though he had asked Ryland multiple times to destroy it.

Jonas had managed to eliminate seven of the enemy while keeping track of Oliver, but he'd been distracted and hadn't climbed up as high as he should have. When Ryland signaled the team to come through the pass, Oliver was to continue climbing upward with Jonas, ensuring there were no more snipers or hidden units. Oliver didn't follow protocol. Instead, he went to ground, stealthily moving back toward the Ghost-Walkers coming through the pass.

Jonas had been too afraid Oliver was going to turn on his team. He had stopped his forward scouting to go after Oliver. The guns above them caught the team as the last man moved out from the rocks of the narrow pass. Half went down with wounds. The other half dragged those wounded to cover and set up return fire.

Oliver became a madman, making matters much, much worse. There was no way to protect everyone from him, and the moment the team members were wounded, he acted as though they were enemies to be fallen on and torn apart, just as he had the assassins Jonas had sought to eliminate earlier.

"I had no choice, Camellia, I swear to you. They were helpless, some in bad shape, the others trying to shoot at the snipers pinning us down and covering the wounded with their own bodies or trying to stop the bleeding to keep those wounded alive. I dragged Oliver off Jeff. Kyle was trying to cover him. Jeff was badly wounded, and Kyle was doing his best to keep him from bleeding out. Oliver kicked Kyle in the ribs and head, and then threw him out into the open where the snipers above us could shoot him."

Camellia gasped, seeing the images in his mind, the way everything happened so fast and the split-second decisions he'd had to make. Jonas used his speed and strength to save Kyle. Running so fast he was nothing but a blur, he caught up to Kyle, realized instantly he had broken ribs and simply carried him, attempting to shield him with his body as he sprinted back to the limited shelter of the rocks. Nicolas Trevane and Ian McGillicuddy, their sharpshooters, gave them covering fire.

Ryland fought off Oliver in an effort to prevent him from killing Jeff. Oliver had torn at Jeff's wound, trying to rip it open further, laughing gleefully, yelling he would tear out Jeff's heart and eat it. He sounded maniacal. Oliver was abnormally strong, nearly crushing Ryland in spite of Ryland's enhancements. It was only Jonas's powerful snapping front kick delivered to Oliver's thigh, giving him a dead leg, that forced him to turn his attention to Jonas.

He dropped Ryland and turned with a cruel, distorted grin on his face. "Jonas. They really think they can stop us. We can kill them all. Let's take them together."

"Oliver, we're sworn to protect these men. They're our friends. Our teammates. We're surrounded by the enemy. Right now, we need to concentrate on killing them, not fighting among ourselves." Jonas did his best to circle around Oliver to put his body between his team and his best friend.

"Weaklings, look at them. No one can take us." Oliver shouted it and then rushed out into the open, exposing himself to the snipers above them on the rocks. Multiple shots were fired. He leapt into the air, giving the enemy the finger and laughing with delight. No bullet touched him. He ripped his shirt from his body, threw it down and declared himself invincible.

He walked slowly back to stand behind the slim wall of rocks and glared at Jonas. "You're either with me or against me. I'm going to kill them all. Everyone. Either they're worthy of living or not. Stand with me, brother."

"You know I can't do that, Oliver."

"Then you're going to die. Right here. Right now."

Camellia winced at the sight of Oliver's snarling, twisted face, a mask now, so distorted, his mouth foaming and bubbling until long strings of saliva hung down on either side of his jaw. The fight was vicious and brutal, a terrible savage brawl more animal than human, two lethal predators coming together in a fight to the death. She had never seen anything like it, and she never wanted to again. Jonas knew he shouldn't share the images with her, his intimate memories of that brutal killing, but he wanted her to understand his fears for their future.

Jonas buried his face in her neck. "Do you see what I'm afraid of for you? For any children we might have together, Camellia? I never want to turn on the ones I love the most. First it was Oliver and then his brothers. Whatever concoction Whitney put into them, he put into me." He tightened his arms around her, holding her to him. The last thing he wanted to do was give her up, but what else could he do if he was going to protect her?

"Jonas, look at me."

Her voice. That soft, gentle tone that wrapped him up in silk and peace. In all the good the world had to give. That was Camellia. Whitney had failed to twist her into

638

something dark or terrible. She was Jonas's personal miracle. He lifted his head and looked down at her, into those eyes that held so many secrets.

His breath caught in his throat at what he saw there. His lungs burned. His heart hurt, thundering in his chest. Camellia's long lashes framed her blue eyes, windows to the soul some said. And if that was the truth, he was looking at love. The real damn thing. Raw. Honest. A gift beyond any price. After what she'd just witnessed, it made no sense, and that meant all the more.

Both of her hands framed his face, her touch delicate, like the wings of a butterfly. So gentle, but he felt them like a brand.

"I see you, Jonas. All of you. Into you. The heart and soul of you. Who and what you are. The good and bad. Everything. You can't hide anything from me, not with Middlemist Red connecting the two of us. I can't hide anything from you. So hear me when I say it would be impossible for you to turn into a cold-blooded murderer or tip over into insanity. You are always in control. Always. I have watched you closely. You strategize. You use your brain. You don't kill mindlessly or easily. You regret every life you have to take. You think you don't have compassion, but it's that wellspring of compassion in you that makes you hurt all the time. At first, in your memories of Oliver, all I could see was the battle because, yes, it seemed brutal and vicious, but then I realized you were doing your best to subdue him, not kill him. You only defended yourself, blocking his blows and trying to land those that wouldn't actually damage him too severely."

"Camellia . . ." He wanted to protest, but she was right. He had done that, but it was Oliver. He'd done everything he could to save him.

Oliver had known what he was doing. In the end, Oliver had given him no choice, at one point coming in close, knife in hand, gripping Jonas to him and whispering that Jonas had to kill him. No one else could do it and it had to be done. It was the only way to save him. He'd said, "If you love me, Jonas, do it. Kill me now before I kill someone I love." That had nearly broken him.

Camellia's thumb brushed along his wet cheek, that sliding caress that turned his heart upside down. "I'm in love with you, and I want to spend the rest of my life with you. I'm not in the least afraid. I just have to know you're willing to risk everything to be with me because you love me that much."

Jonas stared down into her upturned face. He couldn't imagine loving her more. The emotion was overwhelming. Risking his life was one thing. Risking hers was another altogether.

"Jonas, you have to trust someone."

"I trusted Oliver and he trusted me. I let him down, Camellia. I could do the same thing to you." His father hadn't saved his mother, and he hadn't been able to save his father or Oliver.

"But you didn't let him down," Camellia pointed out. "You saved Oliver. You found the strength to do what needed to be done. As for your father, he made his choice, and that was to go with your mother. Jonas, you have to make a choice. You have to decide whether we're worth the risk. I believe in us. Either you do or you don't. But you have to be all in. All the way."

There it was. His woman. Making her demands. Camellia was no shrinking violet. She was magnificent. And she was his. The connection between them was as real as the emotions he had for her. Nothing was ever black and white, the way he wanted the world to be. Issues always came in various shades, depending on the angle viewed. He wanted to spend the rest of his life looking at the world through the angles Camellia did.

He caught her chin and lifted it to him. "I'm choosing you. I love you, Camellia. You already know that. If you're brave enough to take me on, then I'll fight for us for the rest of our lives."

He brought his mouth to hers and instantly lit a fire. The embers had to have been smoldering all along, because the moment her lips parted, it was as though he'd touched a match to a stick of dynamite. They both went up in flames.

He caught at the hem of her shirt. "Arms up, Camellia. This has to go."

She obeyed him, arms in the air, her eyes on his. He dragged her tee over her head and tossed it onto the nearest chair. He slipped his arms around her to find the fastening of her bra.

"We could go inside, Jonas. I do have a bed," she enticed. Her voice was breathy, a little ragged even, but there was that edge of humor he loved.

Her bra slipped into his hand, and he tossed it onto the chair, releasing her breasts into the open air. She was so beautiful to him.

"Out here, honey. Let me have you out here, where I can breathe." The last thing he wanted to do was be inside four walls. He wanted her in his arms out in the open, surrounded by the fragrance of the exotic flowers with the cool breeze blowing on their bodies.

"You can have anything you want," she assured him, her hands dropping to his vest.

She had it off him fast, and he managed to follow it with his shirt while she was coping with her boots and trousers. He did the same. Looking at his woman, Jonas wondered why women had a need for clothing at all. Camellia certainly didn't. As far as he was concerned, she had the perfect feminine form.

Camellia's laughter welled up, more felt than heard. "You just keep thinking that, Jonas." Her arms slid around his neck again, and she tilted her face for his kiss. "Seriously, you can overlook all my imperfections and I'll be happy."

She didn't have any flaws that he could see. Imperfections only made her that much more perfect. He kissed his way from the perfection of her mouth to her stubborn little chin, down her throat, to the luxury of her breasts. He could spend a lifetime feasting on her breasts. She arched her back, giving him better access, at the same time her hands cupping his heavy sac and then gripping his aching shaft with her tight fist, squeezing and pumping until he thought he might go insane if he didn't have her soon.

Jonas lifted her, and she immediately wrapped her legs around his narrow hips to settle over the broad, very sensitive head of his cock. Catching her by her hips, he surged upward as he dropped her weight over him, driving her down onto him. She was scorching hot. Slick. A fiery silken sheath surrounding him, the friction unbelievable.

The cool breeze fanning their bodies and her little cries only added to the heat consuming them from the inside out. He didn't know how long he spent plunging his body into hers. He did press her back to the column at one point, and when that got too crazy, he found the lounge, and they nearly tumbled to the porch floor. Neither cared. In the end, they clung to one another, fighting for breath, bodies scorching hot, dotted with little beads of sweat that the breeze dried on their skin before they managed to find their way inside for a shower and a longer, more subdued but no less satisfying time.

21

"I can't believe what you've done for me, Cami," Marigold said. "I was able to hold my sons on my own without any help. I won't say I wasn't weak, but I did it, thanks to you. Lily came by this morning and checked me out thoroughly. No more internal bleeding at all. She took blood samples and asked me to reiterate how grateful she was that you managed to save some of the poison from the Zenith or whatever it was that my body was reacting to."

Her words tumbled out one on top of the other, far too fast. Camellia didn't know what to think. The Marigold she remembered never talked so quickly in any situation. She thought everything over carefully. Her husband threaded his fingers through hers and pulled her hand tight to his chest. His strange gray eyes moved over Camellia, and his face creased in a slow, genuine smile.

"We owe you so much. Thank you. No

one knows how you managed to do what you did, but all the medical professionals who attempted to treat my wife's condition believed she had no chance of survival. They may not have said it out loud, but we knew what they meant."

Ken Norton brought Marigold's fingers to his lips and kissed them almost reverently. He had once been an extremely handsome man, but he'd been tortured, cut with precision and skill, until his face was a patchwork of scars. Those precise cuts appeared to sweep down his face into his neck and shoulders. What she could see of his arms bore them as well.

"I'm just so grateful I was able to help," Camellia assured them, pouring sincerity into her voice. "Your boys are beautiful, Mari, and they definitely need you." She sank into the leather chair facing the wide stone fireplace. "This room is amazing, Ken. I'm told you and your brother built this house yourselves."

Ken nodded. "We did. We liked having a place to go where no one was around." He winked at her. "Now we're overrun with people. Makes Jack trigger-happy. He sulks because he can't put out his traps anymore. He used to scatter them all around and then put up signs to scare any hikers away, not that we ever got any coming this way."

Camellia laughed. It was impossible not to, especially since Jack glared at his brother and Briony nodded her head.

"Don't look at Ken that way," Briony reprimanded, then turned her full attention to Camellia. "Jack really did that. There were traps everywhere when I first came up here to tell him I was pregnant and Whitney's men were trying to get me. They'd already killed one of the men I worked with in the circus and had made several attempts to kidnap me. I was terrified they'd kill one of my brothers and then force me to abort my baby. Jack was a very scary man back then."

Jack gave a fake groan. "I'm still scary, babe."

Briony rolled her eyes. "It's kind of hard to be scary when you're so good at changing diapers and you can quote pages of how-to-be-the-best-at-parenting books."

When the laughter died down, Marigold stood up very cautiously, as if she was still very weak. She had lost a considerable amount of weight. Both Ken and Briony rose with the intention of helping her, but she shook her head and waved both of them off with a small smile.

"I need to do this on my own." She

walked to the massive fireplace and turned her back on it, leaning against the gray-and-blue rock. Her eyes met Camellia's.

Camellia's heart dropped and then began to accelerate. She didn't want to do this. She preferred to just let the past stay in the past. She would prefer to never know Marigold's reasoning for betrayal. When Mari had been so close to death, it had occurred to her that the rift between them didn't matter. Maybe they were never going to be close again like they had been, but seeing her once vital friend so drawn and gray had made Camellia aware of how fragile life was. She didn't want to live her life with regrets.

She could live with a surface friendship. She didn't have to be super close to be happy for Marigold. She had Jonas. Possibly Jeff and Kyle. Okay. Definitely Jeff and Kyle. They'd slipped under the radar when she wasn't looking, and she already cared for them like they were her brothers. She'd never had brothers and kind of liked the idea.

But she didn't want to do this with Marigold. She nearly leapt up to run. She must have looked panic-stricken because Jonas reached over and took her hand, threading his fingers through hers and tugging her hand until it was snug against his chest, right over his heart.

Right here, honey.

She's going to talk about that night when Ivy was shot. I know she is.

Deep breath. I'm right here.

"I need to tell you what happened between us, Camellia. It was never fair to you. I hated that. I hated it so much," Marigold began.

Camellia shook her head. "It really isn't necessary. It was a long time ago, Mari. I'm happy for you. Happy that you found Ken and your twin. That you have children." She wanted her to stop. *Please let her stop.*

She can't. Clearly, she's needed to tell you for a long, long time.

Marigold took a deep breath and again waved Ken off. "I know what I did had to feel like betrayal to you. It *was* betrayal. I loved you like a sister. I still do. That never stopped. We grew up together. We shared everything Whitney threw at us, and most of it was ugly. We survived it because of each other. I survived his madness because of you. That meant Briony did as well. He took her from me, and he told me as long as I did whatever he said, she could live a normal life with a loving family. If I didn't, he would make her suffer before he had her killed."

Marigold took a firm grip on the stone mantel. She looked as if she might be trembling, but she refused to sit. She stood facing Camellia, making her confession in front of the others.

"He delighted in showing me photographs and later video of his men pointing sniper rifles at her. Sometimes it would just be a laser on the back of her head. He'd call me into his office or lab or greenhouse and just show me whatever he had and smile that smirky smile. He said if I ever told anyone, you especially, and he found out, he would have her killed."

Camellia glanced at Briony and saw tears in her eyes. Jack shifted position just enough that he could wrap his arm around her, drawing her into him, partially blocking her face from the others in the room.

"He knew we hatched escape plans often, and he told me if any of us ever escaped, she would be shot. I don't know how he got wind that someone was planning an escape, but he showed me a video of Briony swimming in a pool. There was a laser fixed on her numerous times. He told me I'd better find out who and report it to the guards or him immediately. If anyone was missing, Briony would be dead."

For a moment she pressed trembling

fingers to her mouth. "I wished a thousand times I had the courage to tell you about her. If it had been my life he threatened, I would have. If he hadn't been threatening Briony, I would never have given you up. I just was so scared for her. I spent my entire life protecting Briony, and I just kept doing it. Then you were caught because I gave you up, and Whitney had his guards execute Ivy as punishment. I will never forgive myself. What happened to her is my fault and no one else's."

Why hadn't she considered that Whitney would do something as heinous as blackmail Marigold emotionally her entire life so she would always feel guilty no matter what choice she made? He had to have taken her twin at an early age, or Camellia would have remembered her. Her heart ached for Marigold and Briony too.

She couldn't help herself. She went to Marigold and stretched both arms up, palms out, as they'd done since they were girls. Mari took her hands automatically. They stared into one another's eyes.

He couldn't break us, Mari. You held out and so did I. We swore he wouldn't break us. Remember that? We made a promise to each other that we'd make it out, and we did.

Marigold nodded, tears running down her

651

face. "We did, didn't we?"

Camellia nodded as well. "Yes." *I don't know if Ivy is really dead.*

Marigold nodded again. *I've wondered myself whether she was alive. I thought I just didn't want to feel guilty.*

I honestly don't think she is dead. But if she is, it wasn't you or me. It was Whitney. Her death is on him.

"I'm really sorry for everything, Camellia," Marigold said out loud, her fingers closing around Camellia's.

"There's no need to be. I would have done exactly the same thing. At least we live close and will have time to catch up. You need rest."

"But you'll come back?" There was a hitch in Marigold's voice.

"Yes, of course." Camellia would have hugged her, but Mari was still too fragile, and she didn't want to bruise her.

"Lydia," Lily greeted. "How nice to see you. How have you been?"

"Good. Everything's been good, Lily. It's been such a good time for me. I've been seeing someone. I never really thought I'd find someone I'd really fall for, but he's a doctor at the research center where Dr. Adams works."

Lily walked beside Lydia Fenamore down the long hallway to the room where Lydia did most of the therapy work for each of the GhostWalkers. "Is he a brain surgeon?"

"Yes, a brilliant man. Dr. Adams thinks very highly of him," Lydia gushed.

Lily unlocked the door and pushed it open. "Brandon Adams has been my friend for a very long time, Lydia. When things went south for us here, he was the first person I thought of to help us, and he came through. As a rule, Brandon is a great judge of character. To my knowledge, he's only gotten it wrong once or twice. What does Jacob Abrams think of your new man?"

Lydia stiffened, stopping just inside the door. She turned to face Lily, moistening her suddenly dry mouth with her tongue several times. Her gaze jumped from Lily's face to look over her shoulder to where Jonas and Gator lounged against the opposite wall. Inside the room, Ryland and Kaden waited.

"What's going on, Lily?" Lydia whispered.

"You tell me, Lydia," Lily asked. "No, don't. I take that back. You tell *them*. They'll know if you lie, and they won't be nice about it. I won't stay, because the methods they use to extract the truth from people who betray us aren't exactly approved by the general population. I suggest you tell them whatever they want to know, although they know most of it already."

She turned and walked down the hall without looking back.

Jonas thought she looked like a queen even with her slight limp. He gestured for Lydia to step all the way inside the sound-proofed room.

"We won't be disturbed in here. You can scream all you want, and you won't upset any of the women or Daniel," Jonas invited, his tone mild.

Lydia gasped and shook her head, but when he came up behind her, she stepped inside because he gave her no choice. Jonas entered the room. Gator followed him in and closed the door. The windows were blacked out on purpose so those inside had complete privacy.

"None of you scare me," she declared, obviously terrified but determined to go on the attack first. "It was so easy to undermine all of you. You're supposed to have this tight bond, but really, you don't, do you? Ryland, you and your wife can't even look at each other. She deceived you over your son, didn't she? Went against your orders and recorded the things your son can do any-way," she taunted.

Ryland smiled at her. "Clearly, you couldn't access her records. If you had, you would have found all the things new mothers want to keep. First steps, first words. Photographs. Little videos of funny moments of the three of us. Daniel dancing, or more like wiggling. Nothing that any other mother wouldn't keep. As for Lily and me, we fight like any couple, Lydia, and then we talk it out and make up. I trust her and she trusts me, so we work it out."

The taunting smile faded from Lydia's face.

"And if you think you caused a break between the two teams, you didn't," Jonas added. "The moment Camellia questioned why we trusted them so much on one hand and on the other seemed distrustful, we all put our heads together and realized something was very wrong. Team Two never felt the break in trust, only Team One, so we knew immediately we had been compromised. We just had to figure out how. You were the logical choice."

Ryland looked her up and down and then shook his head. "You are responsible for so many men dying, Lydia. And for what? Money. You wanted Abrams's money. I hope it was worth it to you."

She lifted her chin, looking defiant and

not bothering to pretend she didn't know what they were there for. "I don't kill people, that's your department."

"You didn't do the actual killing, but you're the one who brokered the contract. You took it out for the money," Ryland continued. "That makes you guilty as hell, Lydia. All those good men who died for absolutely no reason. Oliver wasn't murdered. What you discovered and so quickly reported without investigating any further was a persistent nightmare one of the men had. He had discussed the nightmare with me and with Jonas. We brought in someone we thought could be trusted to help."

Lydia raised her chin. "You can lie all you want, Ryland, but that was no nightmare. It was far too vivid."

"Lydia," Jonas said. "You know anatomy. You are very aware of the human body. Once you recorded what was said, did you actually listen to the recording again before you told Shaker and Tusker that I had murdered Oliver? I don't believe you even listened to it twice."

"Why would I want to relive the murder of my cousin? He was killed in a vile and brutal way. I never want to hear such a thing again. I left it to my older cousin to decide how he wanted to proceed." She was defiant, her belligerence showing in every line of her body.

"It would be impossible for anyone to live through getting their arms ripped from their bodies, and yet in that nightmare, Jeff claimed he did. The blood loss would make it impossible, even for a GhostWalker enhanced by Whitney," Ryland pointed out. "But as you're going to insist on being right, I'm going to show you proof of what really happened."

Jonas's head jerked up. "Ryland." That was the last thing he expected. He knew there was proof of his innocence, but that also meant proof of Oliver's guilt. He didn't want that. "I don't give a damn what she believes about me."

"She needs to know she's responsible for the deaths of all those men — good men. If they had made their way here and killed women and children, she would have been responsible for those murders as well."

Lydia lifted her chin again. "Children that would turn out like *him.*" She gestured at Jonas, sneering.

Ryland pointed to the large screen. "Body cameras are required when we go on missions. These are the actual recordings of what happened. There are multiple recording viewpoints because each man wears his own body cam."

He didn't wait for her reply, he simply started the recording. Jonas looked away. Thankfully, Ryland didn't play any audio. The visual would be bad enough. He'd already relived this time with Camellia, he didn't need to do it again. Jonas turned his back on the screen and pulled out his phone to text his woman.

What are you up to right now?

Working in the vegetable garden with Lily, Daniel and Azami.

I didn't know Azami was here. When did she arrive?

Word went out that there was trouble coming, so she came home and brought her two brothers with her. They're very intimidating.

I'm used to them, but I guess they could be. Jonas knew her. There was something she wasn't telling him. What is it, honey?

Just speculation. Flame, Gator's wife, said she believes Ivy isn't dead. Both Marigold and I always had a feeling Whitney had deceived us. We got into the room, and even though there was so much blood, there was no body, and they didn't have time to get rid of one. We knew all the places they would take her if she was dead. She wasn't in any of them. Do you think he kept her alive somewhere else?

Jonas didn't know how to answer that. He

didn't want to give her false hope. On the other hand, that was exactly the kind of thing Whitney would do.

Lydia began sobbing. "Turn it off. I don't want to see any more."

"Too bad, Lydia. We all had to not only see it, we had to experience it. Jonas had to endure it. That was Oliver, his best friend. You turned this into another nightmare for all of us." Ryland was relentless as only Ryland could be when it came to protecting his team.

I'm sorry, honey. Yeah, I think he very well could have done just that.

Lily said they're going to look for her. Do you think there's a possibility that she escaped?

You knew her better than anyone else. What do you think? Jonas waited. Impatient to be with her. He didn't want to be in this room another minute. Lydia stunk of treachery. He needed to be outside, where he could breathe. With Camellia. Out in the open air. With the plants.

If she's alive, anything's possible. Get out of there, Jonas. Let the others handle Lydia. They're going to turn her over to the general, and she'll be charged with treason. She can't dreamwalk or she would have accessed the files. She only guessed that Lily and Jeff were utilizing his ability based on his brain activity.

That made sense. "Rye, I'm taking off. I'll leave you to it. I'm taking my woman and we're heading to the house. If you need us for anything, we'll be there."

"Thanks for everything, Jonas."

Jonas nodded and left. The moment he closed the door and was out in the hall, he realized he had someone to go to. He wasn't alone.

He stood just outside in the sunlight, listening to the sound of Camellia's voice as she talked to the other women and the little boy. She was on her knees, both hands in the soil. She looked happy and so beautiful she took his breath away. Then she looked up, and her expression turned soft with love.

There was Camellia, waiting for him. She brought him balance. Laughter. Peace. Acceptance.

I love you, Camellia Mist.

She smiled, and for him, it was like the sun coming out. He knew it would always be like that.

ABOUT THE AUTHOR

Christine Feehan is the #1 *New York Times* bestselling author of the Carpathian series, the GhostWalker series, the Leopard series, the Shadow Riders series, the Torpedo Ink series, and the Sea Haven novels, including the Drake Sisters series and the Sisters of the Heart series. She also writes standalone thrillers set in the California backcountry.